REVERIE AND
REDEMPTION

KAYDENCE SNOW

Cover design by Simply Defined Art

Editing by Kirstin Andrews

Formatted by Alexandria Bishop

kaydencesnow.com

For Insomnia
Fuck You

CHAPTER ONE

The sun streamed through the tree branches high above, and the gentle breeze carried the sounds of birdsong. The forest felt welcoming, *wonderous*.

Filled with joy, I smiled up at the sky and held my arms out. A bird landed on my left wrist—a colorful little thing singing a trilling song—and I laughed. Another joined it moments later, and then more and more until I had birds covering both arms and shoulders like a scene from a Disney movie. These birds were my friends, the closest ones even snuggling against my neck.

Then, one by one, they started to take off, flying playfully around me, their wings carrying them higher and higher. I wanted to go with them and be free, but . . .

I frowned at my arms. The birds had pooped all over me, and now my arms were too heavy to flap. I couldn't fly. I stayed stuck on the ground while all my bird friends disappeared into the trees, taking their sweet songs with them.

The forest fell silent; the trees suddenly seemed denser,

blocking out the sunshine. The only sound was the slow, almost too-quiet-to-hear ticking of a clock.

It started to snow. Within moments, it had piled over my feet, and when I finished cleaning the bird shit off my arms and tried to take off again, the snow wouldn't let me. Almost as if it was trying to hold me captive.

The previously vibrant, cheery landscape had turned gray and white, and the sole noise—that ticking—kept getting louder.

The snow had risen up to my knees.

Why was it snowing? Wasn't it summer? And where was that ticking coming from?

Nothing made any sense. I couldn't move. I'd be trapped in this spot, alone forever, unable to get away . . .

And then I felt someone, or *something*, watching me. I tried to turn, but the snow had buried me up to my hips now, and I couldn't see behind me.

And then . . .

And . . .

. . . then . . .

"*Wake up.*" The whispered words were both a demand and an invitation, a caress on my cheek that started to drag me out of my bizarre dream. The voice was distinctly male, with an edge of something like worry riding it.

I groaned and screwed my eyes up against the bright morning light.

As far as dreams went, that wasn't the weirdest one I'd ever had—not by a long shot. Maybe the snow was just wishful thinking, because sweat from the summer heat had already plastered my sleep shirt to my skin. I moved to peel the shirt off, and something poked me in the hip.

My eyes flew open. I wasn't even in my house, let alone in my bed.

I was in the fucking woods, being poked in the hip by a stick while the morning sun beamed down on me as if I were a plate under a heat lamp, waiting for the waitress.

I dragged a hand down my face, equally exasperated and unnerved.

This wasn't the first time I'd woken up in a place I hadn't gone to sleep. What worried me was what often came after.

Something tickled my shin, and I screamed, jolting to my feet and smacking at my legs. I jumped around on the spot, brushed my T-shirt down, shook out my hair, and cursed nature in a weird little anxiety dance. Once I'd assured myself nothing was crawling on me, I turned slowly on the spot to take in my surroundings.

All I could see in any direction were trees, ferns, patches of grass, the occasional bird. There was no sound of cars passing on a nearby road, no hiking track obvious in the dense underbrush, no sign of civilization at all.

Fuck.

I could literally be anywhere. My house had to be at least within a few hours' walk, but Gritton was nestled in a valley, surrounded by forest, accessible only by picturesque winding roads. I could've gone in any direction and ended up in a spot that looked just like this.

At least I still had my socks on. They were pooled around my ankles and filthy, but they'd provide some protection for my feet. Until I ran into a hungry bear. Then I wouldn't have to worry about my feet or anything else, ever again.

Funny that I focused on my socks in that moment, but better to count my blessings than fixate on how I'd probably die in these woods.

No one would even care. I doubted anyone in Gritton would even notice for a week or two, regardless of the fact that I was born there and knew most of the locals by name.

But my plant babies would wither and die.

Do it for the plants. I refused to die without even trying to get home.

I could simply pick a direction at random and hope for the best. But what if I just ended up deeper in the woods and starved to death?

Fucking fuck.

Paralyzed with indecision, I just stood there, looking around with my hands propped on my hips. I sighed and blew a random piece of hair out of my face. At least my hair was short enough that it wouldn't get all matted and caught on anything.

I needed to find a tree to climb so I could get some idea of which way to go, but there were no good trees around. All the ones I could see were giants of the woods, stretching hundreds of feet into the sky. None of the magnificent bastards had a branch within reach.

Guess I'd just have to choose a direction until I found a suitable tree.

"*This way.*"

I whipped my head to the left and frantically searched the area with wide eyes. I'd all but forgotten the firm, deep voice I'd heard in that trippy state between sleep and wakefulness. I was fully conscious now, and I'd definitely heard it —clearer, louder, even a bit less worried.

Shit. Now I was hearing things. Maybe I'd already been stung by something that was giving me auditory hallucinations.

"Screw it." Figuring I had nothing to lose, I walked in that direction.

Really, Reverie? We're blindly following creepy disembodied voices into the deep, dark woods?

Most likely I'd just imagined the directions, my panicked brain creating voices from the rustle of the branches. I mean, my situation couldn't really get any worse, right?

I picked my way through the trees and bushes, careful to watch where I stepped. I walked for what felt like hours —but was realistically probably only half an hour— without spotting a single climbable tree.

Just as despair started to settle in, making me wonder if I should double back and try another direction, I saw it. One pine tree stood at least fifty feet tall, a dwarf compared to all the others around it, and it had a branch about waist high.

"Oh my god!" I rushed over to it, ignoring the pain in my feet. "You have no idea how good it is to see you, Mr. Pine Tree. I need to climb you. I hope you don't mind, but it is a matter of life and death."

Mine, and possibly someone else's.

But I couldn't think about that just yet.

I wasn't exactly an athletic type, but I managed to pull myself onto the low branch and swing my legs over until I was sitting on it. My hands and thighs were already getting scratched up, and I hadn't even climbed three feet off the ground. Doing my best to ignore the pain, I used the trunk to balance, wobbled into a standing position, and grabbed the next branch. This one would be harder than the first, even if I weren't already wrecked and injured.

Making sure my death grip on the branch was solid, I made myself look up. Not *up*, up, into the sky. Just ahead, so my brain could see what was in front of me instead of worrying about plummeting to what was below.

"Holy shit." I leaned forward. A path!

About a hundred feet away, a narrow track wound through the ferns and bushes and around the massive trees. It wasn't remotely visible from the ground, but from just a little bit of a height . . .

"Thank you, Mr. Pine." I kissed the branch, then immediately regretted it and spit out the mossy, earthy, gritty nature that had stuck itself to my mouth.

I scrambled down the tree and walked to the path. It was barely a goat track, but well worn. Without thinking about it too much, I turned left. Turning left had served me well the last time, so I just rolled with it.

Most hiking tracks looped around, went from one point to another, or connected to other tracks. I'd find my way back to a road eventually—hopefully sooner rather than later. By now, the late-summer sun had climbed high in the sky. My skin felt sunburned, my lips and mouth dry. I felt dehydrated and exhausted, but at least the packed dirt was easier on my feet.

After an hour or so, I rounded a bend and saw the end of the path. Rushing forward brought me to an intersection with a wider path, a wooden signpost standing nearby. I leaned against the post and released a sob of relief. Turning left had paid off.

The sign informed me I had reached Frank's Track. Arrows pointed in various directions, indicating the distance to landmarks. I was in the national park near my hometown, and I knew these hiking tracks.

It took about another half hour to walk to the parking area. The public toilets were filthy, but the sinks had fresh cool water. I peed, then drank and drank until my stomach felt as though it might burst, and then I sat in the shade for a while.

There wasn't a single car in the lot, crushing my hopes of begging some hikers for a lift into town. I considered resting longer, waiting to see if anyone showed up, but I knew that would just delay the inevitable. Now that I no longer had to worry if I'd make it through the day alive, I couldn't stop worrying about what I'd find when I got back.

With a resigned sigh, I got to my feet and started walking. Again. Gritton was only about another hour walk, but the mammoth trees lining the curved road provided shade, and the asphalt almost felt soothing on my feet after the rough treatment of the forest floor. I didn't pass a single car, the birds and an occasional rabbit my only companions on the walk.

Of course I'd gone and sleepwalked my ass to the remote woods on the opposite side of town from where I lived. I couldn't have been sensible about it and sleepwalked into the remote woods closer to my house. No, I'd have to walk down Main Street in my *Ghostbusters* T-shirt and my bright blue underwear with the hole at the seam of the left butt-cheek. Not to mention my filthy legs and arms, the tattered socks. As if they didn't think I was enough of a freak already.

I'd resigned myself to a life of loneliness, but that didn't make it easy. The stares and cold shoulders were a bitch to handle on a good day, let alone a day like today.

When Mr. Wallis's driveway came into view on the road ahead, I started building up my emotional armor. By the time I'd walked past his property, I was holding my head high, my shoulders back and my expression stoic. There was no avoiding the walk through town, but I'd be damned if I did it while cowering or embarrassed.

More houses appeared, the properties getting smaller closer to town. By the time I came across the first person, I had a bit of a swagger in my step, as if I were exactly where I wanted to be, doing exactly what I planned.

The boys at Ziggy's Auto all stopped what they were doing, wiping their hands on rags as they stared at me. They never catcalled me or anything like that, but they never acknowledged my existence either.

"Boys." I gave them a jovial nod.

"Wait!" Travis stepped around the open hood of a car. He was a few years older than me and married. "Are you . . . uh . . . want some water or whatever?" He seemed confused —as if unsure why he'd even spoken to me. But he didn't hide the way he looked at my scratched-up legs, my dirty T-shirt, my disaster hair.

I slowed my pace in shock. He'd found a scrap of humanity and was actually showing me some kindness? I glanced up to the sky, sure it might collapse at any moment.

"Nah, I'm good." I waved him off, noting the narrow-eyed looks the others were giving him, and continued on.

Main Street was busy with the lunchtime rush, and I got plenty more reactions. People stopped in their tracks to stare at me, did double takes, craned their necks through the windows of the charming cafés and antique shops. Two elderly women sitting on a park bench openly tutted at me with disapproval.

"Mrs. Jones. Mrs. Douglas. Lovely day we're having." I gave them a wide grin. They'd been good friends with my grandparents; they used to pinch my cheeks and bring me home baked treats. Now I was nothing more than that woman the whole town wished would just disappear.

I forced down a shudder at the thought that they nearly got their wish that morning. Instead I just smiled wider.

The more they stared and whispered and steered their children out of my path, the more pep I forced into my step. I was practically skipping, my grin maniacal, by the time I crossed the main square and the people and buildings started to thin out.

None of them had even asked if I was all right. Dirt and scratches covered my arms and legs. My lips were cracked and dry. I looked as if I'd just escaped a serial killer in the woods. I'd known these people my whole life, and not a single one cared what had happened to me.

I'd stopped expecting anything from them a long time ago, but it still hurt to be treated as less than human.

The local school was on the edge of town. I just had to get past there, and then it was nothing but trees all the way up the winding road to my house on the hill.

"What the hell do you think you're doing?" Vera—Travis's wife—appeared from behind a tree, hissing at me like a striking snake. We'd gone to school together, had even been friends at one point. Now she was a teacher, and I was the town freak.

I kept my pace steady, not in the mood for any more friendly catchups with the locals. "I'm walking home. And what are you up to?"

"Can't you keep your weirdness private? There are children in there." She pointed to the school building behind her as another teacher marched toward us. Mrs. Upton had taught there since Vera and I were students.

I gasped and gave Vera a wide-eyed look. "You're right! How could I forget? They are so tasty before the age of ten. Thanks for the reminder, Vera. I'll come by for a snack later."

They both looked horrified, but I'd walked too far ahead for them to say anything else. I still heard Mrs. Upton's haughty comment though.

"Why is that girl still living in our town? No one wants her here."

Vera replied, but I couldn't make out what she said.

I'd asked myself the same question so many times over the years. Why did I stay? Everyone hated me here. I had no friends. I'd lost my whole family.

Why did I keep putting myself through this?

I'd tried to leave a few times—I'd even gotten as far as packing up half my stuff once—but I just couldn't make myself go. Maybe because at the end of the day, it didn't matter where I went, who I got to know. Everyone would leave me eventually. They'd either hate and fear me, the way my whole town did, or end up like my parents and my best friend and anyone else I ever cared about.

I pushed the thought out of my mind as I walked

through the front gate of my property. Immediately, my shoulders loosened, and I could finally breathe. No one dared step foot past that gate, and that's how I liked it.

That was the other reason I couldn't bring myself to leave. This property, this house, was my sanctuary. I'd grown up here, and all my happiest memories had happened on this plot of land. It was the only thing that made me remember I was loved once. My parents were in every corner of this house, in the photos on the walls, in the furniture, in their bedroom that I hadn't been able to bring myself to open for years.

It was their home. Now it belonged to me.

A few steps up the walkway and the lush garden hid me from the road. At the end of the winding gravel path, I stomped up the front stairs.

"Fucking fantastic," I grumbled when I saw the front door wide open. "Couldn't have closed the door behind you when you went sleepwalking into the damn woods, Reverie? You're an asshole."

I wasn't really worried about anyone breaking in, but I did have a hosta plant in my sunroom that squirrels freaking obsessed over.

With a huff, I locked the door behind me and went to check on my plants. The polka-dot plant was drooping a bit, so I gave it a good watering, but otherwise my little indoor forest looked just fine.

"Pretty green babies," I cooed to them. "Momma's here to give you water and fertilizer and take care of you. I'd never leave you . . . intentionally."

The plants in the farthest corner whispered something.

I gasped, turning around to face them. Of course, it

wasn't the plants—I loved my green babies, but I wasn't so far gone that I thought they could actually speak back to me.

Someone was in my house.

Would this day never end?

I reached for the ice pick I kept lying around to aerate the soil in the potted plants and brandished it in front of me like a knife. I was a split second away from calling out, *Who's there?* but I held it back, rolling my eyes. *Do not get slasher-flick-bimbo-murdered, Reverie. You're better than that.*

". . . is she . . ." The voice came again, from the same spot. Except I was staring right at it, and no one was there.

". . . but if she is . . . don't try . . ." That time it sounded like a different voice. It actually reminded me of the voice I'd heard in the woods. And it didn't sound so much like whispering now that I was focused on it—more like someone speaking really far away.

I stood there for another few moments and contemplated searching the house, but then I dropped my weapon and dragged my ass into the bathroom. Either I'd lost my mind or the exhaustion and dehydration were giving me auditory hallucinations again. Either way, I needed a shower.

After a good hour in the bathroom—scrubbing away dirt, wincing every time soap got into one of my scrapes, sanitizing each injury I could reach, and moisturizing my whole body—I put on my comfiest shorts and T-shirt and headed into the kitchen. My stomach growled almost constantly, *demanding bitch*. Grabbing Chinese leftovers from the fridge, I carried the box over to the couch and started wolfing it down cold.

With my belly full and my body clean and safe, I couldn't avoid thinking about it any longer. *Who had fallen victim to the curse of just plain knowing me?*

It started when I was eleven years old: every time I sleep-walked, I'd wake up to discover someone I loved had been taken from me. And once all my loved ones were gone, anyone I even remotely cared about ended up being next.

So as much as it hurt, I couldn't blame the people of Gritton for staying away.

I hadn't sleepwalked in nearly a year though. I'd kept my distance even from those outside my town. I was a straight-up bitch to almost everyone I met. I literally had no friends; I didn't even have acquaintances. Who was there left to take?

My phone started ringing, the sound carrying through the empty house from my bedroom.

By the time I hobbled to my room, wincing from my sore muscles and scraped feet, the phone had stopped ring-ing. I pulled it off the charger to see half a dozen missed calls and a text message, all from the same person.

I called him back.

"Rev, hey!" Morris sounded rushed. He was my boss from the diner two towns over where I worked a few times per week. I didn't really need the income—my ginseng and herbs brought in more than enough for me to live comfort-ably—but I craved at least a little normality. I liked going somewhere where no one knew me, no one glared at me, no one hated me.

"Hey, Mo, what's up?" I gingerly lowered myself to the bed.

"Can you work tonight?" he asked.

The way I was feeling right now? No way in hell. I opened my mouth to say as much, but he kept speaking.

"Diana didn't show up for her shift this morning. Laura covered it, but now she can't do the dinner shift, so can you cover that?"

"Diana didn't show up? That's not like her." I squeezed my eyes shut and braced myself.

"Yeah." My manager sighed. "I got ahold of her husband about an hour ago. She's in the hospital. Apparently, she just didn't wake up this morning. They're running tests."

"Oh my god." I felt sick to my stomach.

"I know. They have no idea what's causing it."

"Yeah, I'll take the shift. It's no problem."

"Thanks, Rev."

It was the least I could do—considering I was the reason Diana was in the hospital in the first place.

CHAPTER TWO

I hobbled through my front door at nearly midnight. Quimby's was just a low-key family eatery, but it was nearly an hour drive from Gritton.

Everyone had been on edge, all the staff sad and worried about Diana. There were still no updates on her condition. There wouldn't be. Not for weeks or even months, when she finally woke up. *If* she woke up.

My dad never did.

All the wait staff had to fake smiles and pleasantness, but customers pick up on that shit. My feet were bleeding in my shoes, and all I had to show for it was half of what I usually got in tips.

But hey, at least I wasn't asleep in a hospital, no one able to work out why they couldn't wake me.

Despair, even more potent than the exhaustion, made my knees weak. I dropped my bag onto the ground and leaned back against the door. I hadn't turned on any lights, and the only illumination came from the moon, shining through the glass panes of the door.

My tears spilled over just as my ass hit the floor.

Diana was the kind of person who always did her best to stay positive. Her family had been through some hard times, but she never came into work without a genuine smile on her face. I'd been working at Quimby's for just over a year and had kept all the other staff at arm's length. I didn't want to put them in danger. But I just couldn't help feeling something for Diana. We hadn't formed a friendship outside of work or anything like that, but out of all my coworkers, I liked her best. I smiled easier around her. She didn't treat me any differently. We covered each other's shifts.

She was the closest thing I had to a friend.

And now she had fallen victim to my curse—just as everyone always did.

I drew my knees up to my chest and gave in to the sobs. I hated that Diana was in that hospital bed because of me. I hated how much everyone in town hated me. I'd been close to getting lost in the woods and dying that morning. And my feet throbbed. I'd wrapped the cuts and scrapes, but five hours on my feet still resulted in blood pooling in my shoes.

With a pathetic wail, I unlaced one shoe, then the other. The pain as I gingerly pulled them off nearly took my breath away, and I gave in to more anguished sobs.

Everything was fucked.

I threw the shoes across the room, letting loose a frustrated growl that ended on a sob. They thumped against the wall next to the grandfather clock that had been in our family for generations.

I felt pretty sorry for myself. I didn't wallow in it often, but today had been a particularly awful day, and I didn't even have anyone to bitch to. I didn't have anyone to comfort me and tell me everything would be OK. I didn't have anyone to care about me.

"Please, don't cry."

I gasped, opening my eyes wide. That voice . . . it sounded as if someone had spoken right into my ear. As if someone was whispering the comforting words I craved so much. It was the voice I'd woken up to in the woods, the smooth, confident one.

"Completely losing my shit," I muttered as I hauled myself to my feet. I was so distraught that I'd imagined a comforting presence. I thought I'd gotten over my imaginary friend phase in elementary school.

I hobbled to the bathroom, tended to my poor feet and washed up, then fell into bed. I was so emotionally and physically spent that I fell asleep within seconds.

SOMEONE WAS CHASING ME. OR MAYBE some*thing*. I kept looking over my shoulder, but I couldn't make out the threat. I just knew I needed to run away. My heart pounded, my breaths coming in shallow pants as I ran down the middle of a road. No, not a road. I was on a bridge. No, a hallway.

I was definitely in a hallway, rushing past endless doors. A dead end loomed up ahead, and I just knew that once I got to it, that would be the end.

A door on the left opened as I barreled toward certain death. Someone leaned out, wearing a warm smile. I slowed down. He didn't look worried at all. Did he even know about the . . .

I glanced over my shoulder. Someone was chasing me. Right?

"Come in, Reverie," the man said, swinging the door wider.

I walked the rest of the way. Why was I running earlier?

The man with the nice smile stepped aside as I passed through the door, then he shut it behind me with a soft click.

Together we walked across the room. A window and lamps threw soft light over a couple of big comfortable chairs. We sat at the same time. The chairs faced the window, but I couldn't see what was outside. It didn't really matter; this room was so safe and warm.

"Are you comfortable?" he asked.

"Yes." I smiled and tucked my feet under me.

"Good." He relaxed into his chair more, tilting his head toward me as he leaned back against the soft cushions. He had gray eyes and long fingers. Artist's hands.

"What happened to your mom?" he asked.

"She fell asleep."

"That was a long time ago."

"Yeah. She just won't wake up." I frowned. Where was my mom?

"What about your dad?"

"Dad is happy. He's waiting for Mom, but he's free."

"That's nice."

"Yeah." I rested my head on my hand and turned toward him more. It seemed the longer we spoke, the better I could see him. Blond hair in a neat side part, glasses perched on his nose, a chin dimple. He had an average build but was tall.

"What happened to your dad, Reverie?"

"He fell asleep."

"And then what happened?"

"He died. Mom is still asleep, but Dad died before he woke up."

"I'm sorry. Do you miss him?"

"That's OK. I have my plants now. They need me. I think I need them too though."

His lips twitched at the corners, almost a smile. "What about Nora?" he asked while I stared at his lips. They were very good at making the words. "What happened to Nora?"

"She fell asleep too. But she woke up."

"How long was she asleep?"

"I don't know. A long time. Then she woke up, and we weren't friends anymore. I don't have any friends."

There was a long pause. We stared at each other. It wasn't an intense, awkward stare—more like a comfortable silence. His face remained neutral, but I could see something in his eyes . . .

"You have me," he finally said.

"Are we friends?"

He smiled, as if the answer were obvious, but did I know this guy?

I cocked my head. "Who are you again?"

His eyebrows rose the tiniest bit in surprise, but he swiftly hid it away. Those lips opened to form more perfect words, but I beat him to it.

"Who are they?" I asked, looking over his shoulder.

The room was vast, much bigger than when I first

walked in. The door looked tiny in the distance—a distance that had only taken me a few steps to cross. Everything seemed miles apart, all the furniture and walls at an almost comical distance from one another. It looked as if someone had arranged doll furniture in a regular-sized room.

But there was a bar in the corner next to the window. It made no sense for a full bar to be in the room, but there it was, regular size, like the chairs we sat in and the two other figures.

I couldn't quite make them out. I sat up straighter, trying to focus.

"Reverie?" The man with the mouth drew my attention again. "You were telling me about Nora."

"I was . . ." He hadn't answered my question. Did he not see them? "But who are they?"

I pointed this time.

"Who?" He tilted his head, still not turning to look.

"The two men, at the bar there." I raised my voice. As soon as I said they were men, they snapped into focus, as if to confirm my intuition. One of them was dressed in all black and looked wider, more solid, than the one sitting next to me. He had black hair and a dense five-o'clock shadow. He stood behind the bar, arms crossed, staring at me intently.

The other had curly brown hair and an air of levity about him. He stood in front of the bar, leaning back against it on his elbows. He grinned at me with a mischievous look, half amused and half self-satisfied.

"Told you," he said, but I had a feeling he wasn't talking to me, even though his eyes hadn't left mine.

The man in the chair sighed, but by the time I focused

back on him, the chair was empty. I looked back over to the bar, and the other two had vanished as well. The whole bar was gone, a door in its place.

I got to my feet just as something thumped at the door. A chill ran down my spine.

Whatever had been chasing me had found me. I had to run.

I bolted for the other door. It was so far away.

As I reached it, the new door burst open, making me jump.

I glanced over my shoulder as I wrenched the door open and . . .

. . . and . . .

I woke with a gasp, my whole body tense. Forcing a few deep breaths into my lungs, I sat up and turned on the lamp. The sudden brightness hurt my eyes, but it was better than the darkness that seemed ready to wrap itself around me and never let go.

I just couldn't shake the uneasy feeling the dream had left crawling over my skin. I pulled my knees up to my chest and rested my chin on them, frowning. It had definitely been another chasing dream, but something else was there too—something I couldn't quite put my finger on. It felt . . . different.

I grabbed my dream journal, jotted down what I could remember of the chasing dream, and then paused with my pen over the page. I'd dreamed of a bar and a man, a scowl and a smile. *Reverie, you were telling me about* . . . My name on his lips.

I'd closed my eyes and settled back against the pillows

without realizing. I'd never dreamed a specific person, a distinct face, so clearly before.

I tried to remember more, but nothing would come, so I put the journal back in frustration and turned off the lamp. What were we talking about? It felt important. The questions niggled at my brain, but at least thinking about them had banished the lingering sense of unease from the other dream.

Pulling the blanket over my shoulders, I fell back to sleep with visions of long fingers and sparkling eyes in my mind.

It didn't last long. I drifted in and out of unconsciousness for the few remaining hours of darkness, tossing and turning, chasing that blissfully deep sleep but never quite able to grasp it.

I kept hearing voices.

Every time I started to drift, I'd hear snippets of conversation that would drag me back to wakefulness. As soon as I changed sides or turned onto my back or looked over my shoulder, they'd fall silent.

I was pretty sure I was losing my damn mind.

After a while, I just gave in to it. Instead of rolling over to make sure I was indeed alone in my room, I kept my eyes closed and remained still.

The voices kept whispering, and eventually, I realized one of them sounded like the man I'd been speaking to in my dream. Another was that voice I'd heard in the woods—which, come to think of it, belonged to the guy who had been leaning against the bar. The third voice I didn't recognize, but it didn't take a genius to figure out it belonged to the frowny one that had been glaring at me.

I still couldn't make out complete sentences, but I heard enough snippets to jog my memory of our dream conversation. They were talking about my parents and the other people that had suffered my curse. They were talking about me, but I couldn't piece together if they were angry or pitied me.

Probably both. I definitely felt both, so it made sense that they did too, as they were just lingering figments from my dream. It was all in my head.

Right?

With the first hint of grayish dawn light, the voices fell silent, and I did drift off for another few hours. When I woke up midmorning, covers twisted around my hips, I felt confused.

I'd had some weird-ass dreams in my time—it was kind of my thing. But that whispered predawn conversation hadn't felt like a dream.

CHAPTER THREE

I pushed my worries about my sanity aside to deal with my physical demands first. I made myself scrambled eggs and bacon and ate them in front of the TV, watching morning shows. This late in the morning, they were more infomercials than anything, but I liked to have some company over breakfast and coffee.

"Yeah, until you put it all back on and then some." The presenter was interviewing some "weight-loss expert" about the latest diet fad. I couldn't stand her or the phony expert. I argued with the presenter almost every morning; it felt incredibly cathartic to tell her to shut up.

"I'll just keep working on accepting my juicy ass just as it is, thank you very much," I mumbled into my plate before finishing off the last of the bacon. Someone laughed, and I paused midchew. It sounded far away, but also as if it was in the room. More of that bullshit from last night.

I turned the TV off and sat back, coffee in hand, as I closed my eyes and just . . . listened.

After a few moments, a familiar voice drifted by.

". . . she doing with . . ." It was the gruff one I hadn't heard speak in my dreams.

". . . trying to hear what . . ." My guide from the woods, with the smile riding his words.

". . . entirely sure if that's even . . ." And the calm guy with all the questions, to round it out.

I opened my eyes and took a slow sip of coffee, looking around the room with narrowed eyes.

Fuck this shit.

"Nope. Not today, Satan." I shook my head as I got to my feet. I had enough to deal with. I simply refused to worry about whether I was hearing shit that may or may not be real.

I finished half of my coffee, then left the mug on the counter on my way out the back door. Gardening always made me feel better. It had since I was a kid. Getting my hands dirty was just what I needed.

My feet felt so much better after a night in bed, and I didn't bother putting any shoes on. I didn't even bother putting pants on—just marched outside in my underwear and *Golden Girls* T-shirt. I jammed on my favorite wide-brimmed hat, grabbed my basket, and walked on the lush grass to my ginseng garden.

My property—the property I'd inherited from my parents—spanned several acres, and most of the back half I'd dedicated to growing ginseng. It was one of the most profitable plants to grow, but it took five to ten years for a plant to reach full maturity. There was still a market for seedlings and younger roots, and I had rows upon rows of plants in various stages of the growth cycle.

I checked on the seedlings first. It was another hot

summer day, and I didn't dare water them with the sun so high in the sky. I'd give everything a good drenching when the sun started to set.

I spent the next few hours plucking the odd weed, cutting back dead leaves, and just generally spending time with my plants. By the time I finished with the ginseng and then the herb garden in the front and side of the house, I was sweating, thirsty, and hungry again.

After a cool shower, I had a sandwich for a late lunch, then settled in front of the open window in the living room with a book. I put music on, determined to drown out any pesky whispered conversations that decided to make an appearance.

I planned to spend the rest of the afternoon right in this spot—letting the soft breeze wash over me as I lost myself in a story of fantasy and dragons and princesses who saved themselves. I had a lot of ways to keep myself distracted, or occupied, depending on how you chose to look at it. The TV, the books and music, even my plants, all made me feel less alone during the daytime hours, but nothing could truly eliminate the constant loneliness.

I was halfway through a chapter when a knock came at the door. I set my book down with a huff.

There hadn't been a friendly knock at that door in many years, so I was less than enthusiastic to drag my ass away from the comfy couch to answer it. It was usually someone coming to yell at me, or shithead kids playing a prank. Even salespeople and Jehovah's Witnesses avoided my house.

The outline of a man was visible through the frosted

glass panes, his silhouette surrounded by the orange glow of the late-afternoon sun.

I braced myself and opened the door.

"Miss Hofman." The man on the other side greeted me politely but coldly. There was no smile, only a hard look. He wore a plain black suit and white shirt—no tie—his black hair cut close to his head, dark eyes always searching.

"Senior Special Agent Andersen." I greeted him just as coldly, leaning on the door frame and keeping the door as closed as possible.

"May I come in?" He glanced over my head to try to see into my house, but I pulled the door closer to my body.

"Got a warrant?"

"No." His lips thinned.

"Then no." This wasn't my first run-in with the law, or even Andersen himself. He and his minions came around every time someone ended up in a mysterious coma; I was the only person all the victims had in common. I couldn't blame the feds really—I was clearly cursed, and anyone who came close to me was struck down by it. But I hadn't broken the law.

When Nora woke up after three years of unexplained unconsciousness, she told the people investigating that she hadn't even seen me that day. She'd gone to bed, like usual, and then just . . . didn't wake up. Her last waking day had felt like just yesterday to her.

I'd been miles away every time it had happened. There was no way I could've done some awful thing to these people to put them into comas. Still, the agents came every time, their moods even more sour for having had to drive all the way out here on perilous roads, wasting precious time to come speak to an insolent, uncooperative suspect.

Well, they could all kiss my juicy ass. I hadn't done anything.

After a silence I refused to fill, the agent finally asked his questions. "Are you aware that Diana Rivers is currently in the hospital?"

"Yes. Our boss mentioned it. I have to cover her shifts."

"Are you aware why she's in the hospital?"

"Well, I'm not a doctor, so . . ."

He gave me a withering look. "She's in a comatose state that doesn't match any of the regular neural symptoms of a coma. In fact, her brain activity seems to imply she's asleep. Does any of that sound familiar to you?"

"Sure does. Sounds like the same thing my mom is in the hospital for. Still. Have you boys figured out who's doing this?" My tone landed somewhere between sarcastic and angry.

"That's what I'm trying to do." He gave me a thin smile, and I rolled my eyes. "Miss Hofman, what were your whereabouts three nights ago?"

"Hmm." I tapped my chin, squinting into the middle distance as if I really had to think about it. "That was Tuesday night, right? Oh yeah! I was out in the woods, dancing naked in the moonlight with my coven."

He gave me a flat look and jotted something down on his notepad. "Can anyone confirm this?"

"Sure. The other twelve coven witches would be happy to, but I'd need to kill a dove to perform the ritual to reach them in the other realms, and birds are so hard to catch." I winced and shrugged. I was laying it on thick, but I was just so sick of having the same fucking conversation over and over.

"You think this is funny?" He narrowed his eyes, the first sign I was pissing him off. "People are getting hurt, hospitalized. Their loved ones are devastated, and you're standing there cracking jokes about Devil worship?"

I forced myself to remain outwardly calm while my blood boiled. I didn't want to give him any excuse to arrest me. Been there, done that, didn't rate the accommodation.

I had to unclench my teeth to speak. "No, agent, I do not think it's funny that everyone I ever loved or even remotely cared about has been struck down by whatever this is. I'm one of those devastated loved ones too. My mother is in the hospital too. But I don't have any more to say to you than I did last time. I went to bed like usual on Tuesday night. I must've sleepwalked, because I woke up in the middle of the woods off Frank's Track. It's a damn miracle I found the track and didn't die in the woods. I'm fine, thanks for asking." I waved my hand as though he'd actually shown some concern.

"The birds and rabbits I saw can confirm my story. Also, half the town saw me walk down Main Street in my old T-shirt and underwear around noon. I have nothing else to say to you. Feel free to come back if you get a warrant. OK, bye!" I delivered the *bye* with saccharine sweetness and slammed the door in his face, making a point to turn every single lock.

He stood there for a moment, and I could practically feel him stewing on the other side of the door. Then he turned and walked away. Not a total idiot then.

CHAPTER FOUR

It was cold. Not dead-of-winter, snowing cold, but cold enough that my fingers felt a little numb as I reached for the knobby piece on the chess board. I shifted it to another square.

"Your move," I told my companion. He was dressed in all black, except for his white shirt. His long coat brushed the ground below his chair, and he watched me closely with dark eyes, his hands folded in front of his mouth.

"Truth or dare?" he said, lowering those hands to reveal sinfully plump lips and thick black stubble. Without taking those piercing eyes off me, he reached down and moved a chess piece.

A beam of sunshine cut across the chessboard, making me glance up. The tree branches swayed in the breeze and let a latticework of sunlight through.

We were in a park. We were in Central Park. I'd never been to New York.

"Truth then," my companion said, drawing my attention back to the game just as he moved another piece.

"Hey, it was my turn." I frowned at him.

"What did you do to Diana?" he asked, moving another piece.

"What?" Why was he bringing her up? I thought we were having a nice time in New York. I'd always wanted to visit New York.

"Answer the question," he demanded. Then the asshole moved another piece.

"Stop that!" I smacked his hand away, and he gave me a brief surprised look before narrowing his eyes.

"What did you do to Diana? What did you do to your best friend, Nora? What did you do to your mother?" He pushed and pushed, moving a piece with every question.

"Nothing!" I stood up and smacked the board off the table. The pieces all went flying, but Dark-and-Pushy threw an arm out and froze them in midair.

The board and pieces all settled back onto the table, with every piece lined up in neat rows on either side of the board.

"Let's start again," he said calmly, moving one of the knobby pieces forward. "Truth or dare."

Thunder rumbled. I looked up to see that the trees were completely bare of foliage and the sky had turned gray and oppressive.

I fixed the asshole invading my dream with a firm look. "No."

He tilted his head just slightly. "No?"

"No, douchebag. We're in my head, and you don't call the shots here. I've never been to New York, I have no idea how to play chess, and truth or dare has nothing to do with anything. Now, I'm going to go sit on that park bench over there"—I pointed behind me, to a single bench bathed in sunlight—"and wait until I wake up or another dream starts."

He stood to his full height and stepped toward me, his head still tilted. With the long coat and the boots and that intense stare, he was definitely intimidating.

"A lucid dreamer. Interesting," he murmured, more to himself than anything.

He turned as if to walk away from me, and the next thing I knew, I was sitting down again. The guy didn't break his stride; he walked to the door, firmly closed it, then turned back to me.

I glanced around. We were in a dark, bare room, all gray concrete and no windows. A single lightbulb hung from the ceiling, casting the corners in shadow.

"Reverie Hofman." He started taking steps toward me. "What happened to Diana?"

Poor Diana. She was such a sweet person, and now . . . "She fell asleep and now she can't wake up."

"Why?"

I shook my head and fidgeted with my fingers. "I don't know, but I think it's my fault."

"Is it? What did you do to her?" He stood over me, the lightbulb directly above his head making it impossible to see his features.

"I didn't do anything to her." My voice sounded weak, unconvinced.

"Try again. What did you do to her? What did you do to Nora? What did you do to your mother?"

I glanced around the room again, remembered I was dreaming, and folded my arms over my chest. "I didn't do jack shit to anyone. But I'm clearly running low on creativity if this cliché interrogation is the best my mind can come up with."

I couldn't see the expression on my interrogator's face, cast as it was in shadow. Whatever. He'd be gone soon enough. This was clearly a guilt dream about Diana—not the first and probably not the last. My brain just wouldn't give me a break. I felt awful about what had happened to Diana. I felt fucking awful about all of them. Even worse, I felt so *powerless*. I knew it had something to do with me— just like the police did. But just like them, I had no idea why.

My interrogator leaned down to grip the arms of the chair, getting right in my face. "Lucid dream or not, you're going to answer my questions. What are you? What have you done to those people?"

"Or what, big guy?" I brought my face to within a few inches of his.

He smiled slowly, the curve of his lips full of menace. "Or I'll show you just how imaginative I can be with nightmares."

I stared him down for a few moments, then burst out laughing, bumping his chin with my forehead. He pulled back a fraction but kept me caged in with his arms.

"Bitch, please," I said. "There is nothing you can do to me, say to me, or show me that I haven't already put myself through. I know it's my fault all those people are suffering. I have no idea why or how to fix it. And I'm going to live my whole, pathetic, lonely life with that knowledge. Trust me, I'm torturing myself plenty already."

To drive the point home that I wasn't taking any more

shit from a figment of my own imagination, I pressed both hands against his chest and pushed. He didn't budge. Neither did I.

"Damn!" I rubbed his chest. "Under all that baggy clothing and dark attitude, you're *built*. I'm impressed."

He released the chair and stood back up. I followed him, getting to my feet and staying in his space. A wonderful scent teased my senses at his sudden movement, and I took a deep breath of it.

"God, you smell good. What is that? Frankincense or something? What's the fresh undertone?"

He stared at me, wide-eyed. For the first time, he looked as if he had no idea what to do with me. Good. Now that I had control of this dream again, it was time to have some fun before I got dragged back to reality and my shitty life.

I caressed his chest, then moved my hands up to his shoulders. The soft white fabric of his shirt hung loose on his powerful frame, an open V at the front exposing the top of his chest and the hair peeking out.

I'd never dreamed someone in this much detail before. I'd had my fair share of sex dreams, sure, but never had I conjured up someone so . . . singularly specific. Right down to his intriguing scent.

"Maybe I need a taste to figure it out," I whispered, settling my hands on his shoulders underneath the black coat. I kept my eyes locked on his as I tilted my head and leaned in. His head turned, following my movement as I tucked my face into his neck.

As soon as my gaze left his, his hands shot out to firmly grasp my waist. He started to push me away but froze when I caressed the curve of his neck with my nose, taking another deep inhale. His chest rose and fell against mine as he pulled me closer now instead of pushing me away.

I pressed my lips to his warm skin, and he shuddered out a breath, gripping me tighter.

Now this was the kind of dream I wanted. I smiled against his neck, ready to walk him back so I could press him against the wall and have my way with him.

"Sinan!" A familiar voice made me pause. "I told you to leave the poor girl alone. She's not—"

The voice cut itself off, and my sexy interrogator and I both turned to see the guy who'd guided me out of the woods stepping out of a dark corner. His eyebrows were raised, his lips curving into an amused smile.

"Well, well. What do we have here?" He stuffed his hands into his pockets and rocked back on his heels.

Sinan—apparently—stepped away from me as if I were a live wire, a furious look on his face.

"Evil temptress," he gritted out in my direction, then addressed the other guy. "I told you she was not all she seems to be."

"Uh, excuse me." I huffed. "*She's* standing right here."

"Enough of this." The man with the kind eyes appeared from the opposite dark corner, giving the other two reproachful looks. "This isn't what we do."

He snapped his fingers, and everything went dark and . . .

. . . light. A warm, glowing light. It was so warm on . . .

. . . on my face . . .

My eyes flew open and I winced, raising a hand to block the sunlight streaming through my bedroom window. I must've forgotten to pull the curtains closed last night. I rolled over, turning my back to the brightness, only to find a man in my bed.

I yelled and shot into a sitting position, flailing my arms and legs.

Sexy Sinan from my dream was reclined on my bed, one arm tucked behind his head, looking at me curiously. He didn't appear as vibrant and . . . alive as he had in my dream, but it was clearly him.

My legs got twisted in the sheets, and I toppled right off the opposite edge of the bed. I landed on the floor with a thud, pain shooting through my hip.

"Ow!" I shouted, outraged, rolling around until I could wrench the sheet out from under my shoulders and off my face. When I finally got myself free, I brushed my hair out of my eyes and just stared at the ceiling.

"What the fuck?" I asked the flaking paint in the corner.

I'd had some vivid dreams in my time, but I'd never carried them into my waking life. Was I losing it for real? Between this and the voices . . .

I jolted upright again, my hand gripping the edge of the mattress. Slowly, I turned my head to take in the whole bed —the whole *empty* bed.

There was no one there. Just my pillows and the fitted sheet, which had come off one corner.

I didn't know how I hadn't realized it before, but my interrogator was not a new dreamtime visitor. I'd seen him before. He'd been the one glowering at everything from behind the bar. His was the third voice I'd been hearing.

The friendly one with the curly hair who'd guided me out of the woods and comforted me when I cried.

The blond with the kind eyes and artist's hands who'd chatted with me in the armchairs and made me feel safe.

The dark, menacing one who smelled amazing and badgered me about all the people who'd ended up in the hospital because of me.

Sinan.

It was all just dreams, right? My guilt and my loneliness becoming unbearable. My overactive imagination creating vivid characters in my sleep, companions for my waking hours.

I fixed the sheets and headed for the bathroom, telling myself it was just more of my sleep-related quirkiness. Nothing to worry about.

But as I stood under the spray of the shower, I heard voices whispering again, seemingly out in the hall. They were clearer now. Distinct. The unique voices of those three men.

I didn't know what to believe anymore.

CHAPTER FIVE

O ver the next few days, I went about my life as normal. I tended to my gardens, took care of my potted plants, invoiced customers for their orders, made deliveries and trips to the post office, read books, watched TV, ignored the other assholes that lived in Gritton.

Except I wasn't normal.

I went to my waitressing job and covered shifts for the woman who was in a hospital because of me. I thought about going to see her several times but decided against it. We hardly knew each other, and it would be weird and suspicious.

Agent Andersen came in to my work one night. He was talking to my boss when I arrived for my shift and left just as I got there, giving me a hard look down his nose as he passed. I had no idea what Detective Douche told them, but judging by how everyone gave me a wide berth all night, I could probably take a stab at it.

My waitressing shifts were the only times I couldn't

hear the whispers. I tried to pretend they didn't exist, like the mature adult I was, but if anything, they'd gotten more frequent. I was pretty sure they were talking about me. Full sentences—let alone conversations with context—eluded me, but I'd heard my own name and references to what I'd dreamed, even commentary on my outfit one time.

No matter how much I kept treading water deep in the river Nile, the voices were just too distinct, their conversations too specific. They even had expressions I'd never use. I'd heard things like "We know our onions" and "She's bricky, I'll give her that." No way was my brain imaginative enough to come up with all that.

I hadn't had any more sightings of strange men in my bed—or anywhere else, for that matter—but I saw them in my dreams. Almost every dream I had, one of the three weirdos haunted me in there somewhere. They didn't talk to me as they had before; they just stayed back and lurked, watched me. Sometimes I could see all three talking to one another, but I couldn't hear anything. Anytime I tried to approach or speak to them, they'd vanish.

It was beyond infuriating to be blocked from communicating in my dreams, when I actually wanted to, and to be forced to endure their commentary during my waking hours, when I'd give my left tit for some peace and quiet.

As I watered my indoor plants on a cloudy afternoon, I found myself once again obsessing over the whole thing. Maybe I needed to get in touch with a psychiatrist . . . but crazy people didn't question their own sanity, right? So I probably wasn't losing it.

There was only one logical conclusion. Ghosts.

"I think I'm haunted, bro," I mumbled to the fiddle-leaf I was watering, before moving on to the fern in the corner and switching to a spray bottle. "Pretty sure it's not the house. I would've noticed sooner, and I've lived here all my life."

I picked the watering can up again and moved to the peace lilies. "What do you guys think? Huh? I mean, the logical conclusion is that it's me, right?"

"Yeah, could be," a peace lily answered, and the two next to it murmured their agreement. "But could you ease up on the water? I'm drowning here." It spluttered.

"Shit! Sorry." I stopped the stream of water immediately and moved to the next plant. "But why now? Where did these hot-as-sin ghosts come from all of a sudden?"

"Maybe you just need to get laid," the fiddle-leaf piped in.

I gave it a withering look over my shoulder. "Maybe you need to get put in a drafty, dark corner."

Several of the other plants grumbled, outraged at the idea of such heinous treatment.

"I think figgy's got a point," the bamboo in the corner chimed in. It nearly touched the ceiling, and I had to crane my neck to look at it. "It's been, like, six months since that one-night stand from your trip to the Gardening Expo. Maybe you're just horny-hallucinating. Hornlucinating!"

"That's not a thing." I crossed my arms. "And you're lucky you're such a hardy plant. Even if I threw you out in the compost, you'd find a way to survive."

The bamboo blew a raspberry in response. Quite impressive, considering it had no lips or mouth or face to speak of.

"Nah, I think the ghost theory makes the most sense." The peace lilies backed me up again.

"Thank you!" I bugged my eyes out at the other plants.

Everyone started talking at once, arguing about what exactly was wrong with me, while the maidenhair fern started wailing that it needed precisely four sprays of water immediately. I went over and gave it exactly that, only to have it throw a tantrum, complaining it was too much.

I'd just thrown my hands up, beyond frustrated with everything, when I turned around and spotted the very ghost guys the plants and I had been discussing.

All three of them stood in the arched doorway to the sunroom, watching me with varying expressions of amusement. The nice one who'd guided me out of the woods said something around a smile, and the quiet, thoughtful blond laughed. Even surly Sinan cracked a smirk.

"Everyone, shut it!" I called over my shoulder. I couldn't hear what the guys were saying, and it felt important.

I marched over to them, but they turned and walked away, completely disappearing before I reached them.

"Damn it!" I huffed and turned back to the room. All my plants were watching me—another impressive feat, considering the whole no-faces-or-eyes situation.

I almost asked them all what they thought, but then I realized that . . .

. . . that maybe . . .

. . . maybe . . .

My book slipped out of my grip and tumbled to the floor just as I woke up. I'd fallen asleep in the big chair in the corner of the sunroom after I'd watered all the plants and read a chapter and a half.

It was late evening. The hazy afternoon light had disappeared, and everything was pitch black. I could see the stars through the big curving windows that took up part of the roof. This was one of my favorite advantages of living in a remote town—no light pollution. The sky always looked magnificent on a cloudless night.

I settled more comfortably into the chair, content to just stare at the stars for a while, but it didn't take long for my mind to turn back to my dream and my unwelcome visitors.

As though I'd summoned them with my thoughts, the whispers came.

". . . to the plants?" A-hole 1 laughed.

". . . that she can see . . . ," A-hole 2 added in a more serious tone.

". . . something's not right with . . . ," A-hole 3 grumbled.

I'd gotten so used to seeing them in my dreams and hearing them in my waking hours that I could tell who was speaking with just a few words. Frustration bubbled up my throat, making my teeth grind. They'd ruined my moment of peace with the night sky.

"Fuck this." I sat straight up.

I'd been steadfastly ignoring the constant whispers, pretending I wasn't hearing shit, wondering if I was haunted but not willing to fully embrace the idea. I mean, it was all just so . . . *ridiculous*! But they weren't going away, and they were ruining any scraps of contentment I had in my sad little life.

Pretending they didn't exist clearly wasn't working, so screw it. I'd try the exact opposite.

I had no idea how to contact the spirit world or whatever—I'd never done a séance or even played with a Ouija board—but I figured a good place to start would be my intentions and focus. My intentions so far had been to get rid of the voices, my focus on ignoring them in the hope that they would go away. So, my intentions now had to be to accept them, my focus on connecting with them any way I could.

I planted my feet on the ground, rested my hands on my thighs, rolled my shoulders, and took a deep breath. Then another. With the third breath, I let my eyes close gently.

I felt the weight of my body in the chair, the solid ground under my feet. I strained my ears to hear the whispers once more, but that just made me tense up. *Should I say something? Maybe I should speak out loud and say some kind of cosmic welcome?*

I huffed and shook my shoulders out, relaxing my muscles again. I couldn't force it—that would never work. I had to try to just . . . accept whatever came.

Even if it was a whole lot of nothing.

I'd been hearing them, so I decided to concentrate on that. I let my sense of hearing, my awareness, spread out. I could hear the insects outside, the wind in the trees, the grandfather clock in the front room ticking away steadily.

". . . is she doing now?"

A whisper! I didn't let myself react. I didn't let myself recoil from it or clutch at it. I just . . . accepted it.

". . . maybe it has something . . ."

"It looks like she's meditating to me."

I couldn't help myself. I gasped and opened my eyes, a grin splitting my face. That was a complete sentence. I'd never heard a complete sentence before. And it was about me!

The voices disappeared once more, and I tamped down my excited, nervous energy. With more deep breaths, I closed my eyes and let my awareness spread.

After a few moments of calm, I spoke softly. "Yes, I am meditating, in a way. I can hear you, but only in fits and starts. I'm . . . er . . . welcoming you spirits into my house. Or onto this plane."

I cringed, hoping that message went through, then a horrible thought struck me. What if they were some kind of evil trickster spirits, and I'd just set my own personal horror movie in motion?

"Unless you're evil," I rushed to add. "No malicious spirits or energy or anything is welcome in this house. Or this plane."

My heart hammered, but I kept my eyes closed, trying hard to steady my breathing.

"Told you she could hear us!" the excited one with the curly hair said.

"Remarkable," the calm, proper one answered. "Is it possible . . ."

The voices began to fade out. I waited patiently, accepting whatever came or didn't come, having faith that I would hear them again if I was meant to.

Then Curly piped up again. "We mean you no harm, Reverie. We are not malicious."

"We're not *not* malicious," said Sinan.

"That's not helpful." The calm one sounded exasperated.

"Yeah, Sinan," I chimed in. "That's not helpful."

"How do you know my name?" he demanded, his voice definitely louder than a whisper. I was doing it! I was making contact with . . . whatever they were.

"Your buddies said it when they interrupted your attempt to interrogate me in my own dream," I answered.

"You mean when they interrupted your feeble attempt to seduce me?" he shot back.

I had enough in my life to feel guilty about; I was not going to let anyone slut-shame me. "Judging by how close I came to getting into your pants, there was nothing feeble about my seduction." I gave him a satisfied smile—although I had no idea if they could see me, since I couldn't see them.

When no clever comeback came, I peeked one eye open, then the other. I didn't know what I'd expected to see, but there was nothing in the sunroom.

Maybe I'd gotten all I was going to get out of them. I considered closing my eyes and trying again, but I felt really tired. Who would've thought that sitting still with your eyes closed and talking to a snarky, gorgeous man could take it out of you this badly? I flopped back against the oversized, cushy armchair and lifted my arms over my head. The air still felt sticky with heat. I watched the stars again.

"Reverie." The calm one's voice reached me as if he was sitting right next to me—loud and clear. "Can you hear me now?"

"Yeah?" I sat up a little straighter.

"Told you she was a Seheraum," Curly said.

"There hasn't been one in eons," Sinan argued.

"Then how do you explain—"

"Hey!" I cut him off. "Time out! If you're going to be all up in my auditory space, the least you could do is not talk about me like I'm not here. *You're* the ones who are not here."

"You are absolutely correct." That calm voice of reason made my ire subside. "We are in your home and should show more respect."

I could practically see the dirty look he was throwing the other two.

"Right. Now what's a Seheraum?" If they thought I was one of these things, I wanted to know what it was. I got to my feet and headed for the kitchen.

"A conversation for another day perhaps" was the calm response.

I huffed, pulling ingredients out of the fridge for the dinner I'd slept through. "Fine. How about your names then? I'd like to stop referring to you as 'the curly-haired one' and 'the calm one' in my head."

All their laughs mingled, and I couldn't help smiling along as I started to chop onions. I wasn't sure what I was going to cook yet, but my mother had always said, *When you don't know what to make, you grab an onion and start chopping. The meal will come to you by the time you're done.* Onions were in practically everything.

I missed her so much. Tears welled in my eyes, and I couldn't entirely blame the freshness of the onion.

"What's made you so sad all of a sudden?" Sinan asked, his tone not entirely hostile for once.

"Nothing." I gritted my teeth. I didn't spill my guts to anyone, and I wasn't about to start with three disembodied voices. "Names," I demanded.

"My name is Hollis," Curly replied, the usual carefree tone missing from his voice.

"I am Oskar," the calm one added.

"Nice to meet you all, I guess," I mumbled, reaching for the mushrooms. My mood had soured, and I was beyond exhausted. I hated cooking for one.

"I think that's enough for today." Oskar's voice started to fade as he spoke.

"Wait! No!" I pressed my hands flat on the counter and tried to will them to keep speaking, but I knew they were already gone.

I didn't think it was possible to feel any lonelier.

CHAPTER SIX

In the week that followed, I figured out some things about this weird situation. For one, it really took it out of me anytime I tried to reach out to the ghosts. It was getting easier though. I did it every day—sat down somewhere and spread my awareness until they came into focus. Each time, it took less effort to make that connection, and I could keep it open for longer before I started to feel like death and had to take a nap.

They still lurked in my dreams, and they were still as elusive.

I'd learned—or suspected—that one of them always stayed with me. Regardless of what time of day I tried to reach out, one of them always answered, and the others would join the conversation not long after.

Every time we spoke, I tried asking them about what this was, what they were. I still hadn't gathered the courage to ask how it all connected to the people in my life who ended up comatose. They'd asked me about that in my dreams, so I knew it was connected. I just didn't know if I wanted to hear the answer.

My phone rang, the vibration on the coffee table startling me. I set my book down and grabbed it, then took a deep breath when I saw who was calling.

"Hey, Mo." I still put on a pleasant voice.

"Uh, yeah, hi, Rev. Listen, there's something I need to talk to you about."

"Sure, what's up?" I knew what was coming. I'd known since I saw Agent Pain-in-My-Ass in the restaurant. My few scheduled shifts had been canceled by text, and I hadn't been to work since that day.

"I'm sorry, but I gotta let you go," Morris said. To his credit, he actually did sound kind of conflicted about it.

"Oh, really? Why?" I let the hurt out in my tone. As if I didn't already know why.

"Well, there just aren't enough shifts. And you were the last one hired, so . . ."

What a load of shit. We'd been struggling to cover all of Diana's shifts. If anything, they needed more people, not fewer. I didn't respond, letting him sit in the uncomfortable space of knowing I knew that was a flat-out lie.

"Anyway." He finally broke the silence. "Thanks for all your hard work. If it picks up again, I'll give you a call. All the best."

He hung up before I could even respond. Coward.

I pulled the phone away from my ear and gave it a dirty look. Then I flipped it off for good measure.

"*All the best*," I mimicked his voice in a high pitch. "Fuck you too."

I set the phone down and flopped back against the cushions, dragging my hands down my face.

Don't cry. Don't cry. Don't cry.

I growled as tears pushed through anyway. You'd think I'd be used to it by now.

"Reverie?" Hollis's voice sounded as if he was sitting right next to me. I wiped my eyes with my sleeve but kept them closed, pretending he actually was.

"Yeah?"

"Who was on the other end of the telephone? What's upset you?"

"It was my manager from the restaurant where I work. Used to work," I corrected myself.

"They fired you?"

"Yeah." I sighed and wrapped my arms around myself, half pretending it was Hollis comforting me with a gentle touch.

"On what grounds?"

I laughed darkly. "On the grounds that I'm a freak."

"That's preposterous. You're a beautiful bearcat."

"Thanks. I think," I muttered. "They found out that I'm somehow connected to Diana and the state she's in. They're scared."

"No matter. We will find you another position." He sounded so positive and upbeat, but it didn't escape my notice that he'd steered the subject away from my involvement in Diana's hospitalization.

"It's fine." I shrugged. "I don't really need the money. I make more than I know what to do with selling what I grow."

"Do you? How fascinating. Will you tell me more about it?"

"Sure, yeah." I told him about ginseng, how hard it was to grow, how lucrative it was to sell if you could get it right.

That was another thing I'd learned over the past week—more about their personalities.

Hollis was so curious, jumping from topic to topic, and he genuinely seemed excited about everything. He laughed the most out of the three of them.

Sinan laughed the least, but that hadn't come as much of a surprise. He spoke directly to me the least too. He struck me as more the observant type. When they were all with me, I could feel him watching me, listening intently even if he contributed very little to the conversation. At least he wasn't outright hostile toward me anymore.

Oskar balanced the other two with his calm, measured energy. He seemed just as curious as Hollis, but where Hollis jumped around topics, Oskar wanted to learn all there was to know about something before moving on. He always asked the most thoughtful questions.

And he avoided mine with the most tact.

They all avoided the topic of who or what they were—or what *I* was, for that matter. I still half believed I was just mad.

The other half had hopped aboard the ghost-theory bandwagon. There was just no way my mind could hallucinate something in this much detail. They had to be real. They just *had* to be. Or as real as disembodied voices could be.

Hollis and I chatted for nearly an hour. I got comfortable on the couch and kept my eyes closed, and we talked like a couple of friends spending the afternoon together. Eventually we moved on from the ginseng to the house plants, and he had plenty of questions about that too.

The conversation ended when my stomach growled, indicating it was dinnertime.

As I went about making myself some pasta, I realized I hadn't intentionally reached out to connect with Hollis. He'd just appeared, and the next thing I knew, we were having a full conversation. I also wasn't nearly as drained as I usually was, even though we'd chatted longer than ever.

I felt normal—I mean, as normal as I ever did. If anything, Hollis had made me forget about getting fired. He'd made me feel less lonely.

"YEAH, I HAVE LUCID DREAMS FROM TIME TO time," I said to the empty cab of my truck as I drove out of Gritton. "Doesn't everyone?"

"No," Oskar answered. "It's not very common actually. Only an estimated one percent of the population have regular lucid dreams. It is a skill that can be practiced, but just as with all skills, some have more of a talent for it."

"So, what you're saying is I'm talented?" I grinned.

The buildings and houses gave way to trees, but I kept the speed steady as I navigated the winding roads. I had several boxes of herbs to deliver to two restaurants in a town about an hour drive away. For once, I had company on the drive.

"Yes, your talents are unmatched, your abilities incredible," Sinan answered in his default tone—sarcastic. "Can we get on with teaching her how to do it properly, please?"

"Can you get out of my car, please?" I shot back with a wide smile. Two could play the sarcasm game, and I was a pro. "No one invited you."

"No one invited anyone anywhere." He huffed. "This is ridiculous."

"Why do you want me to learn more about lucid dreaming?" I asked, deciding to ignore the asshole. "Does this have something to do with me being a Ser . . . Sel . . . what did you call it?"

"Seheraum," Hollis reminded me. "So we can talk properly. Face-to-face."

I frowned. "We're talking now. Tell me what Seheraum means."

"Some things would be easier to explain if we could all meet on an even plane of existence," Oskar explained . . . apparently.

"Huh?" I was as eloquent as I was sarcastic. "We see each other in my dreams all the time. In fact, I see you in my dreams even when I don't want to."

Like the other night, when I was having a very pleasant sex dream about the blue aliens from a book I was reading. All three of these men had been in the cave as I explored alien anatomy. It hadn't bothered me at the time. Apparently, dream Reverie had an exhibitionist streak. But once I woke up, I was mortified.

Sinan's deep, smug chuckle broke the silence first, and the others soon joined in.

"Shut up! It's not funny!" My cheeks turned red. Why

did I bring that up? But I was fighting my own giggles even as I chastised them.

"That's kind of my point," Oskar said. "You do things in your dreams that you wouldn't in real life. You think differently. You're more in sync with your subconscious. We need to speak with your conscious."

"OK, first of all"—I gave the road ahead a sassy look as I took the turn toward Springfield—"speak for yourself regarding that whole 'wouldn't do things in real life' bit."

"Now, this is getting interesting." Hollis's voice had a good dose of mischief in it. "Care to elaborate?"

"About how I would absolutely, one-hundred-percent have sex with a big blue alien if the opportunity presented itself?" Or that I'd let them watch, or even join in. "No. Don't interrupt me."

"Yes, ma'am," he replied, but he still sounded as if he had a big grin on his face.

"And second, you're speaking with my conscious me right now. So, spill the beans!" I was getting impatient. Yes, it had been hard to have a decent conversation with them at the start —I'd get drained too fast. But now it was nothing. I could chat to them all day every day and not get tired of them at all. I mean, not get tired from the effort of contacting them.

"There are also things we must show you," Sinan said seriously, bringing the mood down, as usual.

"In my damn dreams?"

"Yes" was the frustratingly simple answer.

I pulled into a spot at the restaurant and killed the engine, then took a moment to stare into space, my mood souring.

"I'd like you all to leave," I said, my voice hollow.

After a beat of silence, Oskar asked: "Why?"

"Because I have to get on with work, and if you won't tell me the truth about what's happening here, then all I can do is assume you're figments of my imagination and go back to ignoring you."

"But if you'll just—"

"Now's not the time." Sinan cut Oskar off. "As you wish, Reverie."

It was the first time he'd called me by name and not something vaguely derogatory like *that woman*. It made my throat constrict, but I forced the tears back.

This was ridiculous. They weren't even real.

"No," Hollis piped in.

"No?" I raised my eyebrows, the weepy emotion chased away by indignation.

"No, we're not leaving you."

"Perhaps we should give her some time," Oskar argued gently.

"No. Fuck that. We don't have time to waste. She may not either," Hollis argued.

"What? What does that mean?" Should I be scared here?

"Learn how to lucid dream and we'll tell you everything. In the meantime, we'll be right here, keeping you company. We are not leaving you, Reverie."

He was doing the exact opposite of what I'd asked, but as irritated as that made me feel, it also gave me a weird sense of satisfaction. *Everyone* left me. And here he was, declaring he refused.

Instead of unpacking that psychological mess, I got out of the car and slammed the door harder than necessary.

"You know doors don't keep us contained, right?" Hollis sounded amused.

I stuck my tongue out at them as I grabbed a fragrant box of fresh herbs out of the back of the truck.

"What's that?" Hollis asked.

"You know what it is," I gritted out, walking toward the back door of the restaurant. I'd been chatting to them all damn morning. They knew my plans for today.

"Does it smell good?" Oskar asked. "I bet it does. Dill was my favorite. What I wouldn't give to taste dill once more."

"Really, Oskar?" I shook my head and knocked on the door with my foot. "I expected better from you."

"I know. I'm sorry." He did actually sound sorry. "But we discussed it and reached consensus to try another approach."

"Consen—What other approach?" When had they even talked without me hearing?

The door opened, and the sous-chef smiled at me, wiping his hands on his apron. "Hey, Rev."

"Hello." I smiled back and held the box out.

"We're going to be so loud that you can't ignore us," Sinan said, his voice louder and more obnoxious than I'd ever heard it.

The guy at the door took the box from me, giving me an expectant look.

"Sorry, what?" It registered that he'd said something, but I'd missed it.

"Just asking how your day's going."

"Oh, yeah, not bad. It's a nice drive here through the woods and—"

"Who's this punk?" Hollis cut me off. "You're out of his league."

"Uh . . ." I lost my train of thought. "Sorry. I'm just a bit distracted. I'd better go."

I rushed back to my truck as the poor guy called goodbye after me. My three pains in the ass chattered about him, pointing out all his flaws as I went.

I slammed the door once again when I was behind the wheel, then tore out of there as fast as possible as the sous-chef waved to me.

"Shut up!" I yelled as soon as I'd pulled out onto the street.

"Agree to practice lucid dreaming and we will," Hollis said smugly.

I tightened my grip on the steering wheel, grinding my teeth.

I wasn't exactly opposed to the idea. It just pissed me off that they were only willing to give me answers on their terms. I'd spent my whole adult life doing things my way, making my own decisions. I didn't play well with others.

"If you're going to act like children having a tantrum, then I'm going to treat you accordingly," I said with forced calm.

"What're you gonna do, doll?" Hollis mocked me. "Spank us?"

I ignored the suggestive tone in his voice.

"Take away our playthings?" Sinan joined in. Assholes.

"P . . . parent us?" Oskar added uncertainly, and I frowned.

"Seriously, Oskar?" Hollis groaned.

"I'm sorry! I'm not the best at thinking up humorous quips on the spot."

"I'm going to ignore you until your behavior improves." I pulled into the second restaurant and parked near their delivery door.

"That is actually a very good parenting strategy," Oskar said, dead serious. "Not rewarding unwanted behavior with attention, thus creating—"

"Please, no more psychology," Sinan pleaded, as if this was something they argued about often.

I itched to ask them about it, learn more about them, but I stuck to my plan.

This time when I got out of the truck, I did my best to focus on things in the real world and not the voices in my head. The soft breeze felt warm on my skin, the sun came and went behind fluffy white clouds, and I could hear the sound of cars passing on the main road nearby.

I could also hear Hollis, repeatedly calling my name.

"Reverie. *Reverie*. Reverie! Rev! REV!" His volume increased with every repetition, and I clenched my jaw as I grabbed the first box out of the back of my truck. Bee & Bear Grill was a bigger establishment, and they'd ordered double the amount Cecconi's had.

Their delivery door swung open when I approached. A kitchen hand whose name I didn't remember smiled at me, holding her arms out for the box.

"Hello! Herb delivery!" I practically shouted at the poor girl in my attempt to yell over Hollis, whom she couldn't hear.

"Um, yay!" She made a weak attempt at matching my

supposed enthusiasm, but I caught her frown as she turned to put the box away.

At least Hollis had stopped shouting at me. All three of them were laughing now.

"There's another box," I said at a more normal volume and rushed back to the truck. Resisting the urge to tell them to shut up, I grabbed the second box, hurried back to the door, gave the girl a polite goodbye, and got the hell out of there.

As I pulled back onto the road, the guys continued chattering incessantly—a constant stream of comments on what we passed, questions directed at me, and exchanges between them *about* me.

"Oh, look! Ice cream!"

"I've never had ice cream."

"Hey, Rev, what's your favorite song?"

"Hey, Rev, what's your favorite color?"

"Hey, Rev, what's your favorite plant?"

"Do you think we could make her blush if we read one of her romance novels out loud?"

"Ooh! I'd love to see her blush."

"We can't hold a book open, idiots!"

Sinan even put on a whiny voice and asked, "Are we there yet?"

"Nice one!" Oskar chuckled.

"Thanks! I've seen many young children ask the question. It always seems to produce irritation in the parent."

I had to press my lips closed to keep from saying, *So, you agree that you're acting like children then?*

"I do believe it's working," Hollis supplied. It was so unfair that they could see me and I couldn't see them.

The entrance to the mall came into view up ahead. I seriously considered just shooting past it and driving home, but I pulled into the parking lot. I refused to let them derail my day.

Plus, I really needed to do some food shopping—better to put up with their annoying commentary than go into the market in Gritton. I did all my shopping in other towns, avoiding the general population of Gritton at all costs. While not a city by any stretch, Springfield was much bigger than Gritton or even Quimby Valley. No one knew me here, and that was exactly how I liked it.

I grabbed my reusable shopping totes and the pile of boxes I needed to mail.

With Hollis, Oskar, and Sinan keeping up their chatter, I went to the post office first and sent all my recent ginseng orders off. Then I marched toward the supermarket. I'd been hoping to do some clothes shopping too—I needed a new pair of boots, and I could use some new underwear—but I decided to just grab the essentials and get the hell out of there. The three of them were beginning to give me a headache.

I ran around the supermarket like a madwoman, grabbing the things I needed and throwing them into the cart while the guys maintained a running play-by-play. I probably forgot half the things on my list because I was so distracted.

I rounded the corner into the canned food aisle and screeched to a halt.

The fact that the guys' voices got just a little bit fainter when I suddenly stopped—indicating they were somehow moving along with me and not in my head—barely registered. Most of my focus was on Pippa.

She stood halfway up the aisle, a can in each hand as she glanced at the ingredients on each one.

"Fucking shit," I muttered under my breath, backing out of the aisle and moving away as quietly as I could. This was all I bloody needed. It wasn't the first time I'd seen someone from Gritton when out on my errands. I wasn't the only one who went to neighboring towns from time to time.

But why now—when my head felt as if it was about to explode? And why *her*?

Pippa had been mean to me even when we were kids—before the rest of the town got on board the hate-on-Rev train. She never let an opportunity to torture me pass by.

I found myself in the pet food aisle, blissfully alone, and paused. With one hand loosely holding on to my cart, I leaned the other arm on a shelf and rested my forehead on my wrist.

I should just leave. Abandon the cart and go. I couldn't handle her today.

"Reverie?" Oskar's voice was soft, and I realized they'd stopped shouting at me.

"Please," I whispered. "Please just stop. I need to get out of here before—"

"Ugh! You're like a bad smell." Pippa's voice made my head snap up. She'd made her way over to me and was giving me a disgruntled look. As if my very existence inconvenienced her. "I can't seem to get away from you."

My default defense mechanism kicked in, and I went

into full sarcasm mode. "Thank you for your expert analysis, Pip. You are, after all, the authority on bad smells."

Her nostrils flared in anger, but she didn't give any other indication that I'd gotten to her. She just smiled a fake smile and turned the bitchy up to eleven.

"Poor Reverie. At least I don't talk to myself in supermarkets like a crazy person. Do you even have a dog?" She looked around at the pet food and cat toys surrounding us.

"No, I don't, but at least I don't look like one."

She looked me dead in the eye, any semblance of a smile gone, and cut right into my chest with her words. "At least I still have a family."

Calmly, taking her time, she walked forward until she was level with me, then leaned over and delivered the fatal blow. "What happened to yours, Rev?"

With a satisfied little chuckle, she continued down the aisle.

I gripped my cart tightly, resisting the urge to chase after her and go feral on her ass right in this nice supermarket. But I knew I couldn't. Because she was right. That was why her words hurt so much.

I looked over my shoulder and watched her saunter around the corner. I could've sworn I saw Sinan following her. It was barely a flicker, the faintest shadow of the menacing man stalking after Pippa, raising his arms as if to grab her from behind.

It vanished before I really registered it, and I turned around to stare into my cart. Maybe abandoning my shopping and slinking away like a kicked dog was still the best course of action.

"Reverie." Hollis's voice was no longer teasing or

annoyingly loud. It was calm but not quite gentle. "Lift your head and straighten your shoulders."

I sighed and shook my head. How much longer could I keep going like this, pretending I was strong while crumbling on the inside?

"Come on, doll, lift your head," he demanded again.

With no energy left to fight them, I did as he asked, lifting my head and straightening my spine.

"There you go." I could hear the encouraging smile on his face.

"Let's go home," Oskar suggested. "Keep your head held high and go pay for your groceries. You can fall apart later if you need to."

I nodded but couldn't seem to make my feet move. They were right. I had never given any of those assholes the satisfaction of seeing me upset when they taunted me; I wasn't going to start now. But I dreaded bumping into her again.

"Would it make you feel better to know she had incontinence diapers in her cart?" Sinan surprised a laugh out of me. I hadn't expected that from him at all.

"It could be for her elderly father," I reasoned as a young guy came into the aisle with a basket, frowning at me.

"It could be," Sinan agreed. "But when you consider that she also had puppy pads and Odor-Eaters . . ."

I laughed again. "Damn, she really is the authority on bad smells."

The guy looked worried now. There was clearly no one else here, and I did not have a douchey Bluetooth headset on my ear.

I met his gaze and widened my eyes, leaning toward him. "You don't see them?" I whispered as he leaned away. Then he abandoned whatever he'd been searching for and rushed off.

The guys all laughed along with me as I started moving. I gathered the rest of the items on my list and went through the checkout without seeing Pippa again.

I had a blissful twenty minutes of complete silence on the drive home, and I was the one to break it.

"OK, let's do the lucid-dreaming thing."

CHAPTER SEVEN

Who knew sleeping so much could be so tiring? In the week that followed, all I did was work, eat, and sleep. *So much sleep.* I hardly even missed my waitressing shifts and only managed to read one book the entire week. The time flew.

The guys hung around pretty much all the time now. Or at least one of them did. They seemed to respect my privacy when I was in the bathroom, although I couldn't be one-hundred-percent sure of that. I mean, they never answered when I tried talking to them while on the toilet, but that didn't mean they weren't being sneaky about it.

I wasn't too worried though. They'd literally seen my deepest, darkest dreams. What did it matter if they watched me shaving my legs awkwardly in the shower?

"We'll see you in your dreamscape, Reverie." Oskar's soft voice sounded as if it was getting farther away.

I was lying down on the couch, midmorning on a Wednesday. After tending to my herbs and replying to customer emails, I'd started to settle in to practice dreaming.

"The next time I dream, I want to remember that I am dreaming," I said softly, letting the words fill the empty room and really letting the intention sink in.

Between coaching from the guys and my own internet research, which they insisted on giving their opinions on, I was getting pretty good at it. I already kept a dream journal, so it was easy to learn to identify dreamsigns—the weird things that weren't possible in reality. I'd been reality checking throughout the day by pinching my nose to see if I could still breathe, and at night I always practiced the wake-back-to-bed technique. It involved setting an alarm for five hours after bedtime, forcing myself to stay awake for half an hour after it went off, then falling back to sleep, which made it easier to trigger a lucid dream. After a few days, I also added wake-initiated lucid dreaming to my practice.

I was able to lie down, recite the phrase about remembering that I was dreaming, and ease myself into a lucid dream. I knew I could do it for a longer period of time—long enough to have a proper conversation and get some damn answers already.

Eyes closed, body loose and relaxed, I allowed my breathing to even out and felt myself sinking into the comfortable couch, and then . . .

I was in my elementary school classroom. It looked exactly as I remembered it—colorful letters of the alphabet adorning the wall, kids' artworks covering the big pinboard, shelves full of toys and books at the back of the room. I could hear kids playing out in the yard but couldn't quite see them; the sun shone too brightly through the windows.

I was alone in the classroom.

No, I wasn't.

Sinan, Oskar, and Hollis were there. They sat in the little desks, looking like giants with their legs sticking out underneath and their arms draped over the narrow table-tops. Sinan had one foot resting on the desk in front.

I chuckled at the sight. "Is that comfortable?"

Hollis shrugged, getting to his feet and stuffing one hand into the pocket of his pants. "Sure. This is a dream-scape. It looks and feels however we want it to—even if the two concepts don't match."

They really did look comfortable. Oskar was leaning back, his legs straight and crossed at the ankles. How did he even fit?

Hollis clicked his fingers, and all the tables disappeared, replaced by massive velvet armchairs.

Dreamsign. I noted.

Sinan made a disgruntled sound and sprang to his feet, glaring at Hollis.

"Was that really necessary?" Oskar grumbled. He stood up with more grace but rubbed his back.

Hollis and I laughed. I was pretty sure if I sat in one of those decadent-looking chairs, it would be very uncomfortable. Unless I *made* it comfortable . . .

A child's excited scream drew my attention to the window. I drifted over to it, but I still couldn't see the children outside. I could hear them playing, running around. I could feel the sun on my face. But I couldn't reach them. I frowned, feeling sad and alone as I pressed a palm against the glass.

"What do you see?" Oskar asked. He stood next to me,

looking out the same window. Hollis and Sinan lined up on the other side of him.

"Nothing. I can't reach them." I dropped my hand back to my side.

"Why?" he pushed.

I huffed out a breath, irritated. "Because the glass . . ."

Wait a minute.

I was dreaming.

And I was in control of this shitshow!

I looked up again to find the glass clear, the children playing outside clearly visible. I was one of them, playing with a group of friends in the sandpit.

"I wasn't always this alone," I said.

"She's losing it again," Sinan sighed.

"No, I'm not." I glanced at him. "I was just making a comment."

"Prove it," he challenged.

This was what I'd struggled with the most. I'd figured out how to get my mind into a lucid dream, but I couldn't make it stick. Once my mind entered a dream state, something always seemed to pull me into a proper sleep, and I forgot I needed to remain lucid.

The guys had had to wake me every time, and every time I got frustrated with myself. But I was improving. I was getting better at holding on to my conscious mind. I did it for longer each attempt. I could pull myself back when the dream tried to pull me in.

I could even . . .

I gave Sinan a smug smile and clicked my fingers.

The classroom disappeared, and we were suddenly in a

desert. Nothing but sand and clear blue sky stretched out as far as the eye could see.

"Well done, Reverie." Oskar gave me a proud smile, and Hollis grinned, nodding.

Sinan scowled and looked around us.

"I proved it." I crossed my arms. "I thought you'd be happy."

"He's never happy." Hollis waved his hand.

"I just . . . don't like dry climates," he grumbled.

"OK, then." I rolled my eyes and clicked my fingers again.

This time we were in a rainforest. Verdant green surrounded our perch in the branches of a very tall tree, and pouring rain instantly drenched us all.

With a loud whoop, Hollis jumped to the next branch and swung off it like a gymnast. Oskar held his hands out, palms facing up, and watched the rain gather in his grip. Then he smiled and licked the water off his lips.

To distract myself from the desire to help him out with that—thus probably getting pulled into a sex dream—I turned to Sinan.

He stood on the branch next to me, leaning back against the trunk of the tree, his gaze narrowed. Water ran over his short hair, trickled down his face, and dripped off the tip of his nose.

Mirth bubbled up inside my chest, and I reached out to capture the droplets in my hand. He startled me by springing forward and biting my index finger.

I yelped—more in surprise than anything. It was barely a nip.

"Enough," he said, the gruff voice back, though I still caught the little smile pulling at the corner of his lips.

The rainforest disappeared. Our new location was warm and dry, dark and decadent.

"Oh man, I was enjoying that one." Hollis leaned back on his hands.

I looked around. We were seated on cushions on the ground, multiple rugs overlapping under us, a small table in the middle. Several colorful lanterns hung from the tent poles, but the rest of the space was in shadow.

"I haven't felt rain on my face like that in . . ." Oskar caressed his cheek, staring into space.

"Nor have I," Sinan said. "But we cannot get distracted. She's clearly ready."

"Ready for what?" I asked, curious about how mesmerized Oskar still seemed, but just as excited to get some answers.

"Ask your questions, temptress." Sinan crossed his arms over his chest, smoke gently swirling behind his head. Where had that come from?

I had so many questions I didn't know where to start.

They all stared back at me silently, waiting.

I figured I may as well start at the end. "Oskar, what did you mean about feeling the rain on your face?"

"We can manipulate the dreamscape—change the setting, sounds, smells, et cetera. But we can only work with what is already there. What the dreamer's mind—what *your* mind—is already capable of," he explained.

"You have a very vivid dreamscape, Reverie," Hollis added. "It makes everything feel more real to us."

"OK." I squinted at him, not sure I understood.

"Most people dream in color, but few do so vividly or incorporate taste, smell, sensation. You do, but I guess it's no wonder, considering . . ." Hollis looked to the side.

I would follow that insinuation in good time, but I wanted to know what *they* were before I started digging into my own existential crisis. "So, you can only experience senses in dreams?"

"Yes. To an extent. We can see and hear things in the waking world, but we cannot touch, taste, smell," Oskar elaborated. "We have only what we need in order to observe."

"And we cannot be seen or heard by people in the waking world—or the dreamscape, if we choose to remain hidden," Sinan added. "We cannot be touched, smelled, tasted . . ."

Was it just me, or did he put a little extra emphasis on "smell"? He was subtly teasing me about that time I said he smelled good and tried to have a sex dream with him.

Zero regrets.

"Wait. So, it makes sense why I can manipulate my own dreams. I mean, they're *my* dreams. But how is it that you can do the same to my dreams? Because that just brings me back around to the suspicion that you're all just figments of my imagination."

I knew I was still avoiding my part in this—like why could *I* hear and speak to them in the waking world when no one else could? But the prospect of finding out I was even more of a freak than originally thought made me a little apprehensive, so *excuse me* for delaying the inevitable.

"We are real. I assure you." Oskar leaned forward and gave me a serious look.

"Well . . ." Hollis bobbed his head from side to side.

"Really?" I huffed. I was supposed to be getting answers.

"No, don't get me wrong," Hollis rushed to add, and Sinan picked up the thought for him.

"We may not technically exist on the waking plane, not in the way most humans define living," he said. "But we do exist."

"Are you real or not?" I pressed, losing patience.

"I suppose it depends on your definition of reality." Hollis got that faraway look in his eyes again.

"Seriously? I do not need another existential crisis on top of my current existential crisis."

Oskar chuckled. "We are not figments of your imagination."

"Thank you!" I sighed dramatically. "So, what does this have to do with you controlling my dreams?"

"It is a gift we have." Hollis smiled.

"Or a curse," Sinan grumbled, "depending on how you see it."

"I see it as a tool of sorts. An opportunity," Hollis said.

I looked between the three of them with one raised eyebrow. "Uh-huh, right, yeah, that explains everything. Thanks, guys. Shall we?"

I leaned on the table and started pushing myself to my feet.

"Reverie." Oskar's grip on my hand made me pause. "We don't mean to be cryptic."

I lowered my butt back to the cushion and realized the others were doing the same. All three had jumped up to stop me from leaving. This clearly meant something to them too. They were investing a lot of time in me. Why?

"OK, doll, here's the deal." Hollis threaded his fingers together and leaned forward.

Oskar loosened his grip on my wrist once he saw I was no longer trying to leave. Instead of losing the contact completely, I flipped my hand and held on to his as I focused on Hollis.

"It's not just your dreams we can manipulate. We can manipulate anyone's dreams. Any living human who is asleep is pretty much fair game."

"I went into a horse's dream once," Sinan added, making me laugh.

"I go into dogs' dreams sometimes. It's a nice break. They're so pure." Oskar smiled, and I couldn't help scooting a bit closer to him.

Hollis rattled off the rules they were bound by, ticking them off on his fingers as he went. "We can enter any dream and observe. Choose to remain hidden or make ourselves known to the dreamer. We can change the dreamscape, the subject matter, and the tone of the dream. We can communicate with the dreamer but only in the dreamscape. We can wake them up when we choose, but we can't put anyone to sleep. We can give them a kind of nudge toward slumber, but that's it. Watching and listening in the real world is fair game, but we can't interact. We can communicate with each other and others like us, but it's not a requirement. I think that pretty much covers it?"

He looked between the others. Oskar nodded.

Sinan nodded too. "There are rare exceptions to all the above, of course. Nothing is absolute."

"Extremely rare," Oskar emphasized.

"Right. Extremely rare exceptions. Like me." Solemn expressions met my gaze as I looked at them each in turn. "What are you?"

I didn't know if I was ready for the answer to that, but I was even less ready to ask the other burning question: *What the fuck am I?*

"We don't like to put labels on things." Hollis gave me a teasing look. I grabbed a little decorative cushion and chucked it at his head, and the tassel in the corner slapped him on the forehead—*so satisfying*!

"We used to be men," Sinan said much more seriously.

"We are men still," Oskar argued. "It's just that we no longer belong to the waking realm."

I huffed. "OK, well, now I'm back to the ghost theory."

"I can see why you'd think that." Hollis nodded. "I've never really had to think about how to explain this to someone."

"Yes, it is proving more complex than I anticipated." Oskar frowned.

"Are you kidding me right now?" I raised my voice, and the lanterns in the room flared brighter. "You assholes have refused to give me any answers for over a week, probably been creeping on me much longer than that, and you're telling me you haven't even discussed what to say?"

The three of them shared guilty looks, then Sinan rolled his eyes.

"We are not ghosts, and we are not figments of your imagination. We lived once, just as you are living, then we died. Now we are paying for our sins."

"So dreams are . . . hell?"

"No, no. Sinan is being dramatic." Oskar waved down my rising panic. "We are not being punished. We are here to learn, observe, help where we can."

I frowned, still confused.

"Have you ever heard of the Sandman myth?" Hollis piped in. Oskar and Sinan both rolled their eyes.

"Like, sprinkle-dust-in-your-eye, usher-you-to-dreamland Sandman?" I raised my brows. "Yeah?"

Hollis spread his arms out and gave me a pointed look, as if to say, *You're looking at 'em.*

"Those are just myths, children's stories," Oskar interjected. "What we are, what we do, is not at all like what is told in the stories."

"Yes, but myths and stereotypes come from somewhere," Hollis argued. "And they may be wildly inaccurate, but you can't honestly say it isn't the closest explanation we have to give Reverie an idea of what we do. Plus, different legends have different takes on it. Hans Christian Andersen's 'Ole Lukøje' is probably the earliest written account of Dreamwalkers referred to as the Sandman. Then there's E. T. A. Hoffmann's 'Der Sandmann.' There's Morpheus, god of dreams from Greek mythology; Jon Blund from Norwegian and Swedish folklore; Mos Ene from Romanian folklore; and a few others I'm probably not remembering right now."

Oskar nodded reluctantly. Sinan just scowled at the table.

All the dream stuff and the fact no one was supposed to see them . . . Maybe being in a dream made my mind more open to outrageous things, but it made total sense.

"If you're some version of the Sandman, then what the fuck am I?" I blurted.

"Beautiful." Hollis gave a brilliant smile that I really wanted to return.

"A temptress." Sinan leaned in, his voice melodic. Was he flirting with me?

"You are human." Oskar killed the sexy vibe. "Please don't fret over the idea that you may somehow be *other*. But we believe you may have some special . . . skills."

"Like seeing you three and putting anyone who gets close to me into a coma?" I deadpanned, then gasped, my eyes going wide. "Holy shit, am I the villain? I am, aren't I? I'm the villain, and you three are the super-squad here to take me out."

All three of them talked over one another, reassuring me no one thought I was the bad guy in this scenario.

Eventually, they fell silent. Sinan leaned forward and fixed his dark eyes on me. "I may have thought you were at least partly responsible for what befell those poor souls, but I no longer believe so. We think there may be . . . something else at play."

"Something else." I nodded. "Something related to me and my special skills."

"Perhaps," Oskar agreed.

"In a manner of speaking," Hollis said. "We do not have all the answers, Reverie. We're still figuring it out. I'm sorry."

"It's OK." I gave them each a small smile, glad to know they didn't think I was responsible for the people who ended up in comas. Even if I didn't quite believe it myself, it was nice to hear regardless. "Can you tell me more about me? What does a Seheraum do exactly?"

Oskar finally laid it all out for me: "Seheraum is an ancient term, from *seher*, meaning 'seer,' and *traum*, meaning 'dream.' Seheraum are dream-seers. They—you— are rare, but always there when needed. You have some of the same gifts we do, like the manipulation of dreamscapes, and you can see and communicate with Dreamwalkers. But just as we're limited by existing in the dream realm, you're limited by existing in the waking realm. You can't enter anyone else's dreams, but we can. We can't communicate with people in the waking realm, but you can. And so on."

"OK, but why? What's the point? What am I supposed to do with this?"

"Sometimes, the work we're called to do can't be completed only in the dream realm," Sinan answered. "A Seheraum is kind of like a bridge between two realms."

"You help us." Hollis smiled. "You have gifts so you can use them to help people, both in this realm and yours. Sometimes Seheraum help Dreamwalkers on their path, and sometimes Dreamwalkers help Seheraum navigate their power. There's a reason you can communicate with our kind. Your gifts have profound meaning."

I rubbed my eyes. I needed to process that before I asked for more info—although they seemed to have covered the basics. There was only so much I could handle.

"Wait, do you dream?" I asked, moving the conversation to lighter topics.

"We do not sleep," Sinan said.

"You only experience taste in others' dreams?"

He nodded.

"And my dreams are particularly vivid, right?"

All three of them nodded emphatically.

"Oskar?" I leaned my chin on my hand and looked at him. "What was your favorite dish with dill in it?" I remembered him mentioning something about that.

"I suppose . . . cucumber stew." He smiled wistfully.

I'd had cucumber stew at a German restaurant in the city once, when I'd treated myself to a night in a hotel for my birthday. The day was still lonely, and I didn't really like the stew, but I remembered it.

I brought the flavors and textures back in my mind, determined to make it as close to reality as possible. The creamy potato, the salty ham, the freshness of the dill cutting through, and of course, the cucumbers. Bowls appeared in front of us all, steaming, the scent of dill wafting off them.

Oskar gaped at it, then at me, then slowly picked up his spoon and started eating reverentially. Hollis was eating his too, an appreciative look in his eyes. Sinan scooped some stew up, let it plop back into the bowl again, and dropped the spoon, scowling.

"How is it?" I asked.

Oskar pinned me with such an intense stare any lingering doubts about the guys' reality vanished. No way in hell could I dream up that much emotion in one look.

"Not as good as my mother's," he said. "But pretty bloody amazing."

I grinned, proud of myself.

"So, when you're walking around in the real world," I mused while Oskar finished off his meal, "do you just walk through people? Or do they walk through you accidentally? Does it feel weird?"

"Yeah, it happens from time to time." Hollis shrugged. "But they can't feel anything, and neither can we."

"Can you feel each other?" I asked.

He shook his head. "We can see and hear each other even on the waking plane, but we can only make contact in a dreamscape—with the dreamer and with each other. For example, I can only do this here."

He reached out and smacked Sinan on the side of the head, taking him completely by surprise.

Oskar clicked his fingers, and four large steins of beer appeared. He downed half of his in one go, but the others didn't even notice the drinks.

Sinan sat very still for a few seconds while Hollis eyed him, leaning away slowly. Then, moving so fast I barked a surprised laugh, Sinan lunged. He tackled Hollis, and the little table in the middle wobbled when they both knocked it.

Oskar and I laughed as we steadied the table and the beers. The wrestling match had cushions and limbs flying, but the two men were laughing as much as we were.

"Reverie." Oskar gently tugged on my elbow, and I turned to face him. "Thank you."

"What for?"

"I don't think you understand how precious this is to us, how rare. To be able to taste so vividly, to be able to experience touch . . ." He lifted a hand as though to caress my cheek but let it drop at the last second. "I had hoped we would have more understanding of one another after this conversation, but I never imagined this." He smiled fondly at the other two still throwing each other about the room.

Sinan managed to get to his feet, his coat askew, one boot missing. Hollis launched himself forward and tackled Sinan around the waist, sending both of them flying over the little table in a move worthy of an action movie.

It only registered they were about to crash into us when Oskar wrapped an arm around my back and yanked me to the side.

I laughed as we fell into the cushions, but the laugh faded when Oskar brushed some hair off my forehead and I looked into his eyes. I wanted to kiss him.

And it was my damn dreamscape, where inhibitions were down and minds were more open, so I did.

I closed the distance and pressed my lips to his. He tasted like beer, his lips so soft and warm against mine. After a beat of shocked silence, his eyes fluttered closed and he kissed me back, his tongue darting out to seek permission.

I opened my lips for him, and the kiss turned intense. His hand gripped my thigh, which was suddenly hitched over his hip. My chest pressed against his as I held on to the back of his neck.

A low moan escaped my throat, my entire body sparking with sensation.

Oskar broke the kiss and pulled back to stare at me with wide eyes. He was so sexy with his usually neat hair disheveled, his glasses askew. When had I unbuttoned his shirt?

Before I could push the fabric aside to take a look at what was underneath, he leaned away, putting more distance between us. I looked up and remembered we weren't alone.

Sinan was kneeling behind Hollis, his arm wrapped around Hollis's neck in a headlock, but neither of them were wrestling anymore. They just stared at us.

A cold gust of wind blew my hair back, and I looked up with a gasp.

The tent was gone; only the cushions and rugs remained. Above us stretched the most magnificent night sky I'd ever seen.

I felt both incredibly free and wildly exposed.

Oskar sat up, his back to me, and ran his fingers through his hair.

The others got to their feet, and Sinan started walking toward us as he clicked his fingers.

I awoke with a gasp, still on my bed, still fully clothed, still completely alone.

My body still felt as if Oskar's touch was within reach.

I wanted to reach for him. I wanted him to reach between my legs and . . .

I groaned and rolled to the side, hiding my head under a pillow as embarrassment washed over me. But even that unpleasant sensation didn't make the lust disappear; the ache between my legs persisted.

Despite the embarrassment, I couldn't help grinning under the pillow as I bit my lip. Had our brief make-out session felt as real to him as it had to me? I hoped so, and I wanted to do it again.

I didn't even care if any of this was real anymore. Real or not, they made me feel more alive than I ever had, and I was not about to give that up.

Chapter Eight

I hadn't used the barbecue in my paved patio area since last summer, but it worked just fine. The smell of smoky meat grilling mingled with the sound of chatter and laughter. I smiled as a friend took the tongs from me, commandeering the grill. We clinked bottles, and I took a sip of the beer.

People were milling about, having a great time. Music added to the relaxed atmosphere. Everyone wanted to spend time with me, and I had to make sure to talk with them all. I chatted with a group of girlfriends as I leaned on the gate to my ginseng garden. They were all bright smiles and open expressions.

I felt . . .

. . . good!

Sinan, Oskar, and Hollis sat on a bench at the edge of the patio. Excusing myself, I made my way over to them.

"I'm mad at you three." I propped my hands on my hips, but I was still smiling. Why was I mad at them again?

"But never mind that now. Come help me make more punch."

They shared loaded looks, and Oskar got to his feet. He said something, but I couldn't make it out over the noise of the party.

"What?" I frowned and stepped closer. Again, his mouth moved, but no sound came out. Sinan got to his feet too, coming in close. He looked as though he was yelling, but all I could hear was the meat grilling and people chattering in the distance.

With an exasperated expression on his face, Hollis pointed behind me.

I turned, confused. There was nothing strange to look at.

A drop of water hit my shoulder, and I glanced up to find the sky filled with dark clouds. Wow, that had come on quickly. It was so bright and sunny a moment ago.

As more drops started to hit my arms and head, a burning smell reached me.

I took a few urgent steps toward the barbecue but froze on the spot at what I saw. The meat had turned to charcoal, smoke billowing off the grill. My friend dropped the tongs onto the grill unceremoniously. They made a clanking sound, and everything went quiet. The music disappeared, as did the chatter. Only the sound of the rain could be heard as my friend turned to face me.

I gasped, my hand coming up to cover my mouth.

He had no eyes. There were just red cavities dripping blood onto his cheeks. He lifted one hand in front of his face and opened his fingers, revealing his eyes sitting in the palm of his hand. His head angled toward them, as if he could still see with those empty sockets. Then he tossed his own eyeballs onto the barbecue.

They sizzled on the hotplate, melting into one milky puddle.

The rain was coming down so hard I couldn't even hear the barbecue anymore.

I looked around my yard in horror.

Everyone was facing me; those who still had eyes stared. My friends by the fence all raised their hands at the same time, capturing the eyeballs that rolled out of their sockets.

A couple at the table dug their fingers into their skulls until they pulled their own eyes out.

Everyone's eyeballs were either falling out or getting yanked out. The whole group stood in the torrential rain, staring at me through gory, bloody holes.

I covered my face with my hands. I didn't want to be here.

I didn't . . .

. . . want . . .

"Reverie! Wake the fuck up!" Hollis's voice in my ear pulled me from the horrible dream.

I woke up disoriented, scared, and with a sick feeling in the pit of my stomach.

I was also in a literal ditch getting rained on.

I sat up and pressed my hands to my eyes, breathing a sigh of relief that I could feel them there.

"Rev? Can you hear us?" Oskar's voice almost made me cry out with relief.

"Oskar?" I licked the rain off my lips.

"Yes, I'm here."

"We all are," Sinan added, and I remembered Hollis's demanding voice waking me.

"Hollis?" I had to confirm. And I was actually thankful for the rain—it hid the tears.

"Right here, doll."

I looked around, trying to get my bearings. The tops of tall trees towered over low brick buildings, so I was probably still in town somewhere. The other nearest towns were over a day's walk on foot; no way could I have gone that far in my sleep.

Dark rainclouds covered the moon. Judging by the darkness, it couldn't be anywhere close to dawn yet.

"Are you all right?" Oskar asked.

"Yeah, I'm fine. But someone else out there won't be." I hauled myself to my feet, grimacing. This time, I didn't have socks on. I was in my underwear and a soaked-through faded white MTV T-shirt. I may as well have been naked.

"What do you mean?" Sinan's voice remained even and measured. "About someone else . . ."

I sighed. "That's what happens when I sleepwalk. I have a lovely dream that turns to shit. I wake up somewhere random that isn't my bed. And someone I know doesn't wake up at all."

Silence. None of them had anything to say to that. Whatever. It wasn't as if I'd heard from them in the past few days anyway. They'd pretty much disappeared since that last dream when we talked and I kissed Oskar.

I recognized the street name illuminated by the only streetlamp. Flinders Avenue. I'd ended up at the industrial end of town. Flinders Avenue eventually intersected with

Main Street, but this end was just warehouses and a lumberyard.

At least this time I didn't have to walk through town to get home. The other end of Flinders connected to a winding back road that led to my street. I was more likely to come across a fox back there than any of the locals.

Miserable, drenched in rain and despair, I started walking.

Who the fuck was there even left to take? I literally had no one left in my life.

Even the voices in my head had abandoned me.

"Reverie?" Oskar sounded wary, unsure.

"Oh, you are still here? Great," I deadpanned. Easier to be sarcastic than admit my tangible sense of relief at the sound of his voice. I never felt more alone and worthless than I did walking home after one of these horrid incidents.

But they'd abandoned me once already, and I couldn't just . . . let them back in.

"Of course we are," he said. "We're not going anywhere."

"Uh-huh, yeah, sure." I rolled my eyes and folded my arms over my tits. It was summer rain, coming down hard but not freezing. Not exactly a hot shower either though, and the girls were saluting the night through the thin white fabric.

"It was rather distressing not being able to wake you," Oskar said.

"Yeah, well, it wasn't exactly a picnic for me either."

"This is so dangerous. You could've gotten hit by a car or . . ." Hollis sounded genuinely worried.

"Yeah, but nothing happened to me. Nothing ever happens to me."

The rain came down in steady sheets, and I had to keep pushing my hair off my face. This was the most miserable night of my miserable fucking life.

I stepped on a pebble—the little fucker digging into my heel—and yelped, overbalanced, and nearly fell into a bush by the side of the road. I growled my frustration and kicked at the innocent foliage.

A few deep breaths didn't make me any calmer, but I kept walking. The sooner I got home, the sooner I could warm up and tend to my feet.

"Are you all right?" Oskar asked tentatively.

"Yeah, I'm totally peachy!" I yelled into the rain. "Everything is just fucking *great*!"

"Perhaps we should give you some space," Sinan hedged.

"No!" I turned on the spot, for some reason imagining them behind me. All the anger and snark drained out of me. "Please don't leave."

My voice sounded weak, vulnerable. I hated it, but the thought of them bailing on me was more than I could handle right now.

"It's all right. We're not going anywhere," Hollis assured me.

"We're right here, Reverie. Keep walking. You need to get out of the rain," Oskar encouraged.

I listened to him, trudging along with my head down, no longer even bothering to push the hair or the water out of my face.

"I only meant to offer you some privacy and space." Sinan sounded simultaneously sorry and annoyed.

"I know. It's OK," I told the concrete under my feet. "I should get home in another half an hour. Just stay with me until I get home. Then you can leave if you want to."

"We don't want to—"

"Perhaps," Oskar interrupted, "more serious conversation can wait."

"Yes! Our girl needs a distraction right now," Hollis announced.

Calling me "our girl" was a pretty good start as far as distractions went. I was just some loner with weird dream powers, and they were magical, hot Sandmen I could hear in my head. No one was anyone's anything in this shitshow.

The guys spent the rest of my horrible walk home talking about all the food they longed to taste, telling me about all the things they wished they could do for me—like give me their coat, or carry me, or hug me for warmth—and cracking bad jokes. I didn't laugh or respond at all. I only had enough willpower to keep putting one foot in front of the other.

But the fact that they stayed with me the whole way made me feel warm like no coat or hug could. Made me feel warm deep in my chest in a dangerous kind of way.

As soon as I got inside, I headed straight for the bathroom and jumped into the shower with my soaked T-shirt still on. I adjusted the water to lukewarm so I didn't give myself a shock, then peeled the fabric off. Increasing the temperature bit by bit, I got it to a comfortable scalding level, and blood flow returned to my fingers and toes.

Once my muscles had loosened, I got dressed in fresh

underwear and my *MacGyver* T-shirt, made myself a cup of hot chocolate, and got into bed. My phone told me it was just after two in the morning. I felt exhausted but also too nervous to sleep.

Two sleepwalking episodes had never happened this close together. Months or even years always passed between incidents. What did it mean?

The hand holding the hot chocolate started to shake, and I gripped the mug with both hands, taking a sip.

"Hey . . . ," I croaked, then cleared my throat. "You guys . . . uh . . . you around?"

"We're here." Hollis sounded close, as if he was sitting next to me.

"All of you?"

"We are." Oskar was a little farther away—maybe at the end of my bed?

"Sinan?"

"Over here, seductress." He was definitely in the chair in the corner, on top of my pile of clothes not quite dirty enough to go in the basket yet.

"Thank you for staying with me." I took another sip. I'd never had someone to talk to about my fears when this happened—but maybe I still didn't. They'd disappeared for days without an explanation.

"Why did you think we wouldn't?" Oskar read my mind. "Why did you think we would want to leave?"

I took another sip, frowning into the mug. "Because you already did."

I hated how meek I sounded. I may have felt raw and vulnerable, but I refused to act like a kicked puppy. Sitting up higher on the pillows, I raised my head and my voice.

"After the last lucid dream. You just bailed without so much as a goodbye. Frankly, it was rude to make me believe you're . . . gods of dreams or whatever and then just disappear on me."

I wanted to ask if it was because I'd kissed Oskar, because I'd unwittingly crossed some line, but I held back. They could bloody explain themselves.

"You don't remember?" Sinan's frame flickered in my vision—in the chair, just as I'd thought.

"The lucid dream? Yeah, I'm pretty sure I remember every detail, and I don't recall anything that would warrant this passive-aggressive bullshit. If you're done with whatever this is, just say so."

"Reverie," Oskar said, "we talked about this last night."

"What?" I snapped. I had no memory of that, and I was not about to let these assholes gaslight me. I glared at the spot where I thought Oskar was sitting, and he flickered into view as well, his form muted and transparent but more stable than Sinan's had been a moment ago.

"Last night." Oskar frowned before flickering out of view. "We finally reached you in your dream, and we talked about this."

"No, we didn't," I insisted. "I haven't heard from any of you or seen you in my dreams since that last lucid dream."

"Rev." Hollis's voice made me look to my side, and I found him sitting on the bed with his legs crossed, facing me fully. "We've been here all along. You just couldn't hear us because the lucid dream took a lot out of you. We've been in your dreams too, but you haven't seemed to notice us. You're recharging now, and we're back. We went over this last night."

My brows furrowed. He sounded and looked so genuine. "Sometimes I have dreams I can't remember."

I'd had one of those last night—that feeling I'd dreamed something important, but I just couldn't reach it.

"That's probably what happened." Sinan leaned forward, his elbows on his knees. "You dreamed that you were on a boat and the three of us were with you. You were cracking jokes about a Metallica song." His lips twitched in amusement. "Once our dream selves—your mind's version of us—had disappeared, we were able to talk to you and explain everything."

"I don't remember any of that." I frowned.

"That's OK. You know now." Hollis smiled. "How are you feeling?"

I shrugged, any mirth draining out of me as fast as it had risen. "I'm fine. I'm warm after the shower and the hot chocolate." I downed the rest of it and set the mug on the bedside. "And I managed not to do too much damage to my feet. It's not me I'm worried about."

"Is this about the people who fall into perpetual sleep?" he pushed gently.

"Yeah," I said, my voice low, as I slumped farther down in the bed. "Every time I sleepwalk . . ." I shrugged. What else was there to say? They probably knew it all better than me.

"Do you always walk a long distance from your home?" Oskar asked.

I kept my gaze on the blanket. "Yeah. I mean, the first few times it happened, no, but since I've been an adult, yeah. I always end up in some random new place. I usually don't wake up until the morning though, so thanks for that."

"I'm glad we were finally able to wake you," Hollis said, and I gave him a small smile.

"Me too."

"I have never experienced that," Sinan said. "It was . . . unnerving."

I frowned at him. "What? Not being able to wake someone?"

"Yes. We don't have any control of the waking world. We can sometimes encourage people to be more amenable to sleep, but we can't force them to sleep. But the dream-scape? That's our domain. We can wake anyone up at any time—shove them into consciousness, if you will."

"Until tonight." I sighed.

"Until tonight." He nodded.

"Is that because of my weird dream juju or whatever? Like, is it just another one of my superpowers? Maybe that's why people around me keep falling into comas? I'm, like, projecting my super sleep power or something?"

The three of them shared worried looks.

I folded my arms and lifted my chin. "Don't go having silent conversations about me. What are you three hiding?"

"We're not hiding anything, doll." Hollis moved in closer. "It's just that we don't want to freak you out."

"Freak me out? Everyone I love has ended up in a fucking coma. I just woke up in the literal gutter in my underwear in the rain. I don't think I can get any more freaked out."

"Wait a moment." Oskar leaned forward, frowning. I gave him a "what?" expression.

"Can you see us?" he asked, his eyes widening.

"Oh, that, yeah." I waved my hand dismissively.

All their eyebrows rose, practically disappearing into their hairlines.

"Extraordinary," Oskar breathed, voice full of awe.

"I guess she's recovered from that lucid dream." Hollis's eyes danced with amusement. "And then some."

"Wait a second!" I sat up. "Don't change the subject! What aren't you telling me?"

Oskar's expression closed off. "Perhaps—"

"She has a right to know," Sinan interrupted him. He didn't argue his point or even wait for anyone else's opinion. He just came out with it: "You are not the cause of what has befallen those people. But the *thing* responsible *is* connected to you. We're sure of that now. We just haven't figured out why."

The relief at hearing I wasn't at fault hit me as palpably as the fear that some unknown entity was haunting me and knocking out anyone I got close to.

How was I supposed to get any sleep now?

CHAPTER NINE

Despite the eventful night I'd had, I did actually manage to fall asleep. It was a deep, dreamless sleep that had me waking up way more rested than I should've after traipsing around on the roads in the rain. As I stretched out on the bed, smushing my face into the pillow for an extra few minutes of snooze, I wondered how much of a hand my new dreamy friends had played in helping me sleep and keeping my anxiety dreams away.

They'd all sat in their same spots as I drifted off, talking quietly about nothing important. And when I rolled onto my back and opened my eyes, I was surprised to find them all still there.

"Don't you guys have work to do?" My voice was husky with sleep. "Or anything better to do with your time than watch me sleep like a bunch of creeps?"

"You think we're creepy now?" Sinan raised one eyebrow, his head resting on the back of the chair and his legs stretched out in front of him. "You haven't seen anything yet, temptress."

As if to prove his point, his eyes dragged down my body, then lingered on my legs where they stuck out of the covers. I rolled my eyes but turned away as I sat up, hiding my smile.

"How are you feeling this morning?" Oskar asked, getting to his feet at the same time I did. Unlike Sinan, he averted his gaze from my *indecently* exposed legs like a gentleman. Whatever. They were in my bedroom, and I wasn't about to cover up to make a bunch of men comfortable.

"Pretty good after a nice solid sleep, thank you." I looked over my shoulder and gave him a meaningful smile.

"You're welcome, dollface," Hollis answered for him, winking at me and copping an unashamed eyeful of my ass.

"You guys know I can still see you, right?" I called over my shoulder as I headed for the bathroom. I could hear them speaking in low urgent voices, but I ignored it while I went about my morning routine.

I needed to do a delivery in Springfield today, and I had some ginseng parcels ready to mail too. But as it got closer to the time I needed to leave, my good morning mood was steadily pushed out by the anxiety of what waited for me out there.

Who would be in the hospital today? Would I have to wait for days to find out?

Hollis hovered around as I went about my morning— chatting to me, asking about Pop-Tarts or the plants I was watering, or singing an old-timey song—but I didn't give him much in return. Still, it was nice to have company, especially when I was not in a good headspace.

When I got into the truck, ready to leave, Oskar was in

the seat next to me.

"You all right?" he asked, glancing at my hands white-knuckling the steering wheel.

I blew out a tense breath, nodded, then started the car and pulled out. "Yep. Where are the others?"

"Doing their jobs."

"Where do you guys go? Like, what do you do when you're not here?"

"We go where we're needed. We guide people into the dreams they need to have or out of dreams causing unnecessary distress. We help insomniacs get to sleep where we can. We wake people when they need it. We observe and learn."

"How do you know where you're needed? Do the three of you manage everyone's dreams on the planet?"

"No." He chuckled. "There are many like us. There were many before, and there will be many after."

"Cryptic as fuck, but OK," I mumbled. At least that told me they weren't some kind of immortal godlike beings. And they'd mentioned they used to be human like everyone else.

"And in terms of knowing where we are needed . . ." He shrugged. "We just know. It is one of those things that's hard to explain. Perhaps one of those things we are not meant to understand."

"What are we not meant to know?" Hollis appeared in the middle seat between me and Oskar.

I startled, making the truck swerve too close to the sheer drop into the woods.

"Can you not!" I shouted, righting the car. "Fuck."

Hollis cringed. "Sorry."

"It's OK." I sighed, calmer now that I wasn't staring

down death by epic crash off the side of a mountain. "It's just gonna take some getting used to now that I can see you as well. Please just be careful about popping up out of nowhere when I'm handling heavy machinery."

"You got it." Hollis nodded and pulled a legit pocket watch out of a little pocket on his vest. His waking-world appearance was pretty monochrome, but the watch definitely looked like gold.

"Are you late for something? Does that thing even work?" I asked.

"Yes, it does. But it is kind of redundant. We skip around time zones all the time, so it's rarely accurate, and we don't experience time in the same way. I suppose it's just habit." He slowly closed the watch and ran his thumb over it. After a beat of silence, he added: "It was my father's, and his father's before that."

Any comforting—or invasively prying—words I may have said were replaced by another gasp when I looked in the rearview. Sinan was in the back of the truck. He crouched by the back window, looking out at the forest whipping past.

I grumbled something about being careful what you wished for and focused on the road.

As we approached Springfield, something occurred to me. "Hey, why is Sinan in the back?"

"There's no room for him," Oskar answered.

"Yeah, but the last time you all came for a drive with me, I could hear you all in the cab."

"Uh . . ." Oskar looked at Hollis, and the other man gave it to me straight.

"We didn't want to freak you out."

I gestured for him to continue as I pulled to a stop at a red light.

"We do not have corporeal bodies in the waking world," he explained, "so we can occupy the same space. It's a little odd for us, as we can see each other fully, but we're used to having no sensation. It might be a little unsettling for you though."

I scoffed. "More unsettling than seeing and hearing shit that literally no one else can?"

Sinan appeared in the cab with us, making me jump but laugh at the same time.

"Hey." He gave me a sarcastic smile, but I couldn't stop laughing.

He'd appeared right next to me. If I'd been able to feel him, he would've been completely pressed up against my side. Hollis had moved slightly to make room, and Oskar was now pressed up against the passenger door. They were all . . . *overlapping* was maybe the best way to describe it. Their arms and sides bled into each other while remaining distinct at the same time. They'd never have been able to jam in here with me if they'd been solid. Even just two would've been a tight fit.

It was trippy to look at, for sure, but more fascinating than freaky. Pretty soon my laughter faded, and I just ogled them.

"Wow," I whispered. My eyes roved over the sight, then moved up to meet Sinan's gaze. He was staring at me as intently as I'd been staring at them.

A horn blared, making me jump. It was turning out to be a really jumpy day. I'd been so distracted by my ghost guys I hadn't realized the light had changed to green.

With a wave to the guy behind me, I took off.

When we pulled into the delivery bay for Cecconi's, I killed the engine and gave my companions a serious look. "Before we get out of this car, I need you three to promise to behave."

Sinan slowly raised one eyebrow, as though he immediately saw this as a challenge. Hollis grinned, probably reliving how fun it was to torture me the last time.

"Is she trying to parent us again?" Oskar surprised me by cracking a joke.

I let myself laugh lightly before getting serious again. "I'm not kidding, guys. Last time was a shitshow, and now that I can see you as well as hear you, it'll be even more distracting." I paused, fiddling with the dent in the steering wheel. "Everyone already thinks I'm a weirdo. I don't need to be making it worse. And today is tense enough, considering last night."

I still hadn't heard who'd been struck down, which was surely contributing to my jumpiness.

"We'll behave." Hollis gave me a sincere look, and Oskar nodded in agreement.

"Yes, fine." Sinan sighed. "But you should not be concerned about what others think of you."

"Yeah, well, that's just not how the waking world works," I grumbled as I got out of the car.

Thankfully, they did behave as I delivered the herbs and had a brief friendly chat with the owner. I wanted to be aloof and bitchy so he'd leave me alone—especially after last night—but I had to maintain a good relationship with my customers.

The guys followed me around but didn't try to distract

me, only chatting to each other quietly from time to time. Compared to the last time we'd gone on a delivery together, the difference was night and day. They were good as I spent an obscene amount of time in the post office waiting to send off all my packages. They even kept the commentary to a minimum when I went to a café for lunch—although I wished I could talk to them more while I sat seemingly alone at a little table on the patio.

I hadn't mentioned it to them, but I planned to make one last stop before we headed home. My mom had been in the local hospital here—the closest one to where I lived—for the last nine years. I visited almost every time I came to town.

As I pulled into the hospital's parking lot, the guys all fell silent.

"You don't have to come with me if you don't want to," I told them. "But I'm going to visit my mom for a while."

"Would you like to be alone?" Oskar asked as I started walking toward the entrance.

I gave his question some thought, then shook my head. "Honestly, it would be nice to have some company for once."

Hollis skipped ahead and turned to face me, walking backward. "Then you're stuck with us for—"

Whatever he'd been about to say was cut off by a loud sound—something between a growl of frustration and a wail of agony.

I'd arrived at the hospital doors just as Vera appeared to be leaving. Her face was tear streaked and blotchy, her hair a mess, and she was coming right for me.

Eyes wide, I tried to back away but not fast enough. She

lunged forward and punched me, her fist landing awkwardly on my cheek. Hollis and Oskar moved as if to get between us, but obviously Vera's next swing went right through them. I managed to duck the second blow, and an older couple grabbed Vera and pulled her back.

"Come to finish off the job?" she screamed at me as her parents tried to get her to calm down.

"What?" I backed up farther, poking at my now throbbing cheek. I was pretty sure I knew what this was about.

Sinan paced next to us, his piercing gaze fixed on Vera, his whole demeanor tense and coiled. The others had remembered they weren't solid and stood off to the side, wearing matching expressions of frustration.

"Travis is in the hospital, fucking *comatose*, because of *you*!" She pointed an accusing finger at me, and I felt it like a stab to my gut. "I'm not letting you anywhere near him. I'm going to fucking kill you, Reverie! You don't get to do this to people and get away with it."

"I didn't do anything," I said, my voice small. I suddenly felt like that eleven-year-old who'd just lost her dad. "I'm just here to visit my mom. I'm really sorry—"

"Don't!" Vera yelled again. "Don't you dare say sorry when this is all your fault. My husband is . . ." She sobbed, then recovered. "And it's all your fault."

Her parents finally managed to drag her away, giving me dirty looks as they went. Just in time too. I hated seeing people in pain—it was about the only time I didn't respond to their hostility with sarcasm and a fuck-you attitude. But I could only take so much.

Hollis appeared in front of me, examining my cheek with a hiss.

I turned away from him and started walking back to my car. Being here today wasn't a good idea. I didn't want to risk running into Travis's family and getting another whack to the head.

But the sight of Vera crying between her parents in the parking lot brought me to a halt. I couldn't follow them either.

"Fuck this," I growled and headed back toward the entrance. *I shouldn't have to hide from people. I have just as much right to be here.*

Head held high, I walked through the familiar halls to the ward where my mom lay in an unexplainable perpetual sleep. Not until I reached the room and sat next to her, taking her hand in mine, did I realize only Hollis was still with me.

"Where did the others go?" I asked. I'd closed the door, and it wasn't unusual for visitors to talk to comatose patients anyway, so I didn't worry about anyone hearing me. "Were they called away by the mysterious pull of your duties?"

Hollis leaned on the opposite wall, legs crossed at the ankles, hands in his pockets. "No. They're just taking a closer look at this Travis guy and Diana and . . ." He glanced at Mom's peaceful sleeping form.

"My mom." I smiled down at her. "Hey, Mom. I know you can't see or hear him—hell, I'm not sure you can even hear me—but this is Hollis. He's standing by the wall just over there, looking very dapper, like he's just stepped off the set of *The Great Gatsby*."

Mom freaking loved that movie—and the book. Hollis looked down with a small smile, almost . . . bashful.

Sinan and Oskar walked through the door then—and when I say "through" I mean *through* the closed door. Sinan perched himself on the end of Mom's bed, and Oskar took the chair next to me.

"You should have this looked at while you're here." He raised his hand as if to touch my cheek, then remembered himself. I waved him off anyway.

"I'm fine. What did you find out?"

"Perhaps we can discuss this after your time with your mother," Sinan suggested.

"No." I shook my head. "I've spent my whole adult life wanting to know what the hell this is. I'm done waiting, and I'm done avoiding the painful truth too. Whatever it is, just tell me."

I *had* been avoiding this. They'd hinted at what was responsible for the comas, and I could've pushed for more info at any time. Instead I'd distracted myself with the novelty of having them around. I didn't want to face the potentially painful reality.

But I knew better than anyone that life just didn't work like that.

Oskar leaned back and crossed one leg over the other. "We've confirmed what we suspected. Your mother, the waitress, and this latest victim are all affected in the same way—targeted by the same thing. They are, for all intents and purposes, asleep."

"But they are unreachable by any of us." Hollis picked up where Oskar left off. "We've all tried to enter their dreamscapes, wake them, make any kind of connection. We have failed every time."

"OK . . ." This wasn't really news to me. "And?"

"The dreamscape is our domain," Oskar said. "There is very little we cannot do when it comes to sleep. It is highly unusual to be blocked from entering a dreamer's dreamscape."

"Right . . . but you couldn't enter mine last night either, right?" I was connecting dots; I just didn't know what they led to.

"Yes. We could not reach you in the same way we cannot reach the others."

"OK. What does all that mean?" I asked, getting impatient. "Is it me? I'm, what? Going into other people's dreamscapes when I dream and knocking them out?"

"No. That's not possible," Hollis assured me.

"Yeah, well, no one but me can see you, so *not possible* is not exactly a limitation here."

Sinan cut to the chase. "It's not possible it's you because we know it's someone else."

The air in the room felt thicker somehow, heavy with foreboding, and I braced myself for what Sinan was about to say.

"The only time we cannot enter a dreamscape is when another Dreamwalker is already in it and blocking our access. From time to time, we need to do this in order to deal with a particularly fragile mind, but we can do it at will. The same Dreamwalker who blocked us from you last night is the one responsible for the state Travis is in currently. I'm positive it's the same one responsible for all the people who have fallen victim to this phenomenon."

Sinan got to his feet and looked me dead in the eyes, across the bed of my prone mother. "The only thing we're not sure about is how this is all connected to you."

CHAPTER TEN

I slowly paced the length of my patio, chewing on my thumbnail. Up and down I went as the afternoon sun cast everything in a warm glow.

The guys had explained all they knew at the hospital, but before I'd processed it enough to ask questions, a nurse had come into the room to bathe and change Mom. Oskar and Sinan were called away shortly after that, so Hollis stayed with me on the trip home. We passed the drive in comfortable silence, listening to music, both of us lost in thought.

Oskar appeared around the time I started pacing, just in time for Hollis to disappear. He'd taken a seat on one of the chairs, one elbow resting on the table, his demeanor nothing but patient.

I frowned at him and stopped my pacing. "How do you do that?"

"What?" He cocked his head.

"The sitting and the leaning." I waved at his comfy pose. "Aren't you supposed to be immaterial or whatever?"

"I'm not technically sitting in the chair." He got to his feet to illustrate, passing through the table and moving to a clear space. "We can assume any position on our plane of existence. We can't feel anything but a vague sense of our own beings. I can position my body in any way, and it'll stay there."

To illustrate, he bent at the waist and sat down—on thin air. Then he lifted an elbow and rested it on more thin air, mimicking his exact position from just moments before.

"OK, that's weird. You can stop now." I resumed pacing, relieved to see him back in his spot at the table when I passed. "What's this thing called again? A moron?" I asked, getting to the topic I really wanted to discuss.

"A Maron. It's just a word from Germanic roots that has been used since before I became . . . what I am. The name doesn't really matter. What matters is what it does and why it needs to be stopped."

"Right. Because it feeds on sleep?"

"In a way, yes. It uses its power in a perverse way. It puts people into an unnatural sleep so it can use them to become more powerful, to hold on to this world. And the more powerful it becomes, the more people it can prey on and keep blocked from other Dreamwalkers."

"Because it used to be a Sandman like you guys. So, any one of you could turn into this moron thing?"

"Maron." He smirked. "And we prefer Dreamwalkers, and yes, any Dreamwalker has the potential to turn to the darkness. Usually we catch it fairly quickly though. Keeping ourselves in check is one of our duties—one of the things we get called for. I have never seen one remain unchecked for this long. It's immensely powerful."

"And it's remained undetected and unchecked because of me—because of this weird juju I have."

"It is the logical conclusion, yes. What you have is an exceptionally rare gift. There are only a handful of Seheraum in a generation."

It didn't feel like a fucking gift. "So it *is* all my fault then."

"No." Sinan appeared directly in my path, startling me to a stop. He'd literally just *appeared*, his hazy form not there one second, then right in front of me the next.

"Dammit! Don't do that!" I smacked him on the arm—or tried to. My hand went right through him, and he gave me a withering look. "Can't you all just walk through a door like normal people?"

"We are not normal people." Sinan scowled, not moving an inch. "And no, this is not all your fault. The Maron has used you and your abilities to hide from us. At the beginning, I suspected you were working with it for some reason, but it seems to be using you. You have been its target as much as anyone else."

I deflated and sank into a chair next to Oskar. "I'm just so fucking tired. It feels good to get some answers, don't get me wrong, but I've been fighting an invisible enemy my whole life, and now I find out all I've actually been doing is helping it hurt people. This is bullshit."

Oskar reached for my shoulder, then dropped his hand when he remembered he couldn't touch me. I gave him a sad smile, acknowledging the gesture. It would've been really fucking nice to have some support in that moment, to feel the comforting touch of someone who cared.

But Oskar used his words instead. "You didn't know

what you were dealing with, and you didn't have a Dreamwalker to guide you through your gifts. But you have us now. We'll help you. You're not alone in this any longer."

"Hey." Hollis walked out onto the patio from the sliding kitchen door. I sat up straight, pointing to him while bugging my eyes out at Sinan.

He rolled his eyes.

Hollis ignored us, his expression serious. "We have company."

"Company?" I frowned. I literally never had company. "Like, another Dreamwalker?"

"No. Some joyless man in a suit. He just pulled up outside."

The doorbell rang, and I groaned as I got to my feet. I knew exactly who it was, and he was not welcome company.

When I reached the front door, I opened it just enough so I could fit in the gap with my arms crossed. "Agent Andersen. I wasn't expecting you until tomorrow." I gave him a sweet smile, as if this visit were a pleasant surprise.

The guys joined us, hovering close to watch our exchange.

"Miss Hofman." He gave me a flat look. "You know why I'm here then?"

"I'm thinking it has something to do with this stunning display of violence." I gestured to my sore cheek as if I were an airhead selling it on TV. "Vera did scream at me about her hospitalized husband while she assaulted me. Are you here to take my statement before arresting her?"

His eyes narrowed on my cheek. "She did not mention an altercation," he grumbled.

"Of course she didn't!" I guess that explained why he'd

shown up sooner than usual; Vera had already talked to him.

"Would you like to press charges?" he asked out of obligation.

I seriously considered it, but it wasn't worth the drama. "Nah. I'll let it slide."

He moved on immediately: "Miss Hofman, where were you last night?"

The guys all suddenly stood up to their full heights, tense and glaring. Their hostile energy momentarily distracted me, and Andersen glanced over his shoulder to check what I was looking at.

"Sor—" I shook my head, cutting myself off. I refused to let any form of apology pass my lips to this man. "Uh, last night? I was in my bed, snug as a bug."

"Uh-huh. And what were you doing at the hospital this afternoon?"

"Wow! That's some fast police work, agent." I slow clapped, then waved a dismissive hand. "I was just popping in to pick up some blood bags for my vampire friends. Got delayed by some assault. Super inconvenient, but hey, whatcha gonna do?"

Hollis chuckled. At least someone enjoyed my dry humor.

"Do we have to go through this ridiculous dance every time?" Andersen sighed. "Mrs. Bechamp is beside herself. People are suffering here."

I stood up straight and dropped the smart-ass smile. "If you keep coming here with ridiculous assumptions and no proof, then you'll continue to get ridiculous right back. I know Vera is beside herself—she took it out on me." I pointed aggressively to my cheek. "And not that it's any of your business, but I was at the hospital visiting my mother, who is also in a mysterious coma."

"I'll be checking that with the nursing staff," he said, unaffected by *my* pain, *my* suffering.

"You do that," I said as sarcastically as I could and slammed the door in his face. Every time he came to my house to harass me, I had less and less patience for him.

I heard his footsteps retreating and peeked out the side window. As Andersen walked down the path to the street, Sinan stalked after him, his hands opening and closing as if in search of something to smash over the agent's head—exactly the same way he'd stalked after Pip in the supermarket that day.

I locked the door, then snatched some leftovers and a beer from the fridge before making my way back out to the patio. The sun was starting to set, and it was a nice warm night. Perfect for eating alfresco.

If I hadn't been in such a foul mood, maybe I could have even enjoyed it.

"Reverie?" Oskar sounded calm but in the way people sometimes do when they're really quite mad inside.

"Yeah?" I mumbled around a mouthful of cold pizza. They all sat around the table, watching me.

"Has that man bothered you before?"

"Yep." I took a long pull of beer. "He's been bothering me since . . ." I looked up and to the side. The senior special agent and I had been buddies for a long time. "Since Nora went into a coma when I was thirteen years old. He and I go way back."

"That guy was a dick," Sinan announced.

"Yeah, yep. Grade-A penis, that one," I agreed.

"Nora woke up though, right?" Hollis asked.

"Uh-huh." I swallowed another bite of pizza. "About three years after. Everyone has woken up except Mom, Dad, and old Mr. Greaves. They all tell the same damn story. The last thing they remember is going to bed like they usually do, in their own homes, in their own beds. They have no memory of me being around at all. Next thing they know, they're waking up in the hospital." I shrugged, downing half the beer.

"So why does that man continue to pester you?" Oskar looked angry. I'd never seen him angry.

"Because I'm the only link between all the people. None of them ever incriminate me because I'm never actually doing anything, but I never have an alibi because I'm the town pariah. Plus, the whole town is convinced I'm some evil witch, so they feed him their theories and suspicions. I think on some level he knows it is connected to me somehow, but his police-procedure brain can't think outside the suspect box."

"This is like the witch trials of the seventeenth century," Sinan said. "They had no proof in Salem or England or anywhere then. And they have no proof now. Preposterous."

"Dude! How old are you?" I chuckled.

"I am thirty-one," he answered matter-of-factly.

"No thirty-one-year-old I know witnessed the Salem witch trials firsthand. When were you born?"

He waved that off. "It is of no consequence."

"Sinan is a little sensitive about his . . . experience." A smile tugged at Hollis's lips.

"I am not sensitive," the sensitive one grumbled.

"You can be sensitive at times," Oskar said.

Sinan huffed. "Why are we even discussing this? We have more urgent matters to get to."

"I want to know more about you." I finished off the pizza and leaned back. Darkness had settled around us, and the song of cicadas filled the evening air. "You guys follow me around twenty-four seven. You know everything about me."

"Not everything," Hollis mumbled, more than a little innuendo in his tone.

I ignored him. "I think it's only fair that you share some more personal shit."

"Perhaps another time," Sinan gritted out. "Now, I think we need to go through all the people who have been affected by this and see if we can figure out a pattern, try to predict the Maron's next move."

"I am more than happy to tell you about my human life." Oskar smiled. "But perhaps we should focus on the issue at hand."

"Nope." I gave them a smug look, finished off my beer, and took my time going to the fridge to grab another. When I returned, I settled back in my chair and kicked my legs up on the table. "I'm not telling you shit until you three"—I pointed the bottle at them—"tell me more about yourselves. It's only fair."

"I'm happy to talk about myself." Hollis shrugged, threading his fingers behind his head with an easy smile.

"Of course you are," Sinan grumbled.

I ignored his ass and gave all my attention to Hollis. "So,

where were you born, Hollis? And when? Do you have a last name?"

"I was born in rural Illinois in 1900, and yeah, dollface, I have a last name. It's Adler."

"Hah! I knew you were a Gatsby type." I gave myself a pat on my back.

"What gave it away?" He leaned forward, still smiling.

"Oh, I don't know." I tapped my chin, as if thinking hard about it. "Maybe it was the tweed suit with that crisp shirt and tie, or that devil-may-care attitude, or the way you call me *doll*."

"Maybe." He chuckled.

"What did you do? Before . . ." I gestured vaguely to their incorporeal forms.

"Before I died and became the man of your dreams? I was an investment banker, eventually. I was born on a farm. My parents were simple people, but they wanted more for us boys, so they kept us in school longer than most boys stayed in our town. It paid off. I got myself an education and a real job and set my parents up for retirement." He looked genuinely proud of that—that he'd been able to help his parents in the long run.

"That's amazing, Hollis. I'm sure they appreciated it."

"They did." His eyes got that faraway look people get when reliving the past. "I was twenty-nine when I died. It was just before the Great Depression started."

He looked at Oskar, then Sinan, who both looked back at him with expressions full of understanding. Obviously, they'd shared stories around the proverbial campfire before.

I could sense Hollis approaching the deep pain he always covered with his constant jokes and bright smiles.

Because no one was that chipper all the time. Like my sarcasm, it was just a way to mask the pain.

"My last name is Klein, and I was born in 1854 in Leipzig, Germany," Oskar said before the conversation went there. I almost told him off for cutting into Hollis's story, but then I saw the glance of relief Hollis flashed Oskar's way, and I dropped it.

"I figured it would be Germany or somewhere around there." I sipped my beer. "Your accent kind of comes through sometimes."

He smiled. "Yes, I suppose it would. We gain the ability to understand and speak all languages when we become Dreamwalkers. Accents become irrelevant, really. But I did used to speak fairly good English, and the languages we knew stay with us."

"I guess that kind of makes sense. What did you do in Germany?"

"My family was somewhat well off, and I was able to pursue my passions even when they didn't make me a lot of money. I was a writer, a philosopher, an academic. I worked at the Laboratory of Experimental Psychology in its early days. Until my death in 1886. I was thirty-one years old."

They'd both died so young. I wanted to ask more about it, ask about the people they'd left behind, but Oskar was getting that sadly nostalgic look in his eyes too.

"What's the Laboratory of Experimental Psychology?"

"It was the birthplace of modern psychology." He puffed his chest out. Hollis and Sinan mimicked him word for word as he said it, making me laugh. "I had the privilege of working for Wilhelm Wundt for a time."

"Oh my god! Did you ever meet Freud?" I let my feet drop to the ground and leaned forward.

"Yes, actually. Once, before he started his practice of medical psychopathology." Oskar smiled but didn't give me much more, playing coy.

"What was he like?"

"Actually, he was kind of a dick."

I threw my head back and laughed. "That doesn't really surprise me."

"Yeah, he was a chain-smoker, and I found him to be somewhat arrogant, but he did know how to tell a good joke."

"That is so damn cool." I shook my head, looking between them. This felt like having beers with living, breathing history. The things they must've lived.

"I was born in 1623 in Rabat, Morocco," Sinan announced, and I gave him my attention. "I was a Barbary corsair, and I died at the age of thirty-one in 1654. I did not know any significant historical figures, but I did cross paths on the seas once with some English admiral whose name I can't recall. There. Now you know our backstories. Can we please focus?"

"You didn't tell me your last name."

"Bennani."

"Wait. Barbary corsair . . ." I eyed him up and down, taking in the boots, the loose shirt, the long coat. "Holy shit, you were a pirate!"

"Yes." He narrowed his eyes.

"Wow!" I was legit impressed. With all of them. But to be sitting here talking to a no-joke, actual *pirate* kind of blew my mind. "Did you make people walk the plank? Did you ever get scurvy? Did you do any swashbuckling?"

I had no idea what swashbuckling even was, but his expression soured with every question I threw out, and I was having too much fun.

"Did you bury treasure on a secluded island?" Hollis joined in, his grin as wide as mine.

"Did you . . . steal things . . . from other ships?" Oskar tried his best, but he really wasn't great at thinking on his feet. It made us all burst out laughing anyway—even Sinan's lips twitched in amusement.

"Did you kidnap young maidens and have your way with them on the high seas?" I added.

"It was considered bad luck to have a woman on board," he answered. "And all the women I had my way with came willingly."

All the women? Came willingly? "Did you just crack a dirty joke?" I teased.

"If you really want a taste of my previous life, temptress, join me in a lucid dream and I'll take you on a voyage you won't forget."

Did the night suddenly get hotter? Was it this humid a few moments ago?

I cleared my throat, torn between cracking a joke to lighten the suddenly heavy mood and getting into bed immediately to take him up on that offer.

"Perhaps we should discuss the Maron now." Oskar glanced between me and Sinan with a strange look in his eyes. Was that jealousy?

Hollis just sat back, observing everything with an amused smile.

"Tell us about the first time it happened," Sinan coaxed, his voice gentler than I'd ever heard it, as if he knew this would be difficult for me to discuss.

I downed the rest of my beer and leaned my forearms on the table. "I was eleven the first time. I don't remember any of it, but my mom told me later that I came into their room in the middle of the night and crawled into bed between them. I woke up snuggled against my dad's side. He didn't wake up."

"That must have been very frightening for you." Oskar's gaze was full of compassion.

"It was. He was in a coma for six years and then died of natural causes." I frowned. Would he have lived longer had the Maron not targeted him? "The next one was Nora. Mom told me I kept trying to leave the house, and she kept trying to put me back to bed.

"After that . . ." I took a deep breath. My teenage years sucked a bag of dicks. "After that, Vera and all the other kids stopped being my friends. Everyone avoided me, their parents too scared to discourage it. Even after Nora woke up. A few people tried to show me some kindness in high school—usually new kids—but they'd end up in comas eventually too, and the town just got more and more suspicious.

"Then I left for college, excited to start fresh, but after barely a month . . ." I cleared my throat, working to dislodge the lump in my throat.

"It's OK, *schatzi*," Oskar reassured me. "Take your time."

"It's OK to cry," Hollis said, just as comforting.

Sinan was watching me with a soft, patient expression —for the first time that night.

Their care and attention eased some of the weight on my chest, and I managed to keep the tears in their ducts. "After a month, I woke up one morning on the side of the highway and later found out my mom was in the hospital. I never went back to college."

"Do you have a map?" Sinan asked, a thoughtful furrow in his brow.

"Random, but OK. Uh, yeah, I can bring one up on my phone."

"No, no. It needs to be bigger so we can put markings on it."

"Dude, where the fuck am I supposed to find—" I realized what he might be getting at just as I remembered the big framed map of Gritton and the surrounding area that hung in the hallway. It was a historical thing, showing what the area looked like around the time Gritton was first established.

I rushed inside, took it off the wall, and grabbed a box of Fruit Loops on my way back through the kitchen. Setting the map on the table, I tipped some cereal out and placed red loops in the random places I'd woken up, then purple loops in the places the victims had been discovered.

"OK, so this obviously only shows so much, but college was in this direction." I pointed to the far corner of the table, well off the map. "And I woke up on the highway, like, here-ish." I placed the red loop halfway between the corner and the map. "This is not to scale, obviously, but I was walking in the direction of home."

"Who was after your mom?" Hollis asked while Oskar and Sinan stared at the map.

"Well, I kind of went full hermit for about six months after that, living off insurance money. Then eventually I started to garden, and Mr. Greaves started giving me tips and advice. He lived alone in a cabin off a dirt road in that direction." I pointed over my head to the back of my property. "He wasn't exactly friendly with the townies, but Mom and Dad used to visit him regularly, take him meals, that kind of thing. Anyway, he was in his eighties when he fell into a coma. He's another one that never woke up."

I placed Fruit Loops in the location of his cabin and where I'd woken up in the woods behind our house.

"After that, I consciously started keeping my distance from everyone. No friends, no relationships—only one-night stands and fleeting pleasantries. I did meet someone online through a gardening small business group and hoped that the distance of a digital friendship would keep him safe, but after a few months, I woke up in the woods again, and no prizes for guessing what happened to him. Then it was Diana a few weeks back, then Travis."

The Fruit Loops adorned the map, one for each instance I described, and the four of us just stood around looking at it for a few moments.

"You were trying to save them," Oskar said, "or get to them, at the very least."

I nodded and leaned heavily on the table. It was so obvious with it all laid out in front of me like that. "Why do I have no memory of any of it? Is this a Seheraum thing?"

"Yes, this has to be related to your gifts," Sinan agreed. "But no idea why you can't seem to retain the memory."

"This explains why you sleepwalk every time the Maron attacks." Oskar nodded. "And why your dreamscape is locked to us when you do."

I gestured for him to keep speaking, not having come to the same conclusion yet.

"You are connected," he went on. "This Dreamwalker —this Maron—has been with you from a young age. It's not consciously blocking your dreamscape off to other Dreamwalkers when it attacks. And you're not consciously trying to get to its victims. It's symbiosis."

"All the incidents from when you were younger involved people who were close to you," Hollis said. "Friends, family, old man Greaves who helped you out, a friend you connected with online. So why is it now targeting people you'd hardly consider acquaintances?"

"The attacks are escalating." Sinan voiced my suspicions. "But why?"

CHAPTER ELEVEN

The woods were so beautiful in winter, so pure and peaceful. I tipped my face up to the sky, and delicate flakes of falling snow caressed my skin.

Something hit my hip, breaking the moment, and I looked down to see snow sticking to my pants.

Oskar was standing by a nearby tree, already rolling another snowball. He grinned, his eyes sparkling as much as the white powder all around us, and threw it. I dropped into a crouch to avoid the incoming missile, hastily tapped two handfuls of powder into a ball, set Oskar in my sights, and sent my own snowball flying.

It hit Oskar right in the face, and he dropped the snowball he'd been working on to wipe snow off his nose.

I laughed, tipping my head back and letting loose at the outraged look on his face. The sound cut through the silence of the woods, but it soon died in my throat.

Oh shit! Adrenaline and joy bubbled up inside me as his eyes narrowed—I was in trouble. I turned and ran, pumping my legs as hard as I could, kicking snow up all around me.

All too soon, he caught me. His arms banded around my waist to lift me up and swing me around. We were both laughing now, his grip warm and comforting against the cold.

He lowered me to my feet but didn't loosen his embrace. "Caught you," he whispered, his breath stirring my hair.

"I wanted to be caught."

He rested his forehead on the back of my head and squeezed me a little tighter. I melted in his arms, and the snow started to melt with me. The powder at our feet got mushy, the branches above leaden and dripping.

"Reverie?" Oskar's hold loosened. He sounded confused.

"Yeah?"

"We should probably get back to—"

"No." I spun in his arms and grasped his waist. "Not yet. I love it here."

He smiled at me. "Yeah, let's stay."

Happiness spread through my chest like a pleasant heat. "Kiss me," I said, already leaning into him.

"OK," he whispered against my lips, then closed the distance.

His lips were as soft as the snow, his hands warm against my cheeks. He pushed me back against a tree and hiked my leg over his hip. Our hands roamed as our mouths explored.

The melting of the snow seemed to speed up, scattering drips of water all over us. I licked the droplets off Oskar's cheek, and he gave me a brilliant smile before leaning down to lick some off my neck.

"There you guys are!" Hollis's voice made me look up, but not an ounce of my being wanted to stop what I was doing with Oskar. He seemed to feel the same way, neither of us embarrassed or even surprised to have company.

"Hi, Hollis." I gasped as Oskar rolled his hips against my core.

Hollis chuckled, licking his lips as he took in the scene before him. He sauntered over until he stood right next to us. "Much as I hate to break this up"—he sighed, amusement playing in his eyes—"it's time to go."

He gripped my shoulder with one hand and Oskar's with the other.

I clinked glasses with Oskar, some champagne spilling over the rim of the wide flat glass.

"Come on." Hollis dropped his hands from our shoulders and grabbed his own glass of champagne from a passing waiter. "The fireworks are about to start. I know a good spot to watch from."

He took off, Oskar and I hot on his heels as we wound through a lively outdoor crowd of party people. String lights sparkled over women in flapper dresses and men in dapper suits, who danced and laughed and drank around a pool and elegant fountain. It felt like the set of a Baz Luhrmann movie.

Hollis led us up some stairs to a balcony overlooking the party, just as the first firework zoomed into the night sky and exploded in a dazzling display of color and light. I gasped along with everyone else. All eyes stayed glued to the sky even as the jazz band kept playing a lively tune. The fireworks were mesmerizing, energizing, and I was sure I had a wide-eyed look on my face when they ended. I turned to Hollis, then Oskar, my joy reflected in their gazes.

"Let's dance!" I needed to get this energy out. Grabbing both their hands, I rushed down the stairs and into the thick of the party crowd.

We danced and laughed. The two of them dipped me and twirled me up in the air, passing me between them like a well-practiced team. Oskar spun me around and released me as I kept turning, which sent me straight into Hollis's arms. He pulled me against his chest and started swinging his hips from side to side.

The sultry R and B beat reverberated through my body as Oskar closed in at my back. The three of us moved together, swaying and grinding as if we were in the club and it was an hour before closing time. The people around us seemed to be dancing to a different beat, kicking their feet up and bopping around. But all I could feel was the heady bass and the sensual caresses of four hands all over me.

Hollis pressed his forehead against mine, his nose caressing my own as we moved. I licked my lips; he parted his. His hand wound into my hair while Oskar pulled the strap of my dress down over my shoulder.

As Oskar started kissing my neck, Hollis leaned in . . . then jerked back?

"OK, that's enough of that," Sinan grumbled. Apparently he'd pushed Hollis back before we could kiss.

I leaned my head against Oskar's shoulder and giggled at Sinan's darkening mood. His black coat and deep frown seemed so out of place among the bright, glittery people dancing all around him.

"Come dance with us, Sinan." I held my hand out to him as Hollis leaned in once more, his hands on my swaying hips.

"Temptress . . ." Sinan sighed and pinched the bridge of his nose.

I raised one leg, hooking it around Hollis's hip, and both he and Oskar ground into me at once. Hardness at my core, hardness at my ass, and heat building in my chest.

"Are you two serious right now?" Sinan huffed, looking between my dancing partners.

"What?" Hollis flashed him his brilliant smile.

"We're dancing." Oskar stated the obvious.

"Fine." Sinan rolled his shoulders. "Hard way it is."

He rushed at us, arms spread wide. His body collided with ours, and we all went flying sideways, then splatted into the pool in a tangle of limbs and libido.

I broke the surface and took a deep breath. The sun warmed my face, and the water was the clearest and bluest I'd ever seen. I could see all the way to the white sandy bottom, even though I couldn't reach it.

Salty water slapped the side of my face, and I turned to find Hollis and Oskar splashing each other and laughing under a stunning, cloudless sky. The crystal-clear sea stretched in every direction, with only a sliver of beach in the distance.

Sinan was trying to talk to the others, but they ganged up on him and started splashing him, making me laugh. He gave up and made his way over to me.

"Temptress." He looked me right in the eyes. "I need you to wake up."

"But the water is so warm." I swam closer to him. "It's perfect, like a refreshing bath. It feels so good on my skin."

Sinan gripped my waist under the water—strong hands meeting bare flesh. His drenched clothes stuck to his powerful frame.

"We should get you out of these wet clothes," I half joked, sliding my hands under the jacket and pushing it off his shoulders.

He chuckled, his eyes sparkling like the calm surface of the water. "Why are you always trying to disrobe me?"

I shrugged and leaned into him as Hollis came floating past on his back. Oskar was swimming lazy laps around us.

Sinan's gaze suddenly turned serious, his eyes boring into me.

"Fuck it," he murmured, then slammed his lips against mine. His rough stubble scratched my palm as I caressed his cheek, but his hair felt soft and smooth. His tongue was demanding, searching, and I let him plunder my mouth all he wanted.

Hollis appeared at our side, naked, and the next moment I was kissing him. We were all naked, completely free in the perfect water. Oskar joined us, and then I was kissing him too—kissing them all. As we sank beneath the surface, everything became muted yet incredibly amplified. Every caress, every kiss, every sensation.

We writhed and rubbed and licked, moving together so perfectly it felt like a choreographed dance. Their strong bodies surrounded me, and I reveled in the feel of taut muscles and wiry hair and smooth, hard skin. Their hands were everywhere, touching me just how I liked.

It was the most erotic experience of my entire existence,

and I surrendered myself to it completely. My body sang in pleasure as the soft water around us pulsated. One mouth kissed me passionately, while a second sucked on my nipples. A third licked my neck as a hard length pushed at my entrance.

My head broke the surface just as I released a pleading moan.

But my eyes flew open at the sudden lack of contact.

I found myself able to stand. Water lapped at my ribs, and my toes dug into soft sand. The perfectly clear blue sky had been replaced by dark, fat clouds.

I was already saturated, so I didn't really care that much when it started to rain, but I felt as though I was missing something. I looked around the deserted beach, wondering where they went and why my body was . . .

. . . my body . . .

. . . was . . .

. . . *aching*.

I opened my eyes on a whimper, taking in my dark bedroom and reflexively rubbing my thighs together.

Rain poured down outside, and I released a sigh at the smell of petrichor wafting in through the open window. The movement made me painfully aware of my breasts—they felt heavy and sensitive.

"Reverie." Hollis's voice was barely a whisper. "You awake?"

I rolled my head to the side to find him on the bed with me, his outline barely visible in the darkness.

"Unfortunately." I sighed again. Then I remembered who I was talking to and cringed. "Oh god, please tell me you weren't there for that."

"Oh, I was there." His low voice sounded amused and strained.

"We all were," Sinan whispered from his chair in the corner. I could hardly see him, but he could certainly see me in the bit of light coming in from outside.

Oskar's silhouette crossed in front of the window, but he remained silent as he settled himself on the ledge, one leg up.

I groaned—partly in embarrassment, partly in frustration—while my body continued to undulate gently under the thin sheet.

"Can you all leave, please?" I breathed. I could be embarrassed about my sex dream in the morning. For now, societal conditioning could go fuck itself, because I needed to release this full-body ache.

"Why?" Sinan challenged.

"Because I'm going to touch myself until I climax." I huffed. This was my bedroom, and I was not going to censor myself. "So if you're embarrassed about what you witnessed in my dream, you're going to be mortified at what I'm about to do in real life."

"What if we want to stay?" Oskar whispered, not sounding even a little outraged or even surprised.

"Please, doll." Hollis was so close I'd have been able to feel his breath on my cheek if he were physical. "Tell us we can stay."

Really, Reverie? You're going to get yourself off with an audience? I paused to consider this for just a fraction of a second, but then I thought, *Fuck it*. It wouldn't even come close to the strangest thing that had ever happened to me.

"Stay," I said decisively. Then I dragged my hand down my body until it was between my legs.

I rubbed myself over my underwear, pushing my head back into the pillow and sighing at the relief of contact —finally.

"Holy shit." My mouth fell open. I'd barely made a dozen passes over my engorged pussy, and I could already feel an orgasm coming. I was intimately acquainted with my own body—I could make myself come in five minutes flat if I used my vibrator—but this was something new. My body was so primed I writhed on the bed and gasped in surprise as pleasure shot through me almost immediately.

"Did you just . . ." Oskar sounded curious and disbelieving. I could see his chest rising and falling with deeper breaths.

"Yep." And I was not done. I wanted their hands on me; I craved their mouths and bodies and the connection I'd felt in my dream. But that was not possible, so I was going to have the next best thing and keep going until I was spent.

I pushed my soaked underwear down my legs, taking the sheet with it, and propped my knees up. I had a moment of self-consciousness, but it passed quickly. If I was doing this, may as well go all in.

I felt brazen and powerful as I set my feet wider on the mattress and opened my knees. The air caressed my wet flesh, making me feel exposed in the most carnal way. My hand went back to between my legs, and I ran my fingers through my folds.

"I'm so wet," I gasped.

Three distinct, low groans sounded in the room, sending a shot of thrilling satisfaction through my body.

I rubbed a few slow circles around my clit, then dragged my hands up my stomach, teasing myself as much as I was teasing my audience. I pushed my T-shirt up to expose my generous tits and played with my nipples. The sensations shot right to my pussy, making it clench involuntarily around nothing.

"You have perfect tits, temptress." Sinan's appreciation of my girls pulled a moan from my lips. "I want to feel their weight in my hands, suck them, fuck them."

That heady visual sent my hand down again.

"Yeah, that's it." Hollis leaned in, his low, dirty words close to my ear. "Rub yourself harder. I want to hear that sloppy sound. Fuck, you're so wet."

I moaned again, totally incapable of words.

"I would sell my soul to have the sense of smell in this moment." Oskar surprised me with his declaration and his strained voice.

They may not have been touching me, but their words and their gazes made this feel like way more than my usual alone time. I was definitely not going solo.

Wetness coated my hand, slicking my fingers as I rubbed myself to another orgasm. This one made my back arch and incoherent sounds pour out of my throat. I kept caressing myself gently as I came down, my other hand ghosting lightly over my belly, my ribs, and my tits. I wasn't done. Not by a long shot.

As the rain pelted down outside and my three unlikely companions whispered depraved things in the dark, I brought myself to orgasm at least six times. I'd never done more than three in one session, and I had fun seeing how far I could push my body.

I also didn't want this moment to end. Their voices in my room were so clear, their forms didn't seem so immaterial in the darkness, and my body was so lost to sensation that I could almost feel them touching me. A caress to my cheek, a graze at my ankle, a touch at my neck.

It was easy to let myself believe they were really there with me, really touching me, really in the room. Just for a little while, I let myself fall into the ecstasy of that fantasy.

When my body was spent, I just lay on my bed, completely naked, and listened to the rain as my breathing evened out. Then I went to the toilet and cleaned myself up —because UTIs were not fun.

The guys stayed with me as I drifted off to sleep again. I could've sworn I heard them speaking in low voices as the dream world pulled me under, but I didn't hear what they said. It didn't really matter. They'd stayed, and I was satisfied in a way I hadn't been in a long time.

I slept late into the next morning and woke up to a bright sunny day. The summer sun had banished the rain clouds. I stretched, taking deep breaths of the warm air, before getting my ass up.

I was alone, but I knew one of them would be around here somewhere.

After a nice long shower where I kept smiling like a lunatic every time I remembered another hot moment from the previous night, I made my way into the kitchen with my hair still wet. All three of them were seated at the kitchen island, and they looked up at the same time.

"Uh, morning." I gave them a tentative smile, then

avoided their gazes as I busied myself making coffee. I was starving, but coffee was necessary. "One of you could've put the coffee on," I joke-scolded before grabbing some bread for toast.

When they remained silent, I turned to face them properly. The serious expressions on their faces instantly caused my good mood to start dripping away.

"What?" I looked between them.

Oskar leaned forward, resting his elbows on the countertop. "We need to talk about what happened last night."

The toast popped, making me jump, and I used it as an excuse to look away. I didn't want them to see the hurt in my eyes. I was not ashamed of my sexuality, and even if they regretted getting caught up in the moment, I didn't.

"OK, then. Talk." I kept my chin up, my voice even, digging the knife into the toast a little too hard as I buttered it.

CHAPTER TWELVE

"Reverie?" Hollis said.

I bit into my toast and raised one eyebrow at him.

"What's wrong, doll?"

"Ugh." I rolled my eyes. They were not allowed to play hot and cold with me and continue to use pet names. "Don't call me that. You wanted to talk, so talk." I took another big crunchy bite and shot them a look full of attitude.

"You are hurt." Oskar, the psychological genius, had figured out I used sarcasm as a shield. "Why?"

"Oh, I don't know." I leaned into the snark, waving my toast around. "Maybe because I haven't even had coffee yet, and you assholes want to *talk about last night*."

I glared at them and finished off my toast.

"Rev, this is not about the . . . uh . . . activities we enjoyed after you woke up," Oskar said. Was he blushing? He looked pretty muted and translucent still, but I could've sworn he was blushing.

"Dollface." Hollis used the nickname on purpose. I could tell, because he flashed me a grin when I glared at him. "I think I speak for everyone in this room when I say that we all enjoyed the show you put on last night. Thoroughly. This isn't about that."

Oskar nodded in agreement. Sinan crossed his arms over his chest and cocked his head to the side.

"I don't think she believes you," he said, then got to his feet and walked around the island until he was standing right in front of me. "I never do anything I don't truly wish to do, temptress, no matter how *tempting*. Regret is a waste of energy."

I took a good look into his eyes and saw nothing but sincerity. Sinan may have been a dick about it, but he never lied. I looked at the other two and sighed.

"OK, fine. What's this about then?" I asked, eager to get to the point and avoid any more scrutiny of my fragile feelings.

"It is about what happened before—in your dreamscape," Oskar explained.

I frowned as I poured myself a coffee. "So, you have no problem with the very *real* sex we had—er, I had—last night, but you do have a problem with the gang bang my dream mind cooked up?" I carried my coffee into the sunroom and settled into my favorite chair. "Look, if you're uncomfortable about crossing swords, that's a you problem. You didn't have to hang around and watch my sex dream like perverts."

They followed me into the room and situated themselves among the plants.

"That's just it," Sinan said. "We didn't just *watch* your

sex dream. You didn't just dream *about* us. We actively participated."

I blinked at him a few times. The coffee hadn't made its way to my brain yet, and I was having trouble following. "I'm sorry, what?"

"You know how we talked about the dream realm and the waking realm?" Oskar asked.

I nodded, sipping my coffee.

"And remember how we can feel and taste and experience things in an individual's dreamscape depending on how vividly they dream?"

I nodded again.

"And remember when you were learning to lucid dream, and one of the things you had to overcome was getting pulled into the dream instead of remaining consciously present?"

"Yep." So far so good.

"Well, that's what happened last night, except the other way around. You pulled us into your dream."

I started to nod, then my brow furrowed. "You've lost me. I thought you said you guys don't sleep, let alone dream. Plus, you said you can be present in a dreamscape as observers or as participants. So you're telling me you chose to be participants this time?"

"Not exactly." Oskar looked to the others for help, and Hollis jumped in.

"Consciousness is a tricky thing to explain. You're a conscious being because you're aware of your own consciousness, right? Well, we are conscious beings too, but we have no physical bodies, so it makes our existence a little harder to define."

"Riiiight." I gestured for him to keep going. It was way too early for metaphysical shit, but whatever they were trying to tell me seemed important to them, so I did my best to understand.

"Without physical bodies, all we are is consciousness. That's what defines our existence and makes it possible for us to do what we do. Regardless of how bizarre or amusing or tempting an individual's dreamscape may be, we will always be conscious of the fact that we are just visitors—there to do a job and leave."

"OK. And last night was more play than work? You feel guilty?" I lifted the mug to my mouth to hide the smile. I had a feeling cracking jokes wouldn't go down well, but Hollis laughed anyway, and Oskar cracked a smile too.

Sinan came to stand next to my chair, leaning back against the wall. "Point is, we're not supposed to forget we're in a dreamscape. It's not meant to be possible. Last night, that's exactly what happened. You pulled us all into your dream, and we forgot we were in your dreamscape, only there as visitors. We experienced those moments as fully as you did."

I mulled this over, nodding slowly at my half-empty mug while the caffeine got my brain moving enough to connect the dots.

"Oh my god!" I gasped and shot to my feet. "Are you telling me I dream-raped you? I raped you with my mind? Fuck!"

All three of them burst into laughter, and annoyance replaced my panic.

"I don't think rape is funny, but whatever."

"You didn't make us do anything against our will, doll," Hollis reassured me.

Oskar nodded. "Exactly. You may have pulled us into your dream, but even that wouldn't have been possible if we weren't open to your intentions."

"That's the first time any of us have forgotten what we are and just . . . *felt* . . ." Hollis struggled for words.

"Just existed without expectations," Sinan added.

Wow. OK. I guess it was as good for them as it was for me.

"Is this related to my being a Seheraum?" I asked.

"Most likely, yes." Oskar smiled.

"Is this bad? Should I be worried?"

"No." Sinan's answer was confident and definitive. "It just means you're far more powerful than we suspected. This is new territory for us, but it makes sense. It's a natural extension of your other abilities."

"We just have to practice to make it a tool in your arsenal and not a hindrance—like the lucid dreaming," Hollis explained.

"Right. Got it. I need more coffee." I'd need a *lot* more coffee if unexpected shit like this kept popping up.

I headed toward the kitchen, and after a beat of silence, I heard Oskar ask: "What is crossing swords? How is fencing technique relevant here?"

I laughed my ass off as the others explained context to him.

The rest of the week passed quickly, made easier by how comfortable we'd all become with one another.

Without any other leads on the Maron, the guys stuck to me like glue—well, at least one of them did at all times.

The others more or less patrolled Gritton and the surrounding areas, keeping an eye out for the thing that had been terrorizing me for years. Apparently, it wasn't so easy to make contact with another being on their plane if you hadn't already been in contact with them.

I thought of it in terms of how hard it was to make adult friendships. Like, you wouldn't give your actual number and address to someone you'd only just met, but you might follow them on Instagram. The better you got to know them, the easier it was to get in touch.

So, basically, they were stuck waiting for it to crawl out of whatever nightmarish hole it was hiding in so they could . . . actually, I didn't know what the plan was once they found it.

Note to self: ask SandDudes about ass-kicking plan.

In the meantime, life went on as normal. Well, as normal as it could get when you had three new friends only you could see. Whom you'd furiously masturbated in front of. Who flirted with you all the damn time.

The unresolved sexual tension grew more intense by the day, but it was interspersed with plenty of just . . . being around one another.

"What's the point of having three virile men around twenty-four seven when they can't even help you load heavy shit into the truck?" I grumbled as I hefted the last of the deliveries for the day into the back.

Hollis leaned on the side of the car with his hands in his pockets, eyes fixed on the forest beyond my property. He didn't turn his head as he spoke, but I could hear the smile in his voice. "We have other uses."

"Uh-huh. Yep." I got behind the wheel, started the car,

and took off without waiting for him. He appeared in the passenger seat, his body angled toward mine.

"Rude," he teased.

"Whatever."

"You all right, doll?" The amusement in his eyes dimmed. "You seem a bit extra sarcastic today."

I flipped him off as I pulled onto the main road. "Yeah, I'm fine. I just got my period this morning, and it feels like someone is stabbing me in the uterus—from the inside."

"Yikes." He cringed, and the smart-ass of the group suddenly had nothing to say.

"Are you awkward right now?" I laughed. "Dude, how long have you walked this earth? At least a hundred years? Women don't hide the fact that we bleed from the vagina once a month anymore. It's just biology. Deal with it."

"I know." He chuckled. "I'm fine with it, really. Like you said, I've been observing how society has changed for decades. It's just, when I'm with you . . ." He waved his hand around, searching for the right words. "I don't know. You make me feel real. Like what I used to feel like *before*. When I was just a regular man. Being in that frame of mind sometimes throws me back into old habits."

I made him feel real? That was the most romantic thing anyone had ever said to me.

"Tell me another story about the roaring twenties. Did you ever go to a speakeasy?" He'd made me feel better about my period pain, so if talking about his human life made him feel more real—well, that was a win-win for me. I loved all their stories.

"Of course I did!" He laughed. "A lot of people did, honestly. I even got to see Bessie Smith perform at a speakeasy once. I was so sauced that night I don't remember anything, but I remember that. She really was incredible."

"Holy shit, that's insane! Tell me absolutely every single detail," I demanded. I'd grown up listening to Bessie Smith records. Mom's Gatsby obsession had sparked a love of all things twenties.

As I drove, I listened to Hollis tell me about seeing a legend perform, and I enjoyed every second.

There had been a lot of conversations like this one over the past week. The guys had opened up more and more, telling me about their lives before they became Dreamwalkers. Hollis had told me about practically every person he knew, what his job was like, even the women he'd dated.

Oskar mostly talked about his work at the Laboratory of Experimental Psychology, his philosophy studies, all the things he enjoyed learning about. He mentioned the people in his life here and there, but I didn't want to push.

Sinan was being the most cagey. He rarely answered direct questions and almost never volunteered information. But a couple nights back, when it was just him and me in my room as I struggled to sleep, he told me a bit about what it was like to sail in one of those magnificent ships. His voice rose and fell melodically as he recalled the thrill of a voyage, the feel of fresh salty air on his face, the camaraderie between the crew.

None of them had talked about how they died. I didn't blame them.

"That was the night that George and I . . ." Hollis had moved on to another speakeasy story—one where the police showed up for a raid. He was just getting to the good part when I gasped and slammed on the brakes.

The car in front of us had swerved to avoid hitting a deer and started fishtailing all over the place. The deer disappeared into the safety of the trees, but the car careened into the ditch on the side of the road, flipped once, twice, and landed back on its wheels in the brush, looking utterly destroyed.

I managed to pull over ahead of it, jammed my car into park, and rushed out.

"Fuck, fuck, fuck," I chanted as I ran toward the wreck.

We were on a sleepy, windy one-lane mountain road in the middle of the morning. The wrecked car was the first and only one I'd seen since leaving Gritton. Whatever situation lay ahead, I'd be the one in charge of it.

Please don't be dead. Please don't be dead. Please don't be dead, I pleaded, praying to whatever goddess was out there, as I carefully stepped over the ditch and through the thick underbrush to get to the car.

All the windows were smashed, and broken glass had scattered everywhere. A man slumped forward in the driver's seat, his seatbelt keeping him from draping completely over the wheel, but to my immense relief, the rest of the car appeared empty.

"Hey, hello?" I pulled on the doorhandle. It was stuck, and I had to yank it hard to get the door open. "Can you hear me?"

The man didn't respond. When I reached a shaking hand out to check his pulse, he moaned in pain, and I nearly jumped out of my skin.

I grabbed my cell out of the front pocket of my flannel shirt and dialed 911, then took the shirt off with the phone pressed to my ear. I didn't even know why I'd put the damn thing on over my shorts and tank top that morning. It was hot out.

"911, what's your emergency?" a lady answered, and I rushed to explain the situation. She assured me emergency services were on the way and instructed me on examining the driver.

Once I had him leaning back on the seat once more, he groaned again and lazily blinked his eyes.

"What happened?" he slurred, struggling to keep his head upright.

"Hey, hi. My name is Reverie. What's yours?" I asked in as calm a tone as I could muster—blood covered the front of the man's shirt, and I needed to figure out where it was coming from.

The 911 lady said some more things and then said to keep him conscious if I could. I turned wide eyes to Hollis. I had no idea if that was in his wheelhouse, but I was beginning to panic.

"I'll do my best, Rev." He gave me an encouraging nod, then focused on the man.

I found a massive gash on the man's abdomen, just below his ribs. I couldn't figure out how it had even happened, but it was bleeding like crazy.

The 911 lady said something, then Hollis said something, then Sinan was suddenly there telling me the ambulance was just up the road, minutes away.

It all blurred together. The only thing that stood out distinctly was how glad I was I'd put the flannel on that morning. I would've had nothing to staunch the bleeding otherwise.

* * *

"ARE YOU SURE THIS IS A GOOD IDEA?" OSKAR questioned for the millionth time.

"I'm fine. These deliveries can't wait." Could a few restaurants do without herbs? Sure. Could my ginseng packages go out tomorrow? Absolutely. But in that moment, I just wanted life to continue as normal. Besides, I'd nearly reached town anyway.

All three of the guys were packed into the cab with me. After the ambulance had taken the man away and the police had taken my statement, I'd been free to go. I'd walked back to my truck and gotten on with my day. My three pains in the butt were not on board with this plan, but they couldn't do jack shit about it, so whatever.

I went about my business on autopilot as the guys watched me like hawks and murmured to one another behind my back. I hardly remembered the drive home, but when I let myself into the house, I felt exhausted—my limbs heavy, my head foggy, my soul tired.

In the bathroom, I was horrified to discover flecks of blood on my chest and arms. Nothing too gory, but the ones on my white tank couldn't be mistaken for anything else.

Really, Reverie? You went about your business looking like an axe murderer? Like people aren't afraid enough of you? I rolled my eyes at myself as I ran a bath. The guys were right—I should've come straight home. Not that I was going to tell them that.

I loved baths. I hardly took them in summer because of

the heat, but I just needed to submerge myself in the warm water and get my shit together.

After fifteen minutes, my muscles had already started to loosen, and I could accept that what I'd seen was fucked up. It was OK to be shaken.

"Reverie?" The sound of Sinan's voice made me open my eyes and sit up straighter. Then I realized my nipples were poking out of the pale blue opaque water—courtesy of a bath bomb—and I shrank back down.

All three of them were jammed in the bathroom. Sinan stood by the tub, his arms crossed. Hollis was seated on the toilet. Oskar leaned on the sink.

"Excuse you! Privacy." I glared at them.

"You weren't worried about your privacy the other night," Hollis teased, pointedly trying to get a look at what was under the water.

"Yeah, well . . ." I sighed and leaned my head back on the edge. He kind of had a point, and I couldn't be bothered arguing. "What do you want?"

"We just want to make sure you're all right," Oskar said gently.

"I'm fine," I snapped, then remembered I'd only just been telling myself they were right about wanting me to come home, so I dropped the attitude. "I appreciate it, but I'm going to be OK."

"Good. We need to discuss what happened." Sinan's voice was unyielding.

"Which part?" I raised an eyebrow without opening my eyes.

"The part where you dreamed about the accident you witnessed earlier in eerily precise detail."

My eyes shot open and I sat up straight, nipples be damned. "I what now?"

"The other night," Oskar explained, averting his gaze like a gentleman. "You dreamed about that car, that man, that accident. You don't remember?"

"No." I shook my head. I wrote in my dream journal every damn day. I definitely didn't recall that one. "I have dreams I don't remember sometimes. Everyone does, right? Maybe it's just some kind of coincidence?"

"Seheraum don't have dreams they can't remember, doll," Hollis said. "It's part of your power, your affinity with the dream realm. And the level of detail? It was not a coincidence."

"Except for how it ended," Sinan said ominously.

I just looked at Oskar, and he explained. "In your dream, you were driving along that same stretch of road, that same car in front of you. We were there observing, but we couldn't communicate with you—which isn't that unusual in itself. It's happened plenty of times before. In the dream, the wreck happened that same way. The deer, the car rolling, then you pulled over as fast as you could. The main difference is that in the dream, you weren't wearing that flannel shirt. You ran over to the man, but you'd left your cell phone in the car. You lost time running back to call 911, and when you found his wound, you had nothing but your hands to try to stop the bleeding. He bled too much, and the ambulance took too long. He didn't make it."

"You then dreamed about your parents in the same wreck and not being able to save them," Hollis added. "We figured it was just one of those dreams where your subconscious works through strong feelings about something."

"Are you telling me I saved a man's life today because a dream I can't remember told me to wear a flannel and keep my phone on me?" I gaped at them.

"That's one way to put it." Sinan nodded. "Reverie, we're pretty sure you have prophetic dreams."

"Well . . . shit." I didn't know how to process that information. It had been a really weird day. With my mind turning everything over, I slid back down into the tub until the water covered my ears.

Chapter Thirteen

I sprtized my ferns as I waited for my coffee to brew. Midway through a meandering circuit of the green room, I made a detour to my bedroom and pulled on some thick socks. Summer was on its way out, and while the overcast, cool day wasn't too cold for traipsing about the house in a *Star Wars* T-shirt and lounge pants, my feet were getting chilly.

Sinan followed me around, sighing dramatically as if that would get me to move faster. I just smiled to myself and took my time showing my plant babies some love. Somehow, he managed to keep his comments to himself long enough for me to get my coffee, settle into my favorite chair, and flip my dream journal open.

"OK, ready." I gave him a smile.

"Finally." He flicked his long coat behind him and sat directly in front of me—on literally nothing. I hated it when they sat around on thin air, and he knew it. This was payback for me not jumping into what he wanted to do immediately.

I shot him a narrow-eyed look but decided to focus on the task at hand, flipping to this morning's dream entries. "I've got a chasing dream, some unknown evil after my ass in a restaurant."

Sinan nodded.

"Then there was the one where I was friends with Mariah Carey and I was going with her on tour and she was showing me around her private jet, but also for some reason, it was a cargo plane, and it was filled with crates of bananas."

Sinan nodded again, confirming he'd taken note of that dream as I'd dreamed it.

We'd been doing this for nearly two weeks now. Since the guys decided I had prophetic dreams, they wanted to try to catch the next one, as I didn't remember them. The only surefire way to do that was for one of them to be in my dreamscape during all my sleeping time and take note of the ridiculousness my brain came up with. Then I'd recite what dreams I remembered, and we'd make sure none were missing.

So far, it had proven to be useless. I remembered every single thing I dreamed about. Maybe that day with the car crash had been just a coincidence. Surely I'd know if I was having prophetic dreams, right?

Although until a few weeks ago, I didn't even know I was a Seheraum and could talk to invisible men, so . . . who knew?

"Then the one where I could fly and I was tasting the clouds. They all had different flavors, but I knew the best one was the highest up, and I kept trying to reach it until I dropped out of the sky and started falling."

"I hate the falling ones." Sinan sighed.

"You and me both, dude."

"Don't call me dude. What else?"

"Someone's pissier than usual this morning." I took a slow sip of coffee, watching him over the rim. He just stared back, unamused.

Usually, Hollis or Oskar was on dream-report duty. Sinan had only done this one other time, and it had ended with us arguing. He didn't like my way of doing it. It took up too much of his precious time, took him away from creeping on people's dreams or something. But I was the one having to recite my flagrantly psychotic vivid sleep hallucinations, so he could suck it.

The first few days they'd bombarded me as soon as I woke up, demanding the details of my dreams. That didn't really work for me, considering my brain wasn't fully functioning until I'd had coffee. I'd told them to back off. Now I just did my usual morning routine, then gave them the CliffsNotes version over my morning coffee.

Sinan hated having to wait for anything ever, so there we were, antagonizing one another in my sunroom.

"Is that all?" he pressed.

I rolled my eyes. "No." He knew very well that the only dream I hadn't told him about yet was the sex one.

"Well, do you remember what else you dreamed about? Or have we finally found a prophetic one?" His lips twitched. Just barely, but I'd spent enough time with them to know their subtle tells. He was teasing me.

"I remember it perfectly, thank you very much. Would you like it to have been prophetic?" I asked innocently, leaning forward and maintaining eye contact as I finished my coffee.

He didn't even flinch. "Perhaps."

"Really?" I was genuinely surprised. "I would've thought a man of your age would balk at such things."

"What things?" He leaned in too. We were inches away from each other, and I wished I could close the distance and kiss him—just to see the look on his face. "You still haven't told me the contents of your dream."

He was really going to make me say it. Jerkface. Although the others had too, so why would I expect Sinan to let me off easy?

One thing they all had in common was that they loved making me recount my sex dreams. They were endlessly amused by them and teased me every time. It was flirty, suggestive teasing, but they were ganging up on me—and not in the way I dreamed about.

My erotic dreams had been getting more frequent, and more often they included group sex. Sometimes I dreamed about the three of them, sometimes just faceless dream people. Sometimes they even joined me in my dreamscape, giving me ammo to tease them back about it. But never all at once. Not since that first time in the water when I'd drawn them into my dream.

I'd gotten really good at recognizing when I was just dreaming *about* them—my brain creating scenarios and situations—and when they were actually there, a separate consciousness visiting my dreamscape.

I leaned back again, rested my arms on the arms of the chair as if it were a throne, and tilted my head back just a fraction. Channeling all the confidence I had, I told him.

"The only other dream I remember from last night was the one where I walked into that office building. I was running late for an appointment or an interview or something, and I rushed for the elevator and slipped inside just as the doors closed. Then for some reason there was a bed in there, and the several men in there with me pulled me onto it. Can't really remember how many it was exactly, but there were hands everywhere." I dragged my right hand up my torso, my fingers grazing my cleavage, to emphasize the point. "And cocks everywhere. Like, *everywhere*. Is that the dream you took note of? Any others I'm not remembering?"

Sinan cleared his throat. "No, that's it."

"Great!" I gave him a broad smile and got to my feet. He remained sitting on thin air, and I had a feeling I knew why.

"I have to go," he called over his shoulder.

I turned around to tease him about his outdated sensibilities or having to go jerk off to my sex dream, but he'd already started to dissolve from view.

"I am needed elsewhere. One of the others will be with you shortly." His voice faded from the room too, and I sighed. Alone again.

This was just part of what they did—I knew that—but I hated how suddenly they had to leave sometimes. The unpredictability of it unsettled me. The loneliness always lurked right there, ready to fill the empty space they left with horrible thoughts and aching feelings.

I put some music on to fill the silence and took a shower, then got dressed for the day. The house had never felt so empty until they came along and started disappearing randomly. It was crazy how fast a girl could get used to having three hot, intriguing guys around all the time.

I checked on my herbs, taking note of what was ready for picking, then watered the ginseng before sitting down at my computer to do some invoicing. Ugh! I hated invoicing. So damn boring. I could afford to hire someone to do the financial side of things for me, but I couldn't risk them falling prey to what I now knew was the Maron. So I did it all myself.

After a solid hour of pushing through the boredom to get shit done, I decided to take a break. But when I went to have my fave snack—juicy pickles with peanut butter—I was devastated to find myself out of peanut butter. I hated going into town and avoided it at all costs, but midmorning on a Tuesday would be as quiet as it got, so I put on my hiking boots to take the path through the woods.

The twenty-minute trek through the forest was relaxing, the weather mild and overcast. Perfect for a walk. Not until I stepped off the path and onto the main road, the town center visible nearby, did I start to get nervous.

Breathe, Reverie. You're just going into the corner store and picking up the one thing you need. We'll be in and out in no time.

Determined to get this over with quickly, I picked up my pace, straightening my spine and readying myself for any run-ins with locals. I ignored the few people I passed—their blatant animosity, the narrow-eyed stares, the wide berth they were giving me. I chose to ignore it all.

I lived here too, dammit! And if I wanted to pop into a store to pick up some peanut butter, I was damn well going to.

I marched into the store, found what I wanted, and went through the self-checkout. The one young girl on the register looked about as relieved that the self-checkout existed as I felt.

I rolled my eyes as I exited, then startled at Oskar's sudden appearance. He hadn't poofed into existence the way they often did—he was actually just standing on the sidewalk, looking down the street with his hands in his pockets. I was just so wound up he'd taken me by surprise.

He smiled at me, then frowned when he took in my agitated state.

"Where the hell have you been?" I snapped. A woman came out of the drug store right at that moment, saw me talking sternly to myself, and turned right back around.

"We have all been needed elsewhere." He kept pace with me as I started walking back toward the path. "I came as soon as I could, Rev. I'm sorry. What happened?"

I forced myself to take a breath and give him an apologetic look. "Sorry. Nothing happened. I just hate being around . . ."

My words died in my throat when I spotted the woman who'd just come around the corner, carrying two large iced coffees.

"Fuck." I pivoted to duck into the clothing store I was in front of, then realized I'd be trapped in there with locals and turned in the opposite direction. I'd just cross the street and be done with it. But it was too late.

"Reverie?" Nora, my childhood best friend, stood in front of me, an uncertain smile playing on her lips.

"Hey!" I said too loudly, cleared my throat, and tried again at a more normal volume. "Hi, Nora."

She looked the same as the last time I spoke to her, a few days before she left for college. She still had the freckles over her nose, the slight shoulders. Her honey-blonde hair was shorter now, her hips a little wider, but she was still Nora. We hadn't been friends since the incident, but every time I saw her around town, it felt as if the knife permanently stuck in my gut twisted just a little more.

I hadn't seen her in so long. I'd forgotten how much it hurt. That knife in my gut was trying to catch up on years of undelivered pain.

We stood there awkwardly, taking each other in, not saying anything.

"It's really nice to see you," I blurted like an idiot. It was, but it wasn't. It hurt too much.

Her eyes softened, and she smiled. "It's nice to see you too. You still live around here? What are you up to now?"

"Yeah, still in the same place. I have a business—"

The jingle of the bell over the clothing store door cut my words off. Nora's mother walked out and gave her daughter a bright smile, which withered on her face as soon as she spotted me.

I couldn't have cared less. All my attention was fixed on the little girl in Mrs. Martin's arms. She was maybe two years old, and she had Nora's freckles over her little button nose.

"Nora, let's go." The older woman took one of the iced coffees and turned her back to me. The sweet little girl reached for her mother, eyeing me with wary curiosity.

"Oh my god, Nora." I stared as she took her daughter into her arms. "You have a daughter."

"Yeah." She bounced the baby girl on her hip, and the child smiled.

"She's so perfect. Hi, cutie," I cooed at the adorable cherub. "What's your name?"

"Let's go," Mrs. Martin hissed, putting herself between me and her family. I gritted my teeth but couldn't really blame her.

"Uh . . ." Nora glanced between her mother, her daughter, and me. Then she angled her child away from me. It was a small movement—I'm not sure she even noticed it, but I did. "Better get going. Take care of yourself, Rev."

They walked away. She didn't even tell me her daughter's name. The knife twisted some more.

"Yeah, you too," I said to the empty street, my voice flat.

"Rev?" Oskar's gentle voice made me remember he was still there, that he saw that whole awful exchange.

I couldn't look at him. I just took off, walking fast until I reached the path through the trees, then walking quickly some more. Of course he kept up, remaining by my side.

Nora had seemed tentatively open to speaking with me. She'd treated me like a normal person—an old friend she'd lost touch with. Maybe being away from Gritton, away from this bubble of small-town superstition, had made her rethink her fears about me. But then her mother had come out and . . . and *holy shit*, she had a *daughter*. I guess no amount of distance and time could stop a mother's instinct to protect her child. From me.

I growled in frustration and kicked a tree. "Shit. Sorry, sorry." I immediately apologized to the birch, stroking its trunk and sighing. Tears pricked the backs of my eyes. "Oskar?"

"Yes?"

"Do you think . . . will my mom be OK? Will she wake up eventually?" My voice was low, as raw as my feelings.

Nora was living a whole, full life out in the world. She was an adult, she was married, she had a child, she was back in Gritton visiting her parents. And I was still living in my childhood home, friendless and lonely and half-resigned to the fact that I would never have what she had. A family. A normal life.

The other half of me yearned for it so much it hurt worse than that knife twisting in my gut.

"Honestly"—Oskar leaned on the tree next to me—"I don't know. I don't want to lie to you, Reverie. Once the Maron is taken care of, she should wake up. That's what happens when a Maron is sent on from this plane and yours —all their influence is severed. But we've never known a Maron to be around for this long, a person to be kept in a dreamscape this long. We just don't know what that does to the mind, and we can't get past its blocks to find out. I'm sorry."

"It's OK. Thank you for being honest." I gave him a watery smile, then leaned my head against the tree. Silent tears tracked down my cheeks as I battled to get my shit together.

"You're welcome," he whispered, scooting closer. "Please don't cry, Reverie."

"I can't exactly help it." I sniffled.

"I know. It pains me that I can't do anything to help. I just want to hold you." He sounded genuinely distraught.

"You are helping." I wiped the tears off my cheeks and

looked up to the sky. "Being here with me, telling it to me straight—it helps."

"It's not enough." He sighed, and I saw him shift out of the corner of my eye. As I closed my eyes to block out the sudden blinding sunlight that burst out from between two clouds, I could've sworn I felt a warm, comforting hand on my shoulder.

I looked down, but Oskar was already lowering his arm to his side. Had I imagined it? Was I so desperate for contact that I felt something that wasn't there?

"Let's go home." Oskar gestured to the path, and I nodded.

"Maybe when we get back, I can practice some lucid dreaming? I think I'd like to take you up on that hug." It was the closest we could get to the comfort I craved; beggars couldn't be choosers.

"I'd like that." Oskar gave me a smile as we walked shoulder to shoulder the rest of the way.

CHAPTER FOURTEEN

T he night sky was nothing short of magnificent. Everything glittered. I could see the curve of the Milky Way slashing across the sky, and it felt so alive, so vibrant.

"Wow," I breathed, threading my fingers through Hollis's.

"I know." He tucked his free arm under his head, his gaze fixed on the stars above us—and all around us too. Every direction except down was a tapestry of magic.

Hollis and I lay on a blanket in a grassy field, the land stretching out for miles. I'd asked Hollis to show me something from his life before in one of my lucid dreams. Next thing I knew, soft grass was below me and sharp, clear stars above.

"Where are we?" I asked.

"Rural Illinois. Circa 1910." He lifted onto his elbows and pointed at something on my other side. "That's my family home over there. This is my family's land."

I could just make out the outline of a house and several

outbuildings nearby. They were all dark.

"We used to come out here, my brother and I." He settled back, eyes once more on the sky. "Any chance we could get on a clear night. We'd wait until our parents were asleep and sneak out here and just watch the stars. Sometimes we talked, but often it was just comfortable silence. Just existing with another soul in peace, you know?"

I hummed. I didn't really know. Couldn't say I'd ever experienced that kind of peace, certainly not with another person. But I didn't want to ruin the moment.

"Tell me something you enjoyed seeing," I said. "Something that you never could've imagined during your life here." They all seemed to have mixed feelings about being Dreamwalkers, while I was endlessly curious about it.

Hollis stayed silent for a long time, then finally spoke. "I don't know if it's because of our current surroundings, but the one thing my mind keeps coming back to is space travel. We put a man on the moon. We have space stations and satellites and . . . I don't know. Thinking back to when my brother and I used to lie here like this—it was such a mystery to me. It still amazes me that we figured out how to go to space."

"Yeah. Honestly, when I think about it, it amazes me too."

He turned his head to look at me. "You know, I haven't thought or talked about my life this much since I became a Dreamwalker."

"Really?" I released his hand so I could prop my head up on my elbow. "You guys don't talk about this stuff? You don't discuss it with other Sandmen?"

"Dreamwalkers." He nudged my hip playfully but left

his hand there. "And yes, we have from time to time. Oskar and Sinan know . . . all the important things. But we don't talk about our lives often."

"I'm sorry if my persistent questions are bringing up painful things. I'm just curious. I want to know more about you."

"It's OK." He waved it off. "Honestly, it's been nice to remember some of the good things. Puts some shit in perspective."

"Like what?" I pushed.

"A discussion for another time. I'm too busy now." He put his focus back on the sky.

I sat up a bit more. "Doing what?"

"Waiting for you to kiss me." He smiled smugly.

Instead of replying, I sat up and straddled his hips. The smug expression fell off his face, replaced by surprise.

The look on Hollis's beautiful face was worth losing the mind-blowing view of the night sky. The way his amber eyes reflected the stars above, sparkling just as brilliantly as he looked at me, was just as mesmerizing.

I propped my hands on either side of his head, leaned down, and kissed him. His hands gripped my hips, his fingers digging lightly into the fleshy area, as his tongue darted out to meet mine.

It had started out as a flirty, fun moment but quickly turned more intense. I could feel him getting hard under me, and I couldn't resist rolling my hips against it.

With a desperate moan, Hollis sat up and flipped us so I was on my back and he was nestled between my thighs. His hot mouth trailed down my neck, and I gasped when he reached a sensitive spot.

The stars seemed brighter somehow, more glittery than before—as if my arousal had stirred them up. And they were no longer just above me. They glowed all around and under me too. The blanket floated in infinite space, as soft as a mattress in a luxury hotel.

Hollis brought my attention back to him with a gentle but firm grip on my chin.

"Jealous of the stars?" I teased, rolling my hips against his rock-hard arousal.

"Doll, I'm jealous of anything that has your attention when I don't." He kissed me, his thirsty mouth drinking me in, before pulling back just an inch—just so he could look in my eyes.

"I'm jealous of the stars," he breathed against my lips, his hand trailing down my chest.

"Of the books you read." He palmed one breast, then the other, teasing at my nipples through the fabric.

"Of the plants you tend to with so much care." He dragged his hand down my front and confidently grabbed me between the legs.

"I'm even jealous of your own hands after seeing what they did to you on that rainy night in your bed."

Heat spread down my spine at the reminder of that night, pooling at my core. I reached between us and rubbed his hardness, hoping he would reciprocate. Hollis may have been jealous of my hands, but I wanted his touch more than my own. I craved contact, intimacy, pleasure at another's touch.

Thank the heavens holding us in their infinite grasp, he took the hint and rubbed me firmly. I released the button on his pants; he lowered my zipper. I reached inside and wrapped my fingers around his cock; he tucked his hand into my underwear and his fingers into my wet pussy.

"Hey, guys." Oskar appeared out of nowhere, sitting on the blanket next to us, cross-legged.

Hollis and I stopped what we were doing but didn't move.

Oskar took in our current situation, and his eyes somehow widened in surprise and arousal at the same time. "Oh . . . uh . . . right . . ."

"Don't stop," I groaned, thrusting my hips, practically fucking myself with Hollis's fingers.

Hollis got back to what he was doing, and Oskar looked uncertain.

"I'll just . . . uh . . . ." He shifted as though he was about to get up and walk off the blanket into nothingness.

"Stay." I reached my free hand out to him. "Stay with us. Touch me. Make me feel good."

Apparently, I was super confident about voicing what I wanted in my dreamscape.

Oskar didn't need more convincing. He crawled over to my side and bent down to take my nipple into his mouth. I was suddenly completely nude, at their mercy, and I couldn't think of another place I'd rather be.

I got my other hand into Oskar's pants, and then I had them both in my grip, pumping their cocks in unison. They were slick and slippery, making my job easy—because lubrication happened automatically in the dreamscape. Obviously.

They were both naked now too, both of them touching me. They took turns fingering me and rubbing my clit while their free hands roamed my body.

We floated through space tangled in a ball of flesh and ecstasy.

I came repeatedly on their fingers—or maybe it was just one extremely long orgasm. It felt as if the very stars were touching my skin, dancing over it with their sparkling, effervescent energy, driving my pleasure higher.

Hollis and Oskar came at the same time, in the kind of perfect unison possible only in a dream. Their cocks pulsed in my hands, and their cum came bursting out. Instead of landing all over my tits, it floated away, dispersed, started to sparkle just like the stars.

The sight made me giggle as they lay down on either side of me. "So pretty," I breathed, mesmerized by the sight of it all, the feel of it all.

"I can't say I have ever heard my seed referred to as pretty." Oskar's voice was rough and sexy. Hollis just grunted and nuzzled into my neck.

The stars danced for us, shifting and moving like murmuration. I could've sworn I saw a pair of dark, searching eyes among them, watching us closely.

They kind of reminded me . . .

. . . reminded me of . . .

. . . of Sinan's . . .

I woke up on my living room floor, right where I'd gone into my lucid dream on my yoga mat.

"Dammit," I muttered, rubbing my eyes. I'd lost the lucidity and let my mind pull me into a sleep state after . . . well, after hot dream sex. I couldn't help smiling a little at the memory, and my back instinctively arched.

With a stretch, I opened my eyes and startled.

"Fuck." I reached both hands out to smack the man

above me, but of course they went right through him.

Sinan was hovering maybe half a foot over my head, just chilling casually in midair. The sides of his coat hung down, pulled by gravity or whatever the fuck, while the rest of him defied physics.

"Do you *mind*?" I huffed and sat up, not giving a shit that it sent me through his chest. He moved to sit on the couch, laughing under his breath.

"Did you have a nice magic carpet ride?" he asked.

"Creep." I stretched forward over my straight legs to hide my smile.

"You love it."

I did, damn him.

When I looked up again, Oskar and Hollis had joined us, sitting on either side of Sinan. All three of them appeared more solid, with more color to their features and clothes.

Before any of us could address the horny elephant in the room, Sinan leaned forward.

"Dream report. Go," he demanded.

I frowned. "I didn't have any dreams after the, uh, space sex. How long was I out?"

They shared a look, making me sit up straighter. I wasn't sure if I should be excited at the possibility I'd had a prophetic dream or terrified of what was in it.

"Come on. Spit it out." I got to my feet.

"Try to remember, Rev," Oskar suggested gently. We'd discussed this—how important it was for me to learn to remember my prophetic dreams, that I'd need to practice it like anything else. But I didn't know if I could.

Shaking my limbs out, I sat in the armchair, closed my

eyes, and took deep breaths. A multitude of thoughts raced through my mind, and I quickly got frustrated. I just couldn't focus.

I growled and brought my fists down on the arms of the chair.

"Relax. Take deep breaths," Oskar soothed.

"Perhaps we should do this another time, considering . . ." Hollis trailed off.

"Considering what?" I shot back to my feet, any semblance of focus gone out the window.

"Agreed." Sinan nodded.

"You dreamed of a maze." Hollis kept the explanation to the point. "A hedge maze. There were people all over it. You could hear them through the greenery, but you couldn't reach them. Every time you turned a corner, they'd be gone." He took a breath before landing the blow. "You had a child in your arms. The young girl was crying, and you kept trying to soothe her while you searched for her parents."

"A baby?" I whispered, wide eyes flicking between them. "A baby?" My voice rose higher and higher. "A fucking *baby*? What baby?"

"The only child you've been in contact with recently." Oskar connected the dots for me at the same time they clicked into place in my head. "Nora's daughter."

"No no no no no no no." I laughed maniacally. This could not be happening. What the fuck kind of monster went after children?

But it *had* gone after children before—it had gone after my friends when I was just a child myself. Nora didn't deserve this. Her innocent daughter didn't either.

"Fuck!" I tugged at the roots of my hair. "This is not happening. Do something," I pleaded with them, my voice holding more than an edge of anger.

"I have already checked in on the babe," Oskar said calmly. "As soon as I recognized her in your dream, I made my way over there, even before knowing it was prophetic, just in case. There was no sign of the Maron or even any other Dreamwalker around the house."

"We suspect the Maron only strikes at night." Sinan stood up. "From everything you've told us, that seems to be the pattern. But we will monitor the child throughout the day anyway."

"Yes. Good. Go." I pointed to my front door, as if they couldn't just will themselves to disappear. "All of you. Watch everyone in that house. I don't want that thing anywhere near them."

"Reverie." Hollis approached me, his voice soft. "Doll, everything's going—"

"Don't." I took a step back. "I don't want to hear it. I know you're just trying to make me feel better, but if you really want to do that, then you'll go and watch over them. My best friend does not deserve to go through this shit again."

"We won't let anything happen to them." Sinan nodded, and one by one, they disappeared.

I collapsed onto the couch, my head in my hands, and sobbed. It was the least of all that I had to be upset about, but how fucking sad that I still thought of her as my best friend?

* * *

THE NEXT THREE DAYS WERE LONELY WITH A strong undercurrent of anxiety. I did my best to go on as normal, but it was impossible to focus on anything. The guys weren't around to distract me either, which made it even worse.

They'd assured me one of them could easily keep watch over Nora and her family in case the Maron showed up, but I'd insisted they all go. It didn't seem right to have them here with me when I didn't need them. Not in a life-or-death kind of way—or an unnaturally-long-sleep-or-awake kind of way, I suppose. I had too much other shit going on to worry about unpacking all the ways I *did* need them.

"What a mess," I muttered to myself and dragged my hands down my face.

"Doll, try to sleep." Hollis kept his voice low. He lay in the bed next to me, but I'd hardly slept the past two nights, and I didn't see this one turning out any differently.

"I fucking can't." I huffed, sitting up and flicking the light on.

"Want me to give you a nudge?"

"No." I pointed a warning finger at him.

They had agreed to all hover over Nora and her family twenty-four seven, even though they insisted it wasn't necessary. But they refused to budge on one of them being with me when I slept. They said it was to keep watch for any more prophetic dreams, but I had a suspicion they were worried about the Maron coming after me too.

It was tempting to let them use their dreamy voodoo to encourage me to sleep, but it just didn't feel right, and they knew not to push their luck by doing something I'd expressly told them not to.

So here we were, tense, sleep-deprived, anxiously waiting for the other shoe to drop.

Or maybe that was just me.

"I'm gonna go watch a movie or something." I stood up and pulled on my robe. The nights were starting to get chilly. "You should head back to Nora's."

"I'm staying with you." Hollis got up to follow me. "What movie do you want to watch?"

Before I could argue, Oskar appeared in the middle of my room.

I frowned, irritated that now two of them were here instead of protecting those who really needed it, but then I registered the expression on his face. He looked shaken, disturbed, and he was breathing hard—surely just a residual response from his human life; if they didn't eat or sleep, I was pretty sure they didn't breathe either.

"What happened?" I rushed to his side, arms outstretched to grab his, but stopped at the last second. *Incorporeal, remember?* "Are you OK?"

Hollis went to his other side, looking as worried as I was. "Where's Sinan?"

Oskar looked between us with wide eyes, as though just remembering where he was and that we were in the room with him. He opened his mouth to say something, then closed it several times, shaking his head. He looked haunted.

A heavy weight settled in the pit of my stomach. If a man who had spent 170 years on this planet, who had seen and experienced more than my tiny brain could even fathom, was this shaken . . . he was about to drop something heavy.

CHAPTER FIFTEEN

Hollis moved directly in front of Oskar and leaned in.

"Oskar!" he snapped, and it seemed to work like a mental slap—in place of an actual slap none of us could actually deliver. Oskar's eyes focused, and he looked between us.

"Right. Sorry. Sinan is fine. Everything is fine now." He sat down on the end of my bed, and Hollis lowered himself next to him. I was too wired to sit.

"What does that mean?" I asked. "Did the Maron come? Is Nora's baby OK?"

"Yes, yes, everyone is safe." Oskar gave me a reassuring nod, and my shoulders loosened up some. "The Maron did indeed come. It went for the child."

"Oh god." I covered my mouth with my hands.

"We fought it off, Rev. The babe is still sound asleep in her cot, never even stirred through the whole thing."

"OK." I took a deep breath, a little more tension leaving my body. "OK, good."

"Because we have been monitoring all their dreams, we had a stronger hold on their dreamscapes than any Dreamwalker or Maron possibly could at this time. We had the advantage, and I had no doubt we could fight it off but . . ." He got that faraway look in his eyes again. "I never expected it to be so difficult. It was so strong—stronger than any Maron I've ever seen."

"That makes sense," Hollis said. "We suspected it would be, considering how long it's remained undetected, how long it's been feeding. I've never seen one older than six months, I believe. Hasn't Sinan come across one three years old?"

"Two," Oskar corrected. "The oldest I've seen was left unchecked for nearly a year."

"Why?" I said, and they both looked at me. "Why has this one been allowed to continue torturing people? Torturing me? Why hasn't this mysterious force, or what-ever the fuck is in charge of you all, seen fit to send someone after it before now?"

"We don't know." Hollis's gaze was full of pity, and I couldn't stand it.

"Keep going," I demanded, focusing on Oskar. "What else happened?"

"It battered against our defenses, trying to get into the child's dreamscape, before finally giving up. It was enraged and went for Nora next. But while I protected the child, Sinan swept through the house and woke everyone else up. There's nothing it can do to a waking person. We tried to capture it, banish it, but it left. It fought back and got away from us far too easily."

"What does that mean?" I was getting tense again. "Do

we need reinforcements or something? How do you capture one of these things? How do you *banish it*? Is it something I can help with?"

Hollis nodded. "Considering its attachment to you and the fact that you're a Seheraum, maybe you can help, yes."

"OK, how? How do we take this thing down?" I was so over this shit. I was ready to fight for my life, to rid myself of this demon that had been haunting me since childhood.

Sinan appeared in the room, looking as weary as Oskar but perhaps not quite as haunted. He collapsed in his favorite chair in the corner.

"What the hell are you doing here?" I screeched, wide eyes bouncing between them. "What if it comes back to finish the job? What if—"

"I'm going there now," Hollis cut in. "I'm going," he repeated in a more soothing tone, and when I nodded, he disappeared.

"If that thing is anywhere as drained as I am right now, it's not going to be coming back tonight, probably not for a few nights, now that it knows it has to get through us," Sinan grumbled.

"Man, I have not felt this exhausted since I was human," Oskar agreed.

Sinan leaned his head on his hand. "Wish we could still sleep."

Well, shit. Now I felt like a dick for yelling at them. And I was worried about them both. I hadn't known they could get tired, considering they didn't eat or sleep or anything. They both looked wrecked.

I took Hollis's spot next to Oskar and pulled my feet up, wrapping my arms around my knees.

"Is there anything I can do?" I asked softly. I couldn't even give them a comforting pat on the back. I knew exactly what it felt like not to have anyone to comfort you, and I ached for them and for myself.

Sinan gave me a rare warm smile as Oskar answered for both of them. "No, *schatzi*. But it means the world that you want to."

"Try to get some sleep, temptress." Sinan nodded to my rumpled sheets. "At least one of us should."

I wasn't remotely sleepy, but I took off my robe and climbed back into bed anyway. Oskar flopped onto his back next to me, his legs hanging off the end of the bed, and Sinan draped himself over the chair in a pose that was becoming all too familiar.

"What does it look like?" I asked quietly, endlessly curious about this horrible creature that had ruined my life.

"It is a dark, twisted thing." Oskar kept his gaze on the ceiling. "A thing of nightmares."

If anyone would know about nightmares . . .

"It is monstrous," Sinan added. "Anytime a Dreamwalker gets corrupted, consumed by the idea of holding on and staying in this realm, they start to lose sense of who they are. Not having a corporeal body . . . it's hard to put into words, really, but it means we have to work to remember who we were before. A Maron loses touch with that, with its humanity, until all that's left is an ugly mani-festation of anger and greed."

"The few I've come into contact with had exaggerated features, in a sense. The eyes were bulbous but without color or light in them, the fingers elongated, the nostrils flared. But they were all still recognizable as human. They still had distinctive features and hair and . . ." Oskar trailed off.

Sinan picked up the thought. "I think they start to change in appearance because of what they desire. They crave to remain in the waking realm, desperate to be human again, constantly reaching for something none of us will ever have: to experience life to its fullest with *all* our senses, as we never did when we could. Ironic that in its bull-headed mission to hold on to humanity, the Maron loses touch with just that."

"Fucking poetic justice," I grumbled, making a mental note not to take the world around me for granted. I'd make sure to stop and smell the roses more—literally.

"There was nothing human about this Maron." I could've sworn I felt Oskar's shiver, but it was probably just my own in response to his disturbed voice. "It didn't even speak. Just screeched at us in rage. I'm not sure it even understood us when we tried to communicate with it."

"Oh, I think it understood," Sinan said, his voice low and ominous, and the two men shared a heavy look.

I cleared my throat. "I'm not tired one bit. How about a compromise?" I hurried on before they could insist I try to sleep. "I get into a lucid dream, and we can hang out on the top of a pyramid or in a land made of cotton candy or some shit? Have a break from all this."

"That sounds like a lovely idea." Oskar tipped his head back to smile at me. Sinan shrugged, and I took that as a yes.

I settled down into the pillows and closed my eyes, beginning the now familiar techniques to get myself into the lucid dream. Then I tried to think of a relaxing place to take us. The first thing that popped into my head was a lake my parents had taken me to when I was seven or eight years old. I didn't remember all the details of the trip, and I probably idealized it in my mind, but it had felt like the perfect vacation. I'd played with other kids visiting the park, and Mom and Dad had let me stay up late and eat ice cream for breakfast.

One afternoon I remembered vividly. It was a hot day, and I'd spent most of it in the lake, running around with the other kids. At some point, I ran out of steam and ended up on a blanket under a shady tree between my parents. They were both reading, and my dad ran his fingers through my hair as I watched the wind play in the leaves of the tree above.

That exact spot was where I took Oskar and Sinan. We were alone at the lake in my dreamscape, surrounded by the sounds of nature, the water sparkling in the sun.

"Nice spot." Oskar looked out at the lake. He propped one knee up and rested his arm on it, fiddling with a blade of grass.

Sinan just reclined onto his back and closed his eyes.

I rested back on my elbows, the memory of my father's gentle touch on my head palpable. I missed him so much.

"My parents brought me here for a vacation once," I said. "I don't even remember what the lake is called."

"It reminds me a lot of a lake near Leipzig." Oskar kept his gaze on the water. "I used to take my family there every year."

My breath froze in my throat, and I did my best not to blurt out something insensitive, like *Holy fucking shit, Oskar, you had a family?!* I glanced at Sinan to find him looking at Oskar's back, a carefully neutral expression on his face.

"Would you like to tell us about them?" I asked gently. "Your family?"

"Sinan knows, and I . . ." He shook his head, plucking more grass out and tearing at it.

Really, Reverie?

Fuck, I mouthed. I'd wanted to take them somewhere they could chill, and all I'd done was upset Oskar by reminding him of his long-dead family.

"OK, um, do you want to go somewhere else?" I went to sit up, but Sinan grabbed my arm. He shook his head slightly and pulled me down to lie beside him.

Oskar still hadn't replied; I wasn't even sure he'd heard me. He just kept plucking out that damn grass and shredding it in his agitated grip.

I turned my pleading gaze to Sinan. I had no idea what to do.

Sinan clenched his jaw and squeezed his eyes shut for a few moments, as if having some kind of internal battle. Then he opened them again. "The day that I died, I took twenty-three other men with me," he told the swaying canopy above us.

Oskar paused his grass shredding.

"Earlier in the day, we sailed past a port. My first mate and I discussed sailing in, giving the men a few days rest before the long journey home. The ship was full to bursting with spices, fine silk, tea, gold, and silver. We were one of the few crews that didn't trade in slaves, and that made us a target for other crews at times. We had the biggest haul of my career, and I didn't want to risk losing it. I decided to sail on. The storm rolled in at night, when any notion of turning back was long dead in the water."

Oskar turned to us with a slight frown, captivated by Sinan's story.

"We fought for survival all night, and all night I watched people die around me. Because of a decision I'd made. By the time the ship sank, only a handful of us were left, clinging to debris with no land in sight. I knew I was going to die out there, that the sea would take me in death as surely as I'd sailed it my whole life. I watched them all die before I let go. The last thing I remember, as my head slipped under the water, was the bright first ray of dawn, cutting through the surface into the depths. My first mate's body floated past, his wide eyes illuminated in the light of a new day. I think that was God reminding me in my last moments that this was my doing."

"Sinan . . ." Oskar seemed as lost for words as I felt.

"You didn't know any of this?" I frowned. These guys had been tight for longer than most people lived. Surely, they'd discussed their deaths.

"I did. I just . . . he never told it in so much detail," Oskar clarified.

So why now? Was it for me? I couldn't shake the feeling that it was for Oskar too. Sinan had ripped his chest open and bared his soul to ease whatever spiral of pain Oskar had been descending into.

"It's time I started facing it. For real," Sinan said.

"Brother, I've never seen another Dreamwalker as contrite as you, never known one to have remained for so long," Oskar said.

"What do you mean?" I asked, confused.

"When I died, I was given a choice," Sinan said, directly to me now. "Hollis and Oskar and every other Dreamwalker I've spoken to had the same experience. I could feel this sense of profound peace, just out of reach. All I had to do was take a few steps to grasp it. But there was something else, something drawing my attention back, something I needed to see or do. It's difficult to describe."

"It's like you know all you have to do is keep your eyes forward and put one foot in front of the other, and everything will work out," Oskar explained. "But there's someone screaming for you to turn around. I turned around. We all turned around."

"Exactly. I turned around and remembered what I had done, what I was responsible for. And then I just . . . knew."

"Knew what?" I leaned forward, absolutely enthralled.

"Knew I was a Dreamwalker, although I didn't have the words for it at the time. Knew I needed to help people with the gifts I'd been given while I atoned for my sins. I knew I was not done learning about what it means to live this human life. That I didn't deserve to step into that peace."

"Wait, wait, wait." I held both palms up. "Are you telling me you guys, like, saw the light or whatever, and you were dragged back to hell? Holy shit, is this hell on earth for you?"

"Sometimes," Oskar grumbled in an uncharacteristic moment of fast wit.

"That is a very Judeo-Christian-centric evaluation, seductress." Why did Sinan sound as though he was chastising me and making fun of me at the same time? I glared at him, and he cracked a smile. "No, this is not hell. The concept of heaven and hell as actual places is just something people invented to frame ideas of morality. You've had enough experience with the dreamscape to know that anything is possible."

"True . . . ," I mused. "So does everyone who's done bad things end up as a Dreamwalker?"

"No." Oskar gave me a sad smile. "There are other paths for those who turn away, but we don't know what they are. And not everyone turns away."

"Who gets to decide this shit? Is there, like, a manager we can speak to or . . . ?"

They both laughed, then gave me shrugs.

"Some things are not meant to be known or understood," Oskar said.

"Really? That's your answer? Dude, you spent your whole life studying people and what makes us tick, trying to *understand*."

"Do not call me dude." Oskar frowned. "I do not like it."

I rolled my eyes. "That's not the point."

"The point"—Sinan fixed me with a serious look—"is that you understand why we're here and why we must eventually leave."

I sat up straighter. Was he breaking up with me? Not that we were dating exactly, but . . . what the fuck was this?

"We turn away from the peace, we come back as Dreamwalkers, we spend our time here helping where we are needed and learning about life until . . . until we feel deserving of the peace." Sinan finished speaking, and they both stared at me as I processed.

They wanted to prepare me for the fact that they would

all eventually move on like everyone else did—in their realm and mine.

I remained silent as I flopped back onto the blanket, pondering what I'd just heard. These men were in some kind of self-actualizing punishment escape room. They all felt so horrible about what they had done before dying that they didn't think they deserved peace. My heart ached for them. It ached for them so much I felt as if it would burst if I let it ache for me too. If I let myself think about them leaving me.

So I didn't.

CHAPTER SIXTEEN

I was running through a field. The brown blades of grass or wheat or whatever were so tall I could only barely see over them. The ground crunched under my fast feet as I whipped past, swiping dry stalks out of the way as I ran.

The thing chasing me was dark and huge. I didn't dare look over my shoulder, too scared I'd trip or, worse, get a glimpse of it. It was so fast. I could hear it right behind me, could feel its breath on the back of my neck.

It was the Maron. I just knew it. Now that the guys had told me what it was, I had no doubt what had been chasing me in all my dreams.

I gave up trying to push the wheat aside and put all my energy into pumping my legs as hard as they'd go. The blades stung my face and arms, like a thousand needles landing on my skin with every step. I didn't care. I was getting away from it, and that's all that mattered.

Abruptly, the field ended, and I stumbled out of the tall

grass onto a barren patch of dirt. Just ahead was a sheer drop, a cliff—certain death ahead as well as behind.

Chest heaving from exhaustion, I looked back. The tall grass was shifting not that far away, something moving toward me *fast*. Once it burst out of the wheat, it would swallow me whole without a second's hesitation.

Reverie . . . My name echoed in the fresh air—a whisper and a yell at once. It sounded like someone calling my name from the other side of the field, but also like someone speaking softly next to me.

"Reverie." That time it sounded much clearer. I snapped my head around to see Oskar's face poking out of the tall grass a few paces over. He held his hand out, glancing past me at where the Maron was surely already reaching for me.

I didn't hesitate. I leapt forward and took his hand. He pulled me into the cover of the wheat, pulled me against him . . .

Pulled . . .

. . . me . . .

I woke with a gasp and shot up on the couch. My tight grip on the cushion felt like the only thing keeping me from falling back into that nightmare.

"Reverie?" Sinan softly called my name, kneeling on the ground beside me. "It's OK. You're OK."

I held my hand to my chest, my heart thumping against it. "Fuck me. That was so vivid."

He watched me with those soulful eyes. "It looked like it. You were panting in your sleep, whimpering. I tried to wake you, but I didn't want to startle you."

"Oskar literally pulled me out of it." I released my death grip on the cushion and leaned back against the couch.

"You're with me now." Sinan hovered so close I felt as if I could tilt my head and kiss him. As he ghosted his fingers down my cheek, gently pushing hair off my neck, I glanced over his shoulder.

The grandfather clock in the corner stood in the same spot it had occupied for decades, but the hands weren't moving. The time showed 3:18. Had I forgotten to wind it?

As if my attention startled it into doing its job, it suddenly started ticking—louder than I'd ever heard it, even in the dead of night with no other sounds to fill the silence. And it seemed to get louder with every tick.

"What the hell?" I sat up straighter. Sinan looked over his shoulder to see what had my attention.

The ticking got louder and louder until it became almost painful, and I covered my ears with my hands. Then, all at once, it just stopped, plunging the room into complete silence.

Sinan and I shared a confused glance before getting to our feet.

I'd barely taken one step toward the clock when I froze on the spot.

The little pendulum door on the bottom slowly creaked open, the familiar sound grating in the silent room. Through the inch-wide gap, long, slender fingers creeped out to wrap around the little door.

My eyes widened, and a chill of terror raced down my spine.

The fingers were pitch black, ending in sharp claws that scraped against the wood as they gripped it.

Run. RUN. RUN!

I knew—I just *knew*—that whatever that thing was, I needed to run from it. And it would chase me, just like the thing in the field had chased me.

Just as I realized it was the Maron, coming after me again, the pendulum door burst open.

In the same instant, Sinan sprang into action. He stepped between us and wrapped his arms around me, his long coat swirling around him as he practically tackled me into the couch. But I didn't land on the soft cushions. I didn't land at all. I just . . . kept falling, wrapped in his embrace.

I opened my eyes, and he disappeared. He just vanished, leaving me still falling, clutching at thin air.

I closed my eyes.

Despair set in. He'd left me. Just like everyone else.

Everyone always . . .

. . . left . . .

This time when I woke up, I wasn't gasping or calling out in fright. My eyes just opened as silent tears streaked down my temples and into my hair. Trying to swallow past the lump in my throat, I shifted to lean against the arm of the couch.

Hollis sat in the armchair, one ankle crossed over his knee, head propped on his fist. The flashing glow of the TV illuminated his cautious expression. "That was a shitty nightmare. You all right?"

"So it was a nightmare? The Maron wasn't actually after me?" I whispered.

"Just a nightmare, doll. I'm here to keep the monster away."

He finally registered the tears running down my face and rushed over to me, lowering himself to the couch.

"What's wrong? Why are you crying?" He looked so concerned, so earnest. It made me cry a little more. He reached for my face but then lowered his hand again, frustration creasing his brow.

With a sigh, I wiped my own tears before glancing to the grandfather clock in the corner. It was ticking away normally, looking as benign as it always did. "Just can't shake that dream."

"Want to talk about it?" Hollis drew my attention back to him.

"I don't know. You know how sometimes you have a dream and it's so vivid, or it taps into something so . . ." I fisted the front of my T-shirt, struggling for the right word. "So *visceral* that it just stays with you when you wake up? Like, for a few moments you're not sure what's real and what's a dream?"

"It's been a very long time since I slept or dreamed, but yes, I know what you're talking about." He gave me a sad smile.

"Right, and I guess the distinction between what's real and what isn't is harder to define now, considering . . ." I gestured to him vaguely.

"Oh, I know!" Hollis chuckled, mirth making his eyes sparkle. "It's hard to believe that all this perfection is real." He gestured to himself in the same way I had.

I laughed, feeling a million times lighter already. Sure, maybe I was straight-up crazy and just hallucinating, but how could I not believe he was real when he looked at me like that, when his eyes had so much life in them?

"Tell me more?" He lifted his legs onto the couch, and I scooted back to make room for him. Of course, he could've just lain right on top of me and I wouldn't have felt it, but it felt odd not to move. He was real to me, and I wanted to look into his eyes.

"I had this feeling that if whatever massive thing chasing me caught up, it could swallow me whole in one go." I paused, and he just gave me a small smile, waiting patiently for me to gather my thoughts.

"I've always had the chasing dreams, but it was always some unknown entity or person after me. But this time, I knew it was the Maron on my heels. Are you sure it wasn't? Is it possible that now that I'm aware of it, it's got more access to my dreams somehow? Or maybe it's just a subconscious thing? My brain is inserting it into my fear dreams."

"It's possible." He frowned, not looking at me.

"Which part?"

"Either. Both. But there's no way it would be able to enter your dreamscape without one of us knowing."

"Shit," I breathed, fiddling with the tassel on the corner of the cushion while trying not to freak out. "Can it hurt me? I mean, it's putting people into straight-up comas in real life. Can it kill me in my dreams?" I hated how vulnerable I sounded. I'd spent my entire adult life depending only on myself. It did not come naturally to show weakness.

"No," Hollis said decisively. "There is nothing it can do to you in your dream that would affect your physical body. That's not possible for us ever. I can check with the others, but I'm positive they would've mentioned if they'd ever come across a Maron that could. You are safe, Reverie. Sleep is safe."

"Right." I took a deep breath. "So we're not dealing with a *Nightmare on Elm Street* situation. That does make me feel a little better." A *little* . . .

Hollis must've seen the fear still in my eyes, despite my flawless technique of deflecting with dark humor. He cracked a smile, but his words remained heavy and earnest. "We will keep you safe, Reverie. I promise."

I nodded, lost in thought. "I just can't believe any of this is real. Why me? My life is fucked up enough as it is. Why did it have to pick me to torment?"

He reached up as if to grip my shoulder, then dropped his arm back down. "That's what we're going to find out. I just . . ." He stared into my eyes with so much regret and . . . longing? "I wish I could do more than talk. I wish I could show you support with my actions *and* my words. I wish I could hold you and . . ."

We'd drifted closer as we talked and were practically nose-to-nose; it felt incredibly intimate, and I craved all the same things he was describing. "I wish I could run my hand through your hair," I whispered, voicing my yearning without thinking too much about it. "I wish I could feel your heartbeat under my cheek as you hold me."

His eyes closed, and he released a tortured breath. "When I close my eyes and it's just your voice and your presence, I can almost make myself believe that I'm . . . that I could reach out and touch you."

I closed my eyes too. He was right. I could feel him—his presence, his energy, his soul—right there next to me. So close but an entire plane of existence too far.

"I want to kiss you," I whispered so softly I wasn't sure he'd even hear. I tilted my head forward, a miniscule unconscious movement, my body responding to my words and thoughts.

My lips met warm, soft skin. His lips moved against mine gently. God, it felt so *real*.

He sighed through his nose, and I could feel the warm air on my cheek. I didn't even care if this was a vivid hallucination; it felt so damn good. So I leaned into the moment. I kept my eyes closed against reality and pressed my body up against Hollis.

He returned the sentiment with a grip on my waist and his tongue darting out to lick my bottom lip.

I could feel his hardness between us, the warmth of his back under my touch.

My eyes flew open, and I jerked back.

Hollis opened his slower, blinking at me in a daze.

I'd never seen any of them look so clear, so vibrant, so *alive*.

His eyes took in my lips, my heaving chest, traveled down to where his hand still held my waist. He squeezed, and then his eyes widened and flew back to mine, his gaze reflecting my own shock.

It wasn't possible. They'd all told me it wasn't possible. That when this was all over, they'd fade into oblivion and I'd never see them again. Yet here I was, making out with Hollis on my couch in the middle of the night.

"Fuck." I sat up, and Hollis scrambled to his feet.

I leaned around him to take a wary look at the clock in the corner. This was clearly another false awakening dream, and that *thing* would start chasing me any second now. Could it actually hurt me?

"This is incredible," Hollis breathed, looking between

his solid hands and me. "Rev? What is it?" He glanced over his shoulder to follow my stare.

I kept the clock in my periphery as I stood up.

"God, how I wish this was real." I reached up to caress his cheek. It was the kind of smooth men's faces only have fresh after a shave.

He covered my hand with his and frowned.

"I think . . ." I swallowed hard. Was he really here in the dream with me, or was I just dreaming about him? Could he help me wake up? "Are you really here?"

"What?" He chuckled, squeezing my hand for emphasis. "Of course I am."

There was a clattering on the roof, almost as if a possum had skittered along the edge, but I knew it was no nocturnal critter. It was my nightmare demon, coming for me once more.

My heart started beating out of my chest as I watched the ceiling. Would it burst through the roof? Which way should I run? Why did this room have so many damn windows?

"Reverie?" Hollis placed his hands on my shoulders, worry riding his tone.

"If you're really here, I need you to do your Sandman magic and wake me the fuck up," I rushed out. "I am so sick of running. *Please*, wake me up."

"Rev, you're not sleeping."

"Yes, I am," I gritted out.

Hollis looked more and more alarmed. "You're not asleep."

"I *am* asleep." I shoved out of his grip. "I was asleep in the corn field, and I was asleep when Sinan comforted me and then left me, and this is just another false awakening dream."

"It's not a dream. I'm here. You're here and—"

"Then how do you explain this?" I shoved him in the chest. His very corporeal, solid chest. "How do you explain the fact that we just kissed?"

He looked down at his hands, as though he'd forgotten he had gained a solid body.

"Shit." He ran his fingers through his hair in frustration, then fixed me with a determined look. "I'll be right back."

Before I had a chance to respond, to tell him, *beg* him, not to leave me, he was gone. He just faded right out of there, as they always did.

He left me, as everyone always did.

I backed up, taking shaky steps in reverse until my back hit the wall opposite the clock. I knew I had to run. I knew it was about to come after me any second. I just didn't have any fight left in me.

Wrapping my arms around my middle, I slid down the wall until my butt hit the floor, just staring—frozen—at that fucking clock.

CHAPTER SEVENTEEN

It couldn't have been more than a few minutes before Hollis reappeared. He just popped back into the same spot he'd been standing in earlier, Oskar and Sinan with him. Hollis looked like his old translucent self again; they all had that dreamy quality to them.

"Reverie?" Oskar crouched next to me, a calm look on his face.

"Hey," I said, voice flat, distant. *Hey?* I was in the worst nightmare of my life, and my greeting of choice was a casual *hey*?

"Hollis tells us you're freaking out a bit. Want to tell me about it?"

I sighed. Was there any point? "Hollis and I kissed, and then I—"

"You what?" Sinan turned a murderous look on Hollis.

He rubbed the back of his head, but to his credit, Hollis faced his intimidating friend head-on. "It's not like I was hiding it. I just needed to get us all back here as soon as possible. I told you all the most important things."

"Gentlemen." Oskar's voice demanded attention and scolded them at the same time. "Can we please focus on the lady in distress?"

I snorted. "I'm neither a lady nor in distress."

Hollis crossed his arms and stared me down. "You seemed pretty in distress when I left."

"She's being snarky and sarcastic." Sinan gestured to me while glaring at Hollis. "She's fine. Are you sure you didn't imagine the whole thing?"

"I didn't imagine it. We touched, kissed. I felt it." Hollis looked me dead in the eye as he spoke, and I could practically feel his lips on mine once more.

"Then how do you explain this?" Sinan swung his arm straight through Hollis's head.

Remembering what I'd learned when I practiced lucid dreaming, I pinched my nose and tried to breathe through it.

Oskar sighed and dragged his hand down his face. "Reverie, are you all right?" he asked as the other two continued to bicker.

"Yeah." I released all the air in my lungs in one long breath. "Actually, I think I am now."

"Are you sure?"

"Yeah." I got to my feet and propped my hands on my hips. "I know I'm not dreaming."

"Good." Hollis heaved a sigh of relief. Sweet thing—he'd really been worried about me. "What convinced you?"

"I remembered to do a reality check." I chuckled, embarrassed I hadn't thought of it sooner.

Hollis grinned, proud of me. Sinan's frown didn't

budge though, as if we'd all interrupted some very important things for our silly little game.

I took another deep breath and glanced around the dark room. It looked so . . . *normal* now that I wasn't freaking out anymore.

"Could we perhaps discuss what happened before Reverie's minor moment of incoherence?" Oskar asked.

"We touched, man. I'm not making it up," Hollis insisted.

"We did. I felt it. That's why I was convinced I was still dreaming. It felt so incredibly real." I absently touched my lips as I remembered what his had felt like against them.

"I have been on this forsaken plane of existence for more than three hundred years," Sinan said, his voice heavy with indignant disbelief. "I have never seen a Dreamwalker turn solid. It is not possible."

"Have you ever seen a living person who could see you? Hear you? Communicate with you while wide awake?" I challenged him.

"Not personally, no, but I have heard tales of such Seheraum. None as proficient as you, but I have heard stories."

"Well, then isn't it possible that this is just an extension of that?" Hollis said.

Sinan shook his head, still disbelieving.

Oskar was frowning at the floor, arms crossed over his chest in contemplation. "I suppose, considering our current situation and the logical progression . . . it could be possible."

Sinan rolled his eyes. I rolled *my* eyes and moved to stand right in front of Hollis.

If I did it once, I could do it again.

The only problem was—I had no idea how I'd done it in the first place. I'd have to wing it. I closed my eyes and took myself back to the moment on the couch. We were talking softly; I felt so close to him, so connected and safe. I held on to that feeling and slowly opened my eyes.

Hollis hadn't moved, waiting patiently with his own eyes closed.

With my focus locked on him, on that feeling in my chest, I reached my hand up toward his cheek. I held it a fraction of an inch from his skin and watched his calm, almost serene face. I wanted to kiss him again. I wanted to hold him and feel him and . . .

Before my very eyes, his form became solid. The process was gradual but fast. As if something rushed through him, he got more and more real until I stood in front of a flesh-and-blood man.

I let my hand connect with his cheek, stroking it gently, and his eyes flew open. He covered my hand with his and stared at me in wonder. Then his face split into a massive grin. Letting loose a surprised, delighted laugh, he wrapped his arms around my middle and lifted me clean off the ground to spin me around.

A high-pitched yell burst from my chest. I couldn't believe how good this felt!

When Hollis set me back on my feet, we turned to the others.

"See? I wasn't lying." Hollis flicked a piece of my hair, as if picking me up wasn't enough of a demonstration.

Sinan and Oskar both stared at us with wide eyes and

open mouths. Oskar's eyes held a good dose of curiosity, but Sinan was in pure shock.

"Impossible," he breathed, looking Hollis up and down.

I took a small step forward and held out my hand. "It's not. Let me show you."

Whatever woowoo made this possible, it came from me. I could just feel it in my gut. This was an extension of my ability to hear and see them when others couldn't.

But Sinan didn't run into my open arms as I expected. He took a step back and then another, his brow furrowing, that intense stare fixed on me. His mouth opened and closed several times, but no words came out.

"It's OK, Sinan." I stepped back to give him more space. "You don't have to."

I was bursting with excitement. I wanted to see each of them in all their solid glory, but I wouldn't force it on them. Consent didn't just apply to sexy things.

Instead, I turned my attention to Oskar, the question on my face.

He licked his lips, that mind of his turning and turning —I could practically see his brain running it all through. After a few seconds, he met my gaze and stepped forward.

"Please," he said, his voice low but sure.

"OK." I nodded and smiled. "Uh . . . I don't really know what I'm doing so . . . maybe . . ."

Hollis moved to our side and, to my relief, made a suggestion. "It helped me to close my eyes," he said casually, and Oskar took his advice.

"You got this, dollface," Hollis murmured close to my cheek, then landed a soft kiss there and stepped back.

I put all my focus on Oskar. He stood in front of me with his eyes closed, waiting with infinite patience and calm —unwavering in so many ways. I thought back to the first time we'd kissed, in that dream in the tent. Oskar had seemed surprised, and we'd both been swept up in the fun and spontaneity of the moment. Now that I knew him, I could tell that was something he didn't experience much. I wanted to put that look on his face again. That excited, awed look. Then I wanted to kiss it off his lips and . . .

I reached up. Oskar's features solidified just as Hollis's had. His blond hair looked shiny in the light of the lamps, and I could feel the warmth of his shoulders under my palms just before I touched him.

He gasped, his eyebrows rising but his eyes staying closed. I caressed his shoulders, letting him get used to it, as I moved my fingers up the column of his strong neck. His lips parted as I played with his short hair.

"Is this real?" he breathed.

Hollis patted him on the shoulder. "It's real, brother."

When Oskar finally opened his eyes, I was the one in awe. The gray was bright and unimaginably deep. No dream or my imagination could've done it justice.

He wrapped his arms around my back and pulled me in for a hug. He was so tall he had to hunch to pull me fully against his chest, but I lifted onto my toes, and we held each other tightly for a long time.

"Food!" Hollis's exclamation cut into our intimate moment, and we separated just in time to see him dart out of the room. We followed him to the kitchen, where he stopped and spun around on the spot, looking lost.

"Oh man, I haven't eaten in decades." He opened the

pantry, then changed his mind and dived for the fridge. "*Literally* decades."

He started pulling out random things—milk, Chinese leftovers, a half-empty jar of jam—then went back to the pantry and extracted a bag of flour, some pasta, and a can of corn.

He froze with a jar of pickles in one hand and a box of Pop-Tarts in the other and gave us a wide-eyed look. "I miss food so much."

I smiled and gently took the food from his hands. Poor thing looked totally overwhelmed.

"How about we start with something quick and sweet?" I suggested.

He nodded, and they both perched themselves on stools while I opened the shiny packet and put two Pop-Tarts in the toaster.

Hollis was uncharacteristically quiet as we waited; his palms rested flat on the countertop, and he stared at his own fingers flexing and relaxing. Oskar, on the other hand, jumped out of his seat as soon as he'd sat down. He wandered around the kitchen and dining room, touching everything, pulling cookbooks off the shelf, pressing his hand to the grandfather clock as it ticked away steadily.

The toaster popped, and they both jumped.

I threw my head back and laughed. "Now you assholes know what it feels like every time you just pop up out of nowhere."

I pulled the Pop-Tarts onto a plate and placed it in front of them. They each picked one up, then shuffled the hot pastries from hand to hand, grinning and giggling the whole time. The way they enjoyed every single thing was addictively joyous to watch.

Oskar finally brought the chocolate treat up to his lips and took a big bite. As his thoughtful chewing turned into a frown, Hollis took a bite too. Oskar's face scrunched up, and he lowered the Pop-Tart back to the plate and pushed it away a bit.

"Oh." Hollis cringed. "That is so sweet."

"Like eating a slightly chocolate-flavored spoonful of pure sugar." Oskar nodded.

I laughed again, then louder when Hollis shrugged and kept eating.

"I can make you something . . ." I trailed off when Oskar walked over to the sliding door off the dining room and pressed his nose up against it.

"Rain," he said, then tried to open the locked door. It had started to rain lightly, a soft pitter-patter I hadn't even registered.

I unlocked the door for Oskar and opened it wide. He walked out onto the patio, taking a deep inhale. Petrichor hung heavy in the air—the kind of fresh smell that had me taking the same satisfied breath.

Hollis followed us outside, and the three of us lined up at the edge of the covered patio. We stared out at the grassy patch of yard as the rain continued to fall steadily, softly. I shivered and pulled my cardigan over my body. The nights had started to get chilly. We were in the mountains, so it wouldn't be long before I'd start seeing my breath and have to close my bedroom window at night.

Oskar took a step forward, palms turned up to catch the

droplets. He tilted his head up and released a laugh full of joy and wonder. Hollis stepped out into the rain, and before long, they were both marveling at the feel of the water on their skin.

In a moment that made my heart squeeze in my chest, they exchanged a look loaded with decades of shared experience, then hugged. I'd fucked up a lot of things in my life, but this was one thing I'd done right, and it made me truly happy: I'd been able to make this possible for them.

After that they started . . . well, pretty much *frolicking* in the rain. They spun around in circles, licked it off their lips, splashed each other with the water gathering on the branches of a nearby tree, even got down on their hands and knees and ran their palms over the blades of grass.

It was like watching a couple of dudes on their first trip with their friend Molly.

I was content to stand under the cover of the pergola and watch them, but it didn't take long for them to pull me out onto the grass too. They spun me around and pointed out the amazing, marvelous things in my yard. My soaked hair stuck to my face and my feet were freezing, but I didn't care.

Sinan appeared on the grass, with us but standing off to the side, and we all stopped. He looked spooked but kind of vulnerable.

"You all right?" Hollis asked.

Sinan nodded, his gaze fixed on me, uncertainty creeping into his eyes.

"Let's go check out the flowers in the front yard, Hollis," Oskar nudged gently, and they disappeared around the corner of my house.

"I . . ." Sinan frowned and looked down, swallowing hard.

"It's OK if you don't want this." I stepped closer to him. "I understand."

His head whipped up. "I do. I got scared, but I do want this. Please, Reverie. Let me touch you, for real."

CHAPTER EIGHTEEN

I wiped the gathering raindrops off my eyes, then nodded at Sinan and walked back under the cover of the pergola.

For the first time since I'd started seeing them, Sinan looked nervous. He tried to hide it, but there was no missing the way his hands curled into fists, the way his wide eyes followed my every move.

I couldn't let his nervous energy affect me. I had to focus.

"Take a deep breath with me." I ignored the slight crease in his brow and took an exaggerated inhale before he could question me. He copied me, and we took several steadying breaths together. "OK, now close your eyes."

"Why?"

"Just do it."

He huffed, but he rolled his shoulders and did as I asked.

With the others, I'd simply done my thing at this point, but Sinan was already frowning and fidgeting. He'd question me again before I could even start, I could tell. Then he'd get frustrated, then I'd get frustrated, and this would never happen.

"Think about the last time we touched in my dreamscape," I instructed him. "Think about the last time we were together in this realm and you had an urge to touch me, or feel the sun on your skin, or taste . . . something."

The frown disappeared from his brow, and his body stilled. I wanted to know what he was thinking about, which moments stood out to him, but I made myself focus. I thought about that first time we spoke in my dream, when he tried to intimidate me. He'd smelled so good. I leaned closer, tipping my head slightly to the side.

I thought about the slick feel of his body against mine in that crazy underwater dream, and I licked my lips as I raised my hands.

It happened slower than it had with Oskar or Hollis, but Sinan solidified before my eyes. By the time my fingers connected with the sides of his neck in a gentle caress, he was warm and soft and really *here* with me.

He moaned softly, the sound more emotional than sexual, and slowly opened his eyes. They were dark, almost black in the dim light, but somehow sparkled as he took me in.

"Hey," I whispered as I rubbed his shoulders, giving him time to adjust.

The shell-shocked expression lifted a bit from his features. His lips turned up in a slow smile, and his hands went to my back, resting there gently.

"How do you feel?" I matched the pressure of his soft touch, not wanting to spook him.

"I . . . don't know," he said with a frown, but a chuckle followed—a rich sound from deep in his chest. "It has been such a long time, temptress. This is . . . I cannot express to you how miraculous this is."

"Yes, well, as I've been telling you all along, I'm amazing so—"

"Yes, you are." His dead serious tone cut off my attempt at light-hearted sarcasm.

"Thanks," I mumbled, glancing down. "So, do you want to go feel the rain on your skin or taste the grass or whatever the others are doing?"

Once again I tried to lighten the mood, and once again Sinan shut that shit down.

"No." His hands tightened on my back.

"No?"

"The only thing I want to feel on my skin is you." He pulled me flush with his chest, his fingers digging into my back. "The only thing I want to taste is you."

"Oh" was all I could manage between labored breaths as Sinan closed the distance between us, his lips ghosting over mine.

"Temptress," he breathed against my mouth before pressing his luscious lips against it.

He was being really intense—more than his usual level of intense—but I was kind of into it. OK, more than kind of into it. I'd forgotten that my bare feet were freezing on the cold pavers and that my wet cardigan felt gross against my arms. Sinan's embrace warmed me; his touch, his taste, his smell consumed me. He smelled even better in real life than he had in my dreams. I felt as if I was drowning in frankincense and the fresh hint of sea breeze.

His tongue lapped at mine, his mouth drinking me in as if he were parched and only I could satiate his thirst. Strong hands traveled down to my ass and firmly gripped my soft flesh. For a split second I got self-conscious about the size of my butt, but then Sinan groaned into my mouth as he kneaded the area, and I forgot all about it.

I rocked my pelvis, mindlessly seeking friction, and felt him hardening against me. But before I could reach between us and shove my hand down his pants, Sinan bent slightly, clasped my thighs, and lifted me clean off the ground.

A surprised squeak escaped my throat, but it was swallowed by his kiss. He wasn't letting up. His mouth devoured mine even as he took the few short steps to my patio table and lowered me onto it. I wrapped my legs around his hips and my arms around his neck, kissing him back as fiercely as he kissed me.

How could I let him go after feeling what it was like to really hold him, to be consumed by him? I was not willing to let any of them go.

I pushed the dark thoughts from my mind as I pushed Sinan's coat over his shoulders. He pulled off the sleeves behind his back and let the coat flop to the ground, then broke our kiss to yank his linen shirt over his head with one hand. Apparently that sexy move where guys grabbed the shirt behind their necks and pulled it off in one swift maneuver had been around for centuries.

I peeled my cardigan off at the same time, happy to be rid of the damp material. But before I could get to my T-shirt, Sinan was all over me again. He gripped my waist and stared at my chest. The cold had made my nipples almost painfully hard, and the old white, now see-through T-shirt clung to my body so tightly my areolas were visible through it.

"Beautiful," he breathed, cupping both my breasts in his hands and running his thumbs over my nipples. I was more than a large handful in his grasp, and the view of his fingers digging into my heavy breasts, my nipples sticking out, was obscene in a delicious way.

Sinan covered my left breast with his mouth while his thumb rubbed the right one back and forth. His hot mouth shocked my cold skin. When he sucked the water out of the wet fabric, taking my nipple with it, the heat shot directly to my core, making me squirm.

As I released a low moan, something snapped inside Sinan. He pulled back and fixed me with a stare so blistering I didn't know if he wanted to fuck me or fight me. Either way, his slow exploration was over, giving way to something more urgent, more demanding.

He pushed my shirt up, exposing my tits to the cool air and his hot gaze, then leaned his head in, placing one hand on the table for balance. I had to abandon running my hands all over him so I could prop them behind me and stop myself from falling backward. The new position made me arch, pushing my chest out more, and Sinan groaned into my cleavage. His free hand kneaded one breast as his mouth lapped at the other.

I was so wet, and not from the rain, and he hadn't even touched me between my legs. Tightening my thighs around him to pull him closer, I scooted my ass to the very edge of the table until I felt him—thick and hard and separated from me by nothing more than a few layers of fabric. I threw my head back and moaned at the friction, but the sound of pleasure turned into one of frustration as something cold and hard dug into my inner thigh and he took a step back.

He reached for his hip and unfastened a leather belt with a big sheathed knife attached to it. I'd never noticed it before, probably because all his dark clothing concealed it nicely. He dropped it behind him, forgotten, and I dug my hands into his sides to pull him close once more.

"So impatient, temptress," he teased with a smirk on his lips—lips wet and swollen from sucking on my tits.

"And you're not?" The words didn't come out as teasing and sarcastic as I'd hoped they would. They were all breathy and needy. "You're the one that hasn't gotten laid in three hundred years."

Instead of an answer, Sinan gripped my sleep shorts and pulled, making me scramble to lift my butt and balance so I wouldn't go toppling off the table. He didn't reach for the drawstring of his pants—*actual drawstring*! Was I in a boddice ripper?—the way I expected, and hoped, and almost begged.

"You asked if there was something I wanted to taste." He lowered to his knees, his gaze intent on me. I felt powerful, sensual, and confident in a way I'd never experienced before. I was leaning back on my hands, tits jutting out, legs open, as a strong, powerful man kneeled before my sex. A man I'd brought into existence in this world.

I was about to get rewarded for it, and who was I to say no, really?

Sinan must've read some of this in my gaze, because he didn't waste any time. He spread my thighs wide and leaned in, taking a long, firm lick from the bottom of my dripping core all the way up to my clit.

He wasn't the teasing type. There were no soft flicks of his tongue, no slow exploration of my most intimate area. Sinan knew what he wanted, and he took it. He devoured it with gusto, moaning and breathing hard against my pussy. He licked and sucked and even bit at times, alternating between working my clit and fucking his tongue inside me.

My arms lost their strength, and I collapsed onto my back. Thank goodness Sinan had a firm grip on my thighs, spreading me out for his enthusiastic mouth, because I was starting to shake and quiver.

I moaned, chanting incoherent things, encouraging him to keep going, demanding more. I could've sworn the rain started coming down harder as my back arched off the table and I came on Sinan's face.

His mouth stayed on me, lips and tongue gentling as I came down off the high of my orgasm. As I caught my breath, he got to his feet. One hand circled my clit as the other pushed his pants down over his hips.

I wished it was broad daylight and not the middle of the night. I wanted to see him properly, take in every inch of his body. Instead, all I had was the faint light coming through the kitchen window and throwing seductive shadows.

Sinan had broad shoulders, his body strong and muscular but not overly defined. Black hair sprinkled the top of his chest. It narrowed down between his pecs, then grew dense again below his belly button, the trail leading to his thick cock. He was so hard. I wanted to run my tongue up the prominent vein that ran up the underside of it. I even lifted myself into a sitting position and reached for it, but Sinan caught my hand before I could wrap it around his dick. He brought it up to his mouth and placed a light kiss on my palm.

"I want to touch you," I almost whined.

"I want to feel your touch. I want to come all over your hands, your tits, down your throat." He placed my palm on his chest. "But I want to come inside you first, Reverie."

Well, when he put it like that, it was hard to argue. I settled for caressing his strong shoulder, running my fingers through the wiry hair on his chest as he pushed one finger into me.

"No fair." That time I did whine, and I didn't even care.

"I've thought about what this cunt would feel like squeezing around me more than I care to admit. I never thought I'd actually get to experience it."

"Well, if you keep talking instead of fu—aah!"

He cut off my sarcastic retort by replacing his fingers with his erection and pushing inside me with one smooth, firm stroke.

It had been a good six months since I'd gotten laid, but even so, feeling Sinan inside me was on another level. I felt full and connected to him in a way I never had with any of the one-night stands before. Eyes hooded, mouth hanging open, chest rising and falling with every breath—I didn't doubt we were both feeling similar things.

Remembering what he'd said moments ago, I deliberately squeezed around his cock, then relaxed, then repeated the action a few times, pulsing my inner walls until he looked as if he was about to come from just being inside me.

"So?" I leaned in to lick at his full lips. "How does it feel?"

"Better than I ever could've dreamed." He groaned, and I wasn't even sure if he was cracking a Sandman joke or not.

It didn't matter, because he started to move then, sliding out of me almost completely before thrusting back in all the way to the hilt. Our moans filled the rain-soaked air as Sinan fucked me in earnest. I'd clearly been delusional thinking he was about to come before he started moving, because the man had stamina, and he was done playing.

He watched me closely, eyes tracing my face and body as he sped up his pace, then his intensity. Maybe he wanted to check that I was all right with the rough sex or something, but he would've seen nothing more than wild pleasure on my face and my tits bouncing.

"You feel so fucking good, temptress. *So* good," he panted as he leaned forward. Once again, I was forced to prop myself up on my hands while Sinan flattened both palms next to my hips.

The sound of the sliding door cut through the rain and our moans, and I whipped my head around just in time to see Hollis and Oskar walking out.

"Hey, guys? Should . . ." Hollis spotted us and froze, eyes going wide.

Sinan didn't even skip a beat. His hips just continued to piston at a steady rhythm.

"Sinan," I hissed at him, assuming he hadn't noticed yet, but he was already looking at our new visitors.

"Want me to stop?" he asked, voice strained.

"No," I responded without a hint of uncertainty. I just

didn't know if they'd be all right with it, considering they'd all lived through some pretty sexually conservative times.

I looked back over my shoulder. Hollis leaned against the brick next to the door, licking his lips as he unashamedly watched Sinan rail me. He smirked and slowly rubbed the bulge in his pants. Oskar wasn't so brazen. He avoided my eyes, but his neat slacks didn't hide his erection, and he wasn't leaving either. He just stood at the door, one hand clenched on the frame as he watched.

Sinan firmly but gently gripped my chin and turned my face back to him. "Eyes on me," he demanded through gritted teeth. "They can watch you, but I want your gaze all to myself, temptress."

I couldn't have peeled my eyes off him then if I'd tried. He was beyond sexy, magnetic, all man as he fucked me harder. The table started to rock with the force of Sinan's thrusts, the legs scraping on the paving.

Sweat beaded on his forehead. I moaned and struggled for breath, holding on for dear life as the man above me drove us both to oblivion. My hands were all over him: tugging at his hair, gripping his arms, scraping down his chest, his back, his sides. Animalistic noises poured from both our mouths—desperate, rough sounds that fit right in with the rain pelting the world around us.

Sinan came hard, his whole body tensing as his hips continued to rock. His neck muscles went taut as he let out a long groan; his arms felt like solid rock where I gripped them.

The feeling of his cock deep within me, the palpable sensation of the others' eyes on us, and the cool air on my skin were almost too much for my brain to process. Or just enough, because my own climax hit me a split second after Sinan spilled inside me. The all-consuming pleasure hit me all at once. My pussy felt as if it were on fire in the best way, the heat spreading to every part of my body, from my toes to the top of my head.

It was hands-down the best orgasm I'd ever had. I panted hard as Sinan collapsed on top of me, his head tucked under my chin and his back bent slightly so he could fit. I wrapped my arms around him and locked my ankles behind his back. He gripped my shoulders, his breath heavy on my skin.

We didn't speak or goad each other or crack jokes. We just reveled in the connection, as only two deeply lonely souls could.

After a while, his legs started to shake. I smiled before planting a firm kiss to the top of his head and nudging his shoulder. When he grunted and stood up, pulling out of me, I immediately felt cold and empty.

"I would stay buried inside you until I hardened once more if my legs weren't about to give out." His serious tone and obscenely sweet declaration made me feel a little less empty, at least in my heart.

Sinan helped me sit up properly and wrapped me up in another tight embrace, his lips moving over mine in a languorous, indulgent kiss. I would've happily stayed right there forever, but my stupid body shivered, and goose-bumps rose on my skin. He caressed my cheek, then leaned down to pull his pants up.

"Let's get you inside. It's cold." He picked me up before I could get to my feet. With one hand under my knees and the other at my back, he carried me to the door.

"I can walk, you know," I said.

Sinan cocked an eyebrow. "If you can walk, then I haven't done my job well enough and I ought to take you back outside."

I just shook my head and tightened my arms around his neck—to appease his manhood, not because I secretly liked being carried around after multiple orgasms.

He took me straight to the bathroom. Not until he was lowering me to my feet in the shower did I realize Oskar and Hollis were nowhere to be seen.

"I have to go." Sinan's sudden declaration distracted me from their absence.

"What?" Did I just get smash-and-dashed? By a fucking ghost man?

"I'm needed elsewhere," Sinan explained, a knowing look in his eyes. "I'll return as soon as I can, temptress. I couldn't stay away for a second longer."

His heartfelt words soothed some of the knee-jerk abandonment-issue anxiety, and when he leaned in and kissed me gently, everything felt right with the world again. With his hand still at my neck, thumb stroking my jaw, he faded into his murky, translucent form before disappearing completely.

I sighed and turned the shower on, letting the scalding water attempt to make me feel as warm as a single kiss from Sinan had. It didn't work, but at least I thawed my freezing toes and got clean.

Wrapped in a towel, hair all messy, I walked into my room to find Hollis lounging on my bed with his hands behind his head.

"When did you turn back?" I frowned at his incorporeal body.

"I think it was about the time you came on Sinan's cock," he said, completely nonchalant.

I stumbled trying to pull my panties up, then turned away to hide my blush and the goofy grin on my face.

No. My sexuality is nothing to be embarrassed or bashful about.

Shoulders back, I turned around again to search for my sleep shirt in the bed. Hollis's wide eyes fixed on my bare tits as I dug under the pillow behind him.

With the T-shirt halfway on, something occurred to me.

"Oh shit." I pulled the shirt on the rest of the way and sank onto the bed.

"Hmm?" Hollis looked up at me and blinked a few times. "Sorry, did you say something? I was distracted by your amazing tits."

"Stop. This is serious." I smacked his leg—rather, my hand went through his leg, and I smacked the mattress.

"What's wrong?" He sat up, wiping the smile off his face.

"We didn't use protection." Oh god. Was I about to get pregnant with a three-hundred-year-old pirate's baby?

Hollis searched my face for a few moments, frowning, and I saw the exact second it clicked in his head. His eyebrows rose, and he laughed.

"Don't. I have enough fucking problems." I ran my fingers through my hair.

"Yes, well, unplanned pregnancy is not one of them."

"How do you know?" I threw my hands up. "None of

you have seen this happen before. We don't know what you can and can't do while you're real boys. What if—"

"Dollface. I'm positive." He lifted a hand to shut me up. "When we turn back to our original forms, we take every part of ourselves with us."

"Huh?"

"Everything we brought into the waking world, we take out again. It seems to be like a reset. Clothes, hair, other . . . substances." He grinned.

"Oh." So when Sinan poofed out of here, he took his jizz with him. "Convenient."

"Yep."

"Wait"—I squinted at him—"how do you know that this juju takes care of . . . secretions?"

He lay down again, getting comfortable. "How much detail do you want?"

I wanted all the details, and Hollis didn't hesitate to provide them, telling me about how he got himself off watching Sinan fuck me on my patio table. Apparently, Oskar had been called away just as things got good, but Hollis stuck around for the whole show.

Hearing him describe it got me all worked up again, and even though I'd just had amazing sex with Sinan, I ended up touching myself in bed—exactly as Hollis instructed while he watched and urged me on. I would've preferred to have him do all those things to me himself, but I couldn't make him solidify again. I was too spent, and I fell asleep minutes after my third orgasm for the night.

The next morning, I was pleasantly sore between my legs. The dull ache felt hot whenever I shifted in a certain way—the kind of heat that made me smile as I remembered what had put it there.

The rain had stopped sometime around dawn, just as I fell asleep. The clouds still hung around, but even the lack of sunshine couldn't ruin my mood. All three of the guys had been called elsewhere, and I was enjoying a rare moment of solitude in my sunroom. Had I ever referred to a moment of solitude as *rare* in my life?

My book lay abandoned in my lap as I sipped my second cup of coffee and stared out the window. Everything looked lush outside, as though the reprieve from the harsh summer sun had allowed the plants to take a deep, cleansing breath.

I couldn't stop thinking about the roller coaster of the night before. I oscillated between worrying about what the Maron would do next and replaying the sex in my mind on a constant, pleasure-filled loop. But it wasn't just the sex memories that made it impossible for me to focus on anything. It was the simple fact that I'd finally been able to touch them, hold them, feel their arms around me.

The feelings this new development brought up were scary in themselves; I wasn't sure how to process them. I knew this couldn't last, but I couldn't stop fantasizing about the most mundane, domestic shit.

I imagined waking up with Hollis's arms around me, Oskar handing me a cup of coffee in the kitchen, Sinan giving me a kiss on the cheek as he put on a sunhat and headed out to the garden. I didn't even know if Sinan liked gardening, or if Hollis was the type to sleep in, or if Oskar knew how to make coffee. My brain just kept inserting them into my life, and I couldn't stop myself from daydreaming about it.

I smiled around a sip of coffee, staring into space as the images just kept coming. I could imagine Oskar sitting next to me in this very spot, both of us reading. Sinan and Hollis would be bickering about something in the kitchen, and then they'd come into the sunroom to drag us into the discussion.

Out of the corner of my eye, I caught movement, and the fantasy evaporated. I could've sworn I'd seen something tall and black move through the plants outside. I sat up straight, focusing on the spot.

A shadow darkened the window—barely a whisper of a suggestion of a form, but for an instant I made out the long limbs and fathomless black-eyed stare. The Maron was watching me, and it was getting too close for comfort.

CHAPTER NINETEEN

Hollis had the best sex-face. I loved seeing that cheeky grin disappear as his eyes hooded and his lips parted. He had this habit of licking his bottom lip, leaving it constantly wet, as he watched his length sliding in and out of me. He loved to watch, which wasn't exactly a surprise.

I widened my knees more, trying to take him in deeper, as I gripped the back of the couch behind his head.

It was our third time having sex in the waking world, and it had only been a week since that first night I made them all corporeal. Sinan and I flirted and teased but hadn't had a chance to be together again yet. I'd fooled around with Oskar, but it hadn't gone further than that, and I didn't want to push him.

But Hollis . . . *oof! Hollis* was insatiable, and I was not complaining. It was a Friday night, and the others had been called elsewhere. I'd been popping some corn in the kitchen, preparing for a movie night, when Hollis asked if we could watch porn. I'd nearly dropped the whole damn bowl of popcorn.

We'd barely gotten ten minutes into a threesome video before we abandoned the screen for the real thing, and now here I was, riding him on the couch as he licked that damn bottom lip again.

I moaned and ground myself against his pelvis. I could feel my orgasm coming. Hollis gripped my hips, his gaze intent on his lap.

The pleasure bubbled from my core, getting more and more urgent and then—

My forehead smacked into the cushions as Hollis disappeared out from under me. I groaned and rolled my head to the side, sitting back on my heels.

Hollis had moved next to me so I wouldn't be perched halfway through his dull, transparent form. He dragged a hand down his face and gave me a devastatingly longing look, taking me in from head to toes.

"Fuck, you're beautiful." He reached out as though to caress the curve of my back, then remembered himself and threw his head back.

I took measured breaths as my pussy squeezed around the sudden and rude absence of a hard cock.

"Make yourself come for me, doll." Hollis turned toward me. "I want to watch your face as you—"

"Nah." I sat up, pouting like a kid who's just been told no sweets before dinner—bottom lip sticking out and everything. "It's not the same. I want your cock, not my fingers."

"I'm sorry." Hollis pouted right back.

"Yeah, me too." I reluctantly put my clothes back on after cleaning up the mess between my legs.

This had happened multiple times, but I was getting better at controlling it. Not the whole "dick disappearing in the middle of boning" thing. Just the general "them suddenly losing solid form" thing.

That first night had been a fluke, just me following my gut and doing what felt right. Since then, I'd been practicing it just as I did the lucid dreaming and everything else, and I was getting better. With just one guy, I could keep them corporeal for pretty much the entire day. With all three, though, I got tired and drained after only a couple hours.

"Should we watch a nonpornographic film then?" Hollis suggested, that cute grin back in place.

"Yeah, I guess." I sighed.

"Hey." Sinan appeared on my other side, draped over the couch. I'd gotten used to them just popping in and out of thin air. "You guys about to start a movie?"

"Unfortunately," Hollis and I said at the same time, then exchanged smiles.

"OK then." Sinan frowned at us. "What am I missing?"

"Ugh. Nothing." I grabbed the remote and started flicking through movie options.

"We just got cockblocked by Reverie's special gift," Hollis announced.

"Oh, this I have to hear." Sinan angled himself toward us, and I found myself between the two of them—more attention on me than I wanted when my body was crying from the lack of orgasm.

I dropped the remote on the coffee table, abandoning

the movie idea, and just started eating popcorn as Hollis went into graphic detail about us having sex. By the time I finished off the bowl, he still hadn't gotten to the part where he vanished out from under me, but we were laughing.

With all of us teasing one another and cracking jokes, the mood had considerably lightened. Even Sinan was smiling more than I'd ever seen him smile. It felt like a totally normal hangout with friends on a weekend. With flirting. And the knowledge that I'd had sex with them both. And hoped to again.

At a lull in the conversation, I turned to Sinan, knowing I was about to bring the mood down again. "How's it going? Any sign of it?" Of course, Sinan would've said something right away if the Maron had tried to attack Nora and her family again, but I needed to hear it.

"No sign of it at all," Sinan reassured me. "Oskar is still there and will remain until Hollis goes. I had to attend to another matter before coming here, but we would've heard from Oskar if there was any trouble."

They could communicate with one another via some unexplained dream-realm mind fuckery—like yelling at someone on the other side of town and having them and no one else hear you perfectly. But they weren't really worried about Nora anymore anyway. They only went because I insisted.

I knew all three of them would rather be here with me at all times. After all, the Maron had tried to attack only me in the past week. There had been no sign of it anywhere else.

That first time I saw the Maron lurking in the bushes,

I'd convinced myself it was just my overactive imagination, my worries making me see things . . . for about fifteen minutes. Then I started working myself up. By the time Sinan appeared fifteen minutes later, I was on the verge of a full-blown panic attack. I was terrified that my pain-in-the-ass special gift would do to the Maron what I had done to Sinan, Oskar, and Hollis—that it was only a matter of time before it took corporeal form just as they had.

Sinan walked me down off the ledge and had me calmly explain what I'd seen. Apparently, I'd been daydreaming, and that had provided the evil sleep monster a brief crack into my dreamscape.

"When you daydream, it creates a sort of window between the waking world and the dreamworld. You're still awake, still present in your physical body, but your mind is open," Sinan explained. "We didn't think it was anything to worry about, as the Maron has only struck at night so far, but . . ."

The conversation had then turned from Sinan comforting me to me comforting him as he berated himself for leaving me unprotected. I'd just been relieved to know I wouldn't accidentally bring a literal monster into the world, where it could do who knows what kind of damage. Gritton had suffered enough.

But apparently, my power was closely tied to my will. Every time I had leveled up, I'd been focusing and working on making it happen. I wouldn't make the Maron corporeal by accident, because I didn't want it anywhere near me at all.

Unfortunately, near me was the only place the fucker wanted to be now.

The Maron tried to bash its way into my dreamscape every damn night. It hadn't tried again during the day, but I was making a conscious effort not to daydream. No easy feat, considering the three insanely hot men I now practically lived with.

"It came by earlier tonight," Hollis said, surprising me.

"It did? When?"

"Right around the time you were sliding onto my—"

"Why didn't you call us?" Sinan cut in.

"Because it basically did a drive-by." Hollis shrugged. "It flitted past, saw that Rev was not asleep—probably saw more than it bargained for—and disappeared. I didn't even have a chance to worry about it. I was otherwise engaged."

He flashed me that flirty grin. If I hadn't been so drained, I would've made him solid and given him a smack. Or a kiss. Probably both.

"This is beginning to really sour my mood." Sinan glared at the coffee table.

I waved his comment off. "Your mood was already sour."

"Pretty sure you were born with a scowl on your face. Probably scared the doctor half to death." Hollis laughed.

"Physicians did not concern themselves with childbirth at that time," Sinan responded, not taking the bait, and continued to stare down the coffee table.

He really hated it when things didn't go his way, and the Maron was pretty much giving him double middle fingers as it zoomed in the opposite direction. They tried to capture it every time it dropped in uninvited, but it always managed to evade them. It had had a lot of time to perfect its technique.

There was no way it would get into my dreamscape with all three of them constantly vigilant. I hadn't had a moment alone in a week. Not that I was complaining. It was a nice change from . . . well, my whole life up to that point.

Unfortunately, with the Maron unable to get to me, and my guys unable to catch it, we'd reached a nightmarish kind of impasse.

None of us had said it yet, but we all knew I was the key to breaking it. I was a Seheraum and had all the damn gifts. Didn't take a genius to figure out I needed to use them to defeat the monster. Problem was, I had no idea how to do that—or even where to start in figuring it out. And on a selfish note, I was pretty sure the guys would leave as soon as I took the Maron down; I hated the thought of losing them.

I wasn't sure what their excuse was. They'd pushed me to practice and develop my abilities from day one, but now they all suddenly kept their mouths shut when it came to the obvious solution.

Oskar appeared in the room and leaned on the wall next to the grandfather clock.

"Hey." He gave us an easy smile.

"Hey?" I sat up straight. "What are you doing here? No one's watching Nora."

Sinan rolled his eyes. "I can't with this woman. Someone talk some sense into her."

"Dollface." Hollis gave me a look that edged on patronizing. "Nora is safe. The whole town is safe. The Maron has not once attempted to attack a single other person other than you in over a week. The only time it even appears is right near you."

"Yes, but what if that's what it wants us to think? Maybe it's trying to throw us off so we'll drop our guard and it can go after others."

"It isn't," Oskar said matter-of-factly, then rushed to keep speaking before I could demand what made him so sure. "They are not that calculating. They lose their humanity more and more, remember? They just go after whatever their current sights are set on, like an animal on the hunt."

"We just need to figure out why it has its sights set on you now," Sinan grumbled.

CHAPTER TWENTY

Oskar leaned back against the headrest of the passenger seat, his face tipped to the wide-open window, a hint of a smile on his lips. His hair fluttered in the wind, the usually neat style completely ruined. Every once in a while, he took a deep breath.

I would've closed the windows if I were driving alone, but he got so much enjoyment from it that the nip of the chilly breeze was more than worth it. Summer's sweltering days had officially ended, but the crisp autumn air still wasn't cold enough to put on layers during the day.

I wasn't usually this observant of the weather—other than how it may affect my plants—but Oskar noticed everything. Every time he was corporeal, he made sure to spend time outdoors. Even during the night or cold or rain. *Especially* the rain. He commented on how the leaves changed color, pointed out the shapes he saw in the clouds, named bird species I'd hardly ever noticed, even though I'd lived here my whole life.

All the guys treasured every second, every tactile experience they had in their physical form, but Oskar had a deep appreciation for the natural world. I could talk to him about my herbs or my houseplants for hours, and he wouldn't get bored.

So I was wholly content to sit in silence with him in my truck as I drove to Quimby Valley and he just . . . breathed.

As I turned onto the road leading to town, the sun came out and bathed his face in its warmth. The natural light, along with his widening smile, softened his strong features, and his blond hair shone.

"I will never get sick of feeling the sun on my face." He opened his eyes and sat up straighter.

I smiled and said nothing. We both knew this would have to come to an end soon, but I hated to be reminded of it. Because wherever they were going would surely be better than the lonely, empty life they'd be leaving me to.

I had three deliveries to make, and Oskar insisted on carrying the herbs to my clients' doors, which was fine by me. It felt ridiculously good to have someone *want* to help, and I loved watching him interact with other people. His infectious joy left every person we talked to smiling.

At the post office, I actually did need his help to carry all the packages inside. He saved me a second trip to the truck, and I finished all my errands in record time.

"What do you want to do now?" I asked as we walked down the main strip, sipping on boba tea. Quimby Valley was just big enough to have a place that sold the drink with bubbles of deliciousness in it. Oskar took tentative sips, apparently still undecided on whether he liked it, but he kept wrapping his lips around the big straw, so it seemed to be winning him over.

"I don't care." He shrugged and took my hand with his free one. "As long as I'm with you and I can feel the sun, the air, your touch." He gave my hand a squeeze, and our fingers threaded together. It felt so natural. As if we always walked down streets holding hands and chatting.

My heart ached, but I pushed that feeling away. I wanted to enjoy every second with them.

"I have an idea. Come on." I turned around and pulled him back in the direction of the car. By the time we reached it, his tea was gone, and a pleasant satisfaction filled me that he'd liked something I suggested.

Oskar didn't even question where we were going as I drove out of town, then turned down a small winding road. He seemed content to just come along for the ride.

There was a little-known lookout about twenty minutes outside Quimby Valley—out of our way—only accessible via a series of narrow dirt roads. I hadn't been there in years, and I couldn't think of another person I'd rather go with. The end of the road had space for maybe half a dozen vehicles, but ours was the only car when we pulled up and parked.

"Beautiful spot, *schatzi*." Oskar stared up at the tall trees. Nothing but green, the occasional flash of autumnal amber, and fresh air surrounded us.

"Just wait until you see our final destination." I tipped my head to the side, and he followed me to the start of the uphill path. The sign next to the trail was so faded and covered in moss it could barely be read.

Oskar and I stayed mostly silent as we made our way up at a steady pace, both of us enjoying the quiet and the sounds of birds all around us. My legs soon started to burn, and I was out of breath by the time we made it to the top. The dense trees and bushes came to an end, and we emerged onto a flat, rocky spot.

"Wow," Oskar breathed, standing shoulder to shoulder with me.

"Totally worth it." I nodded.

The other side of the clearing ended in a sheer cliff, and one of the best views I'd ever seen greeted us. Two mountain peaks towered in the distance, a valley stretched below them. Gritton was tucked behind the first peak, not visible from our vantage point and accessible only by a road that stretched around the other side of the mountain. In fact, no towns or even buildings could be seen at all. A few hunting cabins must've been tucked away down there, but as far as we could see, it was all wilderness. The trees covering the landscape gently rolled over everything, like waves.

The sky felt bigger out here. Patches of blue and white mingled above, but the clouds looked friendly, so it wasn't likely to rain.

Despite the challenging uphill walk, neither of us went to the lone bench off to one side. We just stood there near the edge, taking in the magnificence of it all for several long moments.

"Reverie?" Oskar's soft voice drew my gaze to his.

"Yeah?" I smiled.

He opened his mouth, then closed it, a slight frown creasing his brow. Whatever he'd been about to say, whatever he was turning over in his mind, he shook it off and returned my smile. "I really want to kiss you."

"Then kiss me." I wrapped my arms around his neck and tipped my face up.

He squeezed my hips. "I want to do more than just kiss you. I want to have sex with you."

"Oh." I had never had a guy tell me so clearly and matter-of-factly what he wanted. Yeah, there had been dirty "I want to be inside you"–type comments, but the way Oskar said it felt . . . significant somehow. "Well, you know I'm definitely open to that, so . . ."

His lips quirked up, and he wrapped his arms around me. His eyes practically sparkled in the bright open air, and they had the kind of mischief behind them I'd expect from Hollis.

"Excellent," he whispered against my lips, then started walking me backward slowly.

I tried to kiss him, but he moved his head back, and he was so much taller than me. When my back connected with a tree, I let out a little surprised sound, and then realization dawned.

"Wait. Do you mean *now*?" I glanced behind him at the wide-open, public space.

"Yes." He propped one hand on the tree above my head and leaned down to kiss my neck. His soft lips, the teasing little flicks of his tongue, the occasional scrape of teeth—it all sent liquid desire coursing through my body. But . . .

"What if someone comes along?" My voice was breathy, and despite the objection, I didn't push him away.

"So?" He pulled back to look at me, shrugging. "They get an eyeful for a second, and we leave. Who cares?"

I gaped at him. Oskar was quiet, thoughtful, reserved. That he was also sexually adventurous just did not compute.

He chuckled at what must've been a dumbfounded

look on my face. "Look, there were no other cars when we pulled up, and I didn't see any other trails leading up here. The hike took us a good thirty minutes. If someone arrived not long after us, we would've heard the car. My guess is we have at least fifteen minutes before we're interrupted. That's plenty of time."

There's my logical, thoughtful man.

I was going to reply, but I forgot my entire argument when Oskar's hips started to gently roll against mine.

His rock-hard erection rubbed against my pelvis and lower belly, filling me with frustration at the amount of clothing between us. I pulled his head down, and he finally let me kiss him. I sighed into his mouth as his tongue massaged mine.

Without breaking the kiss, he shifted slightly to wedge his knee between my legs, and then suddenly we were like a couple of teenagers—consumed by lust, kisses messy, grinding on each other as though it was the best thing since sliced bread.

Oskar moved his hot mouth back to my sensitive neck as his hand slid under my sweater to knead my breast. I threw my head back against the tree and gasped into the fresh air. The branches swayed lazily in the breeze above us, the peaceful view a complete contrast to the heated, frantic energy coursing through my body.

Aware that our time was limited—because I really didn't want to get caught fucking at a lookout in the middle of the day—I nudged Oskar lightly until he pulled back enough for me to undo his pants. I immediately missed the friction of his leg against my sex, but the trade-off was worth it. Pushing fabric out of the way, I wrapped my hand around his length and stroked the hot, hard evidence of his arousal.

He sighed, a guttural edge to the sound, as he tipped his head back, eyes closed and mouth open. Drunk on that reaction, I stroked him again, my grip a little tighter just so I could watch how much it affected him.

After a few moments, he opened his eyes and looked at me with something slightly unhinged in his gaze. He fumbled with my jeans to get them open, then shoved them halfway down my ass. One hand gripped the side of my face and caressed my jaw, while the other dived into my underpants, fingers sliding through my already slick folds.

Oskar had decided what he wanted, voiced it, and now didn't hesitate to get it. His fingers explored me with confident, firm strokes, and then he pushed two inside. Our mouths came together once more in sensual, gasping kisses.

We clutched at clothes and hair, groaning, desperate and wild as we pleasured each other. Oskar let me set the pace, his fingers pumping inside me in rhythm with how I stroked him. His touch felt so good, heightened by our exposed location, and I fucked myself on his fingers as much as he thrust them in and out.

My orgasm was building, and my movements on Oskar's cock started to get messy and inconsistent.

He pulled his hand away unexpectedly, making me gasp, but I didn't bother complaining. We both had the same idea as we reached for our own pants.

Oskar shoved his down to his knees and stroked himself while he waited for me to wiggle out of mine. I had to remove one shoe to pull a pant leg off, but I gave up on the other one. He looked positively sinful standing there with his hair a mess and his smart mouth swollen as he squeezed his cock—which looked hard enough to be painful. I knew I was in pain every second I waited to have him inside me.

I reached for him, and he grabbed my thighs and lifted me in one swift motion. I wrapped my legs around his waist and my arms around his neck, my breath hitching.

"Oskar, I'm heavy." I winced. I loved my juicy ass and my curves, but I didn't want him to waste stamina on holding me up. "There's a bench—"

"No, you're not," he cut me off. "Shut up and let me fuck you against this *Pinus monticola*."

"Yes, sir." I wasn't going to argue with that.

He held me against the tree, and I reached between us to position him at my entrance. He slid in halfway, then pulled almost all the way out again. I nearly pleaded with him at that point, but Oskar was as eager as I was. With one slow, deliberate thrust, he filled me with his cock until our hips were flush and I felt deliciously full.

"Oh, Oskar," I moaned, trembling from the intensity of the sensations. He pressed his forehead to mine, and for a moment we just breathed the same air as the birds chirped and the breeze caressed my bare legs.

I glanced over his shoulder at the end of the path, the thrill of possibly getting caught making me clamp around the thick cock deep inside me. That made Oskar groan, and he once again brought his mouth to that sensitive spot on my neck. As his lips and tongue started to move against my skin, his hips started to move too.

Every thought about getting caught flew from my mind. Even if someone did walk up while Oskar was balls-deep inside me, I still wouldn't want him to stop. All I could focus on was *him*. His mouth on my neck; his hands gripping my thighs; his hard, tense shoulders under my hands; and most of all, his perfect length sliding in and out, in and out.

His pace gradually increased, making pleasure wash through my body with every stroke. My ass was getting scratched up on the bark, but I didn't care. If anything, the slight pain drove my pleasure higher, making my senses more aware.

"Are you close, *schatzi*?" Oskar panted near my ear before sucking my earlobe into his mouth.

All I could manage was an incoherent whimper. I kept feeling as though I was about to come, but then the pleasure would keep ratcheting up—as if the peak moved higher and higher every time I got close to it. It was the most intoxicating kind of torture.

Oskar fixed me with an intense look as he fucked me in deep strokes, pulling out just a tiny bit before thrusting back in deep. I rolled my hips as best I could, matching his thrusts, grinding my clit against his pelvis. Sweat beaded his forehead, and the murmur of nature around us mingled with our moaning and the sound of skin slapping against skin.

"You feel so good," Oskar said, his voice low and gravelly. "So fucking tight and wet. Oh, you feel like heaven, Reverie. Come with me."

I started falling into ecstasy the moment he started speaking. My gaze stayed pinned to his as my body locked up. Every muscle seemed to spasm, and I cried out so loudly a flock of birds flew off from a nearby tree. Such fierce pleasure shot through me I saw stars at the edges of my vision.

Oskar pressed his whole body flush with mine as he came. His chest heaved, and his hips ground against me. I held him close as he moaned his release into my ear, the sound something between pure delight and excruciating relief.

We panted against that tree for several long moments, and then his arms started to tremble.

"Oskar." I chuckled, running my fingers through his hair. "Put me down."

"I don't want to." He gave me a lazy smile. "I want to stay right here." His hips rolled against mine, in case it wasn't clear what he meant.

I gasped, the movement too much for my hypersensitive pussy.

He kissed me languorously as he lowered me to the ground, and I leaned back against the tree; I'd have to wait for my legs to stop wobbling before I could cover up. Oskar pulled his pants up and got on his knees before me. I gaped when he started cleaning me up with careful, tender swipes of . . . was that a *hanky*?

I didn't know having a guy wipe the sex-mess from your pussy lips and thighs right after he fucked you silly in the woods could be romantic, but fuck, yeah, it was hella chivalrous.

"Thank you," I murmured, a shy smile on my lips. I'd forgotten he came from an era when they thought it necessary to do things like open doors for women and carry handkerchiefs. When he finished, he helped me back into my pants and even held my shoe for me to step into.

I felt like some kind of sexed-up version of Cinderella.

We clasped hands as we turned back to the lookout.

Immediately I spotted two figures sitting on the faded old bench. Instead of feeling horrified, I chuckled under my breath. Because the two people were translucent and looking over their shoulders at us with cheeky grins.

"Gentlemen." Oskar greeted them politely as we walked over—as if he'd simply run into them on a pleasant day and was not at all bothered they'd seen us fucking against a tree. In fact, none of them seemed bothered by the whole "sharing" thing. Or if they were, they certainly hadn't mentioned it.

"How is it that you're all so chill about this?" I blurted before I could remember that thing about looking a gift horse in the mouth.

Hollis cocked his head to the side, becoming solid before my eyes. He grabbed my wrist and pulled me onto his lap. "What do you mean, doll?"

Sinan solidified a split second later and immediately rested his arm on the bench behind Hollis, his fingers going to the back of my neck. Oskar sat down on Sinan's other side and propped one ankle on his knee.

"I mean this." I gestured vaguely to us all, just sitting there casually, comfortably. "You all come from times when people weren't as . . . open-minded, I guess? So how are you all so OK with . . ."

"Sharing your bed?" Sinan raised his eyebrows.

"The roaring twenties weren't just champagne cascades and dancing." Hollis chuckled. "There was plenty of debauchery, including the sexual kind."

"There is much that is forgotten by history, simply lost to time, or erased purposefully by those with an agenda,"

Sinan added. "I have had many women, sometimes at once, and a few men."

"Really?" I hadn't expected that at all.

"It gets lonely out on the seas for months." He grinned.

"People have been having sex for pleasure since the dawn of time"—Oskar tipped his face up to the sun as it reappeared from behind a cloud—"regardless of how hard various cultures and religions tried to put a stop to it. Besides, the three of us have been observing people all over the world for a very long time. One's mind is cracked wide open, whether one wants it to be or not, when you suddenly gain access to people's most private moments, thoughts, dreams."

"There's nothing we haven't seen, doll." Hollis gave me a kiss on the cheek.

"Well . . . OK then." I shrugged. If they were fine with it, who was I to argue?

After a few moments of comfortable silence, Oskar got to his feet. He meandered over to the very edge of the cliff and peered down.

"Have you ever been bungee jumping, Reverie?" he called over his shoulder.

"No." I was all up for new experiences, but not ones that made me wonder if I might die in the process.

"I've always wanted to try it."

I tensed in Hollis's embrace as Oskar lean dangerously far over. "Well, I'm sure I can find somewhere nearby—"

In the middle of my sentence, Oskar jumped. He just threw his hands out to the sides and launched himself face-first off a motherfucking cliff. I let out a panicked scream as I shot to my feet and scrambled to the edge, just in time to see him sailing down like an Olympic diver—feet together, arms out. And then, right before he reached the treetops below, he winked out of existence.

For a moment I was confused, my eyes frantically searching for him.

"Step back a bit," Sinan said, his voice mild but his grip on my elbow firm. He and Hollis stood on either side of me. "If *you* fall, it would actually be fatal."

I stepped back and whirled around, more angry than scared now. As expected, Oskar appeared before me, translucent and grinning.

"That was incredible!" He whooped, eyes shining.

"What the fuck!" I yelled in his face, then made him solid so I could shove him in the chest. "You gave me a heart attack."

"It's all right, Rev." He dropped the childishly gleeful look as he rubbed my shoulders. "You know we can't die."

"No." I shrugged him off. "I do not fucking know that, Oskar. What if—"

"I wanna try it," Hollis announced.

"Don't you dare!" I whirled on him. "We have no idea how this juju works. You could end up stuck as a solid person at any moment, and then you'll splat, and I am not cleaning that mess up."

"Doll, relax." He slowly backed closer to the edge. "We can't remain in this form permanently, and we have full control of when we move through time and space, regardless of it."

Without waiting for a response, he turned around and jumped off the damn cliff.

"Dammit!" I threw my hands up in frustration.

Sinan watched me with a little too much amusement in his eyes.

"Don't you dare!" I pointed a finger at him.

"It's perfectly safe." He shrugged, then fell backward as an evil grin split his face.

I whirled on Oskar. "I blame you for this."

But I didn't register his response. My irritation evaporated when my eyes caught on something over his shoulder: a dark shape in the branches of a nearby tree. Something about it didn't . . . fit.

Oskar must've felt it at the same moment I realized it was the Maron. It crouched in the tree, watching us with creepy black eyes, its body obscured by the surrounding branches. Oskar stepped forward to put himself between me and the monster, one hand on my hip.

Hollis appeared then, already facing off with it, shoulders tense. Half a second later, Sinan joined us too. He blinked into existence in a blur of movement as he lunged for the creature.

It opened its mouth—too wide, too gaping—in what looked like a scream, but no sound came out. And then it vanished.

Sinan released a string of curses. It looked as if he'd missed it by barely a hair.

"How long do you think it was watching us?" I asked, releasing my death grip on Oskar's blazer. When had I latched on to him like that?

"Not long." He took me into his arms. "I think you spotted it barely a second after it showed up."

"We were distracted," Sinan growled. "It won't happen again."

"Why could I see it? I wasn't daydreaming or anything." I didn't want that thing anywhere near me.

"Your power is getting stronger," Oskar explained. "At this stage, you'd be able to see any Dreamwalker, whether they wanted you to or not. Plus, you spent years unaware of the Maron's existence, but lately you've been thinking and worrying and talking about it a lot. It's natural your senses would be more attuned to it."

The mood was well and truly ruined. I shivered in Oskar's hold, only partly because of the dropping temperature. The clouds had grown thicker, and the sun had been keeping the chill off the air.

"Let's head home," Hollis suggested, and we started the trek back down the mountain. They stayed close to me the whole way, Oskar holding my hand while Hollis and Sinan remained in their ghostly forms. Sinan was grumpier than usual, and Oskar seemed deep in thought. Hollis kept chatting, doing his best to lighten the mood even though we didn't give him much back.

"Oh, by the way, I saw signs up for some kind of festival in town?" he said as we neared the end of the track. His persistence had started to work. The others were actually participating in the conversation, and I felt lighter than I had at the top of the cliff.

"Yeah, the Gritton Great Fair is a yearly tradition," I explained. "Started in the late eighteen hundreds, I think, when the town was first established. It's an end of summer celebration, something to do with agriculture and the harvest and whatever."

"We should go!" Hollis floated backward right in front of me.

The others grumbled, and I winced. "I don't know." I hadn't been in years, and I didn't want to deal with the townies being dicks to me. I had enough shit to worry about.

But Hollis latched on to the idea like a dog with a bone, so by the time we reached the car, I'd agreed to go to the stupid festival just to shut him up.

CHAPTER TWENTY-ONE

Main Street was closed to traffic and teeming with people. The Gritton Great Fair tended to bring in a lot of tourists. What used to be a humble small-town celebration generations ago had grown into a big draw for the region, featuring live music, a produce and makers market, baking contests, and all the usual food and games you'd find at a fair.

My shoulders relaxed when I realized there were more faces in the crowd I didn't recognize than those I did.

"Oh, shoot. We missed the wood-splitting competition," I deadpanned.

"Ooh! Food!" Hollis's eyes lit up at the row of food trucks lining one edge of the park, serving everything from ice cream to deep-fried everything. He ignored my sarcasm and grabbed my hand to hurry through the crowd. I looked over my shoulder to make sure we didn't lose Oskar and Sinan, but I shouldn't have worried. Sinan's resting dick face was firmly in place, and the crowd parted for him instinctively. With his long black coat and general aura of violence, he cut an imposing figure. Oskar strolled next to him, hands in pockets, taking everything in.

String lights hung over the street and the park in the main square, and with the dusky pink and indigo evening light, along with the tall trees framing everything, it felt magical.

Hollis beelined for the popcorn stand and ordered the largest serving they had.

"Eight dollars." The guy in the barbershop getup looked as if he would've fit right in with Hollis's time.

"What?" Hollis spluttered, taking the bucket of popcorn. "That's robbery!"

The popcorn guy frowned, and I jumped in to pay before this turned into a scene. "There you go. Sorry about him. He's, uh, a method actor, and his current role is a 1920s banker."

"Uh-huh." The guy looked us up and down as he took the money.

"The cost of eating out sure has increased," Hollis mumbled around a mouthful of popcorn. "Next you're gonna tell me that sixty-nine is now called ninety-six!"

I shuffled him away, trying, and failing, not to laugh.

"Thanks for the popcorn, doll," he said, more serious. "I hadn't considered we wouldn't have any money we could use to . . ."

He looked genuinely stricken, but I waved him off. "Don't worry about it. It's my treat."

"No, that won't be necessary," he said hurriedly as Sinan picked up a handful of popcorn and shoveled it into his mouth.

"Necessary or not, I'm doing it." I crossed my arms.

"This is the twenty-first century, and I am a strong, independent woman. If I want to spend my hard-earned money on a night out with my, er, with you lot, then that's what I'm going to do. Now, I haven't had dinner and I'm going to get myself a corndog and curly fries. What do you guys want?"

All three of them voiced their discomfort with me paying for everything, but by the time I bought a bunch of food and we found a picnic table to sit at, they were over it.

I spotted several townspeople as I went about buying the food. Those manning food stalls served me with reluctant coldness before turning to the next person with big welcoming smiles. I made sure to be extra sweet and polite to them. *Assholes.*

"This is good ale." Oskar held up his second plastic cup of beer and nodded appreciatively.

"Uh, yeah, it's all right, I guess." I shrugged. They had nice things to say about all the food, and even Sinan had flashed a smile as he ate chicken wings doused in sticky sauce.

Pippa walked past at a glacial pace with her husband, openly scowling at me while trying to see as much as possible of the guys. I sighed and downed the rest of my own beer, reaching for the second one. I'd bought eight immediately to avoid having to go back to the crowded bar set up in the gazebo.

"The natives are getting restless." I rolled my eyes. Word must've gotten out I was here with three insanely hot guys, and more and more locals just happened to stroll past our table.

"Yes, I'm keeping an eye on it." Sinan downed his second beer and crushed the cup in his hand, all while glaring at the crowd.

"That's kind of intense." I giggled. Dammit, the beer was getting to me already. "You get used to it. We'll just leave if they get annoying."

"We'll do no such thing." Oskar slapped the table. "We are enjoying our evening and will not be run off from the festivities by a bunch of . . . of . . . douche . . ." He clicked his fingers. "What's that thing you say, Reverie? Douche . . . bins?"

We all burst into laughter.

"Douchebags." Sinan slapped Oskar on the shoulder.

"She also favors douche-canoes."

"Ah, yes, that's it." Oskar nodded.

"When all else fails, a classic 'assholes' will do just fine," I added.

The middle-aged couple that ran the bookstore in town came past, looking personally offended by the fact I was daring to laugh.

"All right, come on." Hollis got to his feet. "Time to have some fun."

"It is harder to hit a moving target." Sinan nodded as he got up.

Those of us with drinks still left to finish chugged them down, and we took off through the crowd.

"Perhaps we could go play ring toss, if the lady is amenable?" Oskar did a subtle little bow.

"The lady is very amenable." I curtsied in the most obnoxious, over-the-top way I could manage.

"Yes, she is," Sinan said close to my ear, grabbing my ass as he passed. I laughed, surprised at the sudden groping and happy at least one of them wasn't hung up on being a proper gentleman in public.

We meandered around the festival, arguing about which game to play first. Everyone had very strong opinions on ring toss, and only Oskar's was positive. Along the way, we picked up more beers, and our evening started to turn into more of a drinking game than anything.

"OK, OK, OK." I held my hands out, my half-empty beer sloshing around in the cup. "We can't just keep walking around arguing all night. How about we draw straws for it."

"Reverie! Hello!"

I made a childish face when I heard the voice behind me, then took a long pull of my beer as I turned to face Pippa.

"'Sup." I belched. I hadn't planned it, but the timing was divine. Hollis giggled behind me.

Pippa chose to ignore it. She always had choice words for me whenever I had the displeasure of crossing her path. I wondered if she spent time writing her scathing insults, then practiced them in front of the mirror.

She stood before me with a fake-ass smile, a handful of friends with her. "Wasn't expecting to see you here," she said, although the tone was more suited to "What the fuck are you doing here?"

"Yes, but you see, I ran out of food, so I came down for that, and there was beer so . . ." I gestured to my cup and then tipped it back.

"Charming." Her lips thinned. "Well, I hope you don't indulge too much. I would hate for these lovely out-of-town people to see anything embarrassing. It would reflect badly on Gritton."

"Oh, you mean like that?" I pointed over her shoulder, where three men my parents' age were having a chugging contest. Pippa turned just in time to see Mr. Jones finish his drink and stumble backward, crashing into a trash can, as the others laughed uncontrollably.

Pippa once again chose to ignore the obvious. "And who are these . . . men you're with?" Her smile became a little more genuine as she checked out my guys.

For the first time in years, I blanked. I didn't have a sarcastic comment ready to fling back at her. I wasn't used to defending relationships. I wasn't used to *having* relationships.

Before my beer-doused mind could completely spiral down a hole of insecurity and self-loathing, Hollis stepped in close and wrapped his arm around my waist.

"I'm her boyfriend," he announced, smacking a kiss to my cheek.

Pippa looked about as surprised as I felt, but that was nothing compared to the look on her face when Oskar closed in on my other side.

"I am also her boyfriend." He took my hand and raised it to his lips for a tender kiss.

Pippa finally recovered and laughed, her friends joining in.

"Are these guys aware of what they're getting themselves into?" one of Pippa's friends asked. I couldn't remember his name, but I wanted to smack the mocking smile off his face. "This one's trouble, dudes—and not the wild-in-the-sack, fun kind. Like, 'just might take you out in your sleep' kind."

"You best watch your mouth." Sinan's voice was low and deceptively calm as he stepped forward.

Shit. This was escalating, and how the hell would I explain things if a fight started and one of them just winked out of existence in front of a whole crowd of people? I fidgeted, ready to shut this down and just go home. But Hollis's grip on my waist tightened, and Oskar rubbed his thumb on the back of my hand.

"Are you her boyfriend too?" Pippa asked mockingly. How the hell were grown-ass adults behaving like this? I shouldn't have been surprised. I'd been dealing with ignorant, immature behavior from people twice their age for years.

"I'm your worst fucking nightmare." The calm had vanished from Sinan's voice, and anger bunched his shoulders around his ears. Only three people standing here knew just how literal his threat was, but the assholes from my town must've seen something dangerous in him anyway. Their smiles disappeared, replaced by wide eyes.

"Sinan." I placed my free hand in the middle of his hard back. "They're not worth it."

After a few tense breaths, the silence stretching out between us all, Sinan turned to face me. People were starting to look our way, and I really did not need to be the center of yet another drama.

"You're worth it, Reverie." He took my face in his hands, his touch gentle, and kissed me. Neither Hollis nor

Oskar released their hold on me as Sinan's lips crashed to mine. They weren't staking their claim with Sinan or being stubborn. They were showing the world they stood with me no matter what, that they didn't give a shit what people thought.

Sinan took his time kissing me. His lips passed over my top lip and my bottom as his tongue darted out in small flicks. I forgot about the people looking on and the people trying to ruin my night. Because my guys were right—it didn't matter what any of them thought. I felt so strong yet vulnerable, so shaky yet supported. I could've cried.

The sound of cheers and whistles made me remember where we were, and I pulled back from the kiss. The townie assholes had left. A few people in the vicinity cheered on our public display of affection, but they quickly lost interest now that we were giving each other more space.

"Thank you," I murmured and cleared my throat. I suddenly felt awkward. "I could've dealt with those douche-canoes on my own, but I appreciate what you guys did."

"Dollface, just because you *can* do something yourself doesn't mean you *should*," Hollis gave me a warm smile.

Considering how hard I was clenching my jaw to stop my tears, I couldn't believe I hadn't cracked a tooth. I refused to show any kind of weakness in front of the people who made my life hell, but it was impossible to ignore how these three made me feel.

Too much. They held way too much sway over my emotions, and it would hurt more than I knew when they left.

"Hey, what's the matter?" Hollis stepped in closer, and they all looked concerned.

"Ah . . ." I turned my eyes up to the sky, blinking rapidly. "I've just never . . . I've never had a boyfriend, or anyone willing to stand up for me like that. Not since my parents . . ."

I hadn't had anyone in my corner for so long I'd forgotten what it felt like. All the other shit making me emotional—I wasn't ready to voice it, let alone discuss it.

Sinan released a frustrated breath through his nose and pointed a finger at me. "This is unacceptable. You are incredible, Reverie, and anyone who makes you feel anything less deserves a slow and painful death."

I stared at him with my mouth hanging open. Laughter started to bubble up in my chest. This whole night had been ridiculous.

"Would you like to go home?" Oskar offered, but I really didn't. I hated feeling like an outcast, and I refused to be forced out when we'd been having such a good time.

"No, I'd like to stay."

"Then would you like to dance?" Hollis held out his hand, flashing me a big grin.

I slapped my palm into his. "Yes."

"I'll return shortly," Sinan announced.

"Where are you going?" I called after him as he walked away.

"To punch something," he said over his shoulder, and the laughter inside me spilled over.

Hollis led me back to the park, where a dancefloor had been set up and a band was playing lively music. Oskar hung back, leaning against one of the poles of the gazebo, while Hollis pulled me into a twirl.

I laughed freely as we danced, moving to the music and

messing around. Hollis was an excellent dancer. He pulled me close and stole kisses, spun me around, and made me forget all about the unpleasantness of earlier.

Sinan joined Oskar by the gazebo, and in the flashes of them I caught while spinning, they looked relaxed as they chatted.

The music changed to something slower, more sensuous. It was late enough that all the families with kids had left, leaving the adults to get drunker and dance as if no one was watching.

Hollis pulled me in close, and I wrapped my arms around his neck. His knee wedged between my legs, and we moved together—hips swaying, gazes locked—while the music drifted around us. The breeze played with my hair, and when a strand blew over my cheek, he reached up to tenderly swipe it back. Pressure built low in my belly with each passing song, and our movements became more indecent by the moment.

Just when I thought I couldn't stand it any longer and was about to drag him home to have my wicked way with him, a hard chest appeared at my back, and a warm hand settled on my hip. The steadying feeling and glimpse of elegant fingers told me immediately who it was, and I rested my head back on Oskar's shoulder. This was bliss . . . or torture. I couldn't be absolutely sure which.

I released a low, soft moan, my eyes heavy, and Oskar cursed softly behind me. Hollis let go of my waist and took a small step back.

"I'd better leave you two to it before this turns into something that could get us arrested." His lips smirked but his eyes were smoldering. I didn't want him to leave, but he had a point. After a lingering kiss to my lips, Hollis weaved through the dancers to join Sinan. The usually grumpy man must've said something teasing, because Hollis smacked him in the stomach and they both laughed.

I smiled, bursting with joy at seeing them so carefree.

Oskar's arms wound around my waist, my back to his front, as we kept moving to the music. Soon, the burning desire inside me had settled to a low simmer. I turned in his arms, and even while the music cycled through a few upbeat tracks, we set our own steady pace. When a slow song came on, it matched us instead of the other way around.

Oskar took my right hand in his and held it to his chest between us. Suddenly I felt like a lady, dancing with a gentleman, in some romantic historical setting.

"I used to dance like this with . . ." Oskar's thumb rubbed my hand gently, his expression losing focus for a moment.

I remained silent, waiting patiently for him to keep talking. Or decide not to. It didn't feel right to pry.

Seeming to come to a decision, he gave me a sad smile. "I'd like to tell you about my life before . . ." He glanced at all the people around us, wary of saying something that could sound crazy.

"Before you came here." I gave him a knowing look, and he nodded.

"Yes, before that. I was married and I had a son."

My feet kept moving automatically, but any semblance of dancing vanished as I stared at Oskar in shock. It shouldn't have been such a surprise—I mean, they'd all had lives before becoming Dreamwalkers and he'd mentioned that he had a family. I guess the specifics of a *wife* and a *son* just made it that much more real to me.

"Her name was Gertrud." Oskar smiled, his mind clearly in the past. "We met in school quite young, married as soon as we could. Heinrich was born within a year. She loved to dance. I used to dance with her just like this."

"Oh." I loosened my hold, reflexively shifting away from him. "I'm sorry."

"No." He shook his head and held me in place. "It's OK. When I thought of her just now, it wasn't . . . I didn't feel guilt for dancing with you. I remembered her fondly. You . . ." He sighed. "I don't know if I'm saying this right. I didn't exactly plan this talk. But you make me remember all the good things about my life before. Like dancing."

I smiled, at a complete loss for words.

"I'm telling you this because I want you to know me, and my family was a big part of who I am."

"They still are," I blurted out. I had no idea if that was the right thing to say, but I didn't want him to feel as if he had to forget them. Certainly not because of me.

"They are. In my heart and my soul. They will always be a part of me. But it was such a long time ago, Reverie. This is the reason it took me longer to . . . embrace the physical intimacy between us."

"I completely understand. And if that's not what you want anymore—"

"It is. I just want you to understand where it was coming from. But the guilt . . . it's complicated. It really has nothing to do with you and how badly I want to be with you. I think it's tied to why I chose to stay in the dream realm."

He took a deep breath before saying the next thing. "I killed them."

"What?" We stopped moving amid the other dancers and just stood there, our arms around each other.

"It's my fault they died. We had planned a trip to Dresden to visit Gertrud's family. The day of departure had been set for weeks, but I insisted we delay so I could finish some work—I don't even remember what was so important about it anymore. We left the following day. There was a track failure; the train derailed. The details aren't important. I lived and they didn't. I fell apart pretty thoroughly after that. About six months later, I took my own life, and here we are."

Jesus. That was some heavy shit.

"Oskar, I am so sorry for your loss. I can't imagine what that was like."

"But you can," he said. "You've lost people too. Maybe not in the same way, but you've lost all those dear to you. I can see that pain in you. That same pain I've carried across time and realms. But you still find strength in yourself to keep going, and you still find joy in life. You smile, you laugh. You have a smart wit and a smarter mouth."

That made me chuckle, and he caressed my cheek.

"See? Just like that. You've made me understand things, learn things, that I've spent decades trying to grasp. I want to enjoy these moments of joy with you. So will you dance with me some more, *schatzi*? I've missed it."

"I'll dance with you anytime you want." I laid my cheek on his shoulder, and we started to sway again.

It felt so good to be in his arms, to have him trust me enough, like me enough, to want to tell me that. I caught

Sinan and Hollis watching us—no longer chatting, just watching—and my heart filled with gratitude for these men. They'd come into my life and completely flipped it over in a matter of weeks, and . . . *fuck*. I was falling for them.

Really, Reverie? You're catching serious feelings for not one but three dudes who don't even technically exist on this plane?

Before I could spiral down that particular clusterfuck of emotions, something caught my eye. Through the crowd of dancers, over by the picnic tables, I could've sworn I'd seen—

Oskar pulled me into a twirl and cut off my view. I stood taller as I let him lead, spinning my head to look in the same direction.

It took me a few moments and another spin, but then through a gap in the crowd, I spotted the Maron. It stood a full two feet taller than any average person here, but clearly no one could see it. They'd all be running for their lives if they could.

There was nothing human about it, other than the general shape of the body—arms, legs, head attached to a torso. Huge animal-like eyes bulged from its head. It had no hair, no clothes to speak of. It seemed to be made of blackness, and its fingers were long and sharp.

I stopped dancing and stared it down. It tilted its head, and if I could have made out its mouth among all the darkness it consisted of, I knew I'd see it smiling at me.

"Shit," Oskar cursed under his breath. Clearly he'd spotted it too. Icy dread seeped through my veins as I watched the monster tower over the crowd of innocent fairgoers.

It tipped its head to look at a man sitting with friends at a nearby picnic table. Lifting one disturbingly clawed hand, it moved it over the man's head, as though gently patting a cat.

Immediately, the man slumped forward, out cold.

CHAPTER TWENTY-TWO

"N o." The single, horrified word tumbled past my lips on a strained exhale.

The Maron walked slowly to another table occupied by a group of women. They were laughing and drinking—having a girls' night out, by the looks of it. All around us people were laughing, dancing, having fun, oblivious to the danger in their midst.

"We need to go after it," Sinan growled.

"We need to get out of sight first." Hollis stepped in close. When had they joined us? I was so focused on the Maron I hardly noticed anything else.

"How the hell did it do that?" I asked. "You said neither you nor it had the ability to just knock someone out like that."

"Its power has grown, mutated over the years." Oskar sounded as sickened as I felt.

The Maron raised its ugly hand again and caressed a young woman in a sundress.

"No!" I yelled it this time, drawing the attention of several people around us.

The woman raised her cup to her mouth just as the grotesque fingers ran over her head. The cup tumbled from her hand, liquid spilling all over the table as she slumped forward.

"Stop!" I yelled. "No! Stop it!" People were staring, moving away. I couldn't have cared less.

The Maron didn't even move to another table. It simply lifted its hand over the next woman.

"Stop it!" My screams became hysterical, and I shot forward. I had absolutely no plan for when I reached it, but I acted on instinct.

Strong arms wrapped around my middle, stopping me before I really even got moving.

"Reverie, no." Oskar's voice was low but urgent as Sinan held me back. I fought against him.

"Stop! Stop it! What do you want?" I screamed at the Maron, twisting in Sinan's grip.

"Rev, dollface, we need to—"

"I want you."

We all froze, staring at the monster as everyone else stared at us. Its voice sounded as though it were both right next to me and calling from far, far away. It was calm and human, deep and monstrous all at the same time. Nothing on the Maron's face moved, but I knew it was speaking to me.

"I want to talk. Let me in. Or I will keep taking them until no one is left standing." It brought its hand down on the woman in its cursed caress, but Hollis stepped in front of me before she fell, blocking my view.

"We have to get you out of here," he gritted out.

"We can't help these people until we get out of sight." Sinan's breath tickled my ear.

"Reverie." Oskar's firm voice snapped my mind into focus, and I looked at him. "We need to move. Now."

Their words finally registered, and logic cut through the overwhelming panic and dread. I nodded, and Sinan released me. We headed back to the path through the woods, rushing past people who openly stared and stepped out of the way of the crazy lady and her three intense companions.

We picked up our pace as soon as we reached the dark path, and once we rounded a bend and ensured we were out of sight, Sinan and Hollis disappeared. Oskar dropped his solid form but stayed by my side.

"What are you doing?" I asked, stumbling over a rock. "Go with them. Make it stop hurting people."

"I will," he reassured me. "I just want to make sure you're OK."

I was so *not* OK. "I'm fine, Oskar. Go."

He stared at me for a moment, then nodded and winked out of existence.

I stood alone on the path. Silence enveloped me, but everything inside felt as if it was screaming and thrashing.

The hoot of an owl made me jump. My eyes were adjusting to the dark; even on a cloudless night, the moon and the stars would've struggled to shine through the dense trees. I should've gone the long way and taken the streets. I still would've felt cold and alone, but at least I'd have had street lights.

I contemplated retracing my steps and doing just that,

but the path was just as dark behind me as in front. I hesitated, wondering if I should return to the festival. After all, the Maron wanted me.

Hollis appeared at my side, startling me more than any of them had in weeks. "Don't even think about it, doll. We got this."

"How did you . . . never mind." I huffed. "What are you doing here? What's happening?"

"Just checking on you." He winked, then disappeared.

I tried to tell myself Hollis wouldn't be so calm if they were having trouble with the Maron, if something had gone catastrophically wrong, but I couldn't quite convince myself. I made myself start walking anyway.

I would just be a distraction if I went back, a spectacle for all the people to gawk at. The guys could handle this. I could trust them.

Tears still pricked at the backs of my eyes though. That thing was attacking innocent people because it couldn't get to me, and I'd just walked away. I was worse than useless.

When I stumbled on uneven ground again and barely caught myself on a tree branch, I cursed bloody murder. It felt good to let my churning feelings out in some way, but the tears still threatened to spill, and my throat remained tight. I remembered my cell phone and used it as a flashlight to light my path.

Sinan appeared just ahead, making me jump again.

"What's wrong?" I demanded, rushing forward.

"Nothing. Get home. Now." He disappeared before I could reach him.

I focused on putting one foot in front of the other.

The weak flashlight on the phone provided just enough

light to see a few feet in front of me. Just enough to see the pitch-black legs and clawed feet of the Maron as it appeared.

I gasped and stumbled back, falling onto my ass and dropping the phone. It landed flashlight up, so I still had enough visibility to see Sinan and then Oskar appear within moments of each other. They lunged for the Maron, and it disappeared. They vanished just as quickly.

The owl hooted again.

My heart was beating so hard it felt as if it might burst out of my ribcage.

I scrambled to my feet, grabbed my phone, and jogged down the path as fast as I dared.

The Maron appeared in the trees to my right. Then Sinan did too, a split second later, already launching through the air to tackle it. Once again, they vanished.

It appeared in the trees to my left next, Hollis on its heels. Then it was in front of me. Then I could've sworn I heard something breathing down my back.

It kept flashing in and out of my space, the guys chasing it unrelentingly, as I ran through the woods. I knew, logically, it couldn't do anything to me. It existed in the dream realm, and I was firmly planted in reality. It couldn't reach me. It couldn't get past the guys.

But being chased by it felt like falling into one of my own nightmares.

I emerged on the other side of the path and broke into a run on the solid surface of the road. Home felt like some kind of sanctuary—as if the Maron couldn't appear in my bedroom just as easily as it had in the woods.

It only appeared one more time, about a block from my house. The streetlight above illuminated its grotesque body even as the pitch blackness of it seemed to absorb the light itself. Oskar and Hollis appeared at once, coming at it from two sides, and they all disappeared immediately.

I wasn't sure when the tears started falling, but they poured down my cheeks as I released a pathetic sound—something between a sob and a growl of frustration. At my front gate, I only slowed down long enough to burst through it. Then I sprinted up the garden path to my front door, took the steps two at a time, and fumbled with my keys.

It must have looked like a scene from a bad slasher film: my hands trembled as I struggled to get the right key into the lock; tears tracked down my face as I kept looking over my shoulder. When I finally got the door open, I launched myself through it and slammed it shut behind me, locking it as fast as my fingers would allow.

I pressed my forehead to the cool glass and gave in to everything I felt. I sobbed, my shoulders shaking as my knees wobbled. That panicked, adrenaline-fueled part of me demanded I arm myself with the bat by the front door and turn on every single light in the dark house.

But a much bigger part of me was starting to take over, and that part didn't give a shit. I was tired—exhausted on a bone-deep level. I had no idea what was happening at the festival—how many people it had managed to attack, how many families would be suffering and scared for their loved ones tomorrow. All I knew was that it was my fault, and I had no idea how to fix it.

So let the asshole come for me. If it could hurt me, it would've done it already. It had had almost my entire life to do so. And if for some reason it suddenly could cause me harm, maybe it should. Maybe then all this would stop. No one wanted me on this planet anyway.

I stayed at the front door until my heart stopped throwing itself against my ribcage, my tears dried up, and a detached kind of calm seeped into my bones. When the grandfather clock started ringing, it didn't startle me, but it did get me moving. It continued to toll the midnight hour as I walked through the dark house. I didn't turn on any of the lights; the window in the bathroom let in enough moonlight for me to see the tap.

I plugged the drain in the tub, turned the water on, stripped down to nothing, and got in.

The water slowly rose around my ankles and ass, up my calves, thighs, and midsection. When it reached just under my boobs and knees, I turned it off. The last few drops from the tap dripped into the clear, warm water, the sound deafening in the sudden silence.

Keeping my knees up and my front flush with my legs, I wrapped my arms around my thighs.

I had no idea why I'd come into the bathroom or run a bath. But it felt kind of nice to sit in the comforting warmth, the silence and the dark. The lack of sensory stimuli seemed to soothe all the jagged, ugly things that had been shaken up inside me, slicing and tearing as they flew about in there.

At some point, tears started to trickle down my cheeks again. I rested my chin on my knees and let them flow into the bathwater.

CHAPTER TWENTY-THREE

The water was still warm when Hollis appeared in the bathroom. I was having a pretty epic stare-off with the tiles, or the middle distance in front of the tiles, but his presence made me lift my head and look at him.

Something in me craved him so much, some invisible tether pulling from the middle of my chest, threatening to unravel if I resisted too hard. He went solid without me even touching him. I didn't think he even noticed. Whatever he saw in my face had put a worried look in his eyes.

"I'm fine." My low, croaky voice still seemed too loud in the confined, dark space.

"You don't look fine, doll." He crouched down, resting his arms on the edge of the tub. "Let's get out of the bath, OK?"

I shook my head. It was a gut reaction, but fucked if I knew what was behind it. I just did not want to move. "I'll stay here."

"You can't stay here all night. The water will go cold."

He dipped his fingers into it and swirled them around, causing ripples to caress my skin.

"Um . . . yeah . . ." I didn't even know what I was thinking or feeling anymore.

"Jesus," Hollis muttered as he got to his feet, somehow looking even more worried. He brushed both hands through his curly hair. For a moment, he stared down at me as if unsure what to do. Then, apparently, he decided the best move would be to get in with me.

He didn't even take off his nice shoes or any of his clothes. He just stepped into the bath and sat down, sending water spilling over the edge.

"What are you doing?" I demanded, sitting up straighter.

"If you're staying here, then I'm staying here."

I blinked at him. "In your clothes?"

He just shrugged and held my gaze. His tweed suit was sopping wet, the bottom half of his white shirt stuck to his washboard abs, and his tie looked like a dipstick. The sight actually drew a smile to my lips before I knew what was happening. A small chuckle followed the smile, and Hollis flashed me the most brilliant grin.

But as fast as the mirth struck, it faded just as quickly. Now that my numb trance had lifted, all the other emotions came flooding in.

My lip trembled as my eyes filled with tears, and Hollis's grin fell.

"Oh, Reverie." He sounded pained, and that made me even more emotional. My shoulders shook, and I started to cry in earnest.

Hollis scooted forward, sloshing even more water over

the rim. Gripping my legs, he lifted one, then the other, and placed them next to his hips. I leaned forward to rest my head on his chest. I didn't even care if I cried all over him. He was wet anyway. I let it all out while he rubbed my back, my hair, my arms. He just let me cry and cry until it started to settle on its own.

It felt cathartic in a way I'd rarely experienced. There was just something about having someone else take care of your emotional needs, someone who welcomed with open arms all the bullshit you needed to purge, and was willing to hold you at the same time. It made it easier to really let go.

"Do you want to talk about it?" he asked gently once I stopped sobbing.

I lifted my head, then splashed my face with the bathwater before sitting up a bit.

"I don't know." I sighed, and he waited patiently. "I was just . . . fuck, Hollis, I was so scared running through those woods. But then I got into the house, and I realized I kind of wished the damn Maron would just get me. Eat me alive or whatever. All those people—not just tonight, but all of them, everyone it targeted over the years—it's all because of me."

The look in his eyes could have easily been mistaken for pity. But it wasn't. It was understanding.

"I know what it's like to blame yourself," he said. "But you are not responsible for what that monster is doing. You are not a monster."

I knew he really did know what it felt like to blame yourself for something—they all did. That was why they were here, after all. But the way he'd said *you*—as if the similarity, the understanding, ended there—unsettled me. It was as if he'd told me I wasn't a monster in the same breath he told me he was.

"What happened to make you stay?" I had no business asking, but I was beyond caring about boundaries, and I didn't have the energy to argue about just how much of this shitshow I could blame myself for. "Why do you think you're a monster?"

He gave me a small smile that didn't reach his eyes, then looked down at the water between us.

"Shit, I'm sorry. You don't have to tell me." I was all over the damn place. I rested my forearms on his shoulders and caressed the back of his neck, feeling like shit all over again.

"It's OK." He sighed. "I was always going to tell you. I just . . . I've been delaying the inevitable because I've been dreading the way you might look at me after."

"Oskar and Sinan both shared their biggest regrets with me, and I don't judge them for it. I still—" I cut myself off before the *L* word could spill out of my mouth and dissolve in the tepid bathwater.

Hollis didn't seem to notice. "I know. But this is different. What they hold guilt over—I understand it, but ultimately, those things were accidents. Things that may have happened even if Oskar hadn't delayed the trip, even if Sinan decided to sail in another direction. What I did . . ." He shook his head, still not meeting my eye. "It was intentional. No acts of nature or circumstance would've made a difference. It was all me."

I didn't speak. Sometimes people needed quiet and space into which to spill their dark souls. I just rubbed the back of Hollis's neck and waited.

"I've mentioned George to you a few times now," he began telling the bathwater. "He was my best friend. I met him a few weeks after moving to Chicago. He helped me find a place to live, told me which streets to avoid if I didn't want to get mugged, took me to my first speakeasy, introduced me to people he knew—people who opened doors to opportunities I never thought I'd have. He was in the banking business too, but within two years of us meeting, he met a gal and fell in love. They got married and she got pregnant, and George wasn't so interested in the speakeasies or the boxing matches anymore. He also stopped being so aggressive in his work. We used to talk about deals and profits and plans to make more money than God, then he talked more about stability and security for his family.

"We grew apart. He was focused on his family. I was focused on making more money than my parents could even fathom. An opportunity came up. A very high-risk, not entirely above-board opportunity. I won't bore you with the details, but in a nutshell, I talked George into investing with me. There was a minimum buy-in, and I didn't have enough cash. He gave me almost all his life savings. The deal did not work out for our benefit. He lost everything. Weeks before his wife was due to give birth, they lost their home. His child was born into poverty—the very thing I'd been working so hard to crawl out of. I knew very well there was a possibility of that happening, and I talked him into it anyway."

He finally looked up at me, all the anguish, the self-disgust, palpable in his expression. "I never even spoke to him again after that. I was so ashamed, but I never had the balls to go apologize. I don't even know what happened to him. A few months later, I caught influenza and died in a hospital bed alone. I deserved worse."

"Hollis." I tried to pull him in closer, but he leaned away.

"Don't try to assuage my guilt. What I did was wrong, and there's nothing you can say that will make me forgive myself."

"I know, but—"

"How are you not disgusted? I expected you to lose any shred of respect you had for me, but you've shocked me once more, because all I see in your beautiful eyes is compassion and understanding."

I raised a brow. "Maybe you need to have some compassion for yourself too."

"Says the girl sitting in the tub in the dark, drowning in her own self-hatred," he quipped right back.

"Touché," I grumbled.

"How about we stop talking about sad things now? This night has been painful enough."

"Agreed. But I don't think I can sleep. I just know as soon as I close my eyes, I'll see the Maron." I shivered lightly, not just because the water was going cold.

"Well, can we at least get out of the bath?"

I sighed and nodded. Hollis stood up first, water sloshing off his saturated clothes. I let him pull me to my feet, then wrapped my arms around his shoulders and kissed him firmly. His wet clothing felt funny against my bare skin.

"Thank you," I whispered against his mouth. "For telling me that. I know it wasn't easy."

His fingers dug into the soft flesh at my hips as a lock of

curly hair fell over his forehead. "Thank you . . . for existing, Reverie."

His grip tightened even more as his mouth sought out mine again. The way he held on, the way his mouth devoured mine—it felt as though he needed to convince himself that I truly did exist. That this was real.

I tugged at his jacket, and without ever breaking the kiss, he peeled it completely off and let it splat into the water. When I snapped his suspender, he jumped and bit my bottom lip. Both of his hands palmed my ass, and I could feel him growing hard against my belly. I was getting wet in more than one way. I wanted to dive right into the sensations, drown in Hollis and his miraculous touch.

Done playing, I pushed the suspenders off his shoulders and impatiently tackled the buttons on his shirt. He finally pulled back a bit to pull it off over his head, and then—

"Why are you standing in the bath clothed?" Sinan sounded amused.

I turned to look at him, but Hollis just redirected his mouth to my neck. "Won't be clothed at all soon enough," he said before licking a long line from my shoulder to my ear.

Sinan—transparent and dressed all in black—was almost invisible in the dark bathroom. But as soon as I saw him, I wanted him, and he quickly became solid. He glanced down at himself, then raised a single strong eyebrow at me as if to say, "So you're doing this from a distance now? Nice."

Shadows fell over his features, and when he stepped up close to the tub, he looked menacing and alluring all at once.

"You're supposed to be taking care of her, not getting yourself off," Sinan said, watching Hollis's mouth on my neck very closely.

"I am taking care of her." I could hear the smile in Hollis's voice. He gripped my thigh and lifted my leg so my foot rested on the edge of the tub. Then, as he deliberately reached between my legs and cupped my pussy, he raised his head from my neck to look at Sinan. "If we all happen to get off in the process, that's just a bonus."

I gasped as Hollis started moving his hand—his whole palm flat against me and rubbing in small, firm movements.

"We?" Sinan raised that brow again, but his gaze stayed fixed on Hollis's hand between my legs.

I reached out and grabbed Sinan's coat. "Where's Oskar? Is he OK?"

"Everything is fine." Sinan caressed my cheek. "Oskar is just doing one more sweep of the town to make sure the Maron is gone."

"In that case"—I licked my lips and swallowed a moan as Hollis increased the pressure—"I don't want to talk about any of it. I don't want to think. I just want to feel."

"Oh, temptress . . ." Sinan dragged his thumb over my bottom lip, pulling it down until I opened my mouth to him. His hand moved to the back of my head, and he gently tugged on my hair. "We'll make you feel *everything*."

Sinan leaned in to kiss me, his tongue plundering my mouth at the same time Hollis pushed a finger inside my pussy. I moaned into Sinan's mouth as I ground myself against Hollis's hand. They were leaving me breathless.

As Sinan palmed my breast, Hollis bent down to suck the other nipple into his mouth. I squirmed between them, wanting to touch them, wanting them to touch me, wanting . . . *more*. Sinan's hand explored my curves in a long caress down my side. He palmed my ass harder than he had my breast, massaging the soft flesh, before dipping lower to join Hollis between my legs.

When his fingers slid through my arousal, feeling the areas where my pussy was stretched around Hollis's finger, Sinan pulled back to stare at me. Hollis lightly bit my nipple, and I gasped and shuddered between them before he released it and straightened. Now they were both watching me with hooded eyes and swollen lips, and I wanted *more, more, more*.

"More," I moaned, sounding like a bad porno. What they were doing to me had obliterated the filter between my brain and my mouth.

"Fuck," Hollis whispered, breathing hard.

"That's it, temptress." Sinan pushed a finger in next to Hollis's. "Moan for us. It's so fucking sexy how it echoes in here."

Like a good girl, I did as I was told, but I couldn't have stopped the sounds passing my lips if I wanted to.

Sinan stepped one foot into the tub, not giving a shit that he still had his pants and boots on. His chest pressed to my back, and his free arm wrapped around my chest so he could grip my breast. Hollis crowded me in from the front and grabbed my hip. They worked well together, pumping their fingers in at the same time, then switching things up and alternating so one slid in as the other slid out. After a few minutes, Hollis focused on my clit as Sinan pumped two, then three fingers in and out.

I wanted more, and they were giving it to me. Every part

of me ached between them, my cries and their groans bouncing off the tiles.

"Your cunt is fluttering around my fingers." Sinan sounded as if he had gravel in his throat, his warm breath at my ear making me shiver. "I think you're about to cream all over my hand."

All I could do was nod and make more incoherent sounds.

"What do you think, Hollis? Should we let her come?" His fingers stopped pumping in and out, and he adopted a much slower, gentler pace.

Wait. What? I opened my eyes and frowned at the devious smirk on Hollis's face.

"Nah. Let's see if we can make her beg for it."

Both their hands disappeared from between my legs, and I whimpered. I actually *whimpered* from the denied pleasure. I almost started begging right then and there, but my stubborn side dug her heels in. They wanted to make me *beg*? *Assholes.*

Sinan held me tighter, his erection rocking against my ass, as Hollis stepped out of the tub. He removed the rest of his soaked clothing, then reached for me.

I slapped his hand away. "Unless you're planning to give me the orgasm you so rudely interrupted, go away." Of course, Sinan still had me in his embrace and he was just as guilty, but logic wasn't exactly my thing in that moment.

Hollis's face lit up with a grin. "Oh, this is going to be fun."

Sinan chuckled behind me and nudged me forward. Hollis moved fast, and before I knew what was happening, he'd picked me up and wrapped my legs around his waist.

"Put me down!" I slapped his shoulder.

"No." He smacked my ass. Between the way the stinging pain made my pussy clench and the fact that Sinan had begun to undress, my response died in my throat.

Hollis carried me down the hall and into the bedroom while Sinan followed, shucking clothing along the way. His coat was left on the bathroom floor, his shirt abandoned in the hallway. He paused in the doorway to my bedroom to toe off his boots, and as he reached for his pants, Hollis threw me down onto the bed, cutting off my view.

I bounced on the mattress, fighting the laughter bubbling up—I was supposed to be mad at them. Swiping my hair out of my eyes, I lifted onto my elbows to find them both standing before me, completely nude. For a second, I wanted to turn on the bedside lamp so I could take in every minute detail, but I decided against it. My eyes had more than adjusted to the dark, and there was something about the faint light coming in through the windows, the way it cast their bodies in shadow. The air, the darkness, felt charged, and I didn't want to wash it away with harsh light.

"How do you want to do this?" Hollis's question was clearly directed at Sinan, even though his eyes stayed on me. I lifted my knees and spread them—an invitation and a challenge. I looked forward to seeing how they planned to do this too.

Sinan's Adam's apple bobbed. "Doesn't matter. The only rule is she doesn't get to come until she begs for it."

I narrowed my eyes at him even as a thrill of anticipation shot down my spine.

Not willing to give in just yet, I quickly sat up, scooted to the edge of the bed, and placed a hand on each of their chests. Sinan was broader, thicker, with more chest hair under my palm. Hollis was leaner, defined, his chest completely smooth. I dragged my hands down—all the way to their erect cocks. Again, there were differences. Sinan's was the perfect size and had a slight kink to the left. Hollis was shorter but thicker. They both felt warm and hard in my hands as I gripped them at the base.

There was something oddly empowering about having two dicks inches from your face, holding them both in a firm grip—having two intense gazes watching your every move. I stroked them, ran my thumbs over the heads, enjoyed the glide of my palms on soft skin. I'd heard the expression many times, but it really did feel like silk-covered steel.

God, I wanted those things inside me. The very thought made me squirm and rub my thighs together. Squeezing Sinan at the base, I leaned to the side and took Hollis into my mouth.

He groaned and threw his head back, and once again I felt empowered.

They wanted to play with denying me release? Well, I'd show them they weren't the only ones with power in this scenario.

As if he'd read my thoughts, Sinan grabbed my wrist, removed my hand from his erection, and walked around the bed to where I couldn't see him. I wanted to turn around and look, but I wanted to keep sucking Hollis into my mouth even more. He made the most addictive sounds, and his hands were tentatively threading through my hair.

The bed dipped behind me, and Sinan's hands gripped my hips. He maneuvered me so I was kneeling on the bed, my lips still wrapped around Hollis. I couldn't stop myself from moaning, the sound muffled by the dick in my mouth, as Sinan rubbed the tip of his cock up and down my slick pussy to spread the wetness.

I was so ready—I'd been ready since before they started fingering me in the bath—and there was no resistance as he pushed at my entrance. He slid right in, and I took Hollis as deep as I could at the same time.

Sinan started thrusting, and I let him set the pace, matching it with my mouth. Hollis's breath came in pants, his hands fisting my hair, his cock twitching. He was close to spilling down my throat, and I wanted to make him come *hard*. If they both finished, then I could find my own release with or without them. I was already on the edge anyway.

But then Hollis stepped back, releasing my hair and pulling out of my mouth. My lips felt tingly and swollen, and my heavy tits swung with every pump of Sinan's hips as I looked up at Hollis, confused.

"Sweet Jesus." His gaze bounced around, taking everything in. Then he turned toward the wall and took several deep breaths. Sinan slowed considerably.

"You OK, baby?" I asked, my voice breathy, aching.

"Mm-hmm." Hollis nodded. "Just need a minute so I don't come in your mouth."

"But I want you to come in my mouth," I whined, putting the pout on a little.

With one last deep breath, Hollis turned to face us again. "But *I* want to come buried deep in your cunt."

Sinan pulled out, which made me rock back, my body pleading for that fullness to return.

"Come do her from behind," he said, his hands kneading my ass. "Her ass jiggles with every movement, and it's mesmerizing." He gave it a smack, and I had no doubt it jiggled for him just the way he liked. The warm sting went straight to my clit, and I wanted him back inside me so badly I nearly gave in and begged.

Instead, I clamped my teeth together and watched Hollis.

He grinned, and I knew he knew I was on the edge of begging for it.

"Nah." He dropped onto the bed next to me. "I want her to ride me."

Oh god, yes please. I tried not to let my face show how much I wanted that as I crawled over the top of him. Sinan surprised me by following, remaining close to my back and straddling Hollis behind me.

Hollis tucked one arm under his head and held his cock up at the base, ready for me to sink down on. I didn't waste any time, positioning my hips and impaling myself on his hardness. We both moaned. That fullness was back, and I wanted *more*.

But, of course, they weren't going to give it to me. Sinan wrapped his arms around me and lifted me until I was upright, my full weight on Hollis. I spread my knees as wide as they'd go and took him in deep.

"Does that feel good, temptress?" Sinan hissed in my ear. He rocked his hips, rubbing his erection, still covered in my wetness, against my lower back. "You like feeling Hollis deep inside you?"

"Yes." I started rocking too, rolling my hips. I couldn't bounce up and down the way I wanted to—Sinan wouldn't let me—but everything felt fucking amazing anyway.

Hollis reached out with his free hand to play with my tits, his mouth hanging open, his hips starting to move with me. I could feel my release right *there*, just on the other side of a membrane-thin barrier. The feeling of being stretched, so deep, and the firm grind against my pussy . . . I panted, moaned, and threw my head back against Sinan's shoulder.

"You want to come?" he asked, and I knew it was a trick, but I said *yes* anyway. *Please* nearly tumbled out after it, but I just managed to keep it in. I was so close I didn't think they could do much to stop it.

Naturally, they found a way. Sinan pushed me forward, making sure I caught myself on my hands on either side of Hollis's head before he let go. Hollis gripped my hips tightly to keep me from moving. They worked so well together I wondered if they were using their Sandman juju to communicate secretly. Two pairs of hands lifted my hips so only half of Hollis's length remained inside, and their fingers dug into my skin and held me in place, keeping my orgasm back once more.

"What the fuck?" I huffed, smacking the pillow.

They both laughed, and the low masculine sound just made me want them even more.

"Hold still for Hollis, and then, if you ask nicely, you can come too," Sinan said. I wanted to jump out of the bed and end this right there and then, let them finish each other off, see how they liked it. But come on—I was sandwiched between two insanely hot men who were giving me sexual experiences I'd only fantasized about. No way in hell was I going anywhere.

Hollis left one hand on my hip and threaded the other into my hair as he started to thrust up into me. His hips pumped up and down at a fast pace. I knew if I just rubbed my clit, I'd be creaming all over his cock within a few swipes of my fingers. Instead, I dug my nails into the sheets and let him fuck me.

Sinan remained at my back, his cock resting at my ass. I couldn't stop myself from shifting back slightly. My body wanted more. I wanted more. I wanted both of them inside me, but it was something I'd never done, and in that moment, I didn't have the words to ask for it.

"You want us both, don't you?" Hollis said, his voice strained. "You want us filling you all up."

"Yes," I hissed, again on the verge of giving in and pleading.

Sinan's finger, already slick with my arousal, pressed against my ass. "Here?" He put more pressure on my hole. "You want me to fuck you here?"

"Yes!" I moaned and finally gave in. "*Please*, god, yes!"

Sinan pushed the finger in slowly as Hollis groaned and came, his neck muscles tense and his chest glistening with sweat. The finger in my ass, the thick cock inside me—I was closer to orgasm than I'd been all night.

They both stilled, and I collapsed on top of Hollis, close to tears from frustration.

"Fuck, just the thought of that . . ." Hollis lightly brushed my hair back.

"Next time." Sinan pumped his finger in and out a few more times, then removed it. "Our girl begged, so let's give her what she needs."

I could've cried again at his words, this time from relief.

They gently got me back to all fours, and Hollis slipped out of me only for Sinan to sink right in from behind. Hollis leaned up and kissed me deeply while Sinan started to move. His hips smacked against my ass as he fucked me deep, barely pulling out before thrusting back in again.

I moaned against Hollis's tongue, and he dropped back against the mattress. With a devilish grin, he shuffled down the bed between our legs until his face was right under all the action. I didn't think anything could surprise me anymore after the last few weeks I'd had, but I gasped when a hot mouth covered my clit from below.

I came immediately. The pleasure tore through me like an electric shock as I called out. Hollis didn't let up. He kept licking and sucking, and he didn't even seem to care that his mouth was practically on Sinan's cock. Sinan's glorious cock that kept pounding into me faster and harder.

I came again, my whole body tingling and floating and sinking all at once. It went on and on as the men in my bed pushed my body to its limits. It only stopped after Sinan slammed into me hard and came too, his seed mixing with Hollis's.

We fell to the side so we wouldn't suffocate Hollis, and he crawled back up to lie down facing me. We were a mess: a dirty, sticky, filthy, satisfied mess. But my mind was blissfully empty, and my eyes drooped.

I felt sated and safe between them, and when I heard Oskar's voice in the room as I drifted off to sleep, I didn't even worry about how much of that he'd seen.

CHAPTER TWENTY-FOUR

I chose the woods as the setting of this particular lucid dream simply because I could easily bring it to mind. It had been the setting of a dream the night before, which had started as a nice stroll through nature and morphed into a nightmare that threw me right back to the night of the festival.

Now, considering the whole point of this lucid dream, I second-guessed my choice. I was alone, having banished the guys from my dreamscape. That made me uneasy too, but we had a plan and I had to trust them. I had to trust myself.

I walked over to a fallen log and sat down, taking in the trees and the birds, the breeze in my hair, the perfect weather.

All I had to do now was wait.

It had been about a week since that night, and the Maron had attempted to contact me several times every night and day since. Whenever it failed, it went after someone else. The guys always managed to stop it—from getting to me or anyone else in the town—but it was relentless.

They were tired and frustrated. I was over it and done letting them fight this battle for me.

It clearly wanted me, and only I could get it to stop.

When I'd raised the idea of letting the Maron come to me—in a controlled, lucid space—they had surprised me by not shutting it down.

Hollis gave me a knowing smile and a squeeze of the hand, while Oskar explained that as much as they wanted to keep me safe, I was strong and powerful, and they needed my help to end this once and for all. We needed to work as a team. They'd just been waiting for me to say I was ready for it. Sinan ground his teeth, but instead of arguing, he just launched into discussing the safest way to do what I suggested.

They wanted to be in the lucid dream with me, but I knew I wouldn't get much out of the Maron if they were there.

I'd surprised myself when I went into a lucid dream and managed to shut them all out completely. I'd woken up to find Sinan almost frantic and Hollis and Oskar looking more worried than I'd ever seen them. I felt bad for worrying them, but the practice runs we'd been doing had made me more confident in my abilities. I felt strong enough to handle the situation.

Fingers crossed that it didn't blow up in my face.

A cool gust of wind made me shiver; I looked in the direction it had come from as I slowly got to my feet. This was my dreamscape, and I was fully lucid. That cool gust didn't belong in my perfectly temperate dream forest.

It was here.

But where? I searched the trees, even high up in the branches, but I couldn't see it.

"You're alone. For once." That creepy voice confirmed the Maron had joined me. Once again, it sounded both far away, as if calling from deep in the woods, and close to my ear.

I spun around, looking for it again. *Keep your shit together, Reverie. This is your dreamscape. It can't hurt you. You run this show.*

"For once?" I scoffed, refusing to raise my voice. "I've been alone most of my life because of you."

"Because of me?" Its laugh sounded like a growl, completely devoid of humor. It appeared then, to my left, about twenty feet away and half-hidden behind a tree. When it spoke, its grotesque mouth didn't move. "Any suffering you've experienced has been of your own making."

It disappeared, and I had to resist the urge to spin around and frantically scan the trees.

Somewhere, deep in the back of my mind, I felt a nudge. *Oskar.*

The guys had agreed to let me speak with the Maron alone, but they would stay close by, just beyond the proverbial doors to my dreamscape. Unfortunately that meant they had no way of knowing what was happening in here, so they planned to "knock" on those doors every so often. I'd let them in when I thought the Maron might be sufficiently distracted to be taken by surprise.

No point letting them in when I couldn't even keep it in sight for longer than a few moments. But at least the knowledge that I could open the doors whenever I chose kept me from losing my shit completely in the face of a literal nightmare monster.

I gritted my teeth and squared my shoulders. No, that was wrong. The guys waiting in the wings weren't the only thing keeping me from losing my shit. I was selling myself short. *I* had the abilities, *I'd* worked on strengthening them, and *I* had a lifetime of grief, sorrow, and anger to fuel my determination.

"So, it wasn't you who kept knocking people I know into comas then?" I let my oldest friend—sarcasm—lend me some strength too. "I am shocked and surprised."

"Oh, it was me." It appeared right in front of me, its depthless eyes mere inches from my face. And it disappeared before the gasp escaped my lips.

"You're not making any fucking sense." I kept my voice even.

"Aren't I?"

I felt rather than saw it this time. It was behind me. Not as close as it had just been, but close enough to reach out and—

I turned slowly, deliberately. It tilted its head and flashed away, reappearing on a tree branch off to the right.

The steady ticktock of a clock drifted on the cool breeze; it reminded me of a bomb timer.

"You've been trying to get to me for weeks." I held my arms out at my sides. "Well, here I am, ready to talk, and you're just going to play games?"

Another nudge at that door deep in my mind—Sinan this time. *Not yet.*

"Games . . ." The voice sounded as it always did—close

and far at once—but I could've sworn I heard a hint of hesi-
tancy in it.

Something seemed to ripple over the Maron's face, like
a combination of static and heat haze, and for a split
second, I saw a face—a real human face. Just as fast, it disappeared. And then so did the Maron.

"Let's play a game then," the voice, near and far,
taunted.

I sighed, more irritated than scared now.

A low melody began to drift on the breeze as the Maron
appeared on my left, a horrid claw reaching for me. It disappeared before I could react, then flashed up on my right,
crouched low to the ground.

It leapt right for me. I lifted my arms over my head and
braced myself, but the impact never came. It disappeared
once more, and I spotted it in the distance among the
trees.

The music was a lullaby, slowed down and low. It
sounded creepy, especially mingling with the incessant
ticking.

"Enough." I stood to my full height, sick of its crap. I
hadn't come here to play, and I ran this show, dammit, so
this sick game of hide-and-seek ended now.

I ignored the third tap on that door—Hollis this time—
and concentrated on changing the setting. I needed to take
all these trees away so the Maron didn't have anywhere to
hide. The first sprawling, clear space that came to mind was
a cemetery.

Really, Reverie? Like this isn't creepy enough already?

But the cemetery wasn't creepy, exactly. Well-manicured
grass stretched out in rolling hills under clear blue sky, and

carefully placed trees dotted the space here and there. Nowhere to hide.

The incessant ticking and the demented lullaby had stopped.

The Maron perched on a large slab of a headstone nearby. We stared each other down, neither one of us saying anything. It wanted to talk, so it could talk.

"Funny that you would choose this place." The voice was still eerie, but it sounded . . . *less* somehow.

"Why is that funny?"

"This is the very place we had our last conversation. Don't you remember?" It tilted its ugly head down and to the side, its focus on the spot right next to where I stood.

Slowly, I lowered my gaze to the headstone next to me, to the simple and familiar inscription: *Here lies Maria Cabral, Beloved wife, mother, and grandmother*, followed by the dates of my grandma's birth and death.

It didn't hit me all at once, the truth of the situation. It came slowly, but the impact still felt like a punch in the guts.

I remembered sitting in the grass in this very spot when the earth beneath the headstone was freshly turned. Mom stood on the other side, crying hard, Dad's arm around her shoulders. It had been a week or two since Grandma died. I couldn't remember exactly what I said that day, but my mom's stern response stuck with me for years, the way only a traumatizing moment in a child's life could.

"Reverie, you are far too old to still have an imaginary friend. Enough is enough." She returned her attention to my dad immediately. I waited a beat for him to defend me, to take the edge off her harsh words, but he was too wrapped up in supporting Mom, in his own grief, too focused on the fresh soil and the tears soaking it.

I was nine years old. Years later when I found myself standing at the grave next to Grandma's—the inscription on the new headstone honoring my dad—my imaginary friend, Christopher, said something. Something consoling and supportive. But now I couldn't remember what. At the time, I didn't respond.

I never responded again. Eventually, I stopped hearing him or seeing him.

I started high school. Weird shit kept happening all around me. I forgot I'd even had an imaginary friend as a child.

But before all that, before that day at the cemetery, I always had Christopher by my side.

He was in my earliest memory. I was bundled up in winter clothes and taking my first solo ride down the slide at the park. Mom's beaming face and spread arms waited for me at the bottom, and Chris stood right next to her, cheering me on.

My parents played along, like all parents do, setting a plate for him at dinner, asking him questions. Then they started to discourage the whole thing as I got older. I guess on that day, by my grandma's grave, Mom just didn't have the patience for the gentle approach.

My mind reeled as I lifted my gaze to the . . . *thing* now standing before me. Its face did that staticky flickering again, this time exposing its shoulders and part of its arm too. Chris stared back at me for a brief moment.

"How . . . ," I breathed. I couldn't figure this out. The

pieces just didn't fit in my head. No, the pieces fit perfectly; they just didn't look the way they should.

"After this, we should play hide-and-seek." The Maron's monstrous black face stayed firmly in place as it spoke, but its voice had lost that faraway quality. Only the close whisper part remained. "That's the last thing you ever said to me. Do you even remember?"

Slowly, I shook my head. "I remember that day, but I don't remember the details. Just how upset with me my mom was."

"What about how upset I was?" This time the whisper had vanished, and its words were pure shouting—near and far, all around me. "It was you and me from the start. I was there for you for everything. And then one day you just decide to stop acknowledging my presence? *How dare you*? You only cared about the people in the waking world, and you forgot about me."

It began to almost vibrate, its mouth—so many teeth—opening and snapping closed, its clawed hands tensing. I battled to keep my breathing steady, to stay calm, but I was losing that battle.

"You had no fucking clue what it was like to be completely alone! To have no one!" It seemed to grow taller, leaning over me with its snarling mouth. "And if you were going to pretend I didn't exist, then I was going to make you see what it felt like."

Not gonna lie—I was scared. If this hadn't been a lucid dream, I'd have already been running, weaving through the headstones as my heart tried to leap out of my chest and that thing snapped at my heels.

I took a step back, unable to fight the instinct.

Like any predatory animal, it lunged for me—the prey. My heart lodged in my throat, and every muscle in my body tensed, but the Maron vanished inches from my face.

I spun around, frantically searching for it. The brilliant blue sky had turned gray with storm clouds. Was it me doing that or him?

It reappeared, perched on my grandmother's headstone. That flickering static thing happened again—this time over its whole body. The messy brown hair and unassuming brown eyes; the painfully familiar outfit of a blue-and-green-striped T-shirt, jeans, and Converse; the big raised scar on his right arm, above the elbow.

"Christopher," I said, half in wonder and half in horror.

"Ah, so you do remember." It held very still, focus intent on me.

"What do you want?" I forced the words out even though I dreaded the answer. This was why I'd come here in the first place—to try to get some answers, some clue as to what we could use against it.

"I want you to suffer." It was Chris's voice, even though it was the Maron staring at me. "You made me suffer when you pretended I didn't exist while you went about your precious little life. You had everything I could never have again. Family, friends, a community, a life. And you could've shared that with me—you were the only one who saw me. You had everything, and I had only you. But you turned away from me. So I took them away from you."

Anger surged up right along with the tears stinging the backs of my eyes. "Nice monologue," I gritted out, "but what the fuck do you want *now*?"

"I want what you've given *them*!" it roared, Chris's voice and the Maron's mingling all around me.

Another nudge came at the back of my mind, and this time I flung the doors wide open, letting the guys into my dreamscape. I was holding on by a thread. I couldn't handle this alone any longer.

"What I've given who? You took everyone from me." A traitorous tear slid down my cheek.

"And yet you still found someone to let into your life who wasn't me. *Three* someones. You spoke to them and let them in and *fucked* them. You even made them real while I became . . ." Its hands flexed, the claws stretching out menacingly. Then it stood up tall. "I want what everyone wants. A life. A real one. And if I don't get it—"

Whatever threat it was about to throw at my feet was interrupted by Sinan's appearance. He leapt through the air, wrapped his arms around the thing made of nightmares, and brought it crashing to the ground.

The Maron's claws caught Sinan in the chest as it rolled onto all fours. But Hollis and Oskar were already there, and they tackled it once again.

Sinan straightened, stumbled, pulled out his knife. The Maron thrashed and flailed like a rabid animal, sharp teeth and claws slashing through the air. Slashing through the men I loved.

They tussled and grunted and threw fists and claws while I stood there stunned, screaming on the inside.

Then I was screaming on the outside.

"No! Stop! Stop it!" I shot forward to . . . I didn't even know. Do *something*. It was hurting them. There was only one Maron and three of them and it was *hurting them*.

"Reverie. No." Hollis shoved me back before kicking the Maron. "You have to focus. Don't lose control of the dreamscape."

I stumbled back.

The Maron took advantage of Hollis's distraction and got to its feet, slashing Oskar's face in the process. Blood flew through the air and splattered across a headstone. The creature roared, its jaw opening so wide it seemed to grow bigger and bigger, ready to swallow us all into its black depths.

Oskar wavered, his hands coated in his blood, his face mangled. He was breathing hard. They all were. Not a bit of Sinan's shredded shirt still looked white. Blood soaked the fabric and ran down his arms, making his grip on the knife slippery.

The Maron lunged, sinking its teeth into Hollis's neck and shoulder.

Don't lose control of the dreamscape.

His words finally registered, and something inside me clicked.

I was in control. This was *my* dreamscape.

Not the Maron's.

Not Sinan's or Oskar's or Hollis's.

Mine.

And I was done losing people.

Everything slowed to a crawl, and a deep calm washed through me.

I took a breath. And another.

Then, as fast as it had all stopped, everything started again. Growls and grunts filled the air, but I'd made my decision.

I didn't just open those doors in the back of my mind; I pulverized them and the proverbial walls they were attached to, and I ejected the three men from my dreamscape.

The Maron turned to face me. It was just it and me again.

I could tell—even though its eyes stayed dark and its mouth didn't move—that it wanted to say something. But I didn't want to hear it. With little more than a thought, I expelled it too. And I ended the lucid dream.

CHAPTER TWENTY-FIVE

I slowly opened my eyes. Oskar and Hollis were leaning over me, in their ghostly forms, while Sinan paced my small bedroom behind them.

"Oh, thank god." Hollis sagged.

I sat up to take them all in, letting my brain register the absence of injuries. No blood, no bruises. Even their clothing appeared perfect, as always.

"Finally." Sinan propped his hands on his hips but didn't come any closer.

"How long was I out after you left?"

"You mean after you *kicked* us out?" Hollis stood up, crossing his arms. Oh shit. I knew he had to be pissed if he was siding with Sinan.

"One minute, twenty-eight seconds. We were worried." Oskar had a deep frown on his face.

I wondered why they were still translucent. Recently, they'd been turning solid as soon as they came near me. It didn't even take a conscious effort for me anymore. Yet here I sat on my bed, and all three of them were pulling a Casper.

Maybe the lucid dream and the ordeal with the Maron had exhausted me. It wouldn't be the first time I'd pushed my abilities and then needed time to recover. But while I did feel kind of drained, that explanation didn't seem right either.

"What the hell was that?" Sinan snapped at me, making me focus. "We had it. For the first damn time we were able to get our hands on it, and you, *you*"—he pointed an accusing finger at me—"just decided to toss us out? What the fuck, Reverie?"

That's when I realized I'd been subconsciously holding my power back from turning them solid. First off, I didn't know what making them corporeal might do to them after how badly the Maron had hurt them. But maybe, even more than that, I just wanted to avoid this argument. They were easier to dismiss when I could wave my arms right through them.

"You're all OK? You're not hurt?" My eyes flew between them.

"We're fine," Sinan barked. "We'd be even better if we'd gotten the damn job done."

I ignored Sinan and let my power make them all solid. Because no matter how much I wanted to dodge this confrontation, I needed to feel them, hold them.

Tears started to track down my cheeks as I scrambled forward and wrapped my arms around Oskar. He hugged me close, and I crawled into his lap.

"We're completely fine, *schatzi*." Oskar stroked my back, his breath warm on my neck. I let the tears flow, emotion washing over me like a wave.

"Is she crying?" Sinan sounded horrified and uncomfortable. "Why is she crying?" Add frustrated to the mix too.

I peeled my eyes open and saw him staring at me, wide-eyed. Next to him, Hollis no longer had his sour face on. He looked as if someone had kicked his puppy.

"Still as devastatingly gorgeous as always, doll." He tried to crack a joke, but he couldn't even muster a genuine smile as he pulled his shirt to the side, showing me the spot where the Maron had sunk its teeth in. "See?"

I stroked Oskar's face, trying to banish the image of it all torn up and covered in crimson, then I went to Hollis. Kneeling on the edge of the bed, I wrapped my arms around his middle and squeezed. He held my head to his chest and rocked us gently from side to side.

"What the fuck is happening here?" Sinan started pacing again. "Has everyone forgotten that there is a cursed *Maron* running around knocking people out? That we nearly had it before Reverie ruined everything?"

I looked around Hollis to glare at Sinan. "Fuck you. As if I could forget any of that. It's *my* life that thing has been making hell, *my* people it's been attacking." My voice cracked, and my vision blurred with more tears.

"No one's forgetting the gravity of the situation," Oskar said before Sinan could be an asshole some more. "I think Reverie was frightened by what she saw."

"It can't hurt us, doll." Hollis tilted my head up and placed a soft, sweet kiss on my lips. "Anything is possible in the dreamscape, but we can't die. Just like it can't die. We're not trying to kill it, remember? We're just trying to banish it."

"I know," I whined. "I just couldn't stand watching you all bleed like that. It felt too real."

Sinan came to stand next to Hollis. "I know that must've been shocking to see, but what did you think was going to happen? This could've been over." He sighed and dragged a hand down his face.

"Yeah, well, I'm not so eager to have this all be over and have you disappear back to the fucking dream realm. *Excuse me* for not wanting to be alone again." I hated that angry tears tumbled down my face.

"That's why you ended the lucid dream?"

"No!" I yelled in his face—not my proudest moment. "I'm just not as devastated about the unintended consequence as you clearly are. I know I'm a fucking idiot for letting this happen, but I can't help that I—"

I cut myself off before I let *that* word slip out. It would only make it even more painful when they did actually leave.

"I didn't realize you were so sick of me that you couldn't wait to wrap this all up," I mumbled instead, throwing a pity party to rival anything Hollis saw in the roaring twenties.

Sinan grabbed my arm and pulled me away from Hollis. He placed my hand on his chest, and I could feel the warmth of him through the white cotton, the strength.

"See, I'm fine." His voice was more gentle, the frustration gone. "Not a scratch on any of us. And if you think a single one of our sorry asses is sick of you, then we are clearly doing something wrong."

I looked up into his eyes, and my vision blurred again. Dammit!

"You're the best damn thing that's ever happened to me." He wiped a tear off my face with his thumb. "And I treasure every second we have together. I love you."

I gasped. He'd said the words I'd been too scared to utter, and he'd said them with such conviction.

Hollis caressed my arm, and I turned to him. The smile on his face practically made his eyes sparkle. "I love you, Reverie," he said, with just as much conviction as Sinan had.

The bed dipped behind me. Oskar moved in close, his hands cupping my shoulders. When I turned my head, he tilted his to look me in the eyes. "I love you. We all do. And we never want to leave."

I felt as if I was floating in their love and care—as if I could do anything, handle anything, with them by my side. The words had already been on the tip of my tongue, and now they nearly demanded to come tumbling past my lips.

"Shit." That's what came out instead. Because Oskar had said they never *wanted* to leave, not that they *wouldn't*. Because Sinan had said he treasured every second with me, not that we had infinite seconds to revel in our love. And Hollis . . . Hollis said so much with his eyes. Expressive amber eyes looking at me with understanding and something broken between us.

"Fuck." I pushed against Sinan's chest, making Oskar lean back. I needed space. I couldn't breathe.

They felt it as strongly as I did, and it was going to end. I wanted to say it back to them, but how could I when I already felt the devastating grief of losing them—and soon?

"Fucking *shit*." I pressed a hand to my chest as I tried

to scramble off the bed. I needed to get away from them, from this feeling crushing my lungs. "Oh god, I can't do this."

"Please don't leave, Rev." Oskar's voice nearly broke, and the raw emotion from my academic, usually calm and collected man stopped me in my tracks.

"We don't know what tomorrow holds, what we won't have a choice about, but today we are choosing to stay. Please don't leave." Hollis was pleading with me not to do to them what had been done to me my whole life. How could I deny him? How could I deny any of them when all I wanted was to live in their embrace forever?

Sinan took my hand, and the tentativeness of the gesture broke my heart. When I held on tightly, he pulled me against him and banded his arms around my back. I wrapped my arms around his neck and lifted one leg, then the other, until I hung off him like a koala.

Oskar closed in behind me once more, his hand gripping one hip. Hollis shuffled closer on my left, and the others made room for him. We were in some kind of group hug that should've been weird and awkward, but it wasn't. It was exactly where I wanted to be.

Hollis nuzzled my neck and sighed, his breath tickling, as Oskar rested his forehead against the back of my head. Sinan kissed the tip of my nose, then my lips. He kept kissing me, soft and slow, until all the tumultuous feelings inside me were replaced with a distracting heat.

Oskar started kissing down the curve of my neck on one side, while Hollis sucked on the sensitive spot behind my ear on the other. With all of them pressed in so close, I could feel each one grow hard. It only spurred on my own desire. Sinan's mouth was relentless, his tongue now pushing past my lips.

Someone rubbed up and down my ribs, caressing the side of my breast, as another hand grabbed my ass and massaged. I moaned against Sinan's tongue, a soft involuntary sound. Was this really happening? All three of them at the same time? I had no idea how this had gone from the worst night of my life to the best, but no complaints here.

I broke the kiss, needing air, and it set them in motion. Oskar scooted to the side so Sinan could lower me to the bed. I hadn't even caught the breath I needed before Hollis kissed me, his hand in my hair. Oskar kneaded my breast as he rocked his erection against my hip. Sinan massaged my bare legs, the pressure increasing the higher he went. He hooked his thumbs into the waistband of my underwear and—

The doorbell rang. *The motherfucking doorbell rang.*

All three of them glared in the direction of the front door.

"Let's just ignore it," I suggested. It rang again—twice, in quick succession. Whoever it was clearly had no patience.

"Better get it, temptress." Sinan got to his feet, and I realized he was shirtless. When had he removed the coat and shirt? I didn't care. I just wanted to run my fingers through the coarse hair on his chest, kiss the taut muscles all the way down . . .

Instead, I thumped my fist on the mattress, got up, and stomped to the door. "This better be good," I said, half to myself and half to whoever was on the other side.

I opened the door and squinted against the brightness of the midday sun. When I saw Agent Andersen standing on my porch, I rolled my eyes and groaned. Cockblocked by the law!

"This is really not a good time," I whined before he could even say anything.

"Oh, I'm sorry, would you like me to come back at a more convenient time for you?" Oh damn. His control had already cracked if he was coming in with that level of sarcasm. "Perhaps a time when you have pants on?"

I stood up straight and lifted my chin. "I am in the privacy of my own home, and there is a very good reason why I'm not wearing pants, thank you very much. Speaking of which, yes, I would like you to come back at a more convenient time. Or better yet, not at all."

I started to close the door, but his hand shot out to stop it.

"Are you aware that several people were . . . taken ill the night of the festival?" He just ploughed ahead. "Six people, all unable to be roused, all seemingly asleep. Does that sound familiar to you?"

I tapped my chin and looked up. "Hmmm, nope. Doesn't ring any bells."

"Three of them regained consciousness after a few hours. Two remained comatose for twenty-four hours. One is still in the hospital."

"Thanks for the update. I'll be—"

"You were present at the festival, according to several eyewitnesses, and you were reportedly acting strange. Can you explain why?"

"I mean, I could, but where's the fun in that?"

"The fun?" His jaw ticked as he ground his teeth. "People are in the hospital, suffering—"

"She was acting strange because of me." Oskar walked up the hall and leaned on the wall behind me, and a petty part of me felt satisfied he'd interrupted Detective Douche.

Andersen raised a single brow, looking between us. "And who might you be?"

"I'm Reverie's boyfriend." Oskar flashed a grin and crossed his arms.

"Yeah." I rolled with it. "We had a fight and I got upset. I guess I get a little dramatic sometimes."

"Uh-huh." Andersen looked beyond exasperated. "And what were your whereabouts after you left the festival?"

"My dick," Sinan announced, coming to join us. He swung an arm around my shoulders, and, *oh lord*, he was still shirtless.

"Excuse me?" Andersen's eyebrows rose so high they merged with his hairline.

"She was with me after the festival. Riding my dick. All. Night. Long."

I had to bite my tongue to stop myself from laughing.

The special agent looked at Oskar with something between frustration and disbelief.

"She was." Oskar shrugged. "Then we made up. She's been with us every night this week."

"And every day," Sinan added.

"Not Tuesday!" Hollis called from behind us. We all turned to see him wander past with a mug of coffee, which he raised to us in a toast. "Tuesday night she was with me. Just me."

"This is not a joke." Andersen focused in on me. "It's not a joke to the people in the hospital or those families worried sick about their loved ones. And it's not a joke to me."

"It's not a joke to me either, but I don't know how many times I can say it's not my fault." I held his gaze, even though I now knew this really was all happening because of me.

"I know you're connected to this somehow." He pointed at me, and Sinan's grip on my shoulders tightened as Oskar stood up straight. "And I will figure it out."

"Good luck with that." Sinan had his menacing voice on; apparently we were all done playing. "In the meantime, don't threaten my woman."

He pulled me back, and Oskar slammed the door in Andersen's face. After a beat, the agent's footsteps sounded on the stairs and then the gravel path.

"What an unpleasant man." Oskar frowned at the door.

"He's just doing his job, I guess." I shrugged and headed into the kitchen. Why was I defending him? Ah yes —the guilt.

"Why are you defending him?" Sinan voiced my thoughts.

"You've lost your speaking privileges for the rest of the day." I pointed at him before opening the fridge. I was starving.

"What did I do?"

I pulled out last night's pizza and arched a brow at him. "She was on my dick?"

Both Oskar and Sinan burst out laughing, and I couldn't help but join them.

"What? It's funny." Sinan reached for the pizza box,

and I slapped his hand away. There were only three pieces left, and my stomach was eating itself.

"You've lost your pizza privileges too."

"It was pretty funny," Oskar said.

"I know. But I nearly laughed, and I've spent years refusing to let that douche-canoe see a single crack in my mask."

They both stared at me as I started eating the pizza cold, their expressions sobering.

"What?" I frowned.

Hollis appeared in the middle of the kitchen, and my power immediately reached out to make him solid.

"He had another one with him in the car. A woman," Hollis said. That explained where he'd disappeared to. "They went to the local police station."

"Whatever." I waved it off, picking up my second slice. Agent Douche had been sniffing around here for this long; he wasn't likely to find anything new now, especially considering he was looking in entirely the wrong realm.

"I'm sorry he's been harassing you for so long," Oskar said.

"And that you've had to deal with it all on your own," Sinan added.

Hollis wrapped his arms around me from behind.

I swallowed the massive bite of pizza in my mouth before mumbling: "It's OK."

It wasn't OK, but what else was there to say?

We fell into silence as I finished off my cold pizza and Hollis banged around the kitchen behind me. Any hope I'd had of picking up where we left off in the bedroom seemed dead in the water.

Oskar handed me a napkin as I finished eating, and Sinan discarded the box while Hollis deposited four short glasses on the counter. They were filled with ice and an amber liquid.

"Bit early, isn't it? What is this?" I asked.

"It's after twelve, and these are old-fashioneds." He gave me a smile and took my hand. The others grabbed two glasses each as Hollis pulled me through the house and onto the front porch.

"Tell us what happened in the lucid dream, Rev." Hollis said it more like an order than a question, but it came out soft somehow. Not in a way that roused my stubbornness. He pulled me down next to him on the porch swing, and the others leaned on the railing across from us.

Once we all had drinks in hand, I sighed and started talking. Between sips of the old-fashioned—which was freaking delicious—I told them all about Christopher, my childhood imaginary friend. Or as it turned out, the Dreamwalker who'd realized I could see and hear him and decided to hang around, then turned into a nightmare monster after I mean-girled him.

"I froze him out, and he turned into the fucking Maron." I scoffed, then polished off the last of my drink. "Men are so fragile."

Oskar chuckled. "Well, now we know where it came from and why it went undetected for so long. That's good. Maybe we can use that."

"How?" I asked. "I mean, how did it go unnoticed for so long?"

"Wait, you said you saw Chris, right?" Sinan asked. "That his true face flashed through, and his voice?"

I nodded.

"Oh shit." Hollis slumped back, making the swing bounce.

"What?" I looked between them.

"It seems Christopher hasn't completely lost his humanity, hasn't completely turned into a Maron," Oskar explained. "That's probably played into how he's remained hidden all this time. That and your very existence. A Seheraum is . . . it's kind of like you scramble the signal, in a way. You do things that shouldn't be possible, so the laws of the waking world and dream world bend when you're around."

"Like the fact that I can see and hear you and now touch you."

"Exactly," Sinan said at the same time as Hollis mumbled: "I love it when you touch me."

"So your inherent power, coupled with the fact that Chris is existing in a kind of duality within himself, makes this a very complex web to untangle—or even see before you walk right into it, face-first," Oskar said.

Hollis leaned forward, serious again. "It also means that, on some level, he's choosing this. Every time he hurts someone, every time he feeds off their sleep to remain here, it's a choice. That his true, original form can still come through, even with how monstrous and alien his Maron form has become . . ." He released a heavy breath while shaking his head. "Man's got some serious issues."

I stared at the sky, trying to process all this.

"He used to read to me," I said, remembering more and more of my childhood companion. "Before I could do it myself. I'd turn the pages and he'd read the words, doing the voices and acting things out."

The nostalgic smile fell from my face. "How does someone so kind and caring turn into something so heinous?"

"We all have light and darkness inside us," Sinan said, his voice low and loaded with disquiet. "He chose the darkness far too many times."

CHAPTER TWENTY-SIX

The sun was kissing the horizon, its orange glow peeking through the trees, when I pulled into my driveway.

"This is getting ridiculous." I sighed. "How am I supposed to get them off my back?"

"One problem at a time." Oskar reached across the center console and turned solid just as his hand landed on my thigh. He'd gone out with me for the afternoon, but during my errands, he'd remained translucent, visible only to me.

We'd wanted to confirm what Andersen and his colleague were doing, and we'd wanted them to think I was alone. As expected, they followed me everywhere I went. They weren't obnoxious about it, but any moron paying attention to their surroundings would've noticed them. Oskar had flitted between them and me, listening in on their conversations as I went about my business.

It didn't exactly come as a surprise, but they suspected I

was doing something to the people falling into comas and were hell-bent on catching me in the act.

"Yeah, well, we're not exactly making much progress on the other problem either," I grumbled.

"Everything will work out, Reverie." Oskar patted my leg. "It has to. Now come on, let's get all this stuff inside before the ice cream melts."

I dragged my ass out of the car after him, and we took all the groceries inside together. He had a good point about the ice cream.

Summer was all but over. The nights had turned chilly, the leaves were changing color, and I didn't go anywhere without a hoodie or a jacket. But today had been one of those random warm days—summer's last breath of heat before she went to sleep.

As we unpacked everything, I couldn't stop worrying about the several insurmountable problems we needed to fix. It had been over a week since my chat with my childhood imaginary friend–slash–literal nightmare monster. I needed to do something to end this mess, but I had no idea what.

I'd tried luring the Maron to another lucid dream multiple times, but it never took the bait. The guys had even reluctantly agreed to stay away one night and let me sleep on my own, hoping it would come, but that hadn't worked either. Plus, I really didn't like sleeping alone. Funny how quickly I'd gotten used to falling asleep with strong arms wrapped around me—and waking up the same way, sometimes with a different set of arms around me.

My only contact with the Maron since that eventful lucid dream had occurred the night after. The creature had appeared in a dream about me running late to something and not being able to find shoes. I didn't even see it; I just heard that disturbing voice far away and close by, Christopher's and monstrous at once.

"Give me what I want, or I'll just keep taking." It said those words and disappeared before Hollis could get to it.

Its demands were clear—I had to meet it in the waking realm and give it a solid form. But what did the idiot think would happen then? I couldn't make it a real boy permanently. I would've already done that with the men I loved if I could. He was fucking delusional.

Delusional yet determined. Because even though it had stayed away from me, it was wreaking havoc on the town of Gritton. It took one or two people every day—sometimes at night, sometimes during the daytime. People just fell down, dead asleep, at their jobs, in the store, at school drop-off. They never stayed under longer than twenty-four hours, but it was freaking everyone out. Understandably.

Andersen had stayed on my ass the entire time and therefore knew I was always at home or elsewhere when this shit happened, but that didn't shake his conviction it was me. Oskar had overheard a conversation about how big my property was and how I could be sneaking off using some path through the woods. The agents also hypothesized that the comas could be a delayed response to some kind of drug. As if I was going around roofie-ing the entire town.

"Reverie." Oskar wrapped his arms around me from behind, making me realize I'd been staring out the window over the sink, lost in thought. "You need to stop thinking about it. Just for a little while. Give your brain a break."

I leaned back against him. "I don't know how."

"Well, I think we can help with that." He kissed the side of my neck and stepped back. His voice rarely sounded playful. That was much more Hollis's thing, and it got my attention.

"Where are Grumpy and Sunshine?" I narrowed my eyes, but Oskar smiled and took my hand.

"I'll show you." He led me out the sliding door, across the patio, and into the yard. The air was balmy, the grass soft and warm under my bare feet, and something sparkled in the distance.

"What's going on here?" I asked, trying to get a better look at the strange glimmering near the back of my garden.

"I'll show you. Come on." Oskar tugged on my hand again. We passed the ginseng and the compost, then finally ended up at the very back of the property, where I hardly ever went.

I'd been meaning to start another patch for the ginseng around here but hadn't gotten around to it. I usually just mowed the flat, grassy area when I remembered and left the surrounding trees and bushes to grow wild. There was a wire fence in there somewhere, and the woods started beyond my property line.

The edge of the property looked just as wild as always, only now it was draped in fairy lights. The pinpricks of light glowed among the foliage, giving the whole thing a whimsical feel.

Hollis and Sinan stood in front of it, a blanket at their feet. Or more like the rug from the living room and every single blanket I owned, plus enough cushions to drown in. Dozens of candles—tall pillars, elegant dinner candles, and squat tealights, some in holders and others just sitting in the grass—created a rough semicircle around the blankets. The flames barely even flickered in the perfectly still night.

"Welcome home, honey." Hollis flashed me a smile, and I detected a hint of nerves in it.

"Wow," I breathed, eyes wide. "This is . . . wow!"

"So, you like it?" Sinan rubbed the back of his neck, then dropped his hand to his side; he looked mad at himself for letting something as petty as insecurity get to him.

"I love it," I said immediately, hoping to squash their nerves. They had nothing to be nervous about. This was the most romantic thing anyone had ever done for me. This was the *only* romantic thing anyone had ever done for me.

My throat tightened with emotion, but I forced myself to swallow past it. "What's the occasion?"

"You." Oskar squeezed my hand and pulled on it once more, leading me the last few steps to the magical spot.

"Me?" I giggled awkwardly. I was not used to having this much attention.

"Yes, you." Hollis cupped my cheek and gave me a gentle kiss. "When I first saw you in the woods, I was confused. I couldn't wake you from the sleepwalking, and that was a first, so I had no idea why I had been called to you. But I stayed because I knew there was a reason, and it didn't take me long to realize you were special— extraordinary. I think I may have fallen in love with you that first day as you traipsed through the woods and muttered to yourself and followed my voice. I can't describe to you how intoxicating it was to be heard."

My heart swelled with every word, but it stuttered at that last bit. Wasn't that why Chris had turned his back on the Dreamwalker calling, why he'd become consumed and obsessed and turned into the Maron? Because being seen and heard was intoxicating for those who existed on the other side of the glass.

"Don't do that." Sinan stepped in closer, caressing my arm. "Don't think dark thoughts. Everything about you is intoxicating, temptress, but that has nothing to do with the Maron. Christopher made his choices, and that's not your fault."

I opened my mouth to argue, but Sinan held a finger up and kept speaking. "And tonight, we are taking a break from the Maron and the agents and all the bullshit we've been dealing with. You deserve a night to just *breathe*, Reverie. To sit under the stars and let us show you how much we love you."

"You've taught us so much about ourselves," Hollis said, "about the world, about love and forgiveness. You are strong and compassionate and so full of life. Tonight, we live it to the fullest."

"Tonight, we celebrate you." Oskar stood by a little table with a bottle in his hands. "We treat you how you deserve to be treated. We worship you like the goddess you are."

I had no idea Oskar had such a flair for the dramatic, but he popped the cork on the champagne bottle with a flourish, making me jump and laugh. Bubbles spilled out and over his hand, matching the feeling welling up inside me: bubbly and sweet and unexpected—just like the champagne. Just like them.

"And how exactly do we do that?" I asked, deciding to roll with it and put everything out of my mind for a few hours.

"We start with champagne." Sinan kissed my neck as he brushed past me to help Oskar pour.

"And strawberries, of course," Hollis whispered close to my ear, then took a little nibble of my earlobe. Sinan handed him two glasses, and he passed one to me.

I took a sip. I'd never been much of a champagne girl, but this stuff tasted pretty good. It was cold and crisp, and the bubbles tingled on my tongue like a precursor to what the rest of the night held.

A strawberry appeared in front of my mouth as I lowered the glass. Oskar was holding it out with a smile. I took a bite and licked the sweet juice off my lips.

"And then what?" I asked, sipping more champagne.

"So impatient." Hollis chuckled. We all settled down on the blankets and cushions.

"And then a light dinner," Oskar said. "You're going to need your strength."

"I am?" I bugged my eyes out and blinked slowly. I had a pretty good idea where this was heading, and I was *so here for it*.

"Always with the sarcasm." Sinan finished off his champagne in one big swallow.

"You know you're meant to sip that slowly, savor the flavor?" I demonstrated, arching my brows over my glass.

"I'll sip you slowly," he muttered, reaching for the bottle.

"Sorry, what?"

"Nothing!"

We teased and joked around while we polished off two bottles and they fed me—literally fed me, refusing to let me pick up a single finger sandwich or mini quiche. The champagne filled me with a pleasant buzzing feeling as I lounged in the warm night air and was doted on by my lovers.

I asked questions about their lives before, and they indulged me with stories of summers on the lake, bare-knuckled boxing, and singing sea shanties. All the while, their hands were all over me. A teasing kiss accompanied every bite of strawberry. Every refill of my drink included a caress on my leg. Every shifting of positions on the cushions had them coming closer, touching me more, teasing me relentlessly.

But every time I tried to deepen a kiss or lean into a tantalizing touch, they'd pull back and distract me with more food or a new story. It infuriated me in the most delicious way.

"Oh shit, we forgot the chocolate." Hollis sat up and reached over to the side table.

I lay reclined against Sinan with my feet in Oskar's lap. Sinan was running his fingers through my hair while Oskar massaged my feet. It was bliss, but this oversight could not be ignored.

"There's been chocolate this whole time, and you didn't tell me?"

"Yeah. Worst boyfriends ever." Hollis laughed as he settled on his belly at my side, a bowl in his hands. "It was supposed to be a dip for the fruit. I guess it's pointless now. I don't know why I brought it up."

He went to get up again, but I grabbed his wrist, keeping him and the bowl of chocolate sauce in place. "I want the chocolate."

"Doll, we don't have any cutlery or anything."

Sinan reached over my head and dipped his finger in the

bowl. "Who needs cutlery?" He held his finger up in front of my face, thick sauce oozing down the digit.

I leaned forward and wrapped my mouth around it. The smooth sweetness exploded on my tongue, and I moaned as I sucked the delicious sauce clean off.

"Fuck cutlery," Sinan said in a low voice. The balmy air had suddenly become charged. Oskar and Hollis watched my mouth intently as I licked my lips. Something low in my belly tightened, and not for the first time that night, I wondered how much more of this I could take before I soaked through my underwear.

"That looks like fun." Oskar dipped his finger into the chocolate and held it out to me. I wrapped my mouth around it immediately. Holding his gaze, I hollowed out my cheeks and sucked on his finger, imagining it was another part of him.

By the time I'd licked every trace of sweetness off Oskar's digit, Hollis was ready with two fingers dripping in chocolatey sauce.

"My turn." He grinned. He'd scooped up so much sauce it was about to drip onto the blanket. I caught a drizzle with my tongue, then licked the front of his fingers clean before sucking them past my lips, taking my time. As Hollis slowly pumped his fingers in and out of my mouth, I had a feeling he was imagining my warm, wet pussy.

"I think I've suddenly developed a sweet tooth," Sinan declared as I finished with Hollis.

Sinan kissed the side of my neck and, with a gentle grip on my wrist, guided my hand over to the bowl. Hollis held the sauce out for him as Sinan lowered my middle finger into the chocolate, and then Hollis took the opportunity to dip another one of my fingers.

In perfect synchronicity, the two men took my sticky fingers into their mouths and sucked.

"Oh shit," I gasped, surprised at the intensity of the sensation shooting down my arms, through my chest, and right down to my core.

I finally soaked through that underwear.

CHAPTER TWENTY-SEVEN

Oskar took the bowl, scraped the last of the sauce out of it, and moved closer to smear the chocolate on my lips and chin. I resisted the urge to lick it off. I wanted him to do it. And he didn't disappoint. First, he licked the sweet stuff off his fingers. Why was it so hot when he got the last little bit off the pad of his thumb? There was just something indescribably sensual about his elegant, masculine hands and those lips—his usually perfect hair already a bit messy as he stared at me and sucked.

Sinan and Hollis finished with my fingers as Oskar leaned in. Sinan gripped my chin and tilted my face up as Oskar got to work licking clean the mess he'd made. He ran his tongue across my lips over and over—top, then bottom, top, then bottom. I tried to catch his mouth in a kiss, tried to lean up to get what I wanted, but Sinan's grip kept my head in place, and Hollis held on to my arm, essentially keeping me at their mercy.

Oskar tortured me with his teasing licks and nips on my

mouth until well after the chocolate was gone. He moved to the few remaining bits on my chin and then kept going. Past Sinan's hand, to the side of my throat, he kissed a hot path down my neck, over my collarbones, down into my cleavage.

As Oskar nudged my legs open and settled between them, Sinan dragged his hand off my chin and down my throat. He toyed with the hem of my dress, his fingers dipping under the fabric. Hollis leaned over and kissed me. I'd been dying for a kiss, and he gave me such a thorough one that I moaned into his mouth.

Sinan's groan reverberated through his chest, and I felt it on my back. His hand slipped under the front of my dress and cupped my breast.

Hollis's assault on my mouth continued. His tongue massaged against mine in a steady rhythm, his lips soft, his teeth teasing at more.

Meanwhile, Oskar caressed my thighs, his hands drifting higher and higher. He bunched my dress up around my hips and leaned down to press a kiss to my heated core, over my underwear.

"Fuck, you're soaked through," he said, nuzzling his face against me. His thumbs rubbed the creases of my thighs and teased at the very edges of the soaked fabric.

Hollis broke the kiss and stared down at me with fire in his gaze. His swollen lips glistened in the candlelight.

"Are you, doll?" He cupped my other breast over the fabric while Sinan circled my nipple on the other. "Are you wet for us?"

"Dripping," I confirmed in a breathy voice. I wasn't

exaggerating. I could feel my arousal trickling ever so slowly down toward my ass.

Oskar dipped his thumbs under the fabric to rub over my bare flesh. He spread the wetness, caressing my folds while avoiding that most sensitive spot. I rolled my hips, seeking friction, as my body begged for more.

Sinan removed his hand from my breast only long enough to push the straps of my dress off my shoulders. Then he tipped my head back and to the side so he could kiss me. I could feel his erection digging into my back, and I made sure to rock against him with each movement of my hips. A hot mouth wrapped around my other nipple—Hollis. With my arms pinned to my sides by the dress, I could only reach Sinan's leg. But on my other side, Hollis sat close enough for me to find his rock-hard length and rub it over his pants.

Between my legs, Oskar finally lowered his mouth to my clit and sucked on it through my underwear. I moaned against Sinan's tongue. With all of them touching me, sucking me, it was too much. It was not enough.

Thankfully, Oskar was done teasing. He pulled aside the soaked crotch of my panties and spread me with his thumbs before taking a long, firm lick. He lapped at me over and over and moaned as if I was tastier than the chocolate sauce that had started all this. He sucked me with fervor, practically devouring my cunt, while his thumbs firmly massaged my outer lips.

Hollis gripped my leg and lifted it, pulling it open wider and hooking it over his hip. His mouth remained on my nipple, sucking with just as much enthusiasm, and Sinan's mouth was relentless on mine; his grip kept me from moving away to catch my breath.

And then Hollis maneuvered his hand under Oskar's chin and pushed two fingers inside me.

I cried into Sinan's mouth, not even trying to kiss him back anymore. He took pity on me and let me moan and writhe as he sucked my bottom lip.

Hollis barely pumped his fingers a few times, and I was coming. It rolled through me, my brain trying to focus on all the sensations at once and just bursting with pleasure when it couldn't keep up.

My bones turned to jelly, and I went limp. Sinan supported my full weight; his grip on my chin loosened and turned into a caress. Oskar took slow, lazy licks as I came down, ending with a loving kiss to my engorged sex. Hollis withdrew his fingers and grinned at his own hand, clearly enjoying how slick it was.

Meeting my gaze, he put one finger into his mouth and sucked it dry. He sighed in pleasure. Sinan's hand shot out and grabbed his wrist before he could bring the second finger to his lips.

"Mine," he declared and pulled Hollis closer. I tipped my head back to watch as Sinan opened those full, soft lips of his and wrapped them around Hollis's digit. He sighed too, even closing his eyes briefly at the flavor. *My* flavor. Damn, why was that so hot? Them tasting me, Hollis's finger in Sinan's mouth . . .

The whole thing felt so *dirty*, but not in a shameful way —far from it. I loved this feeling. I refused to feel shame over anything safe and consensual. But I still got that rush, that exhilaration from doing something that felt forbidden.

I lay on my back with my dress pushed down, exposing my tits, and pushed up, baring my spread legs and still needy pussy. Three men kneeled over me with hunger and sin in their eyes, touching me, tasting me. They were all fully dressed, and I was laid out for them to do with as they pleased.

I felt like a dirty slut in the most delicious, defiant way. I smiled at the thought and shimmied out of my dress and underwear, kicking the fabric away.

"Ready for more, temptress?" Sinan moved, making me sit up.

"Do your worst." I had no fear, no hesitation. My body belonged to them. "But maybe do it naked?"

I liked their bodies just as much as they liked mine. Tonight was a feast for the senses, and I was ready for the next course.

Hollis grinned and jumped to his feet, and the others chuckled. Oskar stood too, and I sat back on my heels, ready to watch. I glanced over my shoulder just in time to see Sinan pull his shirt off. He was barefoot and in nothing but his pants, which he regretfully left on as he settled down next to me. He propped himself up on one elbow, his head close to my waist.

Almost in tandem, Oskar and Hollis got to work on their belts and suspenders. Oskar's dexterous fingers worked on the buttons of his pants next, while Hollis pulled his shirt from his waistband. I didn't know where to look. My eyes bounced from one to the other, feasting on the show they were putting on. For me. All for me.

Hollis undid the top few buttons and the ones at his wrists and pulled his shirt off in one fluid move. Oskar shoved his pants and underwear down and stepped out of them.

I moaned and bit my lip. The strong, lithe thighs; the defined chest and shoulders; the two sets of eyes—so different yet both looking at me with the same intense expression. Both their gazes raked over my nude body, lingering on my full breasts, fixating on the spot between my thighs.

"Goddamn, you are beautiful," Oskar declared as he reached for the buttons on his vest.

"You like that, doll?" Hollis rubbed himself over his pants. "You like watching us undress for you?"

"Yeah." The word came out as a breathy moan, and I internally rolled my eyes at myself for sounding like a porno. But whatever. I had no control of my own voice. I hardly had control of my own body, and I couldn't care less. I spread my knees a little wider, hoping to give them a show while they gave me one.

Sinan's short hair tickled as he nuzzled my waist before kissing the spot. He slowly dragged his hand up the inside of my thigh and ran his fingers over my folds.

"Oh, yeah." He rested his head on my hip. "She likes that a lot."

Hollis's grin could only be described as proud as he unbuttoned his pants and freed his erection. Oskar had gotten rid of the vest and started on the buttons of his shirt, but he'd gotten sidetracked. He wrapped his hand around his cock, watching Sinan's hand between my legs intently.

"Mmm, yep, she likes that too." Sinan continued the running commentary as he teased at my entrance. I ran my hands up my body and started playing with my tits.

Oskar and Hollis were both stroking themselves slowly, shoulder to shoulder, their full focus on me. Sinan slid a single finger inside, making me whimper. I wanted more.

The ends of Oskar's shirt kept getting in his way, and he yanked it up over his head—and got stuck.

"Fuck," he muttered, arms up in the air, the fabric tight around his shoulder. It made me giggle, but that turned into a gasp as Sinan's thumb brushed my clit.

Hollis stepped closer and removed the shirt the rest of the way. He dropped it on the grass at their feet, then shot out a hand to steady Oskar, who'd tripped on his discarded pants. They ended up kind of holding on to each other, completely nude, and their dicks definitely bumped.

Damn. Something in my brain exploded. The possibilities of this dynamic made me so turned on, and I had no idea why. My cunt squeezed around Sinan's finger, and I could feel myself gush with arousal.

"Oh damn, she fucking *loves* that." Sinan was breathing hard, but not as hard as me. "She's practically dripping into the palm of my hand."

One side of Hollis's mouth tipped up into an intrigued smile as he glanced at Oskar. The other man tensed, his head tilting to the side as he contemplated the situation.

"What do you say, Oskar?" Hollis looped an arm loosely around his shoulders. "Want to cross swords for our girl?"

"I . . . maybe?" Oskar looked unsure, but he'd relaxed a bit too.

"I've had sex with both men and women," Hollis declared, and I filed that away to bring up during his next story time. "So I'm down. But no pressure, man." He rubbed Oskar's smooth chest in a part comforting, part suggestive gesture.

"I'm . . . intrigued." Oskar watched me as Hollis slowly dragged his hand down his ribs. "And I love how into it Reverie is." His Adam's apple bobbed as Hollis reached his cock, wrapping his hand around it. "But I'm not sure now is the best time for this."

Hollis immediately released Oskar's length, taking his own in his fist instead. "Fair enough." He shrugged. "Probably warrants a conversation about boundaries anyway."

I glanced down at Sinan, rocking myself against his hand. He shook his head and laughed.

"What?" I sighed as he added a second finger.

"I've had enough time on this earth to know I want nothing but what's clenching around my fingers right now," he declared. "But if one of these two wants to suck me off for your viewing pleasure, I could be down with that."

The image of Hollis kneeling between Sinan's legs . . .

"Oh god." I nearly came just at the thought of it, but Sinan removed his fingers, which made me lose balance and tip forward. I caught myself on my hands. "I need one of you inside me right now."

Out of the corner of my eye, I could see Oskar and Hollis come closer as I tore at Sinan's pants. I didn't care which one of them it was—I just needed a cock inside me immediately.

"Yes, ma'am." Hollis sounded positively delighted. He caressed my ass, grabbing a handful and squeezing.

Sinan helped me remove his pants, and I grabbed his length in a firm grip before he could try to control the situation again. I took Sinan into my mouth as Hollis slid into me from behind. I was so wet and ready for him he met no resistance and pushed in to the hilt. Precum was salty on my tongue as I sucked and licked, relishing how Sinan's abdominals tightened.

I relaxed my throat and took him as deep as I could while Hollis pumped into me in short, deep thrusts. My tits swung heavy under me as I moved between them. I felt dirty and powerful all at once.

"Fuck, that's so hot." Oskar's strained voice made me open my eyes, which I hadn't even realized I'd closed. He was kneeling at my side, his dick so hard it looked as if it would leave a bruise if I bumped into it. He stared at me, at how his friends were filling me. I moaned around the girth in my mouth and felt an aching tightness in my breasts.

His mouth hanging open and his eyes hooded with pure lust, Oskar ran a hand down my spine and grabbed a handful of my ass. Then he reached under and cupped one of my tits before playing with the nipple.

Sinan shuffled back, pulling out of my mouth. I groaned and gave him a frown. He leaned back on his elbows, chest heaving, and took his time before speaking.

"You're going to come on each of our cocks, temptress," he said, watching Hollis fuck me while Oskar touched me all over. "An orgasm for each of your willing victims. And then we're all going to fill you at once."

"Oh god," I moaned, rocking back against Hollis, encouraging him to go harder as I started to tip over the edge.

"Now be a good girl and coat Hollis in that delicious cream of yours. *Now.*"

I was coming before Sinan even finished his order. Oskar pinched a nipple just as Hollis reached down and did the same to my clit, and my whole body locked up with pleasure. It had started as a cresting wave of climax, but they ratcheted it up to a fucking tsunami, and I yelled my release into the night.

Hollis pulled out immediately, and I wobbled, my elbows nearly giving out. Oskar caught me and lowered me gently to the soft pillows.

I sighed, let my body relax, and rolled my head to the side. Hollis lay on his back, his chest rising and falling with deep breaths as he stared up at the stars.

"Shit, I nearly came," he said.

I frowned in confusion. Wasn't that the point? Were they actually . . . trying to hold back?

"Are you fools edging yourselves?" I chuckled.

"Not on purpose." Sinan turned my head toward where he lay sprawled on my other side. "We want to make this last, but just looking at you with your lips swollen and your hair all messed up and your soft curves—makes my dick twitch."

"Take a breather. I got this." Oskar came to kneel between my legs. He surprised me by lifting my hips off the ground while my shoulders remained where they were.

Sinan tucked several pillows under my butt, and Oskar released me. He pushed my knees open as wide as they would go and rubbed his hard cock up and down my slick sex. The pillows had my pelvis tilted up, my lower back arched, and my head and shoulders comfortably situated on a large cushion. The new position made my tits gather up near my neck as if I were wearing a corset, but it made my tummy look flat.

I looked down the length of my body and rocked my hips, begging Oskar to get on with it. I was still tingling slightly from my last orgasm, but I was ready for more. Sinan had ordered me to come on each one of their dicks, and I had a strange, fiery determination to do exactly that.

Oskar obliged, sinking into me and sighing once he was balls-deep. He gripped my thighs tightly as he pulled almost all the way out, then slammed back in.

"Holy fuck." My eyes widened as my legs tried to close of their own volition. Whatever this pillow thing did, it was pussy magic. I could feel him so deep inside me, reaching spots I didn't even know I had. With a satisfied little smile, Oskar dug his fingers into my thighs and kept my legs open wide.

He pistoned in and out at a steady rhythm, and I thoroughly enjoyed the view of him fucking me: the corded muscle of his forearms as he gripped my thighs, his stomach muscles rippling with each thrust, the taut tendons in his neck as he panted through gritted teeth.

Sinan rolled onto his side, propping his head up on his hand. He brushed a strand of hair off my neck and placed a gentle kiss on my shoulder. Hollis appeared on my other side, on his belly, and leaned over me to kiss my other shoulder.

They kept their hands away as their mouths kissed, nipped, sucked all over my chest. They licked paths up my neck, nibbled on my ears, and kissed me in turns, taking my breath away.

Oskar just kept up that steady pace, rubbing those amazing spots inside me.

I threw my head back and cried out as my walls tightened around Oskar. Liquid heat spread out from my core to the very tips of my fingers and toes, to the top of my scalp. I felt as if I were burning up from the inside in the most wonderful way.

The stars twinkled above me as I came and came, and when I closed my eyes from the pleasure, I still saw them, sparking and shining.

Oskar pulled out, and I whimpered. My thighs were shaking, and I didn't think I could close them if I tried.

Hollis and Sinan worked together to remove the pillows and settle me into a more comfortable position. I took my time catching my breath as my lovers caressed my body gently, worshipping me as they'd said they would. Every part of me throbbed with sensation and sensuality, a languid kind of heat filling my veins. I somehow felt tired but invigorated at the same time, but I knew they weren't done with me yet.

Oskar made his way back over after gathering his wits. He settled at my legs and rubbed my thighs. They'd stopped shaking, but it felt amazing to be touched in such a caring way.

No one said anything—no flirty, teasing comments; no lust-filled demands; no dirty talk. It almost felt as if we'd stepped into a dreamscape and nothing outside of it mattered. I felt connected to them in a way I didn't know was possible. We were feeding off one another's energy, our bodies communicating better than any words could have.

Their attentions slowly turned more intense. Hands

gripped tighter; tongues darted out to make the sweet kisses more sensual. I didn't think I'd even stopped craving more pleasure, but now I became acutely aware of how needy I was again already. Oskar's hands moved higher, teasing at my swollen lips, while the others crowded me between them. Sinan rubbed himself against my hip, and Hollis started doing the same on the other side. I lifted my head briefly to take a good look at Oskar. They were all so hard— it had to be painful at this point.

I'd done that. It was because of *me* that three incredible men were so turned on their cocks looked as though they were straining against the silky-smooth skin. It was intoxicating, that thought—that I could do that to them. That they wanted me to.

My pussy clenched, begging for more.

Would I ever get enough of them?

I pushed myself up and straddled Sinan. His hands went to my hips as I took hold of his erection so I could impale myself on it. I slid down all the way, releasing my full weight on him, and we groaned at the same time.

"Fuck." He breathed hard and dug his fingers into my hips, keeping me from moving. "I was going to make you come on my cock, temptress. Then I was going to fuck your ass while one of the others took you from the front."

I moaned, arousal shooting to my core at the picture he painted, but he still wouldn't let me move against him.

"But I can't," he ground out and took a deep breath. "I can't hold back anymore. If I feel your cunt flutter around me, I'm going to spill inside you."

For a brief second, disappointment shot through me. I

wanted what he'd described so badly. But I should've known my boys would never leave me wanting.

A hand dragged up my spine, and then Hollis's voice spoke in my ear. "You want that, doll? You want us all to fill you up?"

I was beyond words, but I managed to grunt something resembling an affirmative answer.

Lubricant oozed down between my cheeks, and Hollis spread it with the tip of his dick. Sinan sat up, making me gasp at the change in position, but it was only so Oskar could pile an obscene number of cushions behind him. When Sinan leaned back again, he took me with him. The pillows let him recline at a comfortable angle, with me resting against his chest.

Hollis pushed, and I made myself relax all my muscles. After a few tentative, shallow strokes, he pushed all the way in, and I lost my breath for a second. My fingers dug into the soft cushions as I just breathed and felt them both inside me. It was a weird kind of pressure, a new sensation, but just the slightest movement had me shuddering with pleasure. Between the two of them, they were touching spots inside me I couldn't even describe.

I forced myself to stay still. I knew as soon as we started moving in earnest, it wouldn't be long for any of us. And I didn't want that without all of them at once.

Doing my best to move only my neck, I looked around for Oskar.

"I'm right here." His voice sounded close behind me. There was some shuffling, and he scooted to my side. I glanced down at his straining erection and licked my lips.

When I looked back up into his face, he took away what

breath I had left in my lungs. His gaze held so much love, as well as something resembling awe. Somehow those warm emotions stayed in his eyes as his expression turned feral with lust.

He ran his thumb over my bottom lip, and I darted my tongue out to lick it.

Behind me, Hollis groaned and rolled his hips. Sinan and I both made needy, desperate sounds at the pleasure shooting between us.

With no time to waste, Oskar settled himself among the cushions with his hip against Sinan's shoulder, close enough for me to take him into my mouth.

For a split second none of us moved, frozen on the precipice of something explosive. Then, almost as one, we started to *fuck*. No other word for it fit. Yes, there was boundless love between us—care and attention and worship—but what we were doing now could only be described as pure, wild *fucking*.

It took a bit to find a good rhythm with so many moving parts, but we figured it out. Hollis pumped into my ass with confident, firm strokes. Every thrust moved me up Sinan's body, and he rolled his hips as much as he could so that he slid in every time Hollis slid out. I just held on for dear life and sucked on Oskar's cock. He thrust his hips up into my face, helping me.

An orgasm washed through me, molten ecstasy coursing through my body. It wasn't as intense as the others had been, but it went on and on, making me feel as though I was drowning in pleasure.

"Fuck," Sinan grunted, and I pulled my mouth off Oskar to watch Sinan come inside me. He stared into my eyes, into my very soul, through his release, his neck tightening up, his hands gripping me as if I was the only thing that kept him tethered to this earth.

I supposed, technically, I was.

Breathing hard, he brushed my hair back from my face and held it gently at the back of my neck. Hollis kept going, his movements becoming jerky.

I turned back to Oskar, who was pumping his hand up and down his slick length. I leaned over and licked the tip, ready to suck him down my throat again. But before I could wrap my lips around him, he released a deep, gravelly moan and came. Thick, hot ropes of cum spurted out to land on my chin, down my neck, and across the tops of my tits.

It was so dirty, so sexy in a way I couldn't comprehend. I had Oskar's cum all over me as Hollis fucked my ass. *Who even was I and how was this my life?*

Pleasure started cresting through me once more as Oskar leaned down to suck on my neck. Sinan palmed my breasts, spreading the sticky mess all over them and using it to rub my nipples.

Hollis finished with a long, deep moan that reverberated through my back. He shoved his hips against my ass as he spilled inside it, then dropped his head down to my other shoulder and bit down.

I threw my head back and released an embarrassingly animalistic sound as the best orgasm of my life tore through me. It ripped me apart from the inside, and I wasn't sure I'd ever be the same again.

We all collapsed in a tangle of sweaty bodies, struggling to steady our breathing.

The stars continued to sparkle as if my world hadn't just been turned upside down.

I stared up at the sky. It was constant, even if most of it remained a mystery to us. It was always there, even behind the clouds. Looking up at the night sky gave me confidence I was exactly where I was supposed to be. As I lay there under the stars' unchanging glow, I realized I felt the exact same way anytime I was around the three men sprawled next to me.

I silently asked the stars why a love so steady and sure had come into my life, when it was destined to leave me bereft.

CHAPTER TWENTY-EIGHT

Thunder cracked in the dark sky above, so loud I clapped my hands over my ears. The walking track through the woods was muddy, even though the rain hadn't started yet. Darkness made it difficult to navigate, and the slippery soil under my feet didn't help.

I could feel the mud squelching between my toes. Ugh! Why hadn't I put on my hiking boots before leaving?

A flash of lightning illuminated the trees and plants for an instant before everything fell into darkness again. Thunder followed close behind, shaking the very ground beneath me.

I picked up my pace, and not just because the gathering storm freaked me out. I needed to hurry.

At the end of the track, I broke into a light jog. The paved sidewalk provided steadier footing, but the thunder and lightning weren't letting up. The wind started to howl, adding to the cacophony. At least the street lamps made it easier to see where I was going.

Rounding the corner onto Main Street, I came to a halt.

The thunder, the lightning, the wind—everything stopped, as if to give me a reprieve so I could fully take in what I was seeing. People packed the street. They stood all over the road and the sidewalk, shoulder to shoulder, barely an inch of space between them.

They were all facing away from me.

The weather returned, lightning providing a too brief warning of the thunder that came fast on its heels. The wind picked up too. It howled in the distance, made the trees sway, and lashed the hair and clothing of all the people standing eerily still.

I took a step back.

One by one, the people started to turn until they were all facing me, looking right at me.

I knew all these people: Pippa and her friends; Mr. and Mrs. Wallis; Mrs. Martin, although I didn't see Nora with her. There were some faces I couldn't attach names to, but I recognized them all the same. The entire town stood in the middle of the street, staring at me.

I took another step back, my eyes darting around all the familiar faces.

Pippa closed her eyes and fell to the ground.

The storm raged harder, and it started to rain.

A few rows back, Vera fell too, then one of her cousins almost immediately after.

The wind whipped the rain about, making it slash down sideways, as people started to drop. They piled on top of each other, like some kind of disturbed puppy pile, until not a single one was left standing.

The rain continued to pelt them, saturating their prone forms.

Lightning flashed and I whipped my head up, locking my focus onto a pair of eyes darker than night.

The Maron was on the other side of all the sleeping people. I couldn't make out its body, but its huge eyes—the size of my entire head—stared down at me from above the treetops in the distance.

I'm having a prophetic dream. The realization washed through me, and I snapped my head to the side.

My Dreamwalkers stood in the window of the drugstore, safe and dry on the other side of the glass, observing everything with wide eyes and tight jaws.

The thunder boomed, so intense I stumbled and . . .

I woke up violently, shooting up in bed and clutching the sheets.

"It's OK. You're OK. I got you." Hollis sat on the bed next to me, rubbing my back. It was ironic—because he wasn't even technically supposed to exist—but his touch grounded me.

With my hand pressed to my chest, I forced myself to breathe deeper, more steadily.

It was morning, earlier than I usually got up, but the curtains had been pulled back, and light flooded the room. A bird landed on a branch outside my window and let loose a trilling song. The joyful sound and calm surroundings contrasted sharply with what I'd just seen in my dream.

"You saw it?" I leaned against Hollis, and he wrapped his arms around me.

"Yeah." He sighed, then after a beat, pulled back to look at me. "Wait, you remember it?"

"Oh, yeah." I'd been remembering bits and pieces of my prophetic dreams, but that was the first one I recalled fully. "I remember the whole fucked-up thing, and I realized it was a prophetic dream too."

"That's fantastic!"

I wished I could be as happy as he was about the progress in my ability, but the experience—and the worries that came with it—disturbed me too deeply. Throwing the covers back, I got out of bed and went through the motions of my bathroom routine. It felt like existing in two realities at once: the banal one where I was brushing my teeth, and the macabre one from my dream that kept playing over and over in my mind.

Hollis was pouring coffee when I made my way into the kitchen, and Oskar stood at the stove frying eggs. Every morning that I came into the kitchen to find one, or all, of them pottering around in there, I couldn't help smiling. But this morning, nothing could lift my mood.

Oskar tipped the scrambled eggs onto a plate and came to stand before me, a sad look on his face.

"I know you're scared." He cupped my cheeks and caressed them gently with his thumbs. "But everything will be fine."

"You don't know that." I shook my head, but he didn't release me. "Not if my prophetic dream is correct, and as far as I know, I haven't had one that was wrong yet."

In place of an answer, he leaned in and kissed me softly. He took his time, his lips caressing mine as I started to relax a little.

"All your prophetic dreams have been accurate," Hollis confirmed when Oskar released me. "But they have a purpose, and they don't always play out in the exact same way."

I plopped down on a stool and poked at the eggs with a fork. "What purpose? Psychological torture?"

"You're sulking." Oskar crossed his arms and gave me a firm look.

"Excuse you—"

"You have those dreams for a reason, Reverie," he interrupted. "You have them so you can change them."

I rolled my eyes.

"Like the one with the car crash." Hollis gave me a pointed look. "You saved that man's life. You're amazing."

"You are incredible," Oskar agreed.

"And unbelievably sexy," Sinan added, appearing next to me and immediately turning solid. "What are we talking about?"

"My shitty dream," I grumbled and abandoned the eggs for coffee.

"Yeah . . ." He trailed off, then held his arms out. I frowned, wondering what the hell he was doing, but then realized he was offering me a hug. Not forcing one on me or avoiding my melancholy—simply offering the comfort if I wanted it.

I slid off the stool and into his arms. With my cheek pressed to his chest, I let his spicy scent soothe me.

"Is it possible, what I dreamed?" I reluctantly pulled away from Sinan so I could look at them all properly—and drink more coffee.

Hollis shrugged. "Honestly, we're not sure."

"Theoretically." Oskar squinted off to the side, as if doing complex math in his head. "Yes, it is possible. We've never seen it before, but we've never seen a Maron capable of forcing people into sleep at will either."

"What happens if a Maron goes unchecked? If we just . . . do nothing and let it play out?" No part of me was prepared to allow that, but morbid curiosity made me ask.

"We don't know. I'm sorry." Sinan gave me a sad smile, then frowned a bit. "I'm just as frustrated as you. It's not often that there is something I don't know."

"So, what do we do? What do *I* do?" Because it was me that thing was taunting, me it wanted to force to do its bidding.

"You've been doing it all along—you just didn't know," Hollis said, unhelpfully.

"Like with the car accident," Oskar explained. "You wore the shirt, you had your phone, even if you didn't know why."

"You trust your instincts. You're a Seheraum, and just like we inexplicably feel the call when we're needed elsewhere, you have something in you that guides you to do what needs to be done. Listen to your intuition, Reverie." Sinan watched me with so much confidence it was hard not to wither from the pressure. I couldn't bear disappointing him, disappointing them all, and failing an entire town of innocent people.

WHETHER BECAUSE I'D WOKEN UP EARLIER THAN usual or because the stupid lucid dream was making me feel gross, I didn't know, but I couldn't eat. I headed out for a walk instead.

As I left my front path and stepped out onto the street, I spotted Andersen's car across the road. Determined to ignore the two shapes in the vehicle and get some fresh air, I started walking in the other direction, but I didn't get far before I changed my mind and turned right back around.

I marched across the road, tension building in my shoulders with every step, and rapped on the driver's-side window—as if they wouldn't have seen me approaching in a huff.

The window lowered, revealing an unamused Andersen and, in the passenger seat, another agent with dull blonde hair tied back into a ponytail. They were dressed casually in jeans and sweaters, and two steaming cups of coffee sat in the cupholders between them. Apparently suits and ties weren't stakeout attire. The woman had a box of donuts on her lap—how cliché. It was open, but the sweet treats were untouched. I'd interrupted their morning. *Good*.

"Good morning, Senior Special Agent Andersen!" I beamed at him, leaning on the top of the car. "Good morning, nameless minion agent whose name I don't know."

They both gave me flat looks, but I caught the woman's subtle eye roll. It made me grin wider.

"Miss Hofman." He nodded. "Can we help you?"

"Help me? Hah!" I threw my head back. "That's a good one. When have you ever helped me in any way whatsoever?"

He sighed. "What do you want?"

Was I taking my frustration and fear out on these two public servants? Yes. Would I regret antagonizing them later? Probably. But did it feel good to see them so bothered? Oh yeah!

"Oh, nothing." I shrugged. "Just thought I might waste some of your time and bug you for a while—like you've been doing to me."

"Ma'am, step back from the vehicle. This is government property, and we could have you arrested for obstruction of justice." The woman leaned over a bit to speak, but Andersen waved her down with a little gesture of his hand.

The fact that she'd reacted to my childish taunting made me practically gleeful. I gave Andersen a sarcastic, surprised look with wide eyes and pursed lips. "Feisty minion you got yourself there. Hey, tell ya what? You go ahead and arrest me, and I'll sue your ass for harassing me all these years. Fun!" I grinned so hard my cheeks hurt.

"Miss Hofman, you need to back up now." Andersen's voice was level but deep with authority.

"Why?" I stood to my full height and held my arms out at their sides. "You're here to stalk—sorry, *investigate*—me, right? Well, here I am. Right in front of you. Do your thing!"

I wasn't even making sense anymore. Part of me kind of wanted them to slap cuffs on me, just to see the looks on their faces when half the town went comatose while they had me in custody.

I vaguely registered the sound of footsteps coming down my garden path, steadily crunching on the concrete. One of the guys was on his way to defuse the situation.

"Although"—I chuckled, a slight edge of mania to the sound—"if you haven't found anything to pin on me so far, I'm not sure what the point is anymore."

"Reverie," Oskar called from behind me, but I ignored him.

"You know what? Let me do you a favor. Not that you've ever done me any! But that's fine. Let me do you a favor anyway."

"Rev," Oskar said gently as his hand landed on my back. The agents spared him a quick glance but remained focused on me. I was in full purge mode. Short of picking me up and carrying me away, Oskar couldn't do anything to prevent this shitshow.

"Just give up. Quit while you still can and leave this hell-in-the-mountains place. Because you're never going to solve this case. Do you understand? You're *never* going to figure it out. Unless you have some buddies in a top-secret X-Files department, you're going to walk away from this whole mess with more questions than answers."

"Reverie!" Oskar barked, and I finally whipped my head around to look at him. He was giving me an excellent *what the fuck* look. Both the agents' eyes narrowed, watching us closely.

I deflated on the spot, immediately feeling like an idiot. *There's that regret kicking in with steel-toed boots.*

"Excuse us, officers." Oskar wrapped his arm around my shoulders, and I leaned into him. "She's not feeling well."

He didn't wait for a response to his lame excuse—just led me away, back up the garden path to where Sinan and Hollis stood at the front door.

I slunk past them and out into the backyard, flopped down onto the soft grass, and moped.

I'd given in to an immature impulse, and now I'd made everything worse. I'd practically told Andersen I knew what was going on. If that wasn't more reason to suspect me, and possibly the guys too, I didn't know what was.

At least he probably thought I was insane now, so hopefully he'd dismiss it as the ramblings of a crazy plant lady.

Eventually, the guys came out and lay down on the grass with me, our heads close together. They stayed by my side until the fresh air and cool ground under my back made me feel better.

CHAPTER TWENTY-NINE

The voices in my head were talking about me again. They were just out of reach—whispered words muffled by the barrier between sleep and wakefulness.

"... and are we sure that this is ..." The one with the kind eyes and artist's hands. *Oskar.*

"... all of us have to be in agreement or ..." My savior from the woods. *Hollis.*

"... have to tell her either way. She has to know that ..." The unyielding pain in my ass. *Sinan.*

I shifted on the bed, burrowing my face deeper into the pillow, trying to hold on to that magical halfway point. If I woke up, they might leave me. I tried to listen harder, but there was nothing but silence.

No, there was more than silence. There was warmth on either side of me. I nuzzled my nose against a bare shoulder, and when I blinked my eyes open, Hollis was looking back at me with a sleepy smile. The arm around my waist tightened. Artist's fingers dug into the covers, and I could feel Oskar's steady, comforting breathing against my back.

Where's Sinan? Reluctantly fully awake, I scanned the room to find him exactly where I expected: sprawled over the chair in the corner, watching me. His boots were next to the chair and his coat slung over the back of it. I liked him like this—relaxed and at home in my space.

"Morning." His soft words cut through the silence.

"I need a bigger bed" was my reply, delivered around a yawn as I stretched. The others shifted next to me.

A loud urgent knock at the front door made me sit up much faster than I planned.

"Who the hell is knocking on people's doors at this hour?" I grumbled and climbed over Hollis, who didn't miss the opportunity to cop a feel of my ass.

Oskar chuckled. "It's nearly nine thirty."

The knock came again, louder, more urgent.

"Yeah, yeah! Keep your pants on!" I yelled as I headed to the door pantsless. Sinan followed close behind.

When I opened the door to find Andersen and his minion standing on my porch, I groaned loudly and dragged a hand down my face.

"Miss Hofman—"

"Come *on*, dude. It is way too early for this shit. I haven't even peed yet. Come back in, like, an hour." I tried to close the door in their faces, but he whipped a hand out and stopped it.

"I need to take you into custody," he said.

Sinan stepped in very close, his body tense. "You're arresting her? What for?" he barked. I could hear the others coming to join us, bare feet slapping on the polished floorboards.

"I'm not arresting you." Agent Andersen glanced at Sinan but addressed me. "I'm taking you into custody for your own protection."

"I'm sorry, I think I just hallucinated." I shook my head and blinked a few times. "*What*?"

Andersen rushed through an explanation: "More than a dozen people were . . . they couldn't be woken this morning. A lot of angry, scared people came to the police station demanding we do something. They were not very happy with our response. They're looking for someone to blame, something to take their anger out on."

"Me." My shoulders slumped, and Sinan wrapped an arm around my waist.

"Yes, you." Andersen sighed, and it registered he was speaking with a sense of urgency but none of his usual hostility. "They're gathering in the town square. More than half of Gritton, and they're talking about coming here. We only have four agents here, plus the sheriff, who looked inclined to join the mob. We can't stop a riot—we just don't have enough people. Our only option is to get you out of here. So, please, just put some pants on and let's go."

"Wait." I didn't entirely trust I wasn't still dreaming . . . or hallucinating. "Do you actually believe that I'm innocent?"

"I can't discuss the particulars of an open investigation," he deadpanned. "What I can say is we've had eyes on you for days now, and I'm positive you haven't come into even fleeting contact with any of the people who fell victim last night. I have no idea what's going on here, but I know your life is in danger."

"Holy shit, did we just become best friends?" I crossed my arms and gave him an amused smile. I probably should have been more concerned about the angry mob gathering pitchforks and torches to come storm my castle. Maybe it was denial. Maybe it was because of the three amazing men I had standing at my back.

"Ma'am, this is a serious situation," Minion Lady said, her patience clearly wearing thin. "We do not have—"

"Oh god!" I ignored her and turned to look at my guys. They'd been completely silent through this whole exchange, and it had just dawned on me why. They'd put the clues together already.

They all wore stoic expressions, their eyes boring into me.

"Everyone is gathering in the center of town. Just like . . ." *in my dream*. It was happening. The Maron was making its big move, backing me into a corner to force my hand. Make it corporeal, or it decimates the town.

A muscle in Sinan's jaw ticked while Oskar stared at the floor and Hollis crossed his arms. They didn't like this one bit more than I did, but they wouldn't try to stop me. We all knew we had to face the Maron. *I* had to face the Maron.

I couldn't change the prophetic dream if I ran from it.

"We really can't delay any longer," Andersen insisted, and he was right. Just not about taking me into custody or whatever. Every second I wasted meant another person potentially falling victim to that monster.

"You can do this, Reverie." Hollis nodded, and they all

looked at me with so much fierce belief it was hard to doubt myself. I didn't have time for it anyway.

I jammed my feet into the flip-flops by the door and rushed down the front steps. The two agents marched ahead of me, shoulders tense, senses on alert. Behind me, the front door closed, and the next moment my Sandmen were by my side in their ghostly forms.

"We'll be right here," Oskar assured me as we reached the street.

"Every step of the way," Sinan confirmed.

I knew they would be, but it still felt good to hear it. We'd talked about what came next after I had that shitty dream and took it out on the nice feds stalking me. None of us particularly liked the plan we'd agreed to, but we all knew it was the right one. We'd barely even had to discuss it—we all felt this undeniable force of . . . conviction? Rightness? Something hard to articulate.

We just hadn't been able to lure the Maron. It was so mad with power it hadn't even slowed down long enough for me to tell it I would give it what it wanted.

The agents headed for the car parked out front, but I veered off and went straight for the track through the woods.

"Reverie!" Andersen yelled after me, and I could hear the two of them running. "What the fuck are you doing?"

"Saving the world!" I yelled over my shoulder, then mumbled to myself: "Or something . . ."

They followed me down the path, and it didn't take long for them to catch up. Andersen grabbed my arm to jerk me to a stop.

"I can't let you do this," the agent barked.

"I'm not asking for permission," I gritted out and, with barely a spare thought, made Sinan corporeal just as he stepped forward to put himself between us.

"Don't touch her." He really did sound like a nightmare, but I didn't have time to dissect why that possessive tone did things to me.

Andersen had already released me anyway. Both agents had taken several steps back and pulled out their guns, staring at Sinan in disbelief.

As much as I wanted to hang around and watch Andersen realize just how wrong he'd been about me all these years, I was on a mission. I turned and kept rushing toward town, wishing I'd chosen literally any other pair of shoes. And maybe taken thirty seconds to put on pants. Goosebumps prickled over my arms, and my breath misted in the cold morning air. The sun wasn't strong enough to penetrate the dense overgrowth in the woods just yet.

I was in underwear and a *Beavis and Butthead* T-shirt—seriously underdressed for the occasion and the weather—but if the whole town had to see me in this state again, at least the underwear was brand new and cute, not saggy with holes in it like last time.

Sinan rejoined us in his ghost form as I neared the town. I could still hear footsteps hurrying behind me and threw him a questioning frown.

"They won't be a problem," Sinan said.

"What did you do?" I asked as the trees thinned and I stepped onto the sidewalk.

Before he could answer, a scream froze us all in our tracks, and our heads whipped in the direction of rising voices. Many people seemed to be speaking at once, and a few shouts rang out. Was that fear or anger? Probably both.

Muttering a curse, I marched up the pavement. Only after rounding the corner did I slow down, my feet carrying me out onto the road until I finally stopped in the middle of Main Street. As in my dream, half the town had gathered here, but they weren't silently staring in the same direction. They were talking over one another, and they looked agitated.

The man who owned the lumberyard—I couldn't remember his name—spotted me first, and before long more and more scowls were being turned my way.

"Ah, shit." I held very still and tried not to let them see the fear in my eyes.

Before anyone could start lynching me, a commotion broke out halfway up the street, then another closer to where I stood. Lumberyard's wife (Mary?) closed her eyes and collapsed, several sets of arms catching her before she could split her head open on the concrete.

These people were falling into comas where they stood. Just like in my dream.

I scanned the crowd for a hint of depthless black, but I couldn't spot the Maron anywhere.

"Why are you doing this? Stop!" someone yelled in the crowd, their words ending on a wail.

In my periphery, I saw the agents inching forward on either side of me, their hands poised at their hips. My guys were standing behind me, as they'd promised they would. I could feel them there, lending me their strength.

I searched the trees and the rooftops. Still no sign of the true monster in our midst.

"We can't spot it either," Oskar said, preempting my question. "It's here, but it won't show itself."

"She won't stop!" Now *that* voice I knew. Vera weaved through the crowd until she pushed to the front, glaring at me with pure hatred in her eyes. "She's just going to keep hurting us until no one's left. And the authorities won't do anything about it! We have to stop her!"

Several voices rose in support—then in alarm as more people fell throughout the crowd. My eyes flew from one victim to the next, trying to find the Maron.

Nothing.

The angry chatter swelled, and the mob started to shift toward me.

Andersen and his minion stepped forward with their hands held out, their guns pulled but still pointed down. "Stop! Everyone needs to go home and let us handle this!"

Of course, the crowd ignored him.

But they weren't going to ignore me.

I was done being ignored.

I was done playing games.

CHAPTER THIRTY

"Enough!" I yelled with more gravity than I thought myself capable of. My shoulders were back, my stance solid, my expression serious. If I weren't in my underwear and an old T-shirt, I would've looked like a bad-ass bitch in that moment.

Everyone quieted down and shrank back from me, fear evident in their eyes. *Huh.* Maybe I looked like a bad-ass bitch regardless. I decided to roll with that instead of getting bummed that several hundred people just recoiled from me in fear.

I scanned the crowd one more time.

"Come out, asshole. I know you're here," I called out.

No answer. The people shifted nervously, exchanging confused looks.

"I'm here!" I held my arms out and slowly turned in a circle. "Isn't that what you wanted? Isn't that why you're attacking all these people?"

More silence. More worried looks from the townies.

The agents eyed me too, their attention flicking between me and the crowd.

Everything was still. No more people dropped unconscious. I couldn't see the Maron, but I could feel it. It was focused on me. Watching, listening, waiting.

Praying to all the deities I could think of that this wasn't a mistake, I lowered my voice and said what I knew would finally bring it out. "I'm done. You win. I'll give you what you want."

Several tense moments passed, and then I saw it. It stood about twenty feet away among the people, its disturbing black eyes watching me.

I took a steadying breath. It tilted its head to the side and looked at Sinan, Oskar, and Hollis one by one. Then it lifted its hand and scraped its ugly claws down the side of a balding man's head. He went down like a ton of bricks.

"Stop!" I took a step forward as people started getting restless again. "I told you I'd give you what you wanted. What are you doing?"

"I'm not interested in another fight." That voice—close by and all around me. Several people looked around in confusion, as if they'd heard it too.

"They're not here to fight you." I gestured to the guys behind me. "They would've already tried by now."

It bared those impossibly sharp teeth in that impossibly large mouth and raised its claws once more.

I did the mental equivalent of snapping my fingers—a fast and easy maneuver—and made my guys corporeal where they stood. People gasped and backed up, looking to each other to make sure everyone had seen the three men appear out of thin air.

"This is what you want, right?" I kept my focus on the monster no one could see yet. "Come here and I'll make it happen."

"Why?" It lowered its hand in a demented caress, and a woman fell, eliciting more frightened, confused reactions from the people. I wished they'd all just leave—for their own safety.

"Because we tried fighting you and it didn't work," I hurried to say, trying my best to keep its attention locked on me. "Because all these innocent people don't deserve what you're doing to them, and I can protect them if I give you what you want."

"Just like that?" It released a short, humorless chuckle, and Christopher's face flickered into focus for just an instant.

"I have one condition." I held my chin high and resisted the urge to fidget or look down. I refused to let it see how scared I was.

It growled, clearly not liking the idea of a condition, even without having heard it. It raised both clawed hands, and I picked my moment carefully. I made it visible, but not yet solid, just as it drew its hands down. A teenage girl and Mrs. Wallis collapsed, unconscious.

Several screams rang out, and people scrambled to get away from the black, nightmarish monster they'd just seen attack two of their own. Some people bolted, disappearing down side streets, while others couldn't take their wide, horrified eyes off the Maron—all reactions to be expected when faced with a literal nightmare.

"I have the power to give you what you want." I

pointed to the guys. "I can make you solid, real just like them."

Several people raised their voices in protest, throwing threats and curses at me. I ignored them. Hopefully, no one would do anything stupid.

"But I can't keep letting you hurt them. Look at them!" I raised my voice, and it actually obeyed, turning its head slowly to take in the cowering people. "They're terrified. I can't let you walk among them in this form. I will give you what you want, but I'll give it to you, Christopher. To *you*. Not to this thing you've become."

The Maron rolled its head, then its entire body flickered, revealing my childhood imaginary friend for a few moments. He scowled at me before looking at the guys suspiciously.

"That's it. Just come here so I can touch you." I drew its attention back to me. Chris wasn't stupid. He'd started out as a Dreamwalker, after all. He knew they wouldn't stop trying to banish him. It might've been easier to convince him to get close if my guys weren't here, but I couldn't pull this off by myself.

"This is a trap," Chris/Maron declared. His form flickered between the two entities, his voice changing as his face did—fluctuating between a normal human voice and that unearthly growl midsentence. "Do it from where you stand."

"I can't." I totally could, but I needed him to get closer to me, farther away from all these people. "For the first time, I need to be able to touch you."

"I don't believe you." He started walking toward me anyway, more Christopher now, with the monstrous Maron form only appearing here and there. He pointed a finger at the Dreamwalkers. "They would never allow this."

"They have no choice." I kept his focus on me. He was still walking slowly, maybe ten feet away now. "They've tried to take you out, and they failed. You're too strong."

He stopped six feet away, uncertainty written all over his face. I wanted to close the distance myself, but I couldn't risk spooking him, bringing the Maron back out.

"We can't let you walk the waking realm as the Maron," Oskar said. We'd agreed ahead of time that I'd do all the talking and the guys would stand in plain sight, looking as harmless as possible, but I was glad he'd spoken up.

"And we can't defeat you." Sinan didn't hide the disdain in his voice.

"This is a compromise," Hollis said. "Stop terrorizing people, and you can have what we have."

Chris's gaze came back to me, the longing in it clear. He didn't want the kind of relationship I had with the guys. He wasn't after sex or romance. He just wanted comfort—to be seen and heard and held, just as he had in his life before. Whatever that was.

I cast my mind back to my childhood, when we'd been friends. He'd played with me while my parents were busy, made me laugh when I hurt myself, stayed with me when I couldn't sleep because I was scared of the dark.

I let myself feel all the warm, nostalgic feelings I had for Christopher. I let it all show on my face as I opened my arms slowly.

"I'm sorry, Chris," I told him genuinely. I really was sorry for how this had all turned out, even if I wasn't to blame. "I was just a kid, and I didn't know what I was doing, what I had. You were always there for me. Now let me be there for you. Let me make it right."

It felt as though everyone held their collective breath—me, the guys, the agents, the entire town—waiting to see what would happen next.

Chris nodded cautiously and closed the distance, holding his arms out for the hug I offered. I gave him a watery smile, reached out, and made sure my power gave him what he'd wanted all this time. *Slowly.* I wanted him to feel it as his heart pumped warm blood through his very real body, as his legs gained weight where he stood, as his arms folded my body into an embrace.

He gasped as I held him tightly, but I couldn't see the awed look I knew was on his face. My chin rested on his shoulder, and he crushed me against him when he started crying.

I let my tears come too, for what had been and what was to come.

"I'm sorry," I sobbed, gripping the fabric of his T-shirt.

"I'm sorry," I whispered as our hug loosened and I dropped my arms.

"I'm sorry," I breathed as he took a deep, stuttering breath and lifted his face to the sky. His cheeks were streaked with tears, but a smile curved his lips when the warmth of the sun hit his face.

"I'm sorry." My voice had gone flat, resigned, and I took a step backward.

Sinan brushed past me, depositing his dagger in my hand, as he moved to my other side. Oskar and Hollis had drifted nearer too, closing in on our right and left.

"You need to leave," Sinan barked, drawing a hard look

from Chris. With Chris's attention diverted, I steeled myself for what I had to do. And it had to be me. We all knew it had to be me in the end.

"What? Rev, I'd like to stay in Gritton. Maybe we could—"

I interrupted him with a knife to the heart.

Sinan had shown me how to get it right between the ribs, had me practice with the blade. I'd made sure to pay attention to what I was feeling when I'd hugged Chris.

Christopher's eyes went so wide it seemed as if they might pop out, and he looked down at his chest. Sinan's dagger protruded from between his ribs, my hand still gripping the hilt tightly as blood gushed from the wound.

He released a pained, wounded sound and raised his eyes to meet mine. The shock and betrayal on his face started to twist into rage.

Tears pouring down my face, I yanked the knife back out, making him shout in pain.

"Goodbye, Chris." I said what I wished I'd said to him all those years ago when I was a kid. Maybe if we'd had a proper farewell, things would've worked out differently.

The guys pounced, grabbing Chris tightly and pulling him back. Once they'd put some distance between us, Oskar, Hollis, and Sinan returned to their translucent forms as they slipped into the dream realm, ready to drag Chris with them.

Except they didn't.

Every muscle in Chris's body tensed, the guys stumbled, and they lost their grip on him. With blood still pouring from his wound, Chris bared his teeth and lunged for me—but the guys got over their shock quickly. They stepped back into their solid forms and grabbed him again.

Chris thrashed against them, and I could feel him thrashing against me too. Even while he tried to get out of their grip, he was clutching at my power, holding on to it with all he had.

My shoulders sagged, and a wave of soul-deep exhaustion swept through me. Horrified, I wrenched my power back from him and strained to hold on.

Oskar wrapped an arm around Chris's throat; Hollis went low, banding his arms around the man's waist; and Sinan had a shoulder and an arm. The three of them moved as one, heaving him backward and turning translucent as they toppled. But once again, Chris resisted. His solid form hit the ground with a smack, and he rolled over, coughing, and got to his feet.

I glanced to my side and barked at the agents: "Do something! Shoot him."

"We can't," Andersen gritted out. "Too many people."

Both agents had their guns raised, but my guys had reappeared, Chris was struggling furiously, and there were so many people behind them. More and more of the townspeople were backing up and even leaving, but plenty remained.

Over and over, my guys battled to yank Chris out of the waking world, draining my power every time they had to come back into their solid forms. I fought with everything I had to force him to release his grip on me.

Chris was a mess. Blood had started to splutter out of his mouth, but he just kept fighting. He had nothing to lose. He snarled and growled like an animal. Like . . .

Just as the thought crossed my mind, the Maron's ugly face flickered over Christopher's for a split second, and I felt its claws dig deeper into my power.

Acting on hardly more than instinct, determination, and terror, I rushed forward. Sinan, Oskar, and Hollis had their hands full just trying to keep Chris in place. They yelled for me to stay back, but I ignored them and shoved Sinan's coat out of the way. Chris bucked, knocking me onto my butt, but I'd grabbed the dagger and held on to it.

I scrambled to my feet, threw myself at Chris, and stabbed him as hard as I could in the stomach. He weakened. I could see it with my eyes and feel it in my power. His grip was loosening.

The blade came free with a sickening squelch, and I stabbed up into the underside of his chin, then somewhere in his shoulder. My throat made a sound between sobbing and screaming while my arm just kept stabbing and stabbing—until eventually my hand came down into thin air, and I stumbled.

Catching myself before I faceplanted, I looked up to see three sets of eyes watching me with worry and fear and love —*so many emotions*. Chris watched me with pure hatred. I didn't have the energy to say anything as the men I loved finally pulled my monster out of my life.

The moment they vanished, I dropped to my knees, beyond exhausted but finally able to breathe. When I looked down at my shaking hands, I expected to see them coated in blood, but they were clean.

Every trace of the Maron was gone.

CHAPTER THIRTY-ONE

The smell of cornbread wafted past me where I sat at my computer, and I abandoned the email I was writing midsentence to rush into the kitchen. This afternoon was the first time in several days I'd sat down to do some work, but I couldn't concentrate. Between the guys disappearing without a trace and having my mom back—not to mention the clusterfuck that had gone down in the town square—it was no wonder I wasn't functioning like normal.

"I thought you were working." Mom raised a brow and pointed a fork at me, but there was no missing the amusement in her eyes.

"I can't be expected to focus when you're out here making cornbread." Our shoulders touched, and we leaned into each other. We'd been doing that a lot—just touching each other. A tender caress here, a squeeze of the hand there, a full hug at least once every hour. As if neither of us could really believe the other was real.

The cornbread sat on the stove, steaming and ready. I took a big inhale of the familiar smell.

"Well, excuse me for making lunch for my daughter." Mom hip-bumped me and reached for plates. Thankfully I'd left everything pretty much how it was before she ended up in the hospital. No doubt that made it easier for her to adjust, and it was comforting to see her moving about the space again.

"You're excused." I picked at the fresh cornbread, burning the tips of my fingers as I popped a piece into my mouth. *Worth it*. It was exactly as I remembered—hot and crumbly against my tongue.

I reached for more, but Mom smacked my hand before I could get to it.

"Ow!" I cradled my hand to my chest, and she rolled her eyes at me. I definitely got my sarcasm from her.

"Tell me more about the ginseng?" She smiled with genuine interest as we sat down at the kitchen table I rarely used, plates heaped with cornbread, pickles, cold cuts, and salad laid out in front of us.

I'd been doing most of the talking since she woke up, but I didn't mind. I wished I didn't need sleep so I could spend even more time with her. We had so much missed time to make up for.

Mom had woken up moments after we finally defeated the Maron, as had the other people who'd fallen victim to it—both those in town and those in the hospital.

I hadn't really been worried about my guys when I got cleaned up and headed to the hospital later that day. I'd expected it to take a while to make sure the Maron was banished, and in that moment, nothing on this green earth could have kept me from visiting my mother.

Mom was already awake when I got there. She was sitting up in her bed and eating what looked like her third portion of Jell-O while doctors and nurses bustled around her.

"Reverie!" She beamed the moment she spotted me, and I burst into tears as I lunged for her. The nurses protested when I climbed onto the bed, but we both refused to move. We lay in that hospital bed all afternoon while they continued to monitor her. She was perfectly fine as far as they could see, but they wanted to be sure before they let her leave.

In the meantime, we talked and held each other, and I cried. A lot. Just like everyone else who had woken from the Maron's comas, Mom had no memory of anything while she was out. The last thing she remembered was going to bed as usual nine years ago. She'd had a sense of something not being right when she woke up, and she'd been worried to find herself in the hospital, but other than some muscle atrophy, she was totally fine. In fact, the constant stream of medical professionals that came through her room marveled at how coherent and alert she was, considering she'd just woken from a years-long coma. They discharged her that evening.

I'd had to help her get around at first, but she seemed to get stronger by the minute. She'd started making me corn-bread for lunch within a few days. Her third rehab appointment was tomorrow, and she still had work to do, but I'd gladly be there with her every step of the way. I could hardly believe I had my mom back.

My soul felt whole again, but my heart was in pieces, and three of those pieces were missing.

"Revy." Mom's gentle touch on my arm brought me back to the present, and she gave me a sympathetic smile. I'd been doing that a lot—zoning out as my brain struggled to process everything.

"Right." I shook it off. "The ginseng. So, I started planting it—"

The doorbell rang, and we both groaned in the exact same way.

"Not another one," I grumbled as we got to our feet.

"There's no damn room left in the fridge." Mom frowned.

I opened the door, and Mom and I gave Mrs. Wallis identical thin-lipped smiles.

"Hello, Mrs. Wallis," I greeted her politely, trying my hardest not to grit my teeth. She stood before us with wide eyes, a covered dish clutched in her hands.

"Hello, dear." She nodded at me, then turned to Mom. "Oh, Felicity, it is *so* good to see you. I am *so* glad you're all right. We were all *so* worried, especially when more and more people . . ." She cleared her throat with a glance at me.

"Thanks, June." Mom raised her eyebrows in a gesture that clearly said, *Is that all?*

"Well, I just wanted to drop this off." She held the dish out. "I know you girls don't need to be worrying about what to eat at a time like this."

After a beat of uncomfortable silence, I took the dish from Mrs. Wallis's hands, putting us all out of our misery. "Thanks. That's thoughtful."

"I also wanted to thank Reverie," she told my mom, and I rolled my eyes.

"She's standing right there, June. You don't need me to translate." Mom had woken up with precisely zero fucks left to give—especially when I filled her in on my life over the past several years.

"Right, of course." Mrs. Wallis fidgeted and faced me. "Thank you, Reverie, for what you did. In the town square that day. You saved us all."

Tears welled in her eyes. Her granddaughter had been one of the people the Maron attacked that day. The girl had already been by with her mom and a basket of muffins.

"That's OK," I replied as awkwardly as I had to everyone else who'd stopped by in the past few days. I didn't know what to say. "You're welcome" felt smug, and "It was my pleasure" just didn't sit right—there was nothing pleasurable about it.

Mom replied the same way she had every other time too. "Don't you think you should also *apologize* to Reverie?" She crossed her arms and tilted her head at the older woman, as if Mrs. Wallis were a child and this was a teachable moment. "You know? For the shitty way you all treated her while I lay in the hospital."

"Oh my . . ." Mrs. Wallis's eyes widened comically, but to her credit, she squared her shoulders and looked me in the eye. "Your mother is absolutely right, Reverie. The whole town owes you a big apology and a debt. I'm genuinely sorry. We all acted like a bunch of nincompoops, and we'll make up for it."

"You see that you do." Mom huffed. "Now, if you'll excuse us, I need to sit down."

She closed the door in the woman's face, and we waited until we heard her footsteps on the gravel before having a laugh. What else was there left to do? I wanted to get these little unwelcome visits over with as fast as possible. But Mom was livid at how hard these people had made my life, and she forced each one of them to feel as awkward and ashamed as she could while they apologized. I actually loved her protectiveness.

And I'd be lying if I said I didn't also love seeing them swallow the fact they'd been wrong about me all these years.

Word must've spread about how we greeted everyone who came, but they just kept showing up! They brought casseroles and baked goods, hand-knitted blankets and home-grown produce. Travis and another guy from the mechanic's even came over and fully serviced my truck and washed it without even asking.

They weren't all thankful and bashful. Some were still avoiding me, refusing to believe what they'd seen. Others had even tried to go to the media about the whole "monster in a mountain town" incident, but they were dismissed as conspiracy theorists, and no one was taking them seriously. No one had managed to get any clear pictures or recordings, and I was pretty sure our friends at the FBI were doing their best to keep this all quiet. For once, I was glad Andersen was sticking his nose in.

It was beyond amusing, and neither Mom nor I wanted to waste time and energy on negative emotions when we were finally together again.

"Wanna take bets on what it is?" I wiggled the dish as Mom lowered herself back into her chair.

"Nah." She waved it off. "May as well throw it right in the trash. We'll never get to it before it goes bad."

"Maybe we can find a way to donate all this food to a homeless shelter or something."

"That's a lovely idea, Revy."

Curiosity got the better of me, and I balanced the dish on one hand while I peeled back the lid with the other. I stared at the pie, my throat growing a lump the size of a baseball as the remaining quarter of my heart spasmed in my chest.

"What is it?" Mom mumbled around a mouthful of food. She was back to eating and only half paying attention to me.

I cleared my throat, but the lump wouldn't budge, and my words came out sounding weak and pathetic. "It's, uh, strawberry custard pie."

"Reverie?" She sounded worried now, and I couldn't blame her. I'd been bursting into tears on and off for days.

"Hollis's mom used to make this. He'd love it if he was here. He'd say it wasn't as good as hers, but he'd love it." Tears spilled over, and my hands started to shake. I gripped the dish tighter and tried to force the overwhelming emotion away.

Of course, it didn't work. Mom wrapped an arm around my shoulders and squeezed. It was the most bitter-sweet moment of my life. I had her back to comfort me after being alone for so long—but I needed the comfort because I'd lost *them*.

I'd told Mom about Sinan, Oskar, and Hollis. I couldn't have avoided it even if I'd wanted to, not when the townies started knocking on our door with food and gratitude and mentions of the Maron. Not when they asked about the three young men who'd fought the monster with me.

The fact that half the town had seen them in the flesh made it easier to tell Mom about it, and by some miracle, she actually believed me. If she hadn't spent years in an unexplainable coma, I'm not sure she would've bought the story of three ghost dudes falling in love with me and helping me slay the dragon.

Minus the raunchy details, I'd told her the whole story, what they told me I was, what I could do, how amazing they all were in their own unique way. She had a lot of questions, but Mom had always been open-minded, and in the end, she just wanted me to be happy.

It felt like a betrayal to her that I couldn't be. Not entirely. Not without them.

"I never even told them I love them," I whined, blubbering like the mess I was.

I'd known it couldn't last—that they'd have to get on with their Dreamwalker duties once we defeated the Maron. I just hadn't thought it would be so sudden and so final. Did they not want to say goodbye? Did they not really love me as they said? Or did it just take longer to banish a Maron than I thought?

It was the not knowing that killed me the most. That and the fact that a big part of me had been hoping beyond hope we could somehow make it work.

"Don't cry, doll. You're killing me." Hollis sounded as if he stood right before me.

I gasped, my whole body jerking at the sound of his voice, and lost my grip on the dish. By some miracle, it didn't shatter on the tiles, but it sent custard and pie crust splattering all over the place.

"Hollis? *Holy shit*! Hollis!" I scanned the room frantically, not even caring about the mess on the floor, while Mom tried to get me to calm down and sit.

"Did she just hear that?" Oskar sounded excited. "Can she hear us?"

"Yes! I can hear you!" I was yelling, which I immediately realized was completely unnecessary, and burst into laughter. Mom watched me warily. I must've looked maniacal, laughing and yelling with my face streaked with tears.

"Temptress. Focus."

Sinan's barked command made me do just that. I took a deep breath and tried to shake out all the excitement coursing through me.

"If you can hear us," he said, "then you can see us. You're the most powerful damn Seheraum that's ever lived. Come on, beautiful. We miss you."

"I miss you too," I whispered.

Mom lowered herself into her chair once more. She looked tired but couldn't tear her gaze off me, as if she were watching a tense moment on TV.

"Remember everything you learned, *schatzi*. Tap into that control. Sit down and meditate if you need to."

Oskar's encouraging words made me want to see them even more. I could just imagine them all standing shoulder to shoulder, right in front of me, hopeful expressions on their beautiful faces.

"I don't think I can sit. I'm too wired." I shook my hands out and tried to focus.

"I can't wait to hold you, baby," Hollis said softly. "Feel

your soft skin under my touch, smell your hair, kiss those lips."

I wanted that too. I wanted it so badly. I realized what he was doing right as they faded into focus in front of me. He was making me *yearn*, put all my energy into wanting them to be here—just like that night on the couch the first time we'd kissed.

They were exactly as I imagined—standing close, watching me intently, hopefully, excitedly.

I smiled, and more tears slipped down my cheeks.

"Hi," I breathed, and then it was effortless. In fact, it felt a lot like breathing; it was so easy to bring them into the waking world. I willed it, and they solidified before me.

They enveloped me, and I gladly let myself drown in their love. They took turns crushing me in hugs and kissing me reverently, but there never came a point when all three of them weren't touching me in some way. I felt whole again as I returned their affection as best I could. I was, after all, just one woman, and there were three of them.

The relief I felt at having them with me, knowing they hadn't abandoned me, was palpable.

"Where the fuck have you been?" I shoved both Sinan and Oskar, one hand on each chest. Then I turned slightly and shoved Hollis for good measure.

My psychotic change in mood and demeanor did nothing to wipe the happy looks off their faces.

"We've been here, with you, the whole time," Hollis said, amusement shining in his eyes—right alongside the love.

"Well, pretty much," Oskar added, and the others gave him narrow-eyed looks. "It did take us a couple of hours to dispatch the Maron. We've been nearby since you left for the hospital."

I remembered the night I woke up in the gutter in the rain. I thought they'd abandoned me then too, but I'd just been drained and couldn't reach them; we hadn't even been able to communicate in the dreamscape. No wonder the same thing had happened again. Yes, I was stronger than I had been then, but that day we fought the Maron had drained me down to my bones. My power had needed time to recharge.

"God, I am *such* an idiot," I groaned, dragging a hand down my face.

"Yeah, but you're *our* idiot." Sinan flashed me a grin as he took my hand from my face and kissed the palm. I couldn't even be mad at that. He'd said I was *theirs*, and they were here!

Remembering that my mom was in the room, I turned to look at her. She sat in the same spot at the table, one arm propped on the surface, mouth slightly agape.

"Mom?" I turned to face her more fully. "You all right?"

"I . . ." She blinked rapidly as a smile pulled at her lips. "I'm sorry. I just . . . I've never seen someone just . . . materialize out of thin air like that."

"You get used to it." I chuckled.

Oskar took a few short steps to stand before her and held out his hand. "Mrs. Hofman, I'm Oskar Klein. It's a pleasure to meet you. Apologies for our rudeness just now. We were just happy to be reunited with Reverie."

"Pleasure to meet you, Oskar." Mom shook his hand and smiled warmly. "No apologies necessary. It's heart-warming to see my daughter so . . . loved."

She flashed me a meaningful look, and I didn't even know how to feel. It was kind of surreal that she was even sitting at the table right now, let alone meeting these guys.

Oskar stepped aside, and Hollis took his place.

"I'm Hollis. Delighted to make your acquaintance, ma'am," he said with a flourish and his irresistible grin. When Mom took his proffered hand, he didn't shake as Oskar had—he bent over and brushed a kiss over her knuckles like the suave gentleman he was.

"Oh! I too am delighted, kind sir!" Mom put on a hoity-toity voice and laughed as Hollis released her.

Sinan was still holding my hand, and he started to rub it with his thumb. Instead of going over to my mom as the others had, he waited patiently for her gaze to fall on him. Then he bowed his head, slowly and intentionally.

"It is an honor," he said, the intensity of his words and actions perfectly on-brand.

Mom held his gaze for a moment, then nodded in acknowledgment and smiled. I could see all the questions bubbling up to the surface—especially for Hollis. She was going to talk his ear off about the twenties, and he'd love every second of it. I was positive.

"Well"—Mom leaned back in her chair and lightly slapped the table—"with three virile men around, all that food won't go to waste anymore."

"Ew! Mom! Who the hell says *virile* anymore?" I laughed as I stepped around the ruined pie to join her. My hunger had returned now that everything else was out of the way.

For now. I still had no idea where we stood or how long

I had with them, but for an afternoon, I was going to enjoy watching them interact with my mom.

* * *

THE GUYS CLEANED UP THE MESS I'D MADE ON THE floor, cleared the table after lunch, *and* cleaned the kitchen. Hollis even made cocktails, and we sat out on the front porch, drinking and talking. They were being perfect gentlemen and had more than won Mom over.

She excused herself midafternoon, saying she needed a nap after all this excitement. She'd been taking two or three naps per day. I could tell she was genuinely exhausted, but I also knew she would've found a way to give us some alone time regardless.

I pulled my cardigan closer around my chest as a gust of wind made me shiver. Oskar scooted closer and wrapped an arm around me. For a while—probably for too long—the four of us just sat there, watching the chilly wind caress the autumnal foliage.

"So . . ." I drew the word out, breaking the silence when I realized I couldn't really enjoy the nature around us. All I could think about was *what now?* I looked at Hollis in the chair on one side, then at Sinan on the chair on the other side, then at Oskar next to me on the swing. They all returned my gaze with knowing looks.

"Yes." Oskar sighed. "We should discuss what comes next."

I held my breath as I pushed against the floor with my feet, starting a gentle rock of the porch swing.

"Reverie, are you all right?" Sinan leaned forward,

resting his elbows on his knees, and fixed me with a worried look.

"I guess that depends on what you're about to tell me." I hadn't been this nervous since I was sixteen and stupidly decided to go to the homecoming dance by myself, even though I literally had no friends there—or anywhere.

"Ah, shit. I'm just gonna say it." Hollis sat up and rubbed the back of his head. He looked nervous, and I got even more nervous myself. "We want to stay, if you'll have us. We know it's unconventional, being with three men, and we know we've only known each other for a few weeks, but we love you. We want to be with you."

I held my breath again, for an entirely different reason. They loved me. They wanted to be with me. They felt just as strongly about me as I did them. But . . . "How? I don't understand. How would it work? You'd just keep doing your Sandman thing and pop up whenever you could for corporeal couple time? I'd grow old and die, and then you'd go on without me?"

Knowing we loved each other and wanted the same things was validating in a way I could hardly express, but I still needed the logistics.

Really, Reverie? As if you'd say no to whatever they were offering?

"How many times do we have to tell you it's Dreamwalkers, not Sandmen?" Sinan grumbled, teasing me. It was odd to have him try to lift the mood for once, but I supposed we'd all changed during the past weeks.

Before I could throw back a sarcastic response, Oskar jumped in. "We wouldn't be Dreamwalkers anymore."

"Come again?" I frowned. "I thought it was life, death,

Dreamwalking until you discover the mysteries of the universe, then the *great beyond*."

Hollis laughed, and Sinan cracked a grin too, but Oskar remained serious.

"Yes, in a nutshell, that's what we always knew. But not long before we banished the Maron, another option became known to us. We just didn't have a chance to discuss it with you before the shit hit the fan. We have completed our journeys in the dream realm, learned what we were supposed to. We have a choice: the *great beyond*, as you put it, or a second chance."

"We would become wholly mortal once more, lose our Dreamwalker abilities, and live out the rest of our lives like anyone else—with you." Hollis watched me intently and swallowed, making his Adam's apple bob. He was nervous. Holy shit, they all were.

"Wait, wait, wait." I stood and turned to face them. "You're telling me you have a choice between eternal peace and me? And you choose *me*?"

They all nodded, looking confident in their decision.

"We've discussed it at length," Sinan said, "and come to realize that perhaps we were meant to find you all along. We've stayed in the dream realm for so long waiting for *you*. The Maron went undetected for so long so we could find each other. You've taught us more about ourselves, about the world, about strength and responsibility and forgiveness, than we've learned in our combined time observing humanity. It would be an honor to spend what time we are gifted on this plane of existence loving you."

"Cherishing you," Hollis added.

"Honoring you," Oskar concluded.

They all stood as one and stepped closer. I was already weeping.

Hollis took my hand. "We know this is a lot to process, and it's such a big commitment—"

"Shut up," I cut him off. "You're all acting like you're asking me to make some huge sacrifice when you're actually making all my dreams come true. I love you." I laughed through the tears of pure joy. "I love you so fucking much, and I can't wait to spend the rest of our lives together."

For the second time that day, I was enveloped in their affection, their devotion and love. We kissed and hugged and laughed together. I felt so light and free I worried I might just float away on the chilly wind, but I knew they'd never let me go.

I was safe and whole, and the loneliness that had haunted me my whole life already felt like a distant nightmare.

NOTE FROM THE AUTHOR

Thank you so much for reading Reverie and Redemption! I really hope you enjoyed it and you'll consider leaving a review. As an indie author, reviews make a massive difference when it comes to my book reaching other readers. Even a sentence or two helps!

ACKNOWLEDGMENTS

Thank you to my therapist and my doctor. I would not even be functioning as a human being if it wasn't for you, let alone writing a damn book!

Thank you to my wonderful, supportive, talented team. To Christine, Kirstin, Jay, Allie, the ladies at Grey's Promotions, my dedicated beta readers, my enthusiastic ARC readers – I feel very lucky to have you all in my corner.

Thank you to every single reader who has ever picked up one of my books. I'm living my dream because you're reading my stories.

Thank you to my husband, John. I wouldn't be the person I am today if it wasn't for you. You are my real life happily ever after!

ABOUT THE AUTHOR

Kaydence Snow has lived all over the world but ended up settled in Melbourne, Australia. She lives near the beach with her husband and their stubborn rescue dog Summer.

She draws inspiration from her own overthinking, sometimes frightening imagination, and everything that makes life interesting – complicated relationships, unexpected twists, new experiences and good food and coffee. Life is not worth living without good food and coffee!

She believes sarcasm is the highest form of wit and has the vocabulary of a highly educated, well-read sailor. When she's not writing, thinking about writing, planning when she can write next, or reading other people's writing, she loves to travel and learn new things.

To keep up to date with Kaydence's latest news and releases sign up to her newsletter here:

kaydencesnow.com

Join her reader group here:
facebook.com/groups/KaydenceSnowLodge

Or follow her on:
Facebook: facebook.com/KaydenceSnowAuthor
Instagram: instagram.com/kaydencesnowauthor/

Also by Kaydence Snow

The Evelyn Maynard Trilogy

Variant Lost

Vital Found

Vivid Avowed

Devilbend Dynasty

Like You Care

Like You Hurt

Like You Should

Like You Know (coming soon)

Standalones

Just Be Her

It Started With A Sleigh

Reverie and Redemption

www.ingramcontent.com/pod-product-compliance
Lightning Source LLC
Chambersburg PA
CBHW060819120726
47909CB00006B/2001